BY HARRY TURTLEDOVE

The Guns of the South

THE WORLDWAR SAGA
Worldwar: In the Balance
Worldwar: Tilting the Balance
Worldwar: Upsetting the Balance
Worldwar: Striking the Balance

COLONIZATION
Colonization: Second Act
Colonization: Down to Earth
Colonization: Aftershocks

Homeward Bound

THE VIDESSOS CYCLE
Volume One:
The Misplaced Legion
An Emperor for the Legion
Volume Two:
The Legion of Videssos
Swords of the Legion

THE TALE OF KRISPOS
Krispos Rising
Krispos of Videssos
Krispos the Emperor

A World of Difference
Departures
How Few Remain

THE GREAT WAR
The Great War: American Front
The Great War: Walk in Hell
The Great War: Breakthroughs

AMERICAN EMPIRE
American Empire: Blood and Iron
American Empire:
The Center Cannot Hold
American Empire:
The Victorious Opposition

SETTLING ACCOUNTS
Settling Accounts: Return Engagement
Settling Accounts: Drive to the East
Settling Accounts: The Grapple
Settling Accounts: In at the Death

Every Inch a King

The Man with the Iron Heart

THE WAR THAT CAME EARLY
The War That Came Early: Hitler's War
The War That Came Early:
West and East
The War That Came Early:
The Big Switch
The War That Came Early: Coup d'Etat
The War That Came Early: Two Fronts
The War That Came Early: Last Orders

THE HOT WAR
Bombs Away
Fallout
Armistice

ARMISTICE

THE HOT WAR

ARMISTICE

Harry Turtledove

DEL REY　NEW YORK

Copyright © 2017 by Harry Turtledove

All rights reserved.

Published in the United States by Del Rey, an imprint of Random House, a division of Penguin Random House LLC, New York.

Del Rey and the House colophon are registered trademarks of Penguin Random House LLC.

Library of Congress Cataloging-in-Publication Data
Names: Turtledove, Harry, author.
Title: Armistice : the Hot War / by Harry Turtledove.
Description: First edition. | New York : Del Rey, [2017] | Series: The Hot War ; 3
Identifiers: LCCN 2017018935| ISBN 9780553390766 (hardback : alk. paper) | ISBN 9780553390773 (ebook)
Subjects: LCSH: Cold War—Fiction. | United States—Foreign relations—Soviet Union—Fiction. | Soviet Union—Foreign relations—United States—Fiction. | BISAC: FICTION / Alternative History. | FICTION / Science Fiction / Adventure. | FICTION / War & Military. | GSAFD: Alternative histories (Fiction) | War stories.
Classification: LCC PS3570.U76 A89 2017 | DDC 813/.54—dc23
LC record available at lccn.loc.gov/2017018935

Printed in the United States of America on acid-free paper

randomhousebooks.com

9 8 7 6 5 4 3 2 1

First Edition

Book design by Liz Cosgrove

ARMISTICE

SOMETHING LIKE GLASS CRUNCHED under the soles of
Harry Truman's shoes as he walked through the ruins of Washington.
Two men with Geiger counters walked ahead of him. They both wore
gauze surgical masks that covered their faces south of the eyes.

They'd offered him one, too, but he'd turned them down. He'd had
all he could do not to laugh at them. He was breathing in radioactive
dust? He might die sooner if he didn't filter it out? To say he didn't give
a good goddamn showed how little language could really do.

Close to half of him already wished he were dead. Then he could
have Bess and Margaret for company again. He'd been flying back from
a political rally in upstate New York when the Russians hit the center of
Washington with one A-bomb and the Pentagon with another. If there'd
been any air-raid alarms at all, they hadn't come soon enough to let his
wife and daughter make it to the shelter under the White House.

George Marshall had been positive the Soviet Union didn't have the
air-to-air refueling capability to let its Tu-4s (monkey-copied B-29s
with Russian nameplates and hood ornaments) reach the East Coast of
the United States. The Secretary of Defense had had the courage of his
convictions. He'd been working late at the Pentagon when the second

bomb hit. Like most of the enormous building (not like all of it—the Pentagon had been too vast for one atom bomb to destroy it completely, a scary thought if ever there was one), he'd gone up in the fire and smoke and ash and dust.

Turning his head for a moment, Truman looked back toward the Capitol. The blast that leveled the White House had also smashed Congress' longtime home. It knocked off the Capitol's dome and left it lying, shattered and broken, on the Mall below. Seeing it there reminded the President of what happened when a tank turret took a direct hit from a large-caliber shell.

"What a mess," Truman muttered. "What a fucking mess!"

One of the men with the Geiger counters turned his way. The morning sun glinted off the fellow's steel-rimmed specs, making him look even less human than he would have otherwise. "What did you say, sir?" he asked.

"I said, 'What a mess,'" Truman answered. "And it is." He'd been an artillery captain during the First World War. He knew how to cuss, all right. But he didn't swear all the time, and he mostly didn't do it for show. He wasn't sorry the Defense Department technician hadn't heard him this time.

"Oh." The man gave back a grave nod. Truman still couldn't see what color his eyes were. He went on, "It sure is. 'Course, we're still hitting those Red bastards harder than they're hitting us."

"Uh-huh." Truman nodded in return. From everything he knew—and he knew more than anyone except perhaps Joe Stalin—that was true. However true it was, it offered scant consolation to him, or to the hundred thousand or so who'd died here along with his wife and daughter, or to the additional hundreds of thousands who'd perished in New York City and Boston, or to their friends and relations.

Philly would have got it, too, only the Tu-4—the NATO reporting name was Bull—with its bomb had gone down short of the target. For the first time since the turn of the nineteenth century, Philadelphia was the de facto capital of the USA because it hadn't got hit.

Not that the United States had one hell of a lot of government to put there. Truman was still alive, but he didn't take up much room. Seven of the nine Supreme Court justices survived; they'd been at a legal convention in St. Louis when the bombs dropped. But Congress was gutted like one of Hemingway's marlins after he finally dragged it into the boat.

Neither House nor Senate had a living, breathing quorum. Governors could appoint new Senators to complete unfinished terms. But if you listened to the Constitution, Representatives had to be chosen in special elections. That took time, and time was in desperately short supply in the United States right now.

More glass clinked under Truman's feet. Till the A-bomb fused it, it had been dirt or sand or concrete. It was glass now, almost the color of a Coke bottle but less transparent and full of imperfections. He stooped, picked up a piece, and held it in his palm. "How hot is this thing?" he asked the men from the Department of Defense. He wasn't talking about the temperature.

They eyed each other. "Well, let's see," said the one with the glasses. He aimed the business end of his Geiger counter at the chunk.

Truman heard a click, then another and another. They came faster than they had when the technicians were just sniffing the air, so to speak. "What does that mean?" the President asked.

"About what you'd expect, sir," the man said. "It's more radioactive than the air—this has to be somewhere close to ground zero but it isn't hot enough to hurt you in a hurry. You can keep it if you want to."

"No, thanks!" Truman had a hard time imagining anything he wanted less. He threw away the atomic glass as hard as he could. It shattered into half a dozen pieces. Sadly, he shook his head. *A tiny bit of destruction on top of the big blast,* he thought. *Looks like destruction is all people are good for.*

But it was an ill wind indeed that blew nobody any good. Among the elected officials the Soviet A-bomb had incinerated was the junior Senator from Wisconsin. Joe McCarthy had been the favorite to grab the Republican Presidential nomination at the upcoming convention. Truman knew too well that, given the Democrats' popularity on account of the war, whoever the GOP chose was odds-on to breeze to the White House (or wherever he'd stay till there was a White House again) come November.

Well, it wouldn't be Tail-Gunner Joe. Truman suspected Stalin had saved America from swallowing a good stiff dose of Fascism. Now . . . Robert Taft had also died. That should have left the field wide open for General Eisenhower. Truman didn't like Ike, but also didn't think him a bad man.

But McCarthyism seemed to be a vampire that hadn't yet had a stake pounded through its heart. A young Senator from California had taken up the cudgels for the late, unlamented (at least by Truman) Joseph McCarthy. Dick Nixon's nose reminded people of Bob Hope's. Nixon might be a lot of things, but funny he wasn't.

That, however, was the Republicans' problem. The Democrats' problem was that their leading candidate still among the living was Adlai Stevenson. Truman admired his principles and his brains. The combination had taken Stevenson a long way (his being the son of a prominent politico hadn't hurt, either). But he was not the kind of man to whom the average little guy readily warmed. And, like every other Democrat in the race, he ran with a uranium-weighted anvil on his back.

Quietly—almost whispering, in fact—Truman said, "It seemed like a good idea at the time."

"Sir?" asked the technician with the specs. Truman still hadn't seen what color his eyes were.

"Nothing," the President said hastily. "Never mind." If those weren't the saddest nine words in the English language, what would be?

He hadn't thought Stalin would retaliate if he used A-bombs in Manchuria to gum up the Red Chinese supply lines and keep Mao Tsetung from gobbling up all of Korea after his men destroyed the UN force near the Yalu. But Stalin must have decided that letting the United States beat up his biggest ally without hitting back would cost him too much face. And here Truman was, a year and a half later, shuffling through the wreckage of Washington, D.C.

"Ask you something, Mr. President?" that Defense Department man said.

"You can always ask. I don't promise to answer," Truman said.

"Sure." The fellow nodded. His eyes were gray, gray as skies that threatened rain. He went on, "Is it true that the Russians' satellites are getting frisky? You gotta understand, sir: my last name is Plummer, but my old man changed it from Plazynski."

Had Truman had a nickel for every time he'd heard a story like that, he would have been too rich to worry about politics. "They're frisky, all right," he answered. "We aren't quite sure how frisky, but enough to make the Russians wish they weren't."

Somewhere up ahead of Ihor Shevchenko, a machine gun suddenly started spitting death and mutilation at the Red Army men. "*Yob tvoyu mat'!*" he shouted at the Poles on the other end of the murder mill. He was of Ukrainian blood himself, but only the pure Russian obscenity let him tell them what he thought of them and their piece.

Without conscious thought, he pulled the entrenching tool from his belt and flipped more dirt onto the heap in front of his foxhole. His shiver had nothing to do with conscious thought, either. That wasn't just any machine gun. It was a Nazi MG-42. During the last war, the terrified Red Army men who had to go up against them tagged them Hitler's saws.

Here was another one in the stinking Poles' hands. How many had they grabbed and hidden as the Russians liberated their country from the Germans for them? (That the USSR had helped the *Reich* assassinate Poland a few years earlier was something that had never crossed Ihor's mind.)

Or maybe the bandits Ihor's section was fighting had got the machine gun from the Polish People's Army. When it formed, it might well have been happy to latch onto whatever weapons it could grab. For that matter, maybe the bandits the Red Army was fighting had come from the Polish People's Army themselves. Poles and Russians never had loved one another. As a Ukrainian, Ihor could have been neutral in their squabble. That the Poles were trying to kill him, though, cost him his detachment.

The MG-42 fell silent. Rifles in Polish hands—Russian Mosin-Nagants and German Mausers—opened up from near the tumbledown barn where the monster dwelt. They had less firepower than it did. It stayed quiet longer than a minute: just long enough to get Ihor's hopes up. Then it roared back to life.

Changing the barrel, Ihor thought. You had to do that every couple of hundred rounds or it would overheat. During the last war, the Fritzes had been far quicker than these clodhoppers were. In the end, it hadn't saved them. In the end, this MG-42 wouldn't save these Poles, either.

"Mortar crew!" Ihor shouted. "What's the matter with you pussies, anyhow? Put some bombs down on that cocksucker!"

He was just a corporal, but he sounded as pissed off as a field marshal. A sergeant had had the company since another MG-42 did for poor, brave Lieutenant Kosior. Nobody was long on manpower these days.

And nobody answered his shout. Had the machine gun taken out the crew? That would be horrible. Mortars were some of a foot slogger's favorite toys. They were almost like dehydrated artillery.

But then 82mm mortar rounds started dropping close to and on the beat-up barn. Ihor whooped every time smoke and dirt fountained up from a burst. Those Poles over there would be shitting themselves with fear. Between whoops, he grunted. It wasn't as if he'd never done that himself.

Planks flew as the mortar scored a direct hit on the barn. The wreckage started to burn. The bandits' MG-42 cut off in the middle of a long, ripping burst.

"Forward!" Ihor called to his men. "But careful, you dumb pricks! They may be conning us."

He didn't want to come out of his foxhole any more than a mouse wanted to come out of its burrow. The mouse was afraid of weasels and foxes and hawks. Ihor had worse things, things that could kill from farther away, to worry about. If you were going to lead, though, you had to *lead*.

"For Stalin!" he yelled as he scrambled toward the burning barn. He didn't love the Soviet leader—few Ukrainians who'd lived through the famines could—but he had to sound as if he did. Some of his men also took up the cry. He was no Chekist. He didn't care whether they meant it or not.

"Fuck Stalin!" a Pole shouted. Russian and Polish weren't very far apart to begin with. And quite a few Poles had had Russian rammed down their throats lately, so they could understand what their Soviet bosses told them to do.

The machine gun stayed quiet. He breathed a sigh of relief—the mortar really had put it out of action, then. It could have slaughtered his company and him if the crew was lying low, but evidently not. He felt like a cat that had just used up one of its nine lives.

Then he laughed, which wasn't something he did every day with rifle rounds cracking past him. He'd long since used up a cat's nine lives. This was probably somewhere close to his nine hundred ninety-ninth.

As if to remind him of that, his leg twinged. A chunk of missing flesh, a nasty scar, and a limp were souvenirs of his nearest brush with death in the Great Patriotic War. They'd even kept him out of the Red Army for a while this time around. Then, as things heated up and more and more sound men went into the sausage grinder, they hadn't any more.

Maybe his leg was trying to tell him something. He flopped down onto his belly in a wide, shallow hole in the ground—say, the kind of hole a 105 or 155 round might have made in the last year of the last war. It was muddy at the bottom, not that he cared.

Cautiously, he peered out and ahead. Motion focused him as if he were a hunting beast. The man who was moving didn't wear a uniform just like his. Without any conscious thought, Ihor squeezed off a burst from his AK-47.

A Kalashnikov didn't have the range of an ordinary rifle. But it was fine out to three hundred meters or so: twice as far as a submachine gun. Only snipers usually needed to hit from farther away than that. And an AK-47 put a lot more rounds in the air than a bolt-action rifle.

One of them hit the Pole, or Ihor thought so. The fellow went down like a man who'd just stopped a bullet, anyhow, not like someone diving for cover.

"Fuck Stalin!" the bandits kept calling. "Why don't you stinking turds go back to Russia and stay there and leave us the hell alone?"

Somebody from the section sounded furious as he yelled back: "Why don't you Fascist bandits quit aiding imperialism?"

Did he really believe the Poles were doing that? Maybe so; some officers seemed to. Ihor didn't care what the Poles were doing, only he wished they would quit trying to do it to him. He wanted to go back to the Ukraine, if not to Russia. He missed his wife. He hoped Anya still missed him, and hadn't found someone else on the collective farm to console her while he was gone.

No matter what he thought about the Poles and their fondness for Fascism, he had to act as if they were all growing Hitler-style mustaches, even the women. If he didn't, the MGB would be more likely to kill him than the Polish bandits were.

Red Army artillery opened up in the rear. Shells rained down on the Poles, who didn't seem to have many cannons of their own. A few short rounds rained down on his section. A soldier a couple of hundred meters from Ihor let out an anguished shriek. The jerks on your own side could kill you regardless of whether they were trying to or not.

The Poles kept fighting even after they lost their machine gun in the burning barn, even after all those 105s came down on their heads. They were much more in earnest than Ihor was. But small arms could manage only so much against the mechanized hardware of the killing industry. Sullenly, bringing off their wounded and as many of their dead as they could, they fell back.

Ihor pushed his section forward fast enough to keep Sergeant Gordeyev happy. Pavel Gordeyev was a decent guy, even in charge of the company. Like Ihor, he kept his head down, did as much of what he was told as he had to, and tried hard not to get himself or his men killed. Ihor had made a bastard of a sergeant have an unfortunate accident once upon a time. He had no impulse to do anything like that to Gordeyev. He hoped like hell none of the clowns he was in charge of had the impulse to do anything like that to him.

Once upon a time—not so long ago, as those things went, but in a past vanished, shattered, forever—Rolf Mehlen had been proud to wear *Feldgrau*. He'd been proud to put on the *Stahlhelm* with the SS runes on the side. He'd been a *Hauptsturmführer*, a captain, in the *Leibstandarte Adolf Hitler*, the outfit that started as the *Führer*'s bodyguards and wound up one of the *Reich*'s crack panzer divisions.

He'd fought till he—and Germany—couldn't fight any more. Then he'd got a doctor to cut out the blood-group tattoo under his left armpit so the victorious Ivans wouldn't give him a bullet in the back of the neck. They hated his kind as much as he hated theirs. He made it to the American occupation zone and got on with his life.

Now here he was, fighting the Red Army all over again. His uniform was of American olive-drab fabric; he had a Yankee pot on his head instead of the familiar German coal scuttle. The uniform was fine. The old helmet had protected better than the new one did, but the Russians killed out of hand anyone they caught in a *Stahlhelm*. That made him not bitch about the American headgear . . . too much.

He didn't bitch about his rifle at all. The Springfield he'd been issued was identical to his old Mauser except for its caliber. The Amis kept their fancy semiautomatic M-1s for themselves. Some guys in the West German army wanted them, but Rolf was happy with the familiar.

No wonder I joined up as soon as the war started over, he thought, using a cleaning rod to pull an oiled cloth through the Springfield's barrel. *What's more familiar to me than fighting Russians?*

Beside him in a smashed house in Liebenau sat Max Bachman. Max was also cleaning his weapon. He'd served in the *Wehrmacht* last time, not the *Waffen*-SS, but he was also an old *Frontschwein* who'd done a long hitch on the Eastern Front. He knew a clean piece was one of the things that'd keep you breathing if anything did.

Sometimes nothing would, of course. The Germans had dug bunches of graveyards in Russia. Chances were the Reds bulldozed and desecrated them all, first chance they got. "Can I bum a smoke off you, Max?" Rolf didn't want to think about graveyards.

"Why not?" Max handed him a little five-pack of Old Golds, the kind that came with American-made rations. One cigarette was already gone. "Keep it," the other veteran said. "I've got a couple more."

"Danke schön." Rolf lit one and stuck the rest in his pocket. He sucked in smoke, then blew it out again. "I burned through the last of mine this morning." He took another drag. Like his own people, the Amis preferred mild tobacco. French cigarettes, Gitanes and especially Gauloises, felt like sandpaper and blowtorches in your lungs. The cheap junk the Russians smoked tasted as if it were stretched with horseshit. For all Rolf knew, it was.

He inhaled again. He'd scavenged plenty of that nasty *makhorka* from dead and captured Ivans, in this war and the last. Even nasty tobacco beat the snot out of no tobacco at all, which was what the *Reich*'s crumbling supply services had delivered more and more often as the war went down the crapper.

Sure enough, Bachman pulled another American pack, this one with Pall Malls inside, from his breast pocket. He tapped one on the palm of his hand to tamp down the tobacco a little, then put it in his mouth and leaned toward Rolf to light it off the one that was already going.

"If you were prettier, I might've kissed you," Rolf said.

"If *you* were prettier, I might've wanted you to kiss me," Max retorted.

Their chuckles were about equally wry. Neither one of them smelled good or had washed his face any time lately. Rolf hadn't shaved in a couple of days. Max hadn't shaved in a couple of days longer than a couple of days.

"You've got gray streaks on your chin," Rolf said. When he used his index and middle fingers to show where on his own jaw, his sprouting beard rasped his fingertips.

"I know." Max shrugged. "Nothing much I can do about it, though. I wonder if I'll live long enough to go gray all over." He tilted his head back and tried to blow a smoke ring, but made a mess of it. Shrugging again, he continued, "Right this minute, the odds don't look so hot, do they?"

"I said the same thing in 1945, but I'm still here," Rolf answered. "I figure I'm like a cockroach—I always skitter away before anybody can stomp on me."

"That DDT stuff the Amis make takes care of cockroaches whether they skitter or not," Max said.

Rolf nodded. "Gotta hand it to 'em. That's good shit. I haven't had a medic spray me in a couple of weeks, but I'm still not lousy."

"Me, neither," Bachman agreed. "Back on the *Ostfront,* we always got gnawed. Lice and fleas and mosquitoes and bedbugs . . ." He mimed cracking something between his thumbnails. But then he added, "Nowadays, the Amis and the Reds both have atomic DDT to get rid of pests like us."

"Hasn't happened yet." Rolf didn't care to dwell on that, either. He stubbed out the cigarette, peeled off the paper, and dumped the last centimeter-and-a-half of tobacco into the little leather bag he wore on a thong around his neck. He didn't have much in there now—he'd gone through it—but he wasted as little as he could.

Max Bachman had one of those little bags, too. For a couple of years after the last war ended, tobacco had been money in the ruins of Germany. Losing his tattoo had cost Rolf two cartons of cigarettes: a small fortune. You smoked only what you didn't need to spend. The reflexes from that time left slowly, if they left at all.

A jeep clattered past, picking its way up the rubble-filled road toward the edge of town. Every so often, the clatter would turn to a bang as a tire climbed over a rock or some bricks and then hit the frame when it slammed back down to the cratered paving. But Rolf never heard the machine stop. The driver might piss blood after he slid out, but he'd get where he was going.

The same thought must have crossed Max's mind, for he said, "Those things are horses with wheels. They'll go anywhere. I'd rather have one than a *Kübelwagen* any day."

"Maybe." For once, Rolf didn't want to argue. The German utility vehicle wasn't bad, either, but he'd feel stupid saying it could outdo a jeep.

"Horses . . ." Bachman's mind took a new twist. "I saw an American cartoon once—I was a printer in Fulda, you know, for us and for the occupying power."

"*Ja, ja,*" Rolf said impatiently. He knew Max spoke English. Sometimes these days, it came in handy. But Max liked to hear himself talk, too. Rolf tried to make him get to the point: "So what was the cartoon?"

"A jeep had a broken axle, with one wheel all askew. A sergeant was going to put it out of its misery by shooting it in the hood with his pistol. He was looking away and had his other hand over his eyes, the way you would if you were putting down a favorite horse."

"Heh." But Rolf realized something more was called for. He went on, "That's pretty good, all right." He'd had to shoot some horses in his time. The LAH was a mechanized outfit, but infantry divisions and even *Wehrmacht* panzer units used a lot of animal transport. During Russian winters, his superiors didn't sneer at horseflesh. *Panje* wagons drawn by Russian ponies could get through drifted snow where nothing else could. And . . . "You get hungry enough, you can eat horsemeat. You can't chop up a jeep and make goulash out of it."

"Nope. That doesn't work," Max agreed. "Some of the horses I ate when times were hard, though, I might as well have been gnawing on old inner tubes."

"I wonder if we were eating out of the same pot of stew," Rolf said with a chuckle. "But you mostly fought farther north than I did, right?"

"Uh-huh." Max paused as Russian guns rumbled off in the distance. As soon as he realized the shells wouldn't come down anywhere close by, he relaxed. He lit a new cigarette. After a moment, so did Rolf.

Bruce McNulty paused at the edge of the churchyard in the English village with the quaint name of Great Snoring. His dark blue U.S. Air Force captain's uniform didn't contrast too harshly with the black suits and dresses most of the mourners had on.

He didn't know whether or not to go sit in one of the wooden folding chairs they were using. There were plenty; not many people had come to Daisy Baxter's funeral. Most of her friends and relatives in Fakenham—a few miles from Great Snoring—had died when the Russians A-bombed the base at next-door Sculthorpe that the USAF and RAF shared.

Daisy'd almost died herself then. But she got over her radiation sickness. *And she caught me instead,* Bruce thought. They'd been parked on a quiet country lane in the middle of the night when a Russian bomber got shot down right above them. They'd jumped out of the car, run in opposite directions—and a flaming chunk of debris came down right on top of her.

He looked down at his hands. He had bandages on both of them. They still hurt from his trying to pull her free, burn ointment or no. Even if he could have done more than he had, it wouldn't have mattered. That chunk of aluminum and steel would have killed her even if it hadn't been splashed with blazing jet fuel.

His heart hurt worse than his hands. They'd been in love. She was a widow; her tankman husband hadn't come back from World War II. For Bruce, it was the first time, or near enough. Everything would have been wonderful. It would have been, and now it wouldn't be.

One or two of the Englishmen and -women had looked back and seen him now. How much did they blame him? Not so much as he blamed himself, surely. If he hadn't been a horny SOB who'd stopped on that black, silent lane for the most obvious of reasons, she'd still be alive.

The coffin, which sat by the open, waiting grave, was closed. No doubt it had been closed inside the church, too. He knew how pretty Daisy'd been. He also knew, too well, that what was left of her wasn't.

The Church of England priest or minister or preacher or whatever you called him was finishing the service for the burial of the dead, mouthing words he must have used countless times before: "Into thy hands, O Lord, we commend thy servant, uh, Daisy, our dear sister, as into the hands of a faithful Creator and most merciful Savior, beseeching thee that she may be precious in thy sight. Wash her, we pray thee, in the blood of the immaculate Lamb that was slain to take away the sins of the world; that, whatsoever defilements she may have contracted in the midst of this earthly life being purged and done away, she may be presented pure and without spot before thee; through the merits of Jesus Christ thine only son our Lord. Amen."

"Amen," Bruce murmured. Somehow, the almost-biblical language from the Book of Common Prayer did ease his heartache, at least a little and at least for a little while. He wished he could have come on time and got the full dose inside the old church. But he'd had to pull more strings and do more paperwork to liberate his motor-pool jeep than he'd expected. So he was late. But, late or not, he was here.

On and on the priest droned. It was almost as impressive as the Latin of a Catholic service would have been. It took you out of yourself. When someone you loved died, what more could you ask for?

The churchyard crew or gravediggers or whoever the quietly waiting men in dark work togs were lowered the coffin and what was left of Daisy Baxter into the new hole in the ground with straps. Then, tugging and grunting, they pulled the straps up from under the coffin and out of the grave. Daisy's mortal remains stayed behind.

After the clergyman murmured a final prayer whose words Bruce couldn't catch, he turned and started back to the church at a slow walk. The people who'd come to the service stood up. A woman dabbed at her eyes with a tissue. An older man with a hook where his left hand should have been used a handkerchief for the same reason.

One by one, the mourners left the churchyard. Most of them filed past Bruce as if he didn't exist. If they knew who he was, they didn't fancy what they knew. But the man with only one hand paused. "You'd be Daisy's Yank, wouldn't you?" he said.

Bruce nodded. "That's right. I saw you a few times at the Owl and Unicorn"—the pub Daisy'd run till the Russians bombed Sculthorpe— "but you're gonna have to remind me what your name is."

"Wilf Davies."

"That's right! Daisy always said what a nice guy you were." Bruce glanced down at his bandaged mitts. "You've got to forgive me for not shaking hands."

"I wasn't worried about it." Davies touched the hook with the index finger of his good hand. "I got me this at the Somme, more than thirty-five years ago now. Could've been the other just as easy." He eyed Bruce's bandages, too. "You did whatever you could, that's plain."

"I couldn't do anything, not—one—damned—thing." Bruce bit the words off one by one. If he let himself think about that, he'd start screaming.

"You tried. It shows what she meant to you." After another swipe at his eyes, Wilf Davies went on, "She was a peach, Daisy was. If I was half my age and single, and if I hadn't caught a packet of my own in the first war, I might've given you a run for your money there."

"I'm not surprised," Bruce said. Plenty of fliers from Sculthorpe, Americans and Englishmen, had tried to get the pretty widow to notice them. Bruce was glad he'd been the lucky one—glad and sorry at the same time. If Daisy'd ignored him the way she'd ignored the rest of them, she'd still be alive.

"You're a bomber pilot, aren't you? She told me you were," Davies said.

"That's right." Bruce nodded again. "I fly a B-29. I'll go back to it once I finish healing up."

"You do to the Russians what they done to Sculthorpe and Norwich and all them places, isn't that right?"

"Officially, I'm not supposed to say anything about what I do," Bruce answered. "Security, you know."

That seemed to be enough to satisfy the mutilated veteran. "I know I shot me a Hun or two before I caught me this," he said, raising the hook. "Have you the faintest notion about how many people you've killed? D'you mind my asking you like that?"

"No-oo, not really," Bruce said, which wasn't exactly a lie but wasn't exactly the truth, either. He spread his hands. "Daisy asked me the same question. I'll tell you what I told her: I don't know. I couldn't even begin to guess."

During the last war, a few Nazi extermination-camp commandants might have got more blood on their hands than he had. Some other American flyers now, and maybe some Russians with them, also might be in the same ballpark. Maybe, back in the day, Genghis Khan had come pretty close. Bruce couldn't be sure. He couldn't say how many he'd killed, not to the nearest hundred thousand. All he could say was, it was a big number.

Wilf Davies clicked his tongue between his teeth. "Do you ever have nights where you can't sleep for thinking about it?"

"A few," Bruce admitted. "Not so many as you'd expect, though. When you fly a bombing mission, any kind of bombing mission, you don't think about the people down below. You can't, not unless you want to lose your marbles. You think about hitting the target, that's all. Once the bombs go, you think about getting the hell out of there."

"Well, all right," Davies said. "I can see that. I didn't think about killing Germans every time I pulled the trigger, but I bet I got a few I don't know a thing about. It's a rum old world, ain't it?"

"Mr. Davies, you said a mouthful there." Bruce wondered how much he'd sleep tonight. Not much, unless he missed his guess.

BORIS GRIBKOV NODDED in relief as Alexei Vavilov said, "Well, we'll let you out of this metal cigar pretty soon."

"Can't be soon enough!" Gribkov exclaimed: a sentiment straight from the heart.

The skipper of the *S-71* mimed being cut to the quick. "What, Comrade Pilot? You don't care for our elegant accommodations?"

"Now that you mention it, Captain," Gribkov answered, "no." Vavilov was only a commander, but Boris gave him the title every officer in charge of a vessel enjoyed. Boris admired the technical skill that went into making and using the submarine (it was a close copy of a German boat, just as the Tu-4 he'd flown was an even closer copy of an American plane). The sub had picked him and his ten crewmen out of the Atlantic after he bombed Washington. It had eluded the U.S. Navy and the Royal Navy and brought the bomber crew back to the White Sea.

It was only a few kilometers from port now—and Boris couldn't wait to escape it. It had been overcrowded even before the Tu-4 crew came aboard. The air inside the stogie-shaped steel tube reeked of unbathed sailors, stale food, diesel oil, puke, and backed-up heads. The chow went from bad to worse. Gribkov scratched his beard. It was coming in nice and thick, even if he'd have to shave it off as soon as he got onto dry land and to a place where he *could* shave.

He'd shave it off if Kem had any places like that, anyhow. He'd never heard of the Karelian town before Commander Vavilov told him they were going there. As Karelian towns went, Kem was fair-sized. It held about 10,000 people.

Murmansk? Archangel? As ports, both cities far outdid Kem. Or they had outdone it. No more. The Soviet Union's only two harbors ice-free the year around, children of the dying Gulf Stream, had both gone up in atomic fire. The *S-71* had stayed underwater, breathing through a snorkel, as she entered the White Sea near Murmansk.

Commander Vavilov got back to work. He ordered the submarine to the surface. The crew carried out his commands almost before he gave them. Boris Gribkov watched the skipper in action with a fascination he'd felt since the moment he'd clambered out of his rubber life raft and aboard the odorous sub.

It wasn't just that the *S-71*'s crew was so much larger than a Tu-4's. Gribkov was much more a tsar than Vavilov. Sure, Vavilov had and used command authority. But he used it more as a team captain than as an autocrat. He had to depend more on the sailors to get what he wanted done than Gribkov did 9,000 meters up in the sky.

Vavilov climbed the steel ladder up to the top of the conning tower and opened the hatch up there. "*Bozhemoi!*" he said. "We've been submerged a devil of a long time. That first whiff of fresh air smells extra good!"

A few seconds later, the fresh air got down to Boris. It seemed wonderful—and then, all of a sudden, it didn't. Gribkov got some of the moist, salt-smelling air from outside and, as the atmosphere inside the boat eddied, a lungful of what he'd been breathing for so long. That was twice as nasty after getting out of his nose for a moment.

"Comrade Captain, permission to come up?" he called.

"Granted, of course," Alexei Vavilov said. "Not much to see, but you're welcome to what there is."

Up the ladder Gribkov went. When he stuck his head out of the open hatch, he screwed up his face and narrowed his eyes. He blinked several times and had to wipe away tears anyhow. He'd lived a long time in a twilight world of dim orange lightbulbs. That big bright thing up in the sky—that was the sun. Even through sea mist, it overwhelmed his startled vision.

"The sky, the water . . . They're pretty wide, aren't they?" he said. He wasn't used to being able to see more than a few meters down in the bowels of the *S-71*. The passageway that led from the forward torpedo tubes back to the batteries and the engine room had irregular zigs and zags for no reason he could find, and was barely wide enough for two men going in opposite directions to squeeze past each other.

Land lay dead ahead. A signal lamp on the end of a pier was flashing Morse at the submarine. Vavilov uncovered the boat's lamp and click-clacked its shutters. Boris had learned Morse once upon a time, but his was rusty from disuse. "What's going on?" he asked.

"Landing instructions," the skipper answered. "Oh, and they'll take charge of you and your men as soon as you disembark. They've got a train waiting to take you down to Petrozavodsk."

"*Khorosho,*" Boris said, hoping it *would* be good. Petrozavodsk was a medium-sized town—bigger than Kem, smaller than Murmansk (or at least Murmansk as it had been)—somewhere to the south. Just how far to the south, he didn't know; he'd never heard of Kem before the *S-71* proposed stopping there.

He and his men could leave Petrozavodsk by rail. Or, if the authorities were in a hurry, they could fly out. Petrozavodsk would have an airstrip, maybe even an airport. Plainly, the Americans hadn't knocked it flat with an A-bomb. That was good. If atomic hell descended on places as unimportant as Petrozavodsk, nothing would be left of the USSR by the time this war finally ended.

Nothing may be left of it any which way, Gribkov thought unhappily.

Vavilov called orders down through the open hatch. He guided the *S-71* alongside one of the piers that thrust out into the White Sea from the low, swampy ground edging it. A mosquito buzzed. Boris automatically swatted at it.

Longshoremen tossed lines to sailors trotting along the sub's deck. They made the boat fast. It was much the biggest vessel tied up at Kem. The rest were fishing boats and one slightly larger gray patrol boat that sported a heavy machine gun and was probably manned by the MGB's border guards.

He wondered whether Chekists would be waiting for him and the rest of the Tu-4's crew. He'd had an earlier run-in with the secret police, when his then-navigator stuck a pistol in his mouth after they A-bombed Paris. But the officer waving from the pier wore khaki with sky-blue arm-of-service colors on his cap and shoulder boards. He belonged to the Red Air Force, then.

Commander Vavilov called down into the *S-71*. The flyers who'd bombed Washington with Gribkov came up one after another. None of them had any more than the clothes on his back. They were all shaggy and none too clean. Boris could tell they smelled bad. He realized he had to smell bad himself.

Longshoremen shoved a couple of planks from the pier to the sub to let the airmen off her. Since she'd cruised under the sea, not on it, Boris didn't have to get his land legs back when he took a few steps on the pier, whose boards and pilings were black with creosote.

Up strode the young lieutenant. He and Gribkov exchanged salutes. He gave his name as Arkady Medvedev and pointed to a truck at the end of the pier. "If you and your men will come with me, sir, we'll go straight to the waiting train."

"Is there any chance we can clean up first?" Boris stroked his beard with his left hand.

But Lieutenant Medvedev shook his head. "Sorry, sir, but my orders are to put you on the train the instant you come in to Kem."

Gribkov sighed. Whoever'd given Medvedev those orders had probably never come within five hundred kilometers of a submarine, and had no idea what life inside one was like. Boris hadn't known anything about that till he boarded the *S-71,* either. But what could you do? "We serve the Soviet Union!" he said, speaking for his men. The stock phrase could mean anything from *Yes, sir!* to *We're stuck with it,* which was what he used it for.

The train had only one car. Medvedev got in with the flyers. The engine driver blew a blast on his steam whistle and chugged out of Kem. The powers that be were treating the aircrew like very important people. For a few kilometers, Boris supposed that was because they were heroes, men who'd avenged Moscow on Washington. Then it occurred to him to wonder just how many well-trained, successful bomber crews the Soviet Union had left. He wished he hadn't had that thought. Once it lodged in his head, it didn't want to go away.

Herschel Weissman nodded to the men who drove and installed appliances for him at Blue Front. "Well, they've finally got the Hollywood Freeway and the Pasadena opened up again," he said. "Took 'em long enough—months longer than they promised."

Along with most of the other guys, Aaron Finch nodded. He'd seen the announcement in yesterday afternoon's paper, and heard it on the TV and radio news. The freeways, which had been one of L.A.'s larger claims to fame, had been out of commission since the Russians A-bombed the city more than a year before.

"For some of the routes we use," his boss went on, "we'll be able to save a lot of time now, getting to where we need to go. The more deliveries we can make, the better off we'll be."

Aaron nodded again. Since the bombs fell on downtown and the port at San Pedro, business had been crappy. That was putting it mildly. Weissman hadn't canned anyone, but he'd cut everybody's hours. Aaron liked that no better than anyone else who'd been an adult during the Depression. You wanted as much work as you could possibly grab. When you had a wife and a son who'd just turned three back home, you *really* wanted as much work as you could grab.

Next to him, Jim Summers stuck up a hand. Weissman nodded. "What do you want, Jim?" he asked.

Aaron wondered the same thing—apprehensively. He and Summers crewed a Blue Front truck together. Summers was a lot bigger and heavier than his own trim five-nine and 150 pounds, but he was also much less fond of hard work. He did what he had to do to get by, but not a nickel's worth more. A nickel's worth less? Yes, sometimes, because he counted on Aaron to bail him out. And Aaron always did.

Now Summers asked, "Boss, do we *got* to go through downtown on them damn freeways? Can't we keep goin' around like we been doin'? I bet them roads glow in the dark from all the atoms in 'em, y'know?" The way he talked said he came from Arkansas or Alabama or some place like that. It also said he hadn't had much education while he was there.

"All the officials and the scientists say it's safe to drive on the freeways now, Jim." The way Herschel Weissman talked, he was holding on to his patience with both hands.

"Huh! Who trusts them folks? All they give a damn about is linin' their pockets." Jim didn't—quite—add *just like you*. He didn't like Jews almost as much as he didn't like Negroes. He'd only recently realized Aaron (whose father had changed the family name from Fink to duck such problems) was Jewish. That made working with him . . . interesting.

"Jim, you don't have to use the freeways if you don't want to," Weissman said. Summers started to grin. Then the man who'd started Blue Front went on, "I'm sure you can find another job where you don't need to go near them at all."

The grin curdled on Jim's face. Aaron half hoped the redneck would turn and walk out. In that case, he'd have to get used to working with someone else. He didn't look forward to doing so; he wasn't the most outgoing of men. But he wouldn't have been heartbroken, either.

It turned out not to matter. Summers had gone through the Depression, too. A job in hand was worth a dozen in the bush. "Well, I reckon I got to take my chances, then," he muttered.

The first delivery Aaron and he made was of a washing machine. It was in Glendale, only a couple of miles from the Blue Front warehouse—

and even closer to the house in the hills where Aaron's brother Marvin lived. Jim grumbled all the way there. "I still say it ain't right," he told Aaron. "Who knows how much o' that fallout shit ain't fallen out yet?"

"Not me." Aaron didn't feel like listening, and tried to deflect him. "But they've got to be checking all the time. That's their job."

"Harry goddamn Truman's job was not gettin' us into a big ole brawl to begin with, an' look how good he done it," Summers retorted. "Just on account of you're smart don't mean you can't fubar somethin'."

That held just enough truth to leave Aaron without a ready comeback. He let Jim bitch till they got to the house with the Spanish-tile roof. Grunting and swearing under his breath, Jim wrestled the new washing machine onto a dolly and down the ramp at the back of the truck.

Aaron did the installation. Before he could, he unhooked the old wringer machine in the laundry room and lugged it out to the curb. "I hope somebody steals it for scrap metal," said the housewife who'd ordered the new one. "Every time I used it, I was scared it'd eat my hand. These automatic washers, they're the greatest thing since sliced bread."

"I hope you're happy with it, ma'am," Aaron said diplomatically. His wife still used a wringer washing machine. Ruth talked about getting a new one, but they weren't cheap, and the Finches had other things they needed worse. She treated the wringer with respect, but she wasn't afraid of it like Mrs. Tompkins here.

Jim went right on pissing and moaning when they drove back to the warehouse. Now, though, he wasn't bellyaching about the radioactive freeways. "Miserable cheap bitch," he said. "She didn't tip us a lousy dime. Jesus Christ, she didn't even give us a glass o' lemonade."

"I thought you didn't like lemonade." Aaron shoved in the truck's cigarette lighter so he could fire up one of the many Chesterfields he went through each day.

"I don't," Summers said, "but she coulda offered."

Aaron thought about saying something to that, but after a moment realized he had no idea what. It made more sense than some of the things Jim came out with, not that that was saying much. And, as Jim intended, it did say something about Mrs. Tompkins. It also said some-thing about him, though chances were he had no idea about that.

For the next delivery, though, they did need to go through down-town. They had to take a TV set to Boyle Heights, on the east side of Los Angeles. It was a big Packard-Bell, with a twenty-one-inch screen in an Early American cabinet. It was, in fact, quite a bit like the one Aaron had bought for himself, though with innards a bit more modern. Still, you could save yourself a good bit of money when the picture had trouble by taking the vacuum tubes to a testing machine in a drugstore and putting in your own replacements when you had to. Only after you found you couldn't fix it on your own was it time to call the repairman.

When they got close to downtown on the Pasadena Freeway, Jim pulled an old blue bandanna out of the pocket of his gabardine work pants and tied it over his mouth and nose to make an improvised surgi-cal mask. He'd done that before when they went through places he thought to be contaminated. Aaron doubted it did him any good, but didn't suppose it hurt, either.

He did say, "That thing makes you look like a bank robber on *Hop-along Cassidy*."

"I don't give a rat's ass," Jim replied.

"Well, take it off before we bring in the TV set."

"I will. We'll be out of the worst of it by then anyways."

The freeways might be working again, but downtown still looked like hell. City Hall was a melted stub, half its former height. Most of the rest was still a field of rubble. Bulldozers and steam shovels kicked up clouds of dust as they leveled things further. They kicked up so much dust, Aaron wondered if he should wear a bandanna, too.

Boyle Heights, by contrast, was a going concern. It was a mixed neighborhood, Jewish and Japanese and Mexican. Some of the shops had Yiddish signs. Aaron spoke Yiddish, but he could no more read it than he could the Oriental characters on other storefronts.

Mrs. Lois Hanafusa accepted delivery on the TV. She offered them orange juice from a tree in her yard, and gave them two dollars each as they headed back to the truck. "Ain't that a hell of a thing?" Jim said when they were on their way back to the warehouse. "A Jap nicer'n a white lady! What's the world coming to?"

"They're all people," Aaron said. By the look Summers gave him, he had no idea what Aaron was talking about.

"Your rifle clean, Jimmy?" Cade Curtis asked.

"Oh, you bet, Captain!" Jimmy answered, and eagerly thrust his M-1 at Cade. Curtis had to inspect it then. As he'd known beforehand it would be, it was sparkling, the woodwork polished and the barrel gleaming. He checked the action. It worked with oiled perfection.

Cade tossed the rifle back. "Way to go!" he said, and gave Jimmy a thumbs-up.

"Thank you, sir!" Jimmy grinned like Christmas morning with a Schwinn under the tree.

Lieutenant Howard Sturgis fell into step with Cade as the regimental CO walked down the muddy trench. Everything seemed quiet for the moment in this little piece of South Korea. Red Chinese trenches zigzagged the earth a few hundred yards to the north. But the Chinks weren't doing more than squeezing off a shot every minute or so, just to remind the UN forces they were still around. They weren't blaring propaganda from their loudspeakers, either. It wasn't peace, or even a truce. On the other hand, it also wasn't stark terror.

Sturgis lit a Camel. He was ten or fifteen years older than Cade, who was getting close to his twenty-first birthday. Sturgis had been a senior noncom in the war against the Nazis. He'd won a battlefield promotion— which he hadn't much wanted—here on the other side of the world.

When he held out the pack to Cade, Cade took one with a murmur of thanks. He hadn't smoked when he came to Korea as a green, green second lieutenant. He sure did now.

"That Jimmy!" Sturgis said, shaking his head. He kept his voice down even though they'd gone far enough so Jimmy couldn't hear. "Fuck me up the ass if he's not a piece of work and a half!" He still talked like a noncom, sure as hell.

"Why? Just because his weapon would pass a white-glove inspection back at boot camp?" Cade said. "Just because he respects officers? Just because he even likes them?"

"Damn straight . . . uh, sir," Sturgis said stoutly. "It's un-American. It ain't natural, not even a little bit. C'mon, you know as well as I do the guy's Asiatic."

Asiatic was Army slang for squirrely, around the bend, nuts. Cade was sure that was how the veteran meant it. But the word had other meanings, too. "Of course he's Asiatic, for cryin' out loud," Cade said. "He can't help it, you know."

"There is that," Howard Sturgis admitted. "Till he pulls a stunt like he did back there, though, you forget about it. I don't even notice what he looks like any more. He could be an ordinary draftee."

"Uh-huh." Cade doubted that Sturgis would have forgotten what Jimmy looked like had he been a Negro. He doubted whether he would have himself. Born in Alabama and raised in Tennessee, he knew the difference between white and black. He didn't get as excited about it as some people from his part of the country did, but he couldn't pretend it wasn't there.

That wasn't what made Jimmy Asiatic, though. Jimmy damn well *was* Asiatic. He'd been born Chun Won-ung, and was serving as a private in the Republic of Korea's army when he drew Cade's notice. Cade stopped the kid's captain from knocking him around. ROK officers had mostly learned to be soldiers from the Japanese, who'd ruled Korea till 1945. Jap officers and sergeants treated their men worse than the SPCA let Americans treat a dog.

After Cade came to Chun Won-ung's aid once, the kid couldn't stay in his unit. His captain would have made him pay and pay and pay. So he'd stayed with the Americans instead. Now the only way—apart from his looks—you could tell he didn't come from Knoxville or Rochester was that he believed in spit and polish and treated officers (especially Cade) with more respect than they deserved.

Off to the east in the distance, somebody's artillery woke up. Cade and Howard Sturgis cocked their heads to one side, listening to that faraway thunder. "Those're Russian 155s," Sturgis said. "Nothin' we got to worry about unless they get a lot closer, but. . . ."

"Yeah. But," Cade agreed. Those were some of the heavier guns Stalin had donated to Mao's soldiers. The Red Chinese didn't have a lot of them, and had to watch how they used the ones they did have. When they trotted them out, serious attacks often followed.

It was funny, in a macabre way. When Cade got to Korea, late in the summer of 1950, it was the biggest show in town. The whole world watched the fight with breathless attention, wondering where the confrontation between Communism and the United States would go.

Now, to its sorrow, the whole world knew. Western Europe, which had just been getting back on its feet after the horror of World War II, had worse horrors visited upon it. So did Eastern Europe and Russia, which took even more terrible beatings in the last war. So did northeastern Red China. Two A-bombs had fallen on South Korea.

And the United States discovered it wasn't immune. Both coasts had got hammered. No one had the least idea how many people were dead. As far as Cade could see, no one much cared. After so many, what were another half-million deaths?

With so much slaughter all around the poor suffering world, it had done its best to forget about the fight in Korea. Everyone not involved in this fight had, anyhow. But it ground on whether anybody else was looking or not. The Red Chinese had an easier time supplying their men than the USA did—all the more so with most West Coast ports and the Panama Canal smashed. Mao's troops held better than half of what had been South Korea before all the fun started.

They wanted more. The artillery fire got louder and closer. It was coming west across the front. Cade looked for the nearest dugout to dive into. He had the feeling he'd need it any minute.

Belatedly, American guns answered the Reds' barrage. That was good, as far as it went. It didn't go far enough. A ripple of fire on the northern horizon, a rising, demented shriek in the air . . .

"Katyushas!" Cade yelled, and threw himself flat where the trench floor met the forward wall.

No time for anything else, not when the rockets were already in the air and screaming down fast. A few launch trucks' worth of them could level most of a square mile in moments. The Nazis had fled in terror the first time the Red Army used them, and Cade didn't blame those krauts one bit. He wanted to do the same. All that held him in place was the certain knowledge that running wouldn't help.

"Up!" he yelled as soon as hell stopped falling from the sky. "Get up and fight, God damn it to hell!" He wondered how many of his men—how many of his uninjured men—could hear him. He had trouble hearing himself. He felt his ears, wondering whether blast from the Katyushas had made them bleed . . . again. Not this time—and that was snot under his nose this time, not type A Rh-negative.

He jerked the charging handle and chambered a round in his PPSh. The Russian-made submachine gun was a better weapon than the M-1 carbine most U.S. officers carried. For street fighting or cleaning out a trench, it was better than an M-1 rifle. All it lacked was range.

Howard Sturgis carried a rifle in spite of officer's rank. He jumped up on the firing step beside Cade. They both started banging away at the oncoming Red Chinese. The Chinks howled in dismay. After so many rockets, you always hoped you'd killed or maimed everyone in front of you.

Another rifle stuttered death at the Reds. Yeah, that was Jimmy. For a stray puppy, he was mighty handy with an M-1. Machine guns and mortars also bit chunks out of the enemy. When the Red Chinese first entered the war, they would have kept coming no matter what. Not any more. Firing as they went, they resentfully pulled back. *Made it through another one,* Cade thought, though cries from his own trenches and from the Red Chinese wounded in no-man's-land reminded him that not everyone had.

Konstantin Morozov and Juris Eigims worked side by side on the T-54's V-54 diesel. It was a pretty reliable, pretty straightforward piece of machinery. Konstantin had learned on the smaller powerplant the

T-34/85 used in the last war. This was Eigims' first fight, but he'd shown he knew what he was doing. And the more maintenance you took care of ahead of time, the fewer emergency repairs you needed later.

"Hand me that eight-millimeter wrench, will you, Juris?" Morozov said.

"Here you go, Comrade Sergeant," the Latvian or Lithuanian answered, passing him the tool. His accent turned Russian to music. At first, he'd resented Konstantin for taking over his tank when he wanted to command it himself. They worked well together now. Working well together kept them both alive.

Morozov used the wrench to tighten a bolt and secure a couple of wires, then gave it back. "*Spasibo*," he said.

"Any time." Eigims wiped sweat on the sleeve of his coveralls. Camouflage netting concealed their tank and several others near the center square in the little German town of Dassel. Eigims leaned away from the V-54 to light a cigarette.

He offered Konstantin one. Glad for an excuse to take a five-minute break, the tank commander took it. "*Spasibo*," he repeated.

"Sure." Eigims blew smoke up toward the netting. Then he said, "Ask you something, Comrade Sergeant?"

"Be my guest," Morozov said expansively.

"Now I thank you," Eigims told him. "Suppose we get the order to go east and turn our tank against our fraternal socialist allies in Poland or Hungary or Czechoslovakia—one of those places. What do we do then?"

Konstantin had heard things about what was going on in the satellites, and how American-backed Fascists were trying to take them out of the peace-loving people's camp and bring them around to favor the reactionaries and imperialists. He didn't know how much of that was true, but he figured some of it was. In the last war, he'd seen that not all the people who filled the smaller countries between the USSR and Germany loved Russians. For that matter, he'd seen that not all the people who lived inside the USSR loved Russians. Just for instance, Latvians and Lithuanians sure didn't.

A puff on his Belomor bought him time to think. At last, he said, "You disobey orders, your story doesn't have a happy ending."

"I understand that, Comrade Sergeant," the gunner said. "But . . . you never grew up in a country that got grabbed when all it wanted to do was mind its own business."

With a theatrical gesture, Konstantin dug his index finger into his right ear. When he pulled it away, there actually was some earwax stuck on his grimy fingernail. He brushed it off on the leg of his coveralls. "Did you say something there?" he asked. "Gun must have gone off by my ear too often. I didn't hear a thing."

The Balt reached out and softly hit him in the shoulder. "I didn't like you for hell when you got this tank, but you're all right, you know that?"

"I don't have any idea what you're talking about," Morozov said. Juris Eigims had put his life in Konstantin's hands when he asked that question. Plenty of tank commanders would have hotfooted it to the company political officer to report him. Konstantin wondered why he didn't aim to do that himself. Probably because Eigims was a pretty damn good gunner, and because he'd quit giving grief. Konstantin went on, "Follow orders, don't make anybody notice you while you're here, and you can worry about all the rest of the crap after the Red Army lets you go."

"You make it sound so easy," Eigims said.

"*Bozhemoi,* it *is* easy!" Konstantin exclaimed. "All the bastards who've got an emblem that isn't the red star are the enemy. If we don't kill them first, they'll kill us. Long as you remember that, it doesn't get complicated."

"But what if they're on the right side and we're on the wrong one?"

"What if they are?" Konstantin said. Eigims gaped at him. Despite the gape, he continued, "Does that make us any less dead if they do kill us?"

"No, Comrade Sergeant," Eigims said in a small voice.

"Damn right it doesn't," Konstantin agreed. "C'mon, then. Smoke break's over. Let's get this son of a bitch running as good as we can so things don't break down when we need 'em most."

A resupply column made it up to Dassel in spite of everything American planes could do. Some of it got to Dassel, anyhow. The drivers swigged vodka and smoked and shook and told stories about the trucks full of ammo and fuel and food that air attacks had torched. But the survivors brought enough shells to fill most of the stowage slots in Konstantin's T-54 and enough diesel oil to bring the fuel tank closer to three-quarters than half. Rations? Those didn't do so well. But Morozov was a Red Army veteran. He was sure he could always scrounge enough to keep going.

He was glad the convoy got there when it did. American eight-inch and 240mm shells started falling into Dassel. They could fire those from thirty kilometers away, far beyond the range at which any reasonable artillery could reply. Not many rounds came in, but a hit from one would bring down a couple of houses and spray shrapnel across several hundred meters. You didn't want to be anywhere near one when it blew up, in other words. You also didn't want one of those gigantic shells to burst on top of a tank, especially if you happened to be inside it. The chances were slim. Seeing it happen once was twice too often for Konstantin.

The regimental CO was a canny young major named Genrikh Zhuk. As soon as the first T-54 made a fireworks display of itself, he ordered the rest out of Dassel, up to within a kilometer of the front line west of town. "No closer," he told Morozov. "We don't want enemy troops spotting us. If they do, those horrible guns will shift their aiming point."

"I got it, sir," Morozov said, saluting more sincerely than usual. To make sure the move stayed secret, they carried it out at night.

Demyan Belitsky found a patch of bushes three meters high that screened most of the tank from view from the west. He stopped behind it. Then he and Vazgan Sarkisyan got out and cut more bushes to finish camouflaging the machine. Driver and loader were the junior crew positions. The men who filled them got more than their share of nasty work.

Every so often, another enormous shell would smash down on Dassel. Konstantin pitied the foot soldiers left behind. A few skinny, raggedy Germans still skulked through the town and lurked in the cellars, too. Konstantin had scant pity to spare for the Fritzes. As far as he was concerned, they could take their chances. They'd come too close to killing him too damn many times.

All of Major Zhuk's cleverness turned out to be for nothing. The next morning, not too long after sunrise, American bombs and guns started pounding the front about twenty-five kilometers south of where Morozov's T-54 sat. It was just distant rumbling to him, but not to the man in charge of the regiment.

Zhuk came on the all-tanks circuit: "We are ordered to pull back toward the southeast. The imperialist aggressors are attempting to force a breakthrough."

By the order, they weren't just attempting it. They were doing it. Konstantin said nothing of that. When he got the tank moving, Juris Eigims gave him a look. Morozov only shrugged. If the gunner wanted to—and if he kept doing his job here—he could dream about living in a pisspot-sized free country as much as he pleased. Because that would be all it was—dreaming.

ISTVAN SZOLOVITS QUEUED UP for lunch. The Frenchmen
behind the counter at the POW camp's mess hall couldn't have looked
any more bored if they were dead. He shoved his tray along and found
himself with a tin of applesauce, another tin of green beans, and a slab
of Spam.

The Magyar behind him in line poked him in the ribs. "Hey, Jewboy, you oughta complain about that," he said.

"Oh, shut up, Miklos," Istvan told him.

Miklos only laughed. He had a Turul, a mythical bird that symbol-
ized Magyar nationalism, tattooed on the back of one hand and the
Arrow Cross, the emblem of the Fascist party that had run Hungary
during the last few months of World War II, on the other. He'd tried to
knock the shit out of Istvan the minute he came into the Hungarian
barracks. Since Istvan had walloped him instead, now—like a surprising number of Fascists—he had his very own pet Jew.

Since he'd literally marked himself as a Fascist, Istvan was faintly
surprised that the Communists who'd taken power in the country after
the war had let him serve in the Hungarian People's Army instead of
shipping him off to a reeducation camp or just shooting him. Along

with being Communists, quite a few of the new bosses—including Matyas Rakosi, the head man—were also Jews.

But Istvan was no more than faintly surprised. Miklos was a Rottweiler of a soldier. Point him at something and he'd do his best to kill it for you. What it was hardly mattered. He just needed a target.

Now, as the bored worker gave him some Spam of his own, he said, "They're discriminating against you. You gonna let 'em get away with that kind of shit?"

More than faintly surprised Miklos knew a word as long as *discriminating*, Istvan answered, "Yeah. Why not? Not like our own army didn't feed all of us pork—when it bothered to feed us anything." He took a mug of coffee and headed for a table.

Hungarians sat with Hungarians, Poles with Poles, Czechoslovakians and East Germans with their own kind. German was the language most likely to be understood throughout the camp.

Miklos swigged from the mug of coffee he'd got, then sat down by Istvan. "This is better chow than the horrible slop we got from our own side, sure as shit," he said. "They give us more of it, too."

"I noticed the same thing," Istvan said.

"Pisser, ain't it?"

"Oh, maybe a little bit," Istvan answered. Along with fighting an atomic war and a ground war against the Soviet Union and its allies, the USA was taking care of the prisoners of war who came in. Most of the guards and cooks and such here were French, but the supplies— everything from cots to canned food—came from America. The rations and the bedding the Yankees gave to POWs were better than the ones the People's Republic of Hungary issued to its own soldiers. If that wasn't daunting, Istvan didn't know what would be.

Miklos made what was on his tray disappear in nothing flat. "I'm going back for seconds," he said. "How about you?"

"I'm all right," Istvan answered. Miklos walked back to the tail of the queue. As long as he was willing to wait to get more, they'd give it to him. They didn't care. They had plenty of everything. Istvan remembered how lucky he'd felt when he stole a pack of cigarettes from a dead American. Now he had all of those flavorful smokes he wanted.

After he dumped his tray and utensils, he put on his cleats and went over to the football pitch. The Hungarian POW team was practicing on one half of it; the East Germans, whom they'd face Saturday, were kicking the ball around on the other. Istvan was a central defender, longer on size, muscle, and the occasional discreet elbow than on speed.

He also used his elbows on his teammates, not too hard most of the time. He wasn't trying to hurt them, just to keep them from getting past him and in on goal. "Watch it, you fucking clodhopper!" one of them shouted.

"I *am* watching it, Ferenc," Istvan answered evenly. "You're supposed to go around me, not through me."

Ferenc said something about the whorehouse Istvan's mother had worked in. The next time the attacking midfielder tried to dribble the ball by him, Istvan kicked it away. No at all by accident, the studded sole of his boot came down on Ferenc's instep, hard. Ferenc squalled and went down in a heap, clutching at his foot.

"What did you go and do that for?" one of the other players said, waving his arms. "You might have put Gabor out of the match!"

Istvan stared back stonily. "Like I give a shit. You talk about my mother and I'll rack you up, too."

There were two kinds of Jews in Hungary—the ones who bent before every slight in the hope that putting up with anything meant they wouldn't have to put up with so much, and the kind who wouldn't put up with anything in the hope that would make bigots worry about giving them grief. Some of the first kind ended up with stomach ulcers. Some of the second kind ended up dead.

Well, actually there was one other kind. Rakosi and the rest of the Jews in his regime did their best to pretend they'd shed their religion the way a snake sloughed off its skin. Maybe they even believed they weren't Jews any more. The trouble with that, as Istvan knew from all the sour jokes he'd heard, was that none of the Magyars believed any such thing.

He waited to see if he'd have a brawl on his hands. But the other footballer must have remembered what he'd done to Miklos. He'd got knocked around himself in that fight, but he'd proved the old adage that it was better to give than to receive. Anyone who could flatten Miklos was someone you didn't care to tangle with yourself.

They had to drag Ferenc off the pitch. The East Germans stopped kicking the ball to watch. Istvan didn't mind that one bit. If they saw he was somebody who paid back any little presents he got, they wouldn't try to give him so many. Or he could hope they wouldn't, anyhow.

No sooner had he got back to the barracks than Imre Kovacs walked in. Despite his name and perfect Hungarian, he was a U.S. Army captain. Like Istvan, he was also what the Communists called a rootless cosmopolite. "So you smashed one of your football buddies, huh?" he said by way of greeting.

How did he know? He knew, that was how. Istvan just shrugged. "Anyone who says dirty things about my mom, he's no buddy of mine."

"I can see that," Kovacs allowed. "Why don't you come on over to the administration building with me? Couple of things I want to ask you." He talked as if the two of them were equals. Maybe that was an American way of doing things. It didn't make what he said any less an order.

"I'm coming," Istvan said. They walked over together as if they were the best of friends.

Once they got inside the administration building, the American captain asked, "How much do you know about the unrest in Hungary right now?"

"Only what I hear from the guys who're coming in now," Istvan answered truthfully. "Nobody talked about any of that stuff while I was still fighting." *Nobody would have dared,* he thought.

"Nobody talked about it, huh?" Kovacs was good at hearing what you didn't say. "Did anybody know about it?"

"*I* sure didn't." Istvan paused to think. "If anybody I knew would have, it was my sergeant. His name was Gergely. He was like Miklos—he went straight from the old *Honved* to the People's Army without skipping a beat. But it wasn't because he was mean. He *was* mean, but he was good, too. Best noncom I ever knew, and it wasn't close."

"Gergely." Imre Kovacs wrote it down. "He's not here, is he?"

"No. He's still fighting or in some other camp—there are others, right?—or he caught something." Istvan had trouble imagining Sergeant Gergely wounded or dead. In his mind's eye, the veteran was still leading unhappy conscripts and still making them perform as if they'd been soldiering since they were twelve. Some people were born violinists, others born chefs. Gergely had been born to command a squad.

The doorbell to the little rented house rang. Marian Staley opened the door. Standing on her front porch was the teenage girl who lived next door. "Oh, hi, Betsy," Marian said. "C'mon in."

"Hi, Betsy," Linda echoed from the front room. She'd just turned six.

"Hiya, kiddo," Betsy said. Linda laughed. Betsy turned back to Marian. "You said sixty cents an hour, right? Starting from now?"

"That's right." Resignation filled Marian's nod and her voice. She was paying the babysitter almost half of what the Shasta Lumber Company paid her. It hardly seemed fair. But she'd got to know Betsy well enough to trust her to keep an eye on Linda for a little while. "Her bedtime is nine o'clock. You can see she's already in her PJ's." She lowered her voice. "Once she's quiet, help yourself to anything in the icebox, too." That was part of the deal these days.

"Thanks." Betsy sounded as if she meant it. Maybe sounding as if that wasn't part of the deal was also part of the deal. Or maybe Betsy was a polite kid by nature. Stranger things had happened . . . Marian supposed.

A few minutes later, the doorbell rang again. Marian opened the door. This time, Fayvl Tabakman walked in. He looked as nervous as if he were going out on his very first date. Marian was nervous, too, but tried not to let it show. She hadn't been out with anyone since she found out Bill got shot down on a bombing mission.

"Mr. Tabakman and I are going to see *Singin' in the Rain*," she told

Betsy. "I don't expect anything bad will happen, but call the movie the-ater if you need to." Weed, California, was anything but a big town. It had one—count it, one—theater. Betsy couldn't very well phone the wrong one.

"Okay," she said. Her eyes widened. "I didn't know you knew Mr. Tabakman! My father says he's great. Dad's a logger, and he's mighty glad there'll finally be an ambulance in town."

More than half the men in Weed were loggers. Day by day, year by year, they thinned out the forests that lay in the shadows of Mt. Shasta. It was dangerous work. Doc Toohey did what he could, but the closest hospital was in Redding, more than an hour south down US 99. The lumber companies hadn't wanted to pay for an ambulance till Tabak-man persuaded them to split the cost among themselves.

"We've known each other a long time," Marian said. "We lived in the same town outside of Seattle, and we were in the same camp after the A-bomb wrecked it." The inmates, or whatever you called them, had tagged the place Camp Nowhere, but Betsy didn't need to know that. Marian knew she'd probably be there yet if not for Bill's military insurance.

"It vas not'ing," Fayvl murmured. The cobbler's English, learned since the war, was fluent but strongly accented. He'd done better in Camp Nowhere than most of the people who washed up there. He'd survived the Nazis' murder camp at Auschwitz. They'd gassed his wife and children and sent them up in smoke. Even more than Marian, he knew what losing loved ones meant.

"It wasn't nothing!" Betsy insisted. "It was great!"

"Huh." Praise made Fayvl uncomfortable. Marian had seen that be-fore. He touched the brim of the old-fashioned cloth cap he usually wore. "We go?" he asked her.

"We go," Marian agreed. She blew her daughter a kiss. "So long, honey. I'll see you later."

"So long." Linda was playing with a doll and a stuffed cat that squeaked. If doing without her mommy for a while bothered her, she hid it very well.

Out they went. Marian closed the front door behind her but didn't lock it. Like her old neighborhood up in Everett, Washington, Weed wasn't the kind of place where you worried about burglars. In Camp Nowhere, people swiped anything that wasn't nailed down. If they saw a way to pry the nails loose, they'd steal those, too.

Marian's yellow Studebaker sat in front of the house. The Seattle A-bomb had set dark cars on her block ablaze; her bright one came through unharmed. She and Linda had slept in it at Camp Nowhere. Now she walked past it. Nothing in Weed was more than a few blocks from anything else. She used the car for shopping and to take Linda places and to get to work when the weather turned bad. Otherwise, shank's mare was plenty good enough.

She wondered how crowded the theater would be. *Singin' in the Rain* was a big hit in the parts of the country that hadn't had bombs fall on them. It took a while to get to places like Weed, and it wouldn't stay more than a couple of weeks. But there wasn't a line or anything. Maybe loggers didn't care about singing and dancing, even in the rain.

The girl who sold tickets looked from Fayvl to Marian and kind of smiled. Marian realized they'd just become an item of local gossip. Well, too bad. Inside, Fayvl got popcorn and boxes of Good & Plenty and Cokes. After they found seats, he said, "I never eat popcorn before I come to America. Many good things I find here. This one I do not expect." He paused. "I find good people here, too."

"You're a good person yourself, Fayvl," Marian said.

A newsreel came on when the house lights dimmed. It showed ruins from New York City, more from Boston, and still more from Europe. Other film was of glum Russians with their hands high marching into captivity past knocked-out tanks. People with TVs had already seen these things, but no station was close enough to Weed to come in. Even radio reception here was hit-and-miss.

Whether or not loggers enjoyed *Singin' in the Rain,* Marian did. Gene Kelly was so good, he should have been against the law. Every so often, Marian glanced over at Fayvl. He seemed to be enjoying the picture, too. Once, she looked his way at the same time as he was looking at her. They both turned back toward the screen in a hurry.

When they got out on the sidewalk again, Fayvl said, "You want maybe a cup coffee and some pie before you go home?"

"Sure," Marian said. "Thanks for asking me out. I've enjoyed this. I didn't know if I would, but I did."

Weed boasted a couple of diners. "We go to the one right by US 97 and 99?" Fayvl said. "Is better, I think."

"Me, too." Marian nodded. "That's the first place I stopped when I came to Weed. I liked the place, and I liked the town. I haven't left since."

"And you sent me card of Mt. Shasta," Fayvl said. "I think, any place must be better than Camp Nowhere. And I know you, and I know Linda, so I come down here to start up mine little shop."

Marian nodded. She liked that he mentioned Linda. He and her little girl had always got on well. Maybe he saw something of his own lost children in her. Marian had never asked him that. If he wanted to talk about it, he would. Till he did, if he did, she figured it was none of her business.

The brassy, redheaded waitress named Babs who'd served her that first day was on duty now. She cackled like a laying hen when Marian and Fayvl came in together. They both ordered coffee. Fayvl got a slice of apple pie; Marian chose blueberry. Babs talked with the guy behind the counter—who doubled as the fry cook—and cackled some more. He rolled his eyes and raised his eyebrows when she got done, but bobbed his head up and down, too.

When the pie and the coffee were gone, Fayvl raised his index finger to show he was ready for the check. "Forget it," Babs said. "On the house. You guys should have a nice time. From what I hear, you both been without one for way too long."

"You don't need to do that!" Marian exclaimed.

"Who said anything about needing? We're gonna, that's all," Babs said in *Wanna make something out of it?* tones. After that, Marian and Fayvl couldn't very well do anything but thank her. If the news about the two of them was going to be all over town, at least the people who'd spread it seemed to think it was good news.

. . .

Vasili Yasevich saw Grigory Papanin across the town square in Smi-dovich. Papanin saw Vasili, too, and turned and left the square as fast as he could without running. Vasili smiled a nasty smile. Papanin had been Smidovich's number-one handyman and number-one tough guy till Vasili showed up from across the Amur.

He had been. He wasn't any more. His nose was mashed and leaned to one side, part of the damage Vasili had done to him when they tan-gled. Grigory Papanin had been a big frog in a little puddle. The Rus-sians here didn't know Vasili'd grown up in Harbin, down in Manchuria. They thought he was a refugee from A-bombed Khabarovsk. Either way, though, he'd learned to be rougher than anyone from a no-account place like this ever could.

A radio speaker was mounted on a pole in the square. It blared out Radio Moscow at all hours of the day and night: tales of victories and of production surpluses mixed in with music. Vasili didn't know how much of what he heard to believe. *Not much* looked like a good guess. Just for instance, Radio Moscow had yet to admit that its signal didn't originate in the Soviet capital any more, and hadn't since not long after the war started.

Not far from the square was the little, barely tolerated marketplace where babushkas and hunters sold what they'd raised or trapped or shot for themselves. The berries and vegetables and venison and birds you found there were expensive, but far better than what you could get at the state food store . . . when you could get anything at the state food store.

"*Zdrast'ye,* David Samuelovich," Vasili called, seeing a familiar face among the people eyeing mushrooms and heads of cauliflower.

"Oh, hello," David Berman answered. The old Jew offered the ba-bushka behind the big, white cauliflowers a price. She just twitched a scornful eyebrow. He came down a few kopeks. This time, she deigned to shake her own head. The haggle was on.

The trouble with money in the Soviet Union was, even if you had it, you couldn't do much with it. No one in Smidovich lived much better than anyone else. No one had a fancy limousine with a chauffeur. Hardly anyone had any kind of car. You couldn't get a car in Smidovich. You might be able to in Birobidzhan, the capital of the Jewish Autonomous Region. Birobidzhan was a real city, if a small one. But if you went from Smidovich to Birobidzhan to buy one, you'd have to drive it back over seventy kilometers or so of unpaved track. Maybe it would still run when it got here, maybe not.

No one here lived in a mansion, either. No one had cooks or housemaids. The residents who did have more than the others—people like Gleb Sukhanov, the local MGB boss—got what they got because they were powerful, not because they were rolling in rubles.

Harbin had also been a city under Communist rules. The slogans there and here differed only in language. Power counted there, too. Power, as far as Vasili could see, counted everywhere. But money also mattered. Money in Harbin gave power in a way it didn't here.

Vasili always wished he hadn't thought of Gleb Sukhanov just then. *Speak of the Devil and he'll appear* had to be a proverb in almost every language of the world. Up through the market square came the Chekist and three militiamen. They all carried submachine guns. Two of them were hustling along a skinny young woman with her hands cuffed behind her.

Putting his head down and slowly turning away, Vasili pretended to be absorbed in the quality of a ptarmigan carcass. Not drawing attention to yourself was the best way to keep from drawing fatal attention to yourself.

But not even the best way worked all the time. Sukhanov proved regrettably quick on the uptake. "There's Berman!" he barked to the militiamen. "And—*Bozhemoi!*—there's Yasevich with him! Freeze, you two! You're under arrest, in the name of the workers and peasants of the Soviet Union! Hands high!"

For a split second, Vasili thought of going for the Tokarev automatic in his jacket pocket. But one pistol against four PPDs was worse than long odds. It was suicidal odds. As David Berman had before him, he raised his hands above his head. When things went down the drain, you could at least try to meet disaster with style.

Not that it would help. The militiaman who wasn't pushing the handcuffed girl along took charge of Berman. He tossed the cauliflower the old Jew had just bought back to the woman who'd sold it, saying, "Here, granny. Where he's going, he won't need this."

Gleb Sukhanov frisked Vasili himself. He plucked the Tokarev from the pocket where it lived. He found Vasili's brass knuckles and clasp knife, but not the little holdout knife in his right boot. Holding the pistol, he asked, "Where'd you get this?"

"From that clapped-out cunt of a Papanin." Vasili saw no reason not to give him the truth. It wouldn't matter now. Nothing would.

He was right. Sukhanov went on, "You—both of you—have conspired to assist in the escape of an inmate of the Corrective Labor Camps, namely this Maria Grunfeld here." The militiamen holding the young woman shook her to leave no doubt about which Maria Grunfeld their boss meant.

Vasili hadn't even known what her last name was. He'd found her when he was walking outside of town. She needed a place to hide. David Berman had lost his wife, and didn't give a damn about anything any more. Vasili'd hoped she would screw him back to happiness in exchange for safety. And it had worked . . . till it didn't any more.

"Hands down and behind your back," Sukhanov said. Vasili obeyed. Cuffs bit into his wrists. The militiaman handcuffed Berman, who was about as dangerous as a kitten.

Off to the town administration center the little parade went. Once they got there, they sent Maria one way and the two men another. Plainly, they already knew what to do with her. She'd go back to the gulag. With Berman and Vasili, they had to start from the beginning.

Foomp! A tray of flash powder going off in front of Vasili's face was almost as bright as an atom bomb. He'd seen one, from just far enough away to take no harm. Once he was immortalized on film, Sukhanov separated him from David Berman.

"The old man will get a twenty-five-ruble bill," the Chekist said, by which he meant a twenty-five-year stretch in the camps. "Ordinarily, we'd give you the same thing without even thinking about it."

Twenty-five years in the gulags? Vasili would be past fifty when they let him out—if he lived to the end of his term, which was anything but certain. He wriggled, trying to make the cuffs hurt less. Nothing did much good. "But?" he said. By the way Sukhanov talked, there had to be a *but*.

Sure enough, the MGB man said, "We still haven't been able to come up with any records on you, not till you showed up here saying you came from Khabarovsk. Nothing to show you were born in the USSR. Nothing to show you ever fulfilled your patriotic obligation during the Great Patriotic War."

Vasili kept quiet. Anything he said would only get him in deeper. That was how it looked to him, anyhow.

"So," Gleb Sukhanov said, "we can send you to the gulag for your twenty-five, or we can send you to the Red Army and let them knock you into shape. You're not that old, and you're all in one piece. That puts you two ahead of most of the recruits they get these days. Your choice—because I'm your friend."

By the way he said it, he really meant it. That was one of the scarier things Vasili had ever heard. How would the Red Army knock him into shape if he came into it this way? Probably by using him up, the way clerks used up paper clips.

But twenty-five years? The war would have to end sooner than that. He might find some angles once they put a uniform on him, too. "Gleb Ivanovich, since you let me pick, I'll be a soldier. I serve the Soviet Union!" He tried to mouth the phrase as if he'd been saying it since he was four. People on this side of the Amur damn well had.

"*Ochen khorosho!*" Sukhanov said. "We'll put you on a truck for Birobidzhan in a few days, then." Apologetically, he went on, "I'm afraid we'll have to keep you in the lockup till we send you off. Can't have you trying your luck in the taiga."

Vasili didn't think he could live in the pine woods that stretched across Siberia. To manage that, you needed to learn how from child-hood, and he hadn't. A rifle didn't hurt, either. That the Chekist worried he might was a compliment of sorts.

The militiamen didn't rough him up when they put him in the cell. The honey bucket had a lid. The bed was a straw pallet, but it was there. They fed him slop. At least they fed him enough slop.

Two days later, they herded him into a wheezing, rattling truck bound for Birobidzhan. *The Red Army!* he thought. *My parents would be so ashamed!* They'd hated the October Revolution and everything it stood for. They'd fled to Harbin to escape it, and taken poison after Stalin's soldiers seized the city in 1945. They'd known what was waiting for them if the Chekists grabbed them. Now the Chekists had grabbed Vasili. What was waiting for him? He'd find out.

Luisa Hozzel stood with the other female *zeks* on the open ground near the barbed-wire fence that separated their half of the gulag from the men's. She thought the count had gone smoothly, but the guards weren't letting them go to supper. Her stomach growled a protest.

Trudl Bachman stood beside her. "What now?" Trudl whispered without moving her lips. They'd been friends in Fulda, on the far side of the Eurasian landmass, before the Russians overran it when they invaded West Germany.

"God only knows," Luisa whispered back, also doing a fine ventriloquist's act. She'd never dreamt she would ever need or gain that jailyard skill, not back in Fulda. She had it, though, and it was damned useful.

Out came the camp commandant, an officer who'd been mutilated too horribly to be useful in combat any more but who could still serve the Soviet Union in a place like this. He had an eye patch and a hook; heaven only knew what his tunic and trousers hid.

He scowled at the German women as if he hated them. No doubt he did. That was all right. He hated the *zeks* from his own country just as much.

He waited. Two hulking guards dragged in a woman in the shapeless, padded clothes prisoners wore. They shoved her. She went down on the dirt. One of them kicked her in the ribs.

"Grunfeld, Maria. Γ887," the commandant said. "Former escapee. Now returned to finish atoning for her crimes, and to finish the additional sentence imposed on those who abscond with themselves. She will begin her time with a month in the punishment cells."

"Heaven help her!" Luisa prison-whispered. Trudl nodded microscopically. They'd each spent a few days in the punishment block after Maria and several other women escaped. They hadn't helped. They hadn't even been in that work gang. But two of the absconders had come out of their barracks. That was all the authorities needed. Sometimes, the authorities didn't need anything. They did as they pleased here.

The *Gestapo* would have been proud of punishment cells. Luisa could think of nothing worse to say about them. They were too low to stand up in, too small to lie down in. You hunched in one corner, because that was all you could do. They didn't even give you a bucket, so you did your business in the far corner like an animal.

Food was nasty black bread and water: not much of either. When they let you out after a month in there, you wouldn't be worth the paper you were printed on. Then you'd go back into your regular work gang and be expected to produce your full work norm right away. If you didn't, if you couldn't, they might chuck you into a punishment cell again.

"Before you try to deprive the Soviet state of *your* labor, think what has happened to Grunfeld, Maria, Γ887," the camp commandant rasped. "Think how you would like it yourselves. Now you are dismissed to supper. Keep thinking about it while you eat."

He walked with a limp, too. If he hadn't stepped smartly in spite of it, the female *zeks* would have trampled him in their rush to the kitchen. Luisa got a bowl of soupy stew and a brick of black bread bigger than the one they would have doled out in a punishment cell. Add in a glass of weak tea from a battered samovar and. . . .

As gulag suppers went, it wasn't too bad. The stew had more cabbage and shredded carrots than nettle and dandelion leaves. There were a couple of bits of what seemed more like potato than turnip, and a chunk of salt fish as big as the last joint of Luisa's index finger. The bread might be black, but it had more rye and oats than ground-up peas or sawdust. Luisa guessed it was about as bad as the war bread that blighted the memories of Germans old enough to have lived through the Turnip Winter of 1917.

After supper came latrine call. That was another dash. You had only five minutes to do whatever you had to do. The boards and trenches gave no privacy. The stench would have knocked Satan off his throne in Hell. Luisa hated the latrines worse than anything else in the camp, which was saying a lot.

Custom hath made it in him a property of easiness. That was some poet or other, whether German or English she couldn't remember. Camp routine had trained her insides to empty completely in those five minutes and in the five after breakfast, and to stay quiet the rest of the day. She wondered if the rhythm would stay ingrained in her after she got out.

Then she wondered if she would ever get out.

Most of the time, she didn't let herself think about that. If you started remembering the world beyond the gulag, you couldn't live inside it. Now, wiping her filthy hands on her trousers, she couldn't help herself.

Fulda. Hot water. A soft bed. A flush toilet. No one screaming at her in a language she barely understood. No mind-numbing, body-ruining labor. And food, all the food she wanted, whenever she wanted it! Eggs and chops and roasts and fruit and pies and cakes! White bread! Butter! Coffee thick with cream! Coffee with whipped cream, Vienna-style! Chocolate! Dear God, chocolate!

"Are you all right, Luisa?" Trudl Bachman sounded worried.

Luisa shook her head. "No. Not right this minute. I've been remembering."

Trudl's eyes widened with alarm. Back in Fulda, they'd been neighbors and friends. Luisa's Gustav had worked in the print shop Trudl's Max ran. They were both veterans, like most German men. When the

Russians came over the border, Gustav and Max went off to fight them . . . again. Luisa had no idea where either man was, or whether they survived. That they'd gone off to fight made their wives suspect to the Reds. Luisa supposed that was why she and Trudl were here now, if they were here now for any reason at all.

"You mustn't remember," Trudl said earnestly. "If you remember what real life is like, this place turns into hell. You have to forget everything about, about before. It's hard enough even then."

It wasn't as if she were wrong. Their gloomy barracks had wooden bunks stacked four and five high. The mattresses were of sawdust wrapped in burlap ticking. They were hard and lumpy. They smelled bad, and they were full of bugs. You slept in all your clothes, with your boots under your head for a pillow. The cast-iron stove in the center of the hall didn't throw much heat, and didn't throw it very far.

This place turns into hell. Luisa didn't think Trudl quite had that right. The gulag was hell any which way, as far as she was concerned. She climbed up into her bunk and took off her boots. Her feet stank, too. She lay down. By now, the boots felt as soft and familiar as her old goose-feather pillow. Her eyes closed. She started to snore.

VASILI YASEVICH HADN'T SEEN much of the USSR after he crossed the Amur. Smidovich had suited him fine . . . till he got stupid, tried to do a couple of other people a favor, and got caught at it. As soon as he said he'd join the Red Army instead of going into the gulag like Maria and David, all that changed in a hurry.

He signed some paperwork in Birobidzhan. They poured him into a Red Army uniform there. It didn't fit. He hadn't thought it would. He had at least expected it to be new. Too much to hope for. The trousers had several rips sewn up less well than he could have done it himself. A patch on the tunic didn't fully cover a bloodstain that hadn't washed out. Both garments were faded and worn.

The rest of the recruits boarded a westbound train with him. Some carried rifles, others submachine guns like his. About one in four had no weapon at all. They ranged in age from fifteen to fifty-five. Vasili was one of the few anywhere near the midpoint.

One of the other fellows, an older man, said, "Well, if we're the best they can do, they're scraping the bottom of the barrel pretty goddamn hard."

"If we're not the best they can do, they would've nabbed some other guys," Vasili answered. "I guess they already have."

They were shoehorned onto the hard wooden benches of a third-class car. Men pulled out cards and dice to make the time go by. Gleb Sukhanov hadn't stolen the cash Vasili had on him when he was seized, so he got into the games. Most of the new soldiers were born suckers. He made money.

They went through the ruins of Blagoveshchensk, ruins smashed so completely that even the Red Army recruits crossed themselves and said things like "Christ, have mercy!" and "Lord, have mercy!" A sight like the slagged corpse of Blagoveshchensk was more than enough to make the most hardened atheist into a believer. The Trans-Siberian Railway was operating again, though, even if the rest of the city wasn't.

How many men had Stalin used to get the railroad running again? How many had he used up? Mao had done the same thing in Harbin after the Americans dropped the A-bomb there. Vasili had been one of the men cleaning up in the Manchurian city, luckily not too close to where the bomb went off.

His new comrades noticed that he reacted less to the devastation than they did. One of them—the older guy who'd said the Red Army was scraping the bottom of the barrel—asked, "How come it doesn't bother you?"

"It bothers me, but I've seen it before," Vasili answered. That much was true. He went on, "If the one that got Khabarovsk had blown a kilometer farther west, I wouldn't be looking at this shit now." That was the story he'd told since he got to Smidovich, and he was sticking to it.

Another man said, "I'm from Khabarovsk, too. I was in Birobidzhan when it hit. Whereabouts did you live?"

"Near the center of town."

"But that's where it came down. That's what they say, anyhow."

"I know. I was over on the west side, visiting a lady friend." Vasili sketched a female shape with his hands. "She was somebody's wife, but she wasn't mine. If I'd been a good boy that night, I would have gone up in smoke. But here I am."

"Here you are, all right," said the fellow who really was from Khabarovsk. "You better look for more sins to commit, on account of you've got a brand new chance to get blown up."

Some of the sins the recruits suggested argued that they had a lot of experience along those lines. So did the way they talked. Russian in Smidovich was infused with *mat*, the filthy slang that came from prisoners, political and otherwise. That made sense; plenty of the locals had served their sentences but were still forbidden to go back to their homes on the far side of the distant Urals. But these guys swore all the time. Vasili wondered if Stalin needed soldiers so badly, he'd throw even *zeks* at the imperialist aggressors.

On and on the troop train rolled. Vasili learned at first hand just how vast the Soviet Union was. He also saw that Blagoveshchensk wasn't the only city on the Trans-Siberian Railway the Yankees had A-bombed. No matter how totally flattened the cities were, the train tracks always went through.

How many Russians were sick with radiation sickness? How many had died? Stalin worried no more than Mao had.

But the line stopped just short of Moscow. Vasili was sure it couldn't work that way in normal times. Didn't the Trans-Siberian Railway run as far as Leningrad? How many times, though, and how recently, had the Americans hit Moscow? How much was left of it? Anything at all? Even Stalin's daredevil—or conscripted—workers hadn't punched the railroad through the ravaged Soviet capital again, not yet.

Trucks took the new men farther west. Transferring from the crowded train was a slow business. Once Vasili was on a truck—no one had bothered to take off the Chevrolet emblem that showed it came from America—he jounced along roads that would have been bad even in Manchuria.

One of the old-timers, a man who'd been born in the nineteenth century, shook his head in wonder. "I came this way for the Tsar in 1916, and for Stalin in 1944, and now here I am again," he said.

They rolled through the night with no lights. Vasili slept five minutes here, ten minutes there, with big bouncy stretches in between.

When dawn came, the convoy pulled off the road. Workers, many of them women, concealed the trucks with nets and grass and branches. More women came to the trucks and doled out bowls of shchi. It wasn't that good and there wasn't that much of it, but Vasili was hungry enough to lick his bowl clean. He wasn't the only one.

"We'll make a *zek* out of you yet," said a fellow who'd plainly seen a lot of hard use. The guy laughed, for all the world as if he were kidding.

"Why are we hiding here during the day?" a kid asked. He was barely old enough to have zits; the next razor that touched his face would be the first.

"What do you want to bet American planes'll shoot us up if we keep heading west while they can see us?" the well-used man said.

"But we're beating the Americans! The radio tells us so every day," the kid bleated.

"Maybe the Americans don't listen to Radio Moscow," Vasili said. A true believer of a monk hearing for the first time someone claim there was no God could have looked no more shocked than that youngster in a uniform as secondhand as his own.

One truck rear-ended another not long after the darkness came and they set out again. The rest of the convoy, including Vasili's truck, had to go off the road and through a field, guided by swearing soldiers. The field wasn't much rougher than the roadway had been.

This time, they stopped before sunup. In the distance, Vasili heard what sounded like thunder and was probably artillery. Officers moved from truck to truck, talking to the men. Pretty soon, one came to the Chevrolet that carried Vasili and his equally unenthusiastic fellow soldiers.

"We're in Poland," the young lieutenant said. "Polish Fascists have risen up against the People's Republic. We have to help put down the reactionaries and keep open the supply lines to the bigger war against the Yankee imperialists farther west. Do you understand?"

What Vasili did understand of that, he didn't like. Even so, he chorused "We serve the Soviet Union!" with the rest of the men. He'd long since learned that was always the right answer.

They got ammunition. Most of the men knew how to handle their weapons. Vasili didn't, but the PPD wasn't exactly hard to figure out. With a couple of magazines of 7.62mm pistol cartridges, he could fight. He could if he lived long enough to learn how, anyhow. Shouting and cursing, officers urged the new soldiers forward. His first lesson would be coming soon.

Red Army shells rained down around the foxhole where Rolf Mehlen crouched—where he cowered, if you wanted to get right down to it. He was scared just this side of shitless. He'd known a hell of a lot of brave men, in the last war and in this one. He'd never met anyone who could stay calm and relaxed under a heavy bombardment.

The biggest trouble was, this was God playing dice with the universe, even if that damn Jew of a physicist said He did no such thing. Whether you lived or died wasn't up to you. If a shell landed where you happened to be, you wouldn't be there any more. It was that simple. How good a soldier you were didn't matter. It was all luck.

A lot of it was luck any which way. When a stream of machine-gun bullets met your running path, whether one of them hit you or not didn't have much to do with you. But you could hunch yourself down small and bump up your chances that way. And you had some idea when to run, and in which direction.

When the big guns bellowed, you huddled and you hoped. And you came out the other side and did some more fighting . . . or else you didn't.

Rolf knew he would be doing more fighting pretty damn quick. The Ivans didn't shell like this to cover a retreat. When the artillery let up, they'd come. They would have gulped their hundred grams of vodka so they'd quit caring, and they'd be screaming *Urra!* at the top of their lungs. If some nasty little god particularly hated him, they'd have panzers with them.

The shelling stopped. As soon as he was sure it had, Rolf stuck up his head. The sooner you spotted the enemy, the sooner you could start killing him. You tried to do it before he got close enough to kill you.

Just because you tried, that didn't mean you would. Rolf fixed his Springfield's bayonet. He made sure he could grab his entrenching tool in a hurry. You could do all kinds of evil things with an entrenching tool.

They were stirring, out there more than a kilometer to the east. Rolf glanced north. "Max?" he called. "You still there, Max?"

Max Bachman popped up twenty meters away, like a rabbit coming out of its burrow. Rolf had always thought Bachman looked rabbity anyway. "No, I'm not here," the printer answered. "I'm taking leave on the Riviera. I'll be back week after next."

"Funny," Rolf said. "Funny like a belly wound. They're going to rush us, you know."

"They're going to try," Max said. "They haven't got me yet. Maybe they won't this time."

"That would be nice." Rolf looked toward the Russians again. "Happy fucking day—here they come."

"*Urra! Urra!*" Sure enough, that Russian yell made the hair stand up on the back of his neck. The Ivans didn't come on in the human waves they'd used so often during the last war. They knew better now; they'd been learning better even then. They'd figured out how to fire and move, probably from their German foes. One group would spray the opposition with bullets while another advanced. Then the second group would flop down and start shooting and the first would leapfrog past it.

All that made them much harder to kill. It gave them a better chance to kill you, too.

But Rolf was well dug in. He had a parapet thick enough to stop bullets in front of his hole. The shelling hadn't blown away the branches and bushes he'd stuck on and in front of the parapet. As the Ivans learned tactics from his side, Germans had learned about camouflage from the Red Army.

A good shot could hit out to eight hundred meters with a Springfield, as with a Mauser. Rolf didn't wear his marksman's badges—decorations with the swastika were illegal and would get you summarily killed like a *Stahlhelm*, both. But he'd earned them, and the knack didn't go away.

The rifle bucked against his shoulder. A distant khaki figure fell over. He worked the bolt and swung the rifle a little to the right. He fired again. Another Russian crumpled.

He ducked down as he reloaded this time, and came up half a meter from where he'd been. The foxhole didn't give him much room to move, but he used what he had. He fired again, and scored another hit. Then he fed a fresh five-round clip into the magazine.

A bullet cracked past him. A moment later, so did another one. The Ivans had noticed his muzzle flashes, then. That was a shame. He had to keep shooting, or they'd overrun him. He sighed, fired, and swore. He didn't like missing.

Mortar bombs started dropping among the oncoming Red Army soldiers. Rolf whooped when a burst sent a Russian cartwheeling through the air. In the next foxhole over, Max also let out a cheer.

Then three fighter-bombers—obsolescent prop jobs—with RAF roundels zoomed by, so low he could almost reach up and touch their tail wheels. They rocketed and machine-gunned the Ivans. One dropped napalm that torched twenty meters of ground.

Good Russian troops, like good German troops, would have kept coming in spite of everything. But an awful lot of good Russian troops had gone up in atomic fire. The ones who were left broke sooner than they might have. They'd done their duty, they'd paid for it, and they'd had enough.

"Let's hear it for the *Jabos*," Max said.

"Sure is better to have them shooting with us than shooting at us," Rolf agreed. By the end of the last war, *Luftwaffe* ground-attack planes had grown scarce as eagles' teeth. The LAH had been worked over from above by English Typhoons like these in the west and by Soviet Shturmoviks in the east. Yes, it was definitely better to give than to receive.

Thinking of Shturmoviks made him cast a wary eye skyward. But no, the Russians weren't hitting back that way. And they hadn't thrown any panzers into this attack, at least not around here. Maybe even Russian vastness had limits.

Hoping it did, Rolf lit a smoke. Over in the next foxhole, Max was doing the same thing. A cigarette after living through a fight was as nice as one right after screwing. Had he heard that from Gustav Hozzel or back in the last war? He couldn't recall. Gustav, these days, was too dead to ask.

"You know what I hear?" Bachman said.

"No," Rolf said, "but whatever it is, I know you're gonna tell me."

Unfazed, the other German nodded and went on, "The radio says the Russians are having trouble with their satellites. That could be how come they're not able to put a roll of coins in their fist when they throw punches here."

"Only a *Dummkopf* or an *Arschloch* believes the *Scheisse* that comes out of the radio." Rolf left it to Max to decide for himself whether he was a jerk or an asshole—his generosity just then knew no bounds.

"I believe the Poles and the Czechs and the Hungarians don't want to dance at the end of Stalin's puppet strings," Max said.

"Well, Christ, who would?" Rolf said.

"They were just as thrilled about dancing at the end of the *Führer*'s strings, hey?" Max said.

Rolf gave him a dirty look. "I didn't see you peel off your *Feldgrau* and go join the partisans," he snapped.

"No, I had my side and they had theirs," Max said. "But I'll tell you, with some of the things we did it's no wonder they fought us so hard and hated us so much. I should know. I did some of them myself."

"Fuck 'em. Fuck 'em all," Rolf said flatly. He'd done a lot of things like that, too. "Far as I'm concerned, they deserved every damn bit of it—and some more besides." He squeezed the coal off his smoke with thumb and forefinger and saved the butt in his little leather bag. Waste not, want not.

Ihor Shevchenko crawled through weeds and bushes and bricks towards a new-looking farmhouse that had taken a square hit from a 155. Not much was left of somebody's hope for the future, in other words.

Ihor's hope for the future was that no foragers had visited the place before him.

He was careful where he put his hands. Any place Poles had lived, you found broken bottles, and they could slice you up. Once upon a time, most of them had held vodka or schnapps. Stuck between Russians and Germans, the Poles drank both. They drank enough to make Ihor good and sure they were related to Russians, and to Ukrainians like him.

Was that motion, up there ahead in the ruins? Ihor carried his Kalashnikov everywhere he went. It lay by him when he slept, and across his knees when he squatted to take a dump. He had the bayonet in a sheath on his belt. It made a good enough general-purpose knife.

The man who warily looked out of the farmhouse wore khaki darker and greener than was usual for a Red Army uniform. His helmet was halfway between what the Fritzes had used and the American pot in shape. That made him a Pole, no two ways about it.

He had no idea Ihor was there. From less than fifty meters off, Ihor could have bagged him easy as you please. But the shot might have brought the bastard's buddies running—and Ihor's buddies with them. He didn't want a skirmish. He just wanted to scrounge.

So he tried something else instead. In Ukrainian, he called, "Hey, *Polyak!*" He pitched his voice just loud enough to carry to the smashed building. He went on, "You understand me when I talk like this?" Ukrainian was a little closer to Polish than Russian was, and maybe a little less likely to make the guy wet his pants.

The Pole almost did anyway—he damn near jumped out of his shoes. He started to bring up his rifle. It looked like a Mauser, but the Poles had used home-built copies of the German piece during the last war. Then he must have realized Ihor had the drop on him anyway. "*Tak,* I follow you," he said.

That was what Ihor thought he said, anyhow. *Tak* meant *yes* in both Ukrainian and Polish, which set them apart from the Russian *da*. Ihor said, "Want a truce, just you and me, while we go through that place and split whatever we find in there?"

"I want you to get the fuck out of my country," the Pole said. "But you could have killed me and you didn't, so why not?" He leaned his rifle against his leg. "Yeah, I'll split with you."

Cautiously, Ihor came up to his knees and then to his feet. He kept the AK-47 ready to fire, but didn't aim it at the Pole. As he walked up to the farmhouse, he said, "My name's Ihor."

"I'm Miecyslaw," the Pole said. When they got close enough, they shook hands. Miecyslaw added, "You're a goddamn crazy Russian, is what you are."

"Who's a Russian? I'm from right outside of Kiev. Stalin fucked us up the ass before he fucked you, but Hitler fucked us even harder, so what are you gonna do?"

"The Nazis gave it to us pretty bad, all right. They had Stalin in bed with them at first, remember," Miecyslaw said.

Ihor shrugged. "Don't blame me, man. I'm not Molotov. I didn't have anything to do with it—except some Fritzes shot me not far from here during the last war."

"If you weren't crazy, I'd be glad to do it now," Miecyslaw said. "Stalin murdered my cousin at Katyn—he was a captain, and he never came back after the Reds caught him."

"I thought the SS did the dirty work there," Ihor said. That was what the USSR had always loudly insisted.

But Miecyslaw looked like a man about to gag. "That's shit," he said. "It was the fucking Chekists, nobody else but. At least a lot of the Nazis wound up dead. The Chekists are still doing what they did back then."

Ihor couldn't even tell him he was wrong, because he wasn't. Anyone who lived in the Soviet Union lived in fear of Lavrenti Beria, who ran the MGB. As long as Stalin lived, Beria would thrive. And Ihor couldn't imagine Stalin dying.

"It's a fucked-up pussy of a world, all right," he said. The Pole nodded. While they weren't trying to kill each other, they could agree on that much. And if they did try to kill each other, well, didn't that just show what a fucked-up pussy of a world it was?

Neither took his eye off the other as they searched the smashed house. Neither fully trusted the other not to start shooting if he saw the chance. Neither meant to give the other that chance.

They found some canned goods. Miecyslaw looked revolted. "Canned at a canning plant in the Russian part of Germany," he said.

"I'll believe you," Ihor answered. He could read Russian and Ukrainian, but anything in the Roman alphabet was gibberish to him.

"The only thing I ever wanted to do with Germans was kill them, not eat their crappy tinned sauerkraut," Miecyslaw said.

"Is that what this is?" Ihor had nothing against pickled cabbage. Russians pickled plenty of their own. But he'd hoped for something more interesting. "Whoever lived here took all the booze with him when he left." Plainly, the family that lived here had escaped: no bloodstains, no stench of death. Ihor continued, "What a rotten thing to do."

"*Tak.*" Miecyslaw eyed him. "You talk funny, and you've got that goddamn Red Army uniform on, but you aren't that bad a guy."

"Neither are you," Ihor allowed.

"Why are you taking orders from that butcher with a mustache, then?" Miecyslaw said. "Fight for freedom instead."

"Where are your tanks? Where are your planes? Where are your A-bombs?" Ihor said. "You cocksuckers may shoot me, but there'll be nothing left of your shitass country by the time the Red Army gets through with it. When I gamble, I want decent odds."

Miecyslaw flinched. Ihor knew what that meant: the Pole had just heard things he hadn't wanted to tell himself. Ihor had felt that way when he first joined the fight against the Hitlerites. It looked as if they were going to overrun the whole Soviet Union. They didn't, though.

But the Soviet Union was bigger than Germany, far bigger. It could trade space for time. The Poles facing the Red Army couldn't.

"I ought to kill you right here," Miecyslaw said, which was a common reaction when somebody told you things you didn't want to tell yourself. "Then some other Pole won't have to later on."

"Well, you can try," Ihor answered, unobtrusively making sure his

Kalashnikov had the safety off. "But you've been around the block a few times, right? You take a whack at something like that, it doesn't come with a guarantee."

"Ahh, screw it," the Polish rebel said. "You could have done for me before I even knew you were there. I owe you that much, anyway. I wish to Christ we could've found some hooch in here."

"Me, too," Ihor said with feeling. "Something better than the hundred grams they issue us every day. That crap, it's as cheap as they can make it. It sure tastes that way."

"At least you get the fucking hundred grams," Miecyslaw said. "With us, we have to find it before we can drink it."

"Maybe you should come over to the Soviet side, then. They'd fill you full of vodka if you did." Ihor meant every word of that. The Red Army treated defectors well . . . till they weren't useful any more, anyhow. *Then* it shipped them off to one gulag or another. Miecyslaw's horselaugh said he knew that as well as Ihor did. They parted, if not friends, then no worse enemies than they'd been when they met.

Miklos hit Istvan on the shoulder, not *quite* hard enough to leave a bruise behind. "Go knock the shit out of those Fritzes, Jewboy!" the Arrow Cross veteran boomed.

Istvan Szolovits eyed him like an entomologist putting a magnifying glass on some nondescript species. "You're as crazy as a bedbug," he said, sticking to the insectile theme. "You fought alongside the Germans. Now you want me to thump 'em?"

"Those were Adolf's Fritzes. These are just Stalin's," Miklos said scornfully. "These assholes deserve whatever happens to 'em."

"You're a retread," Istvan pointed out. "How do you know they aren't, too?"

That wasn't the only relevant question. The other one was, *What did you do while you fought for the Arrow Cross?* For most of the war, Admiral Horthy had protected Hungary's Jews. After Horthy got ousted for trying to make a separate peace with Stalin, Ferenc Szalasi hadn't—

which was putting it mildly. Close to half a million got shoved onto trains from Budapest to Auschwitz. Only luck and not especially Jewish features had saved Istvan. Was Miklos one of the Arrow Cross goons who'd helped the SS do the shoving? *Better not to know,* Istvan thought.

Meanwhile, Miklos said, "Me, I like to fight. I volunteered. How much you wanna bet the Fritzes are all conscripts?"

A conscript himself, Istvan left that alone for a moment. He didn't like to fight. He didn't even like football all that much. But it gave him a place among the POWs, so he played.

And Miklos was likely to be right—likely, but not certain. How many Fritzes could work up much patriotic zeal for Stalin's German minions? Probably about as many as the Magyars who were eager to march off to war for Matyas Rakosi. Still . . . In sly tones, Istvan said, "You never can tell. If Rakosi took an Arrow Cross guy, the Germans might have some real soldiers who used to be Nazis to stiffen the rest."

"Could be, I guess. If you find any of those suckers, give 'em a knee in the nuts for Hungary—and for yourself." Miklos punched Istvan in the shoulder again, harder this time.

Both football sides wore uniforms of their national colors: red, white, and green for the Hungarians and gold, red, and black for the Germans. Both Germanies had adopted those colors—or been made to adopt them—after the last war. The Weimar Republic had used them before. Hitler's *Reich*, like the Kaiser's a generation earlier, fought under red, black, and white.

The referee and the linesmen, like all the officials in the prison camp's football league, were German-speaking French underofficers. They took even less guff from the players than most officials were in the habit of doing.

Fweet! The man in black blew his whistle. The Hungarians started the action, but the East Germans quickly stole the ball. These two teams were better than the ones the Czechoslovakians and the Poles fielded. Hungarian pros were playing some of the best football in the world when this new war started. The POW side wasn't within kilometers of them, but tried to imitate their buccaneering style. And Germans just generally seemed to be good at everything—everything except winning wars, anyhow.

Here came a Fritz in a gold top, as confident as if it were 1940 and he was invading France. He was confident to the point of arrogance, in other words. He dribbled past Istvan like a man who expected no more trouble than he'd get from a stump.

Then Istvan stuck out a foot, stole the ball, and backheeled it to one his his midfielders. The German did an almost comic double take. He also took a longer look at the man who'd just picked his pocket. "Why, you filthy, stinking kike!" he exclaimed.

"Up your mother's dry, smelly cunt, *Scheissekopf*!" Istvan said sweetly. Having established that they loved each other as fraternal socialist brethren, they got on with the match.

Pretty soon, another German stomped on Istvan's instep. The POWs played by rougher rules than professionals could get away with. Istvan hopped for a few steps till the pain went down a little. He bided his time. After a bit, with the referee down at the far end of the pitch, he planted an elbow in a Fritz's solar plexus. The German folded up like a concertina and tried without much luck to breathe.

Istvan stood over him. "There you go, diving like a frogman!" he shouted. For some reason, the Fritz didn't answer.

Trotting down the pitch, Istvan waited for a whistle, or for the linesman to wave his flag to show the referee he'd fouled. Nothing happened, though some of the Germans watching the match screamed things that weren't love poetry. He'd got away with it. People got away with breaking the rules a lot of the time. Istvan supposed things would have been even worse without rules. They were bad enough as it was.

That German took a while to get back on his pins. He didn't move any too well after he did, either. Football wasn't some sissy American game. If the Fritz had to come off, his side would go on without him. Substitutions weren't in the laws.

Not too much later, a Hungarian let out a shriek when something horrible happened to his knee. That was ruled a foul. Before the Mag-

yars could take their free kick, though, they had to drag him out beyond the touch line. They went on with ten, and the match went
downhill from there.

It ended a 2–2 draw, with nine Germans and eight Hungarians still
standing. Istvan was one of them, though blood from his nose dribbled
down his chin and onto his shirtfront. After the referee blew the final
whistle, he shook his head and said, "Listen to me, you stupid *cons*—
this is supposed to be a game. Don't kill each other between the white
lines. Weren't you on the same side not so long ago?"

"Not on the pitch, we weren't!" a German shouted. Several of the
Hungarians nodded.

The man in black had no weapon but the whistle. But when he blew
four long blasts on it, French soldiers with American M-1s came running. "Enough *Schweinerei*!" he said. No one seemed to want to argue
with 7.62mm persuaders (though the Yankees, for reasons Istvan didn't
fully understand, called the caliber .30-06). The footballers glumly
mooched off the pitch, each side to its own supporters.

Miklos folded Istvan into a bear hug. "Hey, that was great!" the tattooed goon said.

"My ass," Istvan said.

"No, it was," Miklos insisted. "You don't let anybody fuck around
with you, do you?"

"Not if I can help it." Istvan's voice sounded funny in his own ears:
his nose was all stuffed up with blood. He realized how tired he was,
though war took a harsher toll than football could. After a pause for
thought, he went on, "You give somebody the chance to fuck around
with you, next thing he'll do is fuck you over."

"Man, you got that right!" Miklos hugged him again. Istvan didn't
say anything, but it hurt. He'd got elbowed himself, a time or seven.
Once Imre Kovacs, that Hungarian-American officer, had said he was
too smart for his own good. He wondered why, if he was so goddamn
smart, he kept playing football.

JURIS EIGIMS CAME UP to Konstantin Morozov with the air of a man approaching a partly trained bear that might bite off his arm if it forgot itself. The Balt looked first this way, then that. At last, satisfied that neither their driver nor their loader could hear, he spoke in a low voice: "Comrade Sergeant, may I say something to you?"

"Are you sure that's a good idea?" Morozov thought he knew the kind of thing the tall, blond gunner was likely to say. He wasn't at all certain he wanted to hear it.

"Mm, it depends," Eigims answered judiciously. "If you're the kind of guy who reports people to the MGB, I'd better keep my big trap shut. But I don't think you are."

"I never have." Morozov loved the Chekists no more than any other Russian who didn't belong to their corps. Just the same, he added, "If you think you can talk me into treason to the *rodina*, you'd better walk away."

"Treason? No, Comrade Sergeant." Eigims shook his head. "But how likely does it look to you that the Soviet Union's going to win this war?"

Instead of answering, Konstantin lit a *papiros*. The small ritual bought him time to think. He offered Eigims the pack. With muttered thanks, the gunner also lit one of the Russian-style cigarettes with a long paper holder. Their T-54 sat under trees between Einbeck and Northeim; they'd got shoved out of Dassel. Even so, the tank commander said, "You never can tell. Nobody would have given a kopek for our chances in September 1941, either."

"That's true." Eigims bit the words off short. When the panzers rolled through the Baltics on the way to Leningrad, he wouldn't have needed to shave. He'd probably cheered the Germans as liberators then; everyone in the Baltics except the Jews had. But Hitler's soldiers never got into Leningrad, and after a while the tide ran the other way. Which was why Eigims was a Red Army tank gunner these days.

"Remember it, then," Morozov said.

"I do, Comrade Sergeant. I serve the Soviet Union."

"When you feel like it. When you can't get away with anything else." In a different tone of voice, that would have been a denunciation. As it was, Konstantin was ribbing Eigims, and doing it broadly enough so neither one doubted that was all he was doing.

Eigims said, "I remember, sure, but this is different. The Americans can hit a lot harder than Hitler did."

"So can we," Konstantin said. "We've talked about this before, Juris. Do we need to do it again?"

"Do we need to get killed for nothing?" the gunner returned. "We had the USA and England on our side the last time. Who's on our side now?"

"China is," Morozov said loyally. Eigims rolled his pale, cold eyes. Konstantin added, "And the satellites."

"They're trying to get out of orbit, and you know it. The brass are pulling men away from the line here to fight back there. Is that good news?"

"You think I'm an idiot? Of course it's not good news," Konstantin said. "But what are we supposed to do about it? You think the enemy will give a shit about your politics? If you don't blow his dick off first, he'll sure as hell blast yours."

German sergeants must have been saying the same thing to the men they led from about 1943 on. And the junior Fritzes must have listened, too, because they'd fought the Red Army like mad bastards till they couldn't fight any more. Now maybe it was the Red Army's turn to fight like that. Sometimes all your choices were bad.

Juris Eigims' mouth twisted. He didn't want to listen to what Morozov was saying. He didn't want to be in the Red Army, either. Had he been a little older during the last war, he might have picked up a rifle and tried to keep the Russians out of his tiny, worthless, tinpot country. Konstantin could read him much too easily.

He said something else: "Don't bug out, man. You might have one chance in four of making it through the line to the other side without getting caught. The other three, some bored Chekist puts down his cigarette long enough to plug you in the back of the neck. Then he picks it up again and finishes it. Even if you sneak over to the Yankees, fifty-fifty they get overeager and shoot you before you can give up. C'mon. You're no dope. You know fucking well I'm right. Are those betting odds?"

"Nooo." Eigims said what he obviously didn't want to.

Konstantin stood up, walked over to him, and thumped him on the back. "So it's a fuckup. A lot of soldiering's a fuckup. Hell, a lot of life's a fuckup. Ride it out the best way you can and hope it gets better, that's all. I don't know what else to tell you."

"Fuck your mother, Comrade Sergeant," Eigims said sadly. With *mat,* how you said something was more important than what you said. Not everyone who hadn't grown up speaking Russian got that, but the tank gunner did.

So Morozov had no trouble translating the all-purpose obscenity into something like *Well, you're right, goddammit.* "Yours, too. In the mouth," he said, which meant, more or less, *Damn straight I am.* He continued, "Shall we see if they've got any fuel and ammo for us?"

"Pretty hard to fight a war without 'em," Juris Eigims agreed.

That was also true. The uprisings in Poland and Hungary and Czechoslovakia did more than siphon off men who should have kept fighting the imperialists. They kept supplies from getting through to the troops who *were* still fighting the imperialists. As Eigims said, not good news.

Vazgan Sarkisyan looked up from the T-54's engine. He and Vladislav Kalyakin were poking around in there with wrenches. The diesel had been farting out too much black smoke even for a motor of its kind. If the enemy spotted your exhaust long before you could see his, he had plenty of time to cook up something nasty for you.

"Thanks, Comrade Sergeant," Eigims said. "You let me blow off some steam, anyhow."

"Everybody needs to do that once in a while," Konstantin answered. "I know you don't love Russians. But you've got to remember, you are where you are. You go off the rails, you won't like what happens after that."

Revetments camouflaged with usual Red Army attention to detail protected the ammunition store and the fuel bowsers. Morozov and Eigims had almost got to the fuel-storage area when the shriek of jet engines low overhead sent them both diving for cover.

The planes were American F-80s with unswept wings. They were almost as outmoded as FW-190s . . . except when no more modern fighters were around to shoot them down. Now, for instance. They had rockets under their wings. They carried heavy machine guns. Each one hauled a bomb below its fuselage. They unloaded their ordnance on the tank regiment.

Konstantin used a rugby tackle to take Eigims down. They both flattened out while the planes bombed and strafed before zooming back off to the west. Blast picked Morozov up, then slammed him to the ground like a bad-tempered wrestler. He fought to breathe. Blast could kill you even if no fire or jagged steel touched your body.

The attack couldn't have lasted longer than a minute or two. It only seemed to go on forever. When Konstantin doggedly stumbled to his feet, he looked back in the direction from which he'd come. Plumes of greasy black smoke rose to the uncaring sky.

Eigims' boots pounded beside Morozov's. Pretty soon the Balt, taller and with longer legs, outdistanced him. It didn't matter much. Tree cover or not, *maskirovka* or not, their tank was one of the machines that burned. Kalyakin and Sarkisyan lay near the flaming corpse like rag dolls tossed aside by a child having a tantrum. Konstantin and Eigims stared at each other. If Eigims wanted to desert now, the sergeant didn't know what to say that might hold him back.

Harry Truman had named General Omar Bradley his new Secretary of Defense. The only civilian he could have chosen who had the necessary clout was Dwight Eisenhower. Since Ike was busy running for President as a Republican, that wouldn't have worked so well.

Bradley and other new Cabinet members served without Senate confirmation. The Senate wasn't yet a functioning body again. The House was in even worse shape. Truman understood he set horrible new precedents every day of the week, and twice on Sundays. For all practical purposes, he ruled by decree. He figured the USA would sort things out later if it won the war. If it didn't, whether things got sorted out stopped mattering.

Though highly competent, Bradley was a bit of a comedown after George Marshall. Of course, after Marshall anyone this side of God and Winston Churchill would have been. "I have good news, Mr. President," Bradley said now.

"Good. I could use some," Truman answered.

"Believe me, Mr. President, I understand that," Bradley said. "Well, the report from the South Pacific is just in. As far as the physicists can tell, the test was successful in every way."

"All right. I suppose it's all right, anyhow." Truman still wasn't altogether sure. Even before this war started, scientists had told him there was a step up from the A-bomb. When you talked about A-bomb explosions, uranium or plutonium, you talked about the equivalent of thousands of tons of TNT. One of those bombs could rip the heart out of a big city, or knock a smaller city flat.

Those were fission bombs. When you added hydrogen to them and used them to trigger the bigger boom, you got what the fellows with the tweed jackets or lab coats called a fusion bomb, or sometimes an H-bomb for the hydrogen. When you calculated how strong they could be, you had to think in terms of millions of tons of TNT, not thousands. One of them wouldn't just wreck part of Manhattan, the way the Russians' A-bomb had. An H-bomb would level all five boroughs, with Jersey City and part of Long Island thrown in for a bonus.

"What's left of the island where they touched it off?" Truman asked.

"Eniwetok? Not much, sir," Bradley said. "That's the short answer. I can give you a longer one, but that's what it boils down to. Quite a bit of Eniwetok has boiled down, as a matter of fact."

"I believe you. God help us all," Truman said. "No sign of any Russian planes close enough to spy the blast?"

"None picked up visually or on radar," the Secretary of Defense replied. "Submarines, of course, are much harder to spot, so we can't be a hundred percent sure the Russians don't know."

"We can never be a hundred percent sure about the damn Russians," Truman said bitterly. He and his top generals and spies hadn't dreamt Stalin would strike back if the Air Force A-bombed Manchuria. How many millions had died from that miscalculation? And . . . "Any notion of how close they are to an H-bomb of their own?"

"We think they're still some distance behind us, Mr. President," Omar Bradley said. "But anyone who claims he's certain about the Russians isn't as certain as he imagines he is."

" 'A riddle wrapped in a mystery inside an enigma.' " Truman quoted Churchill on Russia. And Churchill had been talking just after the outbreak of World War II, when Stalin and Hitler were still making like bosom buddies. Uncle Joe's USSR hadn't got less opaque since. No one in the West had expected the Bull bomber, the B-29 copy that gave Stalin a plane able to deliver A-bombs. And no one had expected that, two years after he got the Bull, he would have A-bombs to deliver.

So Russian physicists and engineers were bound to be working on the H-bomb as hard as their American counterparts were. Underestimating them would be deadly dangerous.

"Yes, sir," Bradley replied. "You can't very well say he was wrong, either."

"He sure wasn't. We've found that out the hard way," Truman said. "Any news from the other big project?"

"Long Reach?" With obvious regret, the Secretary of Defense shook his head. "We're doing everything we know how to do to get what we need there, but so far we just haven't had any luck."

"Too bad," Truman said. "Be sure to let me know the minute we learn anything on that front. The minute, you hear me?"

"Of course, Mr. President. We have the parallel project running with Red China, naturally. If Mao makes a mistake, it'll be the last mistake he ever makes."

"That would be nice. Chiang Kai-shek would think so; you bet he would. But Chiang either wants Mao's head mounted on the wall above his sofa or served up medium-rare with an apple in its mouth."

"Er—yes," Bradley said, looking revolted at the idea that the President might mean it literally. And Truman pretty much did. Chiang Kai-shek had gone from running the most populous country in the world to lording it over an island a little bigger than Maryland. Would he hate the man who'd reduced him so? Had Napoleon hated the English after they sent him to Elba? Oh, maybe just a little.

Napoleon's second act was mercifully brief. Chiang didn't want a Waterloo if he invaded the mainland. So far, Truman had kept him from doing any such thing. So had his own sense of self-preservation. If Mao Tse-tung were to have an unfortunate accident, though . . .

"I have one more question for you, General. Then I'll let you go," Truman said. "If the war should end fairly soon, can we pick up the pieces and make . . . something out of this mess, anyhow?"

"We've broken an awful lot of eggs, sir," Omar Bradley answered. "The omelette we end up with will be overcooked and ragged around the edges, but we'll have to eat it anyway."

"Won't we just?" Of themselves, Truman's eyes went to the black-framed photos of Bess and Margaret on his desk. So many millions had died. Somehow, he wasn't astonished God had made him feel that to the fullest. He only wished the Lord had taken him instead.

Bradley saluted and left his office. Philadelphia, these days, had more ground- and air-based radar sets and antiaircraft guns surrounding it than any other city on earth. The Russians might get through anyhow. You never could tell. All you could do was make things hard for them.

The President threw himself back into work. Work was the only anodyne he had. The harder he worked at winning the fight overseas and putting the domestic scene back together, the less he'd think about the mess he'd already made of things.

A report said the harbors in the San Francisco Bay were finally functioning at close to their prebomb level. That was progress. It would help keep the war in Korea, the war that had spawned the bigger war, sputtering along a half-forgotten while longer.

He read a scrawled letter from a man down in Cajun country who complained that the increase in shipping out of the Mississippi was fouling up his crab and oyster harvest. Truman sighed. Nice to know that someone could get upset about such mundane troubles. He went back to the job, and kept at it nineteen hours a day.

A week later, the phone rang. It was Omar Bradley. "Sir, we have a Long Reach positive," he said. "The resources have been in place for some time, all but one, and now we're in a position to use that, too."

"Execute the plan, then," Truman said. "We'll see what happens, that's all. The Russians will feel it whether we get everything we want or not."

"I'll give the order," Bradley said, and hung up.

Bruce McNulty had flown his B-29 out of Sculthorpe, west of Norwich, till a Russian A-bomb blew the air base off the map. Now he was stationed at a strip not far from Dundee, up in Scotland. That gave him a few hundred miles of head start when he flew against the northwestern Soviet Union, and let him reach deeper into the vast country.

He'd delivered as many A-bombs as any pilot still alive. His superiors chose to think that was because he was so damn good at what he did. And he *was* good; he knew that. He'd been a bomber pilot during the last war, too, though on mediums, not heavies. He was smart. He was careful.

He was lucky. He knew only too well how lucky he was. Every time you went up there over Russia, you played Russian roulette. So far, the loaded chamber hadn't come up when he spun the cylinder and pulled the trigger. Plenty of men just as good as he was had flown against the Reds and not come back. As far as he could see, skill had damn little to do with that.

As long as the brass thought otherwise, he didn't waste time telling them they were full of shit. He accepted promotions and decorations. But why had that goddamn chunk of flaming wreckage come down on Daisy Baxter's head instead of his? Dumb luck, nothing else but.

Because he was hot stuff to the brass, he got sucked into Operation Long Reach. He was one of the decoy pilots: that was what he got for sticking with an obsolescent aircraft. But even the decoys in Long Reach carried A-bombs.

The briefing officer was a lieutenant general. Bruce had never seen that before. He didn't suppose he would ever see it again, either. He didn't know everything there was to know about Long Reach. What his superiors didn't tell him, the MGB couldn't pull out of him in case he got shot down and captured.

He knew for a fact, however, that whoever'd hatched Long Reach wasn't thinking small. You didn't use an A-bomb to distract the enemy or a three-star general to explain a mission unless something pretty juicy was in the works.

Something, say, that made D-Day look like a beach party by comparison.

"Petrozavodsk—that's where you're going." The general pointed to it on a map. He hadn't offered Bruce his name. Bruce had the feeling that, if he asked for it, the senior man would refuse to cough it up. The officer continued, "It's east of Leningrad, on the western shore of Lake Onega.

The railroad up to Murmansk goes through it. So does some shipping—that's a big lake. It has, oh, 125,000 people, something like that."

"It won't after we get through with it," Bruce said. "Looks like a decent target, all right. How come we haven't hit it sooner than this?"

Instead of answering, the three-star general said, "You tell me."

Bruce eyed the map. He didn't need long. "Oh," he said. "Bad air route. Finland shields the short trip."

"There you go." The general nodded. Like Switzerland, Finland was a neutral. When Stalin knocked her out of the last war, he could have turned her into another Communist satellite. He hadn't. He'd let her stay free and democratic . . . as long as she didn't tick him off. She repaid him by banning military flights through her airspace, and by going after violators with her small but ferocious fighter force.

"So you'll want me to go down through Karelia?" Bruce asked. The Reds had a lot of flak guns and air bases up there. Odds of coming back didn't look great.

But Mr. Three Stars said, "Nope. You have our permission to attack by way of Finland. In fact, you are ordered to do so. How you get out, of course, will be up to you."

"By way of Finland?" Bruce echoed, wondering whether he'd heard straight. The lieutenant general nodded—he had. He said, "But the Finns have radar—they'll spot me. And, chances are, they'll let the Russians know we're coming." This time, the general only shrugged. Bruce threw his hands in the air. "Sounds like you want the Reds to know we're on the way, dammit!"

The senior officer sat mute for several seconds. At last, grudgingly, he said, "You do need to bear in mind that you are just one part of a larger operation."

"A trout grabs a worm, and a fisherman has himself a fish supper," Bruce said.

"That's about the size of it," the three-star general agreed.

"But the worm still gets eaten," Bruce observed. The lieutenant general might have been carved from basalt. Sighing, Bruce continued, "You have to forgive me, sir. I've never been a worm before."

"Are you declining the mission?" the three-star man asked. "If you are, tell me right now, so I can assign it to someone else."

If you are, tell me right now, so you can kiss your Air Force career goodbye. The general didn't say that. Bruce had been in the service long enough to hear it even so. He sighed again. "No, I'll take it on. What the hell? The Finns and the Russians may be laughing too hard to shoot straight."

"I can't talk about the Finns. If Long Reach goes according to plan, I swear to you that the Russians won't think it's funny," the lieutenant general said. "You will be playing a major role in the war, I promise. I shouldn't tell you even so much, but you're going into danger for your country, and I think I owe it to you."

"Thank you, sir," Bruce said.

"I'll give you your flight plan and your orders," the three-star general said. "You can brief your crew from them. Good luck to you all."

Bruce's copilot was a burly Texan named Wally Hickman. "Godalmightydamn," he said. "Reckon I better start praying for real." He was given to such benedictions as *Yea, though I walk through the valley of the shadow of death, I will fear no evil, for I am the orneriest son of a bitch in the valley.* Not this time.

"Almost sounds like they want us to get shot down," said Ezra Jacobs, the radioman.

"Nah." That was the navigator. Phil Vukovich had got his law degree after the last war, only to put the uniform back on for this one. He was relentlessly precise, as a good navigator and a good lawyer needed to be. "What it sounds like is, they want us to get noticed."

"That's how it looks to me, too," Bruce said. "There's other stuff going on. Whatever it is, we're only a piece of the puzzle. Anybody who doesn't want to join in, you don't have to. I won't say boo if you don't." The B-29 had a crew of eleven. Nobody backed out. Bruce nodded. "Okay. We're all a bunch of damn fools. Now we fly the mission."

Taking off in a B-29 with a ten-ton bomb in its belly was an adventure. This bomb had DAISY chalked on the casing. The engines were strong enough to get the giant plane airborne . . . as long as everything went right. Only after the landing gear went up did Bruce's sphincter unpucker.

As soon as they crossed the Finnish border, Ralph Sutton, the man in charge of the plane's electronics, said, "We're getting radar signals."

"Getting queries, too, in English and German," Ezra Jacobs added.

"Don't answer," Bruce said. "Ralph, start releasing window." The strips of aluminum foil drifting in the air would confuse radar sets— for a while.

"Will the Finns tell the Russians we're on our way?" Wally asked.

"Answer that one and you win the sixty-four dollars," Bruce said. "Now that they know we're here, I'm going down to the deck. No point making things easy for 'em. Ralph, keep the window coming."

"I'll do it," the radarman replied. He didn't report any fighters on their tail. That might have meant something, or it might not. The window fouled up his set, too. Other American planes would also be heading for Petrozavodsk, or Bruce figured they would. Putting all your eggs in one basket was dumb.

The B-29 crossed from Finland to Soviet Karelia between Värtsilä and Sortavala, which had both been Finnish till Stalin took them away in the Winter War. Bruce started puckering again. If Russian radar was vectoring MiG-15s toward him, he'd die. He couldn't even bail out. The B-29 was too low.

Phil Vukovich guided the plane toward Petrozavodsk. Al Reynoso, the bombardier, made sure the weapon was up to snuff. It had a two-minute delay to give the bomber a chance to escape. Bruce was glad to give the order to let it go. The antiaircraft guns around Petrozavodsk were waking up. They shot blindly and high, but with a lucky hit it wouldn't matter.

A dozen miles behind the B-29, hell blossomed on earth. Two blast waves smacked the plane, one straight through the air, the other, a beat later, reflected from the ground. Bruce weathered them and hoped to make it back to the good old UK one more time.

. . .

Radio Moscow was playing Shostakovich's symphony about the siege of Leningrad. Boris Gribkov turned up the radio. "I like this one," he said, a way to ask the other flyers in the barracks outside of Tula whether they minded. Nobody said anything, so he didn't turn it down.

Radio Moscow had been playing a lot of martial music lately. The people who ran things were doing whatever they could to get everybody else to want to go on with the war. It wasn't easy. Tula lay south of Moscow. The Germans had briefly taken it during the desperate winter of 1941, but only briefly. No American A-bomb had touched it. But on the way down from Ukma and Petrozavodsk, Boris had seen more horror and devastation than he remembered from the whole of the Great Patriotic War.

Halfway through the second movement, the symphony . . . stopped. Somebody at the studio yanked the tone arm off the record so abruptly, the scratch of needle against grooves seemed almost gunshot-loud. Silence followed. Radio Moscow hadn't gone off the air. Boris could still hear the hiss of the carrier wave. But that was all he could hear for a minute, two, three, four.

"What the devil?" somebody said, which was exactly what he was thinking.

Then a voice came on: "Comrades, this is Roman Amfiteatrov." The newsreader with the mooing southern accent had replaced Yuri Levitan when the first A-bombs struck Moscow. How long ago that seemed now! After another, shorter, pause, Amfiteatrov continued, "Comrades, people of the ever-triumphant Soviet Union, I apologize for the interruption to your musical program. But it cannot be helped, for I bring you the harshest of news."

"*Bozhemoi!*" Boris said, along with three other men. They hadn't talked that way when Moscow and Leningrad and Kiev sprouted monstrous mushroom clouds. They'd just told people to roll up their sleeves and keep fighting. For the most part, people had, soldiers and civilians alike. So what could make Amfiteatrov sound like . . . this?

"The criminal Yankee air pirates have destroyed the city of Omsk, in the southern region of the Ural Mountains. To carry out their murderous assault, they used a bomb of dreadful, unprecedented power, stronger even than the A-bombs that have been the currency of this imperialistic conflict."

Amfiteatrov paused again, and gulped. His voice seemed heavy with unshed tears. *He sounds like someone whose father just died,* Boris thought. Looking back, he realized that moment was the one when he began to understand what must have happened.

"Here, then, is what I must tell you, my friends—here is what I must tell all the peace-loving Soviet people, and all the peace-loving people of the . . . world. Please excuse me." Amfiteatrov's voice did break then. In the background, funereal music began to play. Gooseflesh prickled up on Boris' arms. Roman Amfiteatrov went on, "I have to report that the Great Coryphaeus of the Soviet Union, our beloved leader, Marshal Iosef Vissarionovich Stalin, by unhappy chance and malignant fate, happened to be in the city of Omsk, encouraging its workers and peasants to continue their brave Stakhanovite struggle against capitalism and Fascism, when the Americans destroyed the city with this new and altogether abhorrent atomic weapon. Thus, my friends, there can be no doubt that Marshal Stalin, unique among mankind in wisdom and courage while he lived, now belongs to the ages and lives no more." He fell silent. The strains of the mournful orchestra behind him swelled.

Tears that felt hot as molten lead burned down Boris Gribkov's cheeks. He buried his face in his pillow and sobbed like a heartbroken child. He hadn't cried like that when his own father died during the Great Patriotic War. He'd got the news weeks after it happened, but even so. . . . He'd lived almost his whole life with Stalin at the helm of the USSR. Take away that strong hand and who could imagine what would happen?

For a moment, he felt embarrassed to show his grief so publicly, but only for a moment. Everyone else in the barracks was weeping and wailing the same way. Part of that might have been fear of being seen not to regret Stalin's passing, but it was only a small part. Everybody had to feel stunned. How could you not, when the man who'd ruled the country the past thirty years was no more than radioactive dust?

"Who can hold the Soviet Union together now?" someone howled. That struck Boris as much too good a question.

A moment later, Roman Amfiteatrov did his best to answer it: "Marshal and Deputy Premier Lavrenti Pavlovich Beria has issued the following statement: 'I am as shocked and as filled with horror and sorrow as every other Soviet citizen at the untimely passing of the great Stalin. Even without him, though, the struggle against imperialist aggression continues. I shall do everything in my power to bring it to a victorious conclusion.'"

No one in the barracks said anything to that or about that. The flyers had acquired their sense of self-preservation over a lifetime. Beria sounded as if he was in charge—indeed, as if no one else possibly could be. He'd made Stalin a viciously effective boss of the MGB for years. But did the USSR really want a blubbery Mingrelian telling its more than 200,000,000 people what to do? Even more to the point, did the Soviet Union want to take orders from the leader of all the Chekists?

Boris knew that that prospect failed to fill him with delight. But he was only a pilot, someone far from the levers of political power. What would the men who could grab for those levers have to say?

"The country now enters into seven days of mourning," Amfiteatrov said. "All business not connected with the war or with immediate emergencies of health and safety is suspended for that period. At the conclusion of the mourning, a memorial service in praise of the undying memory of Comrade Stalin will be held. Stay tuned to Radio Moscow for further bulletins."

Shostakovich's Leningrad symphony started playing—from the beginning. No one had any notion where the needle had been when some studio engineer jerked it off the record. Boris noticed that Roman Amfiteatrov didn't say where Stalin's memorial service would be held. That made more sense than the bomber pilot wished it did. If the Soviet people found out where the service was, so would the enemy. One more American A-bomb, or whatever this super A-bomb was, and the USSR wouldn't have anybody left to run things.

Everybody in the barracks started talking at once. The main themes were *I can't believe it, What will the country do now?*, and *I feel worse than I did when my own father died*. Maybe some men thought they had to say such things to keep from drawing suspicion from others. But the ones who spoke sounded as if they meant every word. Boris believed they did. Why not, when he felt that way himself?

No one said anything about changing how things worked in the Soviet Union now that Stalin was gone. That was one more thing Boris noticed only in retrospect. With Stalin dead, everything else seemed trivial. The reason was simple. With Stalin dead, everything else *was* trivial.

WHEN THE CAMP COMMANDANT ANNOUNCED to the assembled *zeks,* women and men, that Stalin was dead, tears ran from his good eye. Luisa Hozzel stared at him in astonished disbelief. She wouldn't have imagined that ruined visage would cry if the man's mother were devoured by starving wolves in front of him.

The guards at the gulag also wept. And so did the prisoners who came from within the Soviet Union's borders. Some of the *zeks* wept louder and harder than the camp guards.

She wondered if they'd gone insane. How had they all wound up in this terrible place in the middle of nowhere? Obeying Stalin's orders, his minions had arrested them and shipped them here. Shouldn't they be celebrating his death, not bemoaning it?

But then she remembered her younger self, and how she'd felt at the end of April in 1945. "It's like when Hitler died," she said to Trudl Bachman in her prison-yard whisper.

"It is, *ja,*" the other woman from Fulda agreed. "No one knows what will happen next, and everybody's scared."

Trudl hadn't been so quiet as she might have been. Most of the time, the camp guards would have made her sorry. Not this afternoon. They were too stunned to do their jobs as well as they might have. They were even too stunned to fuss about the count. When the commandant limped away, they just dismissed the *zeks* to supper.

That supper was no different from any of the other horrible suppers Luisa had eaten since coming into the gulag. She finished everything, licking her stew bowl and making sure she didn't miss a crumb of black bread. Latrine call was the same as always, too. Afterwards, though . . .

Some of the women in the barracks couldn't stop crying. Luisa would have bet they hadn't wept that way when they lost husbands or lovers or brothers in the last war. When Hitler died, most Germans were too numbed by the disaster overwhelming their country to mourn like this. Not the Russian *zeks*, though.

Part of Luisa wanted to cheer because Stalin wasn't around any more. She had the sense to keep quiet, though. If she was lucky, she'd draw a long stretch in a punishment cell. She'd come out all stooped over and pale as a ghost. If she wasn't, either she wouldn't come out at all or the Russians here would mob her instead of turning her over to the gulag administrators.

"Will they send us out into the woods tomorrow?" Trudl asked. "The order said everything would shut down except for the war effort."

She spoke in German to Luisa, but some of the Russian women could follow the language. Nadezhda Chukovskaya said, "That order was for people, ordinary people. We're just *zeks*. Bet your cunt they'll send us out."

She was short and chunky and bad-tempered: no one to mess with. She came from what the Russians called the socially friendly elements. She was a thief or a swindler, not a political prisoner. That put her in the upper class of prisoners here in this classless labor camp in a classless society. And she was a dyke as obnoxious as any horny man. She had all sorts of connections, in other words.

Not surprisingly, then, she knew what she was talking about. After roll call and breakfast the next morning, out the *zeks* went, with guards carrying machine guns to keep them in line. Luisa and Trudl worked a long saw together, back and forth, back and forth. Sooner or later, the pine whose trunk they were attacking would fall over.

They never hurried, except when the guards made them. Most of the time, they clung to the age-old pace of slaves the world around: the slowest they could go without getting in trouble. Today, the guards yelled less than usual. The men seemed as overwhelmed by Stalin's death as the Russian women were.

One of them kept dabbing at his dark, narrow Asiatic eyes with his tunic sleeve. "Terrible thing," he said, over and over. "Terrible thing." He spoke better Russian than Luisa did, but not much better.

"Too bad Stalin is dead," Luisa said: as much sympathy as she had in her.

"Too bad, *da,*" the guard agreed. "He great man. He make great country. Now he gone." He wiped his eyes again.

Luisa couldn't even tell him he was wrong. Without Stalin's driving energy, the German invasion would have crushed Russia, and the world would have been a different place. Better? Worse? It all depended on who you were. But different.

"What do you think will happen now?" Luisa asked. "Will the war go on? Will there be peace now?"

"*Inshallah.*" The guard shrugged skinny shoulders. He wasn't a hulking Slav; his uniform was all right as far as length went, but hung loosely on his shoulders and chest.

"I've heard that word before, but I don't know what it means," Luisa said. "It's not Russian, is it?"

"Not Russian, no," the swarthy man agreed. "Is Arabic. Means *is the will of God.*" He suddenly remembered he was supposed to be a symbol of atheistic Communism. With an embarrassed cough, he continued, "Only old saying now. *Whatever happens, happens*—like that."

"I understand." Luisa wondered if she could use the guard's slip against him. MGB men weren't supposed to spout religious sentiments. From what she'd gathered, they especially weren't supposed to spout Muslim sentiments.

Even if the USSR was supposed to be godless and classless and free from national turmoil, the Russians were the big wheels. They were nervous about Kazakhs and Uzbeks and Kirghiz and Chechens: Muslim groups the Tsars had conquered and the commissars still controlled. Had Hitler overcome Stalin, the grandchildren of his settlers probably would have been nervous about Byelorussians and Russians and Ukrainians the same way.

As things were, Germans had plenty of other reasons to be nervous about Byelorussians and Russians and Ukrainians—and about Kazakhs and Uzbeks and Kirghiz and Chechens.

"You forget I say, hey?" the guard said. "I not work so hard you, all right?"

So he recognized that he'd put his foot in it, too. "However you want." Luisa made it sound as if she were going along without thinking much about it. The guard's smile showed a gold front tooth. Sometimes you didn't need to put on a fancy show to finish a bargain. You didn't even have to say it was a bargain . . . as long as you both knew.

Almost apologetically, the swarthy man said, "You still gots to do somethings, or you gets in trouble and I, too."

"Oh, yes. Of course," Luisa said. The best bargains were often the ones other people didn't notice at all.

"You know, one time I see Stalin," the guard said proudly. "I in Victory Day parade in Moscow. March past reviewing stand, him on it."

Luisa had seen the *Führer* at a rally or two. Admitting that, these days, was bad form. If this war ended with the USSR giving in to America, would admitting you'd once seen Stalin turn into something you didn't want to do? Would whoever took charge of Russia—it looked like Beria now—try to pretend Stalin and everything he'd done had never happened?

She wouldn't be a bit surprised if it worked like that here. It sure had in Germany. Any tree bent the way the wind was blowing. Either it bent, or it broke.

She'd bent herself. She'd had to. If you didn't bend at all, the gulag would kill you. It might kill you anyhow. But she hadn't broken. She wasn't sleeping with a barber, say, for the sake of an inside job and better food. She could still look at herself in the mirror. Or she could have, if only she'd had one. It might have been just as well that she didn't.

Somewhere behind Cade Curtis, the American loudspeakers started howling in Chinese. Cade had always thought Chinese was a godawful language. Hearing it through loudspeakers at ear-hurting volume did nothing to improve it.

Cade had learned the little bits of Chinese a soldier from the other side would naturally pick up, and no more. He could say things like *Drop your weapon!, Hands up!,* and *You stupid piece of shit!* Somebody had told him the last one was literally *You stupid turtle!* He didn't know whether he believed that or not.

Anyway, though, his Chinese stopped almost as soon as it started. He didn't understand the American propaganda, which only made it more annoying. But every so often, he caught the name *Stalin,* so he could make a pretty good guess as to what all the too-loud blathering was about.

We just turned your best friend in the world into a charcoal briquette, the guy on the record would be saying. *We turned his whole goddamn country into a charcoal briquette. If you don't want to turn into a charcoal briquette yourself, come on over to our side.*

But the Red Chinese had loudspeakers of their own. The propaganda duel could get as ferocious as the one fought with 105s and 155s. The American piece hadn't been going on for very long before the other side started yelling back in English.

"Chairman Mao has declared that, come what may, the revolutionary struggle will continue till ultimate victory," the enemy propagandist thundered. He sounded like an American from the Midwest. Maybe he had a gun to his head, or maybe he really believed the crap he was spewing. He went on, "The victory of the proletariat against capitalism and imperialism is inevitable. Setbacks may come, but the cause goes ever forward."

"Boy, what a crock of bullshit," said someone at Cade's elbow.

"Bet your ass it is," Cade agreed. Only then did he turn around to see who'd delivered that verdict. "Jimmy! You know what? You sound like you were born in the States." He wasn't kidding. Accent, intonation— the private born as Chun Won-ung sounded as if he'd been lapping up apple pie since he had baby teeth.

He grinned. "I born in these trenches, Captain, when you take me away from that asshole." His English grew by leaps and bounds, but sometimes he got stuck in the present indicative.

The asshole in question had been his company CO, Captain Pak Ho-san of the ROK Army. The Republic of Korea, the U.S. ally, wasn't much more democratic than Kim Il-sung's Commie People's Democratic Republic of Korea. The peasants in the ROK Army couldn't stand the Jap-trained aristocrats who gave them orders, and it was mutual.

Not for the first time, Cade wondered what would happen when their unit went back to the USA—if it ever did. Would they pass Jimmy on to some other outfit staying in South Korea? (He was sure as sure could be that South Korea would have American soldiers in it for many years to come.) Or would they find some way to bamboozle the brass and smuggle him across the Pacific? Except for his looks, Jimmy already made a better American than most of the guys Cade knew who came from Florida or South Dakota.

"Shame we don't get Kim Il-sung same way we get Stalin," he said now. "And Mao, he gotta be shitting himself. Forget the crap the Chinks pour out of the loudspeakers. He gotta know he next."

"Yeah." Cade eyed Jimmy. He called the Red Chinese the same thing every other dogface in Korea called them. All those dogfaces called Koreans gooks. Cade hadn't heard Jimmy say that. The guys in the regiment had pretty much quit using it since they acquired him. Anybody who called *him* a gook would be lucky just to lose teeth and not to end up holding a lily.

The American loudspeakers started over again with the same shrill, incomprehensible spiel. It must have finally driven a Communist captain or major around the bend, because the enemy started lobbing mortar bombs at them. "Hit the deck!" Cade yelled, and fit action to words.

Those loudspeakers weren't that far behind the front line. Short rounds could easily kill his men—or him—by accident. Or the Red Chinese might decide to punish soldiers along with propaganda outlets. And Cade hated mortars anyway. They didn't make big, loud bangs going off, and they kind of whispered in, so the bursts were liable to take you by surprise.

Naturally, the Americans started shooting back. Naturally, because the men who ran things believed in the big stick, they didn't shoot back with mortars alone. They started throwing 105mm rounds at the Red Chinese loudspeakers. Naturally, the slant-eyed bastards to the north started throwing 105s back. Some machine guns opened up, too.

This wasn't the first skirmish Cade had seen that started because of dueling liars. Whoever said *Sticks and stones may break my bones, but words will never hurt me* hadn't visited the Korean trenches.

An American M-2's deep, nasty bark punctuated the rest of the fireworks. All the Red Chinese privates had to be swearing at their psychological-warfare officers. A .50-caliber machine gun was one of the deadliest man-reapers God ever made. The thumb-sized slug was made to pierce light armor. It would pierce flesh out past a mile and a half. Somebody far behind the barbed wire, far behind the trenches, far behind the damn loudspeakers that had started everything, could be walking along happy as a clam . . . till he walked into a gift from one of John Browning's brainchildren. He wouldn't do any more walking after he met Ma Deuce.

Damn! The Chinks had a heavy machine gun of their own. They hadn't made it themselves; they'd got it from their comrades to the north. The Russian Dushka was powered by gas, unlike the recoil-operated Ma Deuce. Nothing was wrong with the Soviet model, but the Americans had turned out far more of theirs. That Dushka on the other side of the line, though, would rearrange your face just as permanently as the heavy machine guns in the U.S. arsenal.

Tracers from the Russian beast in Red Chinese service flew past, inches above the parapet top. The balls of fire looked as big as golf balls. They reinforced the message that those bullets really weren't anything you wanted to get in the way of.

Which didn't mean you could keep lying here on the muddy trench floor or in dugouts carved into the forward wall. As soon as you figured you could simply ride out a bombardment, that would be the time the Red Chinese officers would send men across no-man's-land if they caught you napping.

So Cade scrambled to his feet and shouted, "Up! Gotta keep the fuckers honest!" He jumped onto a firing step and looked out across the wire-strewn moonscape that separated his trenches from the ones the Chinks infested. Sure as hell, black-haired men in quilted, dun-colored uniforms were slithering forward, deadly as so many cobras.

The M-2 and a couple of rifle-caliber machine guns were already raking no-man's-land. They all lived in nests strengthened with sandbags and cement. Only bombs or direct hits from heavy artillery could take them out. The Red Chinese needed to know the rest of the American trenches were also inhabited.

Cade squeezed off a burst with his PPSh. He liked the Red submachine gun better than both the M-1 rifle and the much lighter M-1 carbine officers were supposed to carry. It was murderous out to a couple of hundred yards, and it didn't care how you abused it. He ducked, moved, and fired again

Jimmy squeezed off a few rounds from his M-1. Other dogfaces were up and shooting, too. The Red Chinese had got more pragmatic about expending men than they were when they first swarmed south across the Yalu. When they saw it wouldn't be a walkover, they pulled back. The mostly undamaged loudspeakers picked up the war again.

Marian Staley fiddled with the radio. When you lived in Weed, California, fiddling with the radio was a fact of life. Weed was too small to have a station of its own. You picked up the ones that broadcast from places like Redding to the south and Klamath Falls to the north.

You picked them up when you could, anyhow. Their words and music often hid behind veils of static. KFI in Los Angeles was much farther away. Especially at night, though, it often came in better. It had a high-power signal, and it was what they called a clear-channel station. No other stations in the western USA broadcast on 640 kilocycles.

Tonight, though, even KFI was having trouble. Interference ran up and down the dial. Marian wished she had a shortwave set. Then she could listen to broadcasts from all over the world. But she didn't. She had what she could afford: this cheap, secondhand piece of junk.

She went almost to the high end of the dial before she found a station that came in well enough to listen to. This signal started in Sacramento. The three familiar chimes told her it was an NBC station. They were playing a Glenn Miller record from the last war.

Linda looked up from her dolls and stuffed animals. "Why are you dancing around like that, Mommy?"

"I used to dance with your daddy when they played this song," Marian answered. "I was remembering, I guess you'd say."

"Oh." Linda paused. Marian thought she was going to leave it there, but she didn't—she said, "I miss Daddy."

"So do I, sweetheart." Marian stopped dancing. She was still remembering, but not in a way now that made her want to sashay around the living room. "So do I, every single day. I guess I always will."

"Me, too," Linda said. Marian doubted that. By the time Linda grew up, she'd barely remember Bill Staley. If she'd been just a little younger when the Russians shot down his B-29, she wouldn't remember him at all.

And maybe it wouldn't have been such a horrible thing if she didn't. Bill hadn't been in that Superfortress to drop chocolate and roses on the Reds. They'd killed him before he could bathe some town of theirs in atomic fire. Marian hadn't thought about that—hadn't had to think about it—till the Russian A-bomb hit Seattle.

Nothing like a smashed house and a mild dose of radiation sickness to make you understand what your husband did for a living, she thought bleakly. Even if Bill had come home, she wasn't sure she could have lived with him again, knowing what she knew. How many lives had he taken before losing his own? He wouldn't have thought of it like that. He couldn't have, not if he wanted to stay sane. To him, they would have been cities, or maybe just targets.

But if you'd been just outside the bull's-eye yourself, what an A-bomb hit wasn't a target any more. It was you. It was personal. The people in the bomber way up there were murderers.

Her husband had been a murderer. The government had paid him to be a murderer. How could she have looked the other way?

"Mommy?" Linda said.

"What is it, honey?" Marian was glad for something to distract her from her own dark thoughts. She hadn't even noticed that the Glenn Miller record was over and the radio was plugging White King D.

"Do you dance to that song with Mr. Tabakman now?"

"I . . . never have," Marian said slowly.

"Do you want to?"

"I don't know. Maybe one of these days," Marian answered, more slowly still. "Maybe not to that song. Maybe to another song. When I hear that one, it reminds me how your daddy's not coming back."

"Does Mr. Tabakman have a song he doesn't want to dance to with you, too?" Linda asked.

"I'm not sure, but he probably does." Marian remembered that Linda was in the first grade. *Little pitchers have big ears,* she thought. She and Fayvl had done a lot of talking in Camp Nowhere, especially after Bill got killed. Of all the people Marian knew, Fayvl best understood what she was going through. How not, when the Nazis gassed his family at Auschwitz?

The three NBC chimes sounded again on the almost-forgotten radio. A neutral tone followed. "It's exactly eight o'clock," the announcer said, "and it's time for the network news."

After another brief pause, a different voice said, "This is Lowell Thomas, with the NBC news on the hour." Thomas had a deeper, richer voice than the Sacramento announcer. NBC picked the best to deliver the news the whole country listened to. He went on, "President Truman has offered Russia and Red China the same peace terms the late Joseph Stalin refused: return to the *status quo ante bellum.*"

"What does that mean?" Linda asked.

"It means the way things were before the war." Marian was glad to field a question that wasn't so personal.

"So far, no answer has been received from Lavrenti Beria. No one in the United States can yet be sure how tight Beria's grip on power is," Thomas said. "In his statement, the President urged the new Soviet leader to consider an old nursery rhyme:

All the king's horses and all the king's men
Couldn't put Humpty together again.

He warned that, if the fighting should go on much longer, the whole world would be as smashed as Humpty Dumpty."

Linda laughed. "How come they're talking about Humpty Dumpty on the news? Humpty Dumpty isn't real! They're silly!"

They were and they weren't. FDR wouldn't have talked about Humpty Dumpty. Marian was certain he wouldn't, not in a Fireside Chat and for sure not in a diplomatic communication to another country. But Harry Truman was the kind of man who called a spade a goddamn shovel.

And the comparison fit only too well. America had lost cities up and down the West Coast, and in the Northeast. Next to Europe and the USSR, the USA was still in good shape. The Suez Canal and the Panama Canal were gone. No one had any idea how many millions of people had died.

The really scary thing was, it could get worse. The H-bomb that finally settled Stalin's hash was even bigger than an A-bomb. The United States had to be building more of them. The Russians had to be working on them, too, as hard as they could. Drop a few of those, and what did you get?

All the king's horses . . .

Fighting in Germany, fighting in Korea, uprisings in East Europe—

the news went on. A pitcher for the St. Louis Browns hit three home runs in a game. His teammates were calling him H-Bomb Garver. Marian didn't know whether to laugh or cry when she heard that.

Like the government, the stock market had relocated to Philadelphia. What there was of it had, that is. It had sunk like a stone since the A-bombs wrecked Washington, New York City, and Boston. Lowell Thomas reported it had lost another four and seven-eighths points today.

Marian thought that was too bad, but it wasn't as if she had money in the market herself. Like so many people who'd made it through the Depression, she looked at stocks the same way she looked at sticking quarters into the one-armed bandits in Las Vegas or Reno. They at least fed you free drinks if you stuck a lot of quarters into the slots. From everything she'd heard, Wall Street—or whatever they called the stock market now that it was in Philly—wasn't so generous.

Another commercial came on, this one plugging Old Golds. *Half the country's up in smoke. Why not send your money the same way?* Marian shook her head. The slogans she came up with wouldn't send Madison Avenue wild. She wondered what had happened to Madison Avenue, and where the surviving advertisers were plying their trade these days.

Music returned, this time a song by a bluesman named Fats Domino. It was too raucous for her taste. "C'mon, Linda," she said. "Time to start getting ready for bed."

"Aww, Mommy! Another half hour?" Linda said, and the nightly dicker began anew.

A car door slammed in front of the house on Irving. Aaron Finch looked out through the curtains on the living-room window. "Here's Roxane and Howard," he said, as temperately as he could. When you married someone, you married her whole family. Ruth's first cousin and her husband didn't always fill him with delight.

"Be nice," his wife said. "And you'd better not start singing 'Ding-dong, the witch is dead!' You hear me? Just don't."

"Aye, aye, sir," Aaron said, as he might have to the skipper of one of the merchantmen he'd sailed on during the last war. He'd tried to join the Army right after Pearl Harbor, but he'd turned forty not long before and he wore Coke-bottle specs. The recruiters laughed at him.

And so he'd faced the U-boat wolfpacks in a bunch of wallowing tubs. One of the ships he'd crewed had shot down a German plane in Anzio harbor. He'd had as many scares and close calls as your average Navy guy, in other words. In exchange for those scares and close calls, his grateful government had allotted him exactly no benefits. That disgusted him, but what could you do?

Howard and Roxane Bauman had politics well to the left of his. Howard, an actor, had had trouble finding work since he declined to tell the House Un-American Activities Committee whether he was now or had ever been. Aaron didn't think Roxane ever had carried a card, but she was more strident than her husband. As far as she was concerned, the war was all America's fault.

Would they regret Joe Stalin's death? Oh, just a little. That was what Ruth's warning was all about.

Leon, on the other hand . . . Aaron and Ruth's son had just turned three. They'd read him *The Wizard of Oz* and as many other Oz books as they had. He'd seen the movie when it got rereleased early this year. And he started singing "Ding-dong, the witch is dead!" at the top of his lungs just before the doorbell rang.

"Make him stop!" Ruth exclaimed.

"Don't worry about it," Aaron said as he opened the door. Roxane and Howard wouldn't know why Leon was singing that particular song just then. Even Leon didn't know why he was singing it just then. He enjoyed making as much noise as he could, that was all. He was one hell of a smart three-year-old, but he was a three-year-old.

Aaron shook hands with Howard and hugged Roxane. Ruth's cousin was about her age but, in Aaron's perfectly unbiased opinion, not nearly so pretty. No matter how abrasive she could get, Aaron tried not to hold it against her. She'd brought Ruth over to his brother Marvin's place while he was staying there after the last war ended. That was how the two of them met and, indirectly, how Leon came to be.

Howard's nostrils twiched. "Something smells good," he said.

Ruth stuck her head out of the kitchen. "Beef stew," she said. "Be ready in about half an hour."

"Sounds great." Howard rubbed his stomach in anticipation. Aaron wondered how well he was eating these days, with parts few and far between. Roxane was bringing in some money because she could type and file, but nobody got rich on that kind of work. He suspected Ruth invited her cousin and Howard over as often as she did so she could feed them square meals.

"Can I get you guys something to drink?" he asked. Had it been up to him . . . But it wasn't up to him. He tried to think of it as charity, like sticking pocket change in the *pishke* for Hadassah. And sometimes that worked, and sometimes that didn't.

"Scotch and water, please, Aaron?" Roxane said.

Howard nodded. "That'll work for me, too."

"Okay. Follow me." Aaron went into the kitchen to play bartender. Ruth also asked for scotch. Aaron built the drinks, and used a church key to open a bottle of Burgermeister for himself. He raised the Burgie in salute. "*L'chaim!*" he said.

"*L'chaim!*" everybody echoed, even Leon. Glasses clinked. *To life!* was a nice, safe toast. Nobody could argue about it or disagree with it. He wondered whether he'd be able to say that about the rest of the evening.

For the moment, he didn't need to worry about that. He got Leon to show off. He spelled out simple words with the wooden alphabet blocks he'd made for his son: CAT, FAT, DOG, HOG, PIG, BIG. Leon had a little trouble with the last two, but read the rest with the greatest of ease.

"Kid's a genius!" Howard said, suitably impressed.

"Oh, at least," Aaron said, which got a laugh. "Now the next question is, will he ever make a living?"

Howard laughed again, but when he said, " 'Ay, there's the rub,' " his voice had an edge to it. No, he wasn't doing so well these days. He glanced down at his glass, seeming surprised to find it empty. "Any chance of a refill?"

"Oh, I expect that can be arranged," Aaron said, though he was only halfway down his own beer. He made another drink and handed it to Howard. "Here you go."

"Much obliged!" Bauman said. "How do you want to toast this time?"

"How about *L'shalom*?" Aaron suggest. "To peace!"

"*Omayn!*" Ruth said, and drained her first drink. She didn't ask for another one. Like Aaron, she thought a little was good but a lot was not so hot.

Howard and Roxane also drank. How could you not drink to peace in a world that had seen so much war? Then Roxane said, "It would have been a whole lot better if this stupid war had never started." She added, "Can you make me another drink, too?"

"Uh-huh," Aaron said, even if he wasn't sure that was such a great idea. As he mixed scotch and water and ice cubes, he asked Ruth, "How's dinner coming, babe?"

Ruth used a potholder to take the lid off the big aluminum kettle on the stove. She stirred the stew with a wooden spoon and poked at a potato with a serving fork. "I think we're ready. Let me take the salad out of the icebox, and you can all help yourself."

Howard Bauman wasn't a great big man; he came within half an inch of Aaron's five-nine. He took enough to feed a couple of basketball players. Yes, this was the kind of spread he didn't get to see every day. After he made it disappear, he went back for seconds.

So did Roxane. There wouldn't be a lot of leftovers. As she worked her way through the new helping, she said, "The war wouldn't have been so horrible if Truman hadn't started dropping A-bombs." She didn't quite spit when she said the President's name, but she came close.

"We'd still have peace if North Korea hadn't blitzed into South Korea." As soon as *blitzed* came out his mouth, Aaron knew he'd have a quarrel on his hands. Comparing Communists to Nazis was guaranteed to make Roxane's blood boil. He gave a mental shrug. It wasn't as if Finches never argued.

"Can we say *L'shalom!* and just leave it right there? Please?" Ruth was more peaceable than her husband and her cousin. "*L'shalom!* in the world and *L'shalom* at the table?"

"Let's do that," Howard said. Roxane looked at him as if he'd stuck a steak knife in her back. Their marriage was less placid than the one Aaron and Ruth enjoyed.

But the two couples managed to get through the evening without a screaming row. That didn't always happen. As Roxane and Howard left, Aaron even managed to say "Hope to see you soon" without sounding like too big a liar. He wondered if he ought to try the acting game himself.

STALIN WAS DEAD. Every time the thought ran through Ihor Shevchenko's head, it brought something new with it. He remembered hunger, hunger to the point of starvation, in the Ukraine when he was a kid. Stalin was going to get rid of the kulaks and collectivize the countryside if he had to kill everyone in sight to do it. He damn near did, too. *Damn* near.

And with that hunger came fear. If you didn't care to do Stalin's bidding but he didn't manage to starve you to death, you might say something unkind about him. If you did, it could cost you a bullet at the base of the skull. Or, if you had a different kind of bad luck, you could vanish into the chain of gulags for ten years or for twenty-five.

No wonder so many Ukrainians greeted the Nazis with flowers and with bread and salt when Germany invaded in 1941. After Stalin's famine, Hitler seemed a liberator. But not for long. Pretty soon, most Ukrainians saw that Hitler made Stalin look good by comparison.

Most, Ihor among them. Not all. Some of his countrymen enjoyed helping the Fritzes kill Russians and Jews. Some used the chaos to try to set up a Ukraine free of Russians and Germans. Some of them stayed in the field for years after the Red Army drove out the *Wehrmacht*.

Ihor had fought in the Red Army. He'd come to respect Stalin for his strength and his indomitable will. He hadn't forgotten the 1930s, but the way Stalin made the Soviet Union fight the Hitlerites made him forgive a big part of them.

He'd ended the war wounded, and gone back to the kolkhoz for what he expected to be the rest of his life. The USSR had come out of the Great Patriotic War one of the two greatest powers in the world. That was nice. That was something you could be proud of. It was something you could brag about while you sat around drinking.

But a new war when the country was still trying to pick up the pieces from the old one? Kiev went into the atomic furnace, along with so many other cities around the world. For a while, Ihor's old wound kept him from having to go back into the Army. Then, after enough healthier men had got themselves shot or blown to bits, it didn't any more.

So here he was in Poland. The Poles who'd rebelled against their People's Republic and the Soviet Union didn't love Stalin. They cheered when they found out he was dead. Ihor wondered how loyal the Poles who made up the People's Republic were. The only man he figured the USSR could rely on was the Minister of Defense. In addition to his place in the Polish cabinet, Konstantin Rokossovsky held marshal's rank in the Red Army.

A Pole came out of a foxhole waving a white flag. "Don't shoot him, boys!" Ihor called to the section he led. To the Pole, he called, "Are you surrendering?" He guessed the bastard would understand.

And the fellow did. "Fuck your mother, no!" he answered in fluent Russian. "What kind of clodhopper are you? I just want to parley. Do you know what parleying is?"

Stung, Ihor said, "I know an asshole when I hear one. Come ahead and parley, asshole. I'll take you back myself."

The Pole did come forward, a big grin on his face. He kept holding the flag high. Now that he'd found out how much he and Ihor loved each other, he wanted to keep reminding him not to open fire. He didn't know Ihor had greased one of his own sergeants. Ignorance, in his case, was bliss.

"Well, move along," Ihor said gruffly, gesturing with his AK-47. "If you want to let our officers get their hands on you, that's your lookout."

"We have Red Army prisoners. If I don't get back in four hours, we start doing things to them," the Pole replied.

That might make Ihor's superiors think twice about flaying the bandit a centimeter at a time, or it might not. Soviet officers thought soldiers were as disposable as hand grenades. Soviet marshals—like Rokossovsky, for instance—thought officers were disposable the same way. Stalin thought Soviet marshals were.

But Stalin had been disposed of himself. The Polish bandit reminded Ihor of that: "What are you going to do now that Iosef Vissarionovich is trying to give the Devil orders?"

"Why are you asking me? I'm just a corporal," Ihor said reasonably. "I do what they tell me, or they chop my dick off."

As if on cue, an MGB man popped up from behind a boulder. "Halt!" he shouted. "What are you doing, moving back from the line?" If he didn't like what he heard from Ihor, he'd shoot him, and probably win a promotion for doing it.

Ihor nodded at the Pole. "This bandit wants to talk with our officers. I'm taking him back so he can do it."

The Chekist tapped his shoulder board. It showed him to be a first lieutenant. "Fine. I'm an officer. What have you got to say, *svoloch*?"

"Takes a scumbag to know a scumbag," the Pole answered with the air of a man who'd heard worse. "I don't want to talk to a piece of shit of a Chekist. I need a Red Army officer, a real soldier."

He'd just said things Ihor had wanted to say for his entire life. Ihor knew better than to let his face move by so much as a millimeter. If the MGB lieutenant knew what he was thinking, he was a dead man. The Pole might be a bandit, but he had a flag of truce to protect him. Ihor didn't.

Face purple as a bowl of borscht, the secret policeman choked out, "Take him, then. Take him fast, or he'll never get there."

"You talk big," the Pole said. "What will you do when they wise up and put strychnine in Beria's soup or something?"

"They won't," the Chekist replied. Ihor wasn't so sure about that. *He* didn't want Stalin's porky henchman calling the shots. But even if Beria wasn't commanding the MGB, what difference would it make? This MGB guy wouldn't lose his job. Ihor couldn't imagine the Soviet Union without its secret policemen.

"Come on," Ihor said. He wondered for a moment whether the Chekist would shoot the Pole in the back. And he had an itch of his own, right between the shoulder blades. But they got away from the first lieutenant.

"You see?" the Pole said. "You see? This is how come we don't want you sons of bitches giving us orders any more."

"If we don't, who would?" Ihor answered his own question: "The fucking Germans, that's who. And then they'd be on *our* ass again."

"We stand on our own two feet," the bandit insisted.

"Oh, horseshit," Ihor said, and the Pole went as dusky as the MGB man had before. Since the end of the eighteenth century, Poland had had maybe twenty years where it was really independent. How long would it last even if it did manage to kick out everyone in the Red Army from Marshal Rokossovsky on down?

Here came a company of Soviet soldiers, with a couple of T-34/85s to put some metal in their fist. The tanks were obsolete, but obsolete tanks knocked the crap out of none. A sergeant saw the white flag and took Ihor and the Pole to the young lieutenant in charge of the company.

"What do you want?" the kid asked the local.

"A cease-fire around here till you people work out what you're going to do without Stalin," the Pole answered. "If peace breaks out, why get people killed for nothing? If it doesn't, you can always start up again."

The lieutenant shook his head. "I can't do that, not without orders from my superiors. And you know as well as I do, they won't give orders like that."

"In the name of Christ, do it on the left, then." The Pole really did speak Russian well. *On the left* was slang for *unofficially* or *through the black market.*

But the kid didn't have the nerve. "I can't," he repeated. "They'd cut my balls off. And besides, if we clear you out of here, I don't have to worry about you any more." He turned his pale eyes on Ihor. "Take him back to where he came from."

"Comrade Lieutenant, I serve the Soviet Union!" Ihor would have loved a local truce. But he had to follow orders, too—as long as other people were watching, which they were here. His chunk of the war would go on.

Someone knocked on the door to Harry Truman's office. "Yes?" the President said. The door opened. In came his private secretary. Truman nodded to him. "What's up, Mike?"

Mike Rogers laid a sheet of paper on his desk. "Cable from Minister Patterson in Bern, sir," he said. "Just now decoded." His voice was soft and even. Truman was still getting used to him. He suspected the man was queer, but that wasn't the kind of thing you could ask. Rogers had passed an FBI vetting—if he was queer, he wasn't getting blackmailed about it or anything. He was plenty capable, that was plain. Rose Conway, who'd served Truman before, died in the bombing of Washington.

Truman unfolded the paper. "From Switzerland, hey?" he said. That was one of the places where Americans and Russians still talked with one another. Not many neutrals were left in Europe.

"That's right," Rogers said.

"Have you looked at it?" Truman asked.

"No, sir. I didn't think it was any of my business." Mike Rogers sounded slightly shocked at the question.

"Okay. But the world won't end if you do. You need to know what's going on. If anyone thought you'd be sending Moscow smoke signals, somebody else's behind would warm your chair," Truman said. Rogers seemed pained again, this time, no doubt, at the homely figure of speech.

Truman peered through the lower half of his bifocals to read the decoded cable. *Minister Turginov says Soviets interested in your defini-*

tion of status quo ante bellum, Dick Patterson wrote. *Acceptance possible if control over satellites conceded. Turginov states—unofficially—Beria's position unstable.*

The President muttered to himself. He knew how much he was playing things by the seat of his pants. A lot of the State Department's experts on the Soviet Union—hell, a lot of the State Department—had got smashed when that first Russian Bull got through. But he still had one man whose judgment and expertise he respected.

"Do me a favor, Mike," Truman said. "Put a call through to George Kennan at the Institute for Advanced Studies at Princeton. If you don't get him, leave a message for him to call me back as soon as he can."

"I'll take care of it right away, Mr. President," Rogers said. He was as good as his word, too. Five minutes later, the phone on the President's desk jangled. When Truman picked it up, his private secretary told him, "I have Mr. Kennan on the line."

"Terrific! Put him through, then."

After a few clicks and pops and hisses, Kennan said, "Is that you, Mr. President?"

The diplomat's patrician tones made Truman more than usually conscious of his own Missouri twang. Not long after the last war ended, Kennan had first proposed the policy of containing the USSR's expansionism. He'd got on well with George Marshall when the soldier headed up Foggy Bottom. After Dean Acheson took over as Secretary of State, he hadn't liked Kennan so well. Kennan and Marshall were both used to being the brightest bulb in the chandelier. While nobody's dope, Acheson wasn't quite in that class. Kennan might have let him know it.

Kennan hadn't wanted MacArthur to go north of the thirty-eighth parallel in Korea, much less all the way to the Yalu. Few others had seen danger in that, but he had. And danger had been there, too. Being right was often its own punishment, which explained why he'd been at Princeton and not working for the government. It explained why he was still alive, in other words. And few living Americans knew more about what was going on in Russia. "I just now got a cable from Patterson in Bern," Truman said, reading it to Kennan. When he finished, he said, "How does that look to you?"

"I think you ought to give the Russians the guarantee they want for the Eastern European countries," Kennan said at once. "I understand that we've hurt them worse than they've hurt us, but I would be surprised if we have the manpower to make them liberate Poland and Czechoslovakia and Hungary and their part of Germany. I know perfectly well we *don't* have the manpower to occupy the USSR. Hitler thought he did, and look how well that turned out for him."

"Hitler didn't have the A-bomb or the H-bomb," Truman said.

"I understand that, Mr. President, and I thank God for it, but the bomb is too fat a screwdriver to fit every screw's thread, if you know what I mean," Kennan replied.

Truman sighed heavily. "Well, it's not as if I can tell you you're wrong, no matter how much I wish I could."

"Russia's impossible, sir. It always has been," Kennan said. "No matter what Hitler thought, it's too big to occupy. Unless you kill every single Russian, it's going to be a great power."

"That's how it looks to me, too. I was hoping you'd say something different, doggone it. We can't even run them back to the border they had in 1939, can we?"

"Not unless you want to start a bunch of little wars—just to name one, Hungary and Romania still can't stand each other. And the little ones would only build towards another big one."

"We can't stand another big one. We can't really stand any more little ones." The President sighed again. "For the next big one, the Russians'll be able to get at us as easily as we can get them, won't they?"

"You would know that better than I would, sir," Kennan replied. "But from what I do know, it seems mighty likely to me."

"Okay. I'll get back to Patterson, then, and let him know I don't mind if the Russians keep holding the satellites down. The people who live in those countries may have a thing or three to say about that, though."

"Yes. They may. And then you'll have the enjoyable job of making the Russians believe you don't have anything to do with that." George Kennan paused. "Assuming you don't, of course."

"Mm-hmm. Assuming." Truman said nothing more about that. The CIA had been trying to stir up trouble for Russia in the satellites since shortly after the last war ended. Till the new one heated up, the American spies hadn't had much luck. The President found a different question: "Do you think Beria will be able to hold on to the top slot there?"

"I doubt it. Beria scares all the other Soviet big shots, because he has a nice, fat dossier on every single one of them," Kennan said. "It would be like J. Edgar Hoover taking over the United States."

"There's a cheerful thought!" Truman had neither liked nor trusted the FBI director. Hoover hadn't had anything like the power Beria enjoyed in Russia or Himmler'd had in Germany, but he'd had too much for the chief cop in a democracy. But Hoover was up in smoke now, too, along with so many other people who deserved it so much less. The FBI was doing the best it could with each city's agents acting pretty much on their own. So far as Truman could tell, the Reds weren't doing much harm here. He asked, "Who'd be in that horse race?"

"Molotov, of course. Malenkov. Bulganin." After a moment, Kennan added another name: "Maybe Khrushchev, too."

"Never heard of him," Truman admitted.

"He's an up-and-comer. Ran the Ukraine. Was a political commissar at the battle of Stalingrad. *Nye kultyurny,* the Russians say— uncultured. Playing the peasant buffoon may have kept him alive while Stalin was slaughtering anyone who seemed halfway clever. He's short and squat, with a bullet head and warts. But you don't want to get in his way, or he'll bulldoze you."

"I'll remember him, then," Truman said. "But for now, it's Beria." He laughed in lieu of banging his head against the wall. "Aren't we lucky?"

"Now that you mention it, sir," Kennan replied, "no."

Vasili Yasevich didn't mind Poland. It put him in mind of what the Soviet Union would have looked like if it were cleaner and the people worked harder. True, the part where he was had been fought over more than once in the last war. Not all the damage had been repaired, and now this new uprising was wrecking what had been. But nothing in Smidovich compared to the houses and churches and farms he saw here.

Some of the guys in his squad had come this way before. One middle-aged fellow named Yuri, whose smile showed a mouthful of gold teeth, started laughing when he trudged past a Catholic church. "What's so funny?" Vasili asked.

"Last time I was here, back in '44, I got shot right in the ass," Yuri answered. "They lugged me in there, laid me on a pew on my belly, and patched me up. I bet my blood's still on the wood. Shit, I spilled enough of it. I was out of action for a couple of weeks. Then they plugged me back in like a goddamn lamp."

"Maybe we won't have to fight too much longer, now that things are different." Vasili had learned to talk around Stalin's death. Too many men got upset if you spoke about it too openly. It was as if they'd lost their own fathers, not the tyrant who'd sent them out to get killed.

When his outfit got the news, he'd had to fake sobbing and wailing to keep from looking like a white crow to everyone else. To him, Stalin was the monster who'd taken over from the monster named Lenin. They'd run his family out of Russia and into exile in Harbin. He had no genuine reason to be sorry Stalin wasn't breathing any more.

A rifle cracked up ahead. Yuri hit the dirt with a speed that spoke of lessons learned in a hard, hard school. Vasili was a split second behind him. "Watch yourself, kid," said the man with the bankroll in his mouth. "You get shot once, you find out you sure the fuck don't want to get shot twice. Shit on me if they'll slap another wound dressing on my hairy ass in that church."

"I hear you," Vasili said. "Where do you think that round came from?"

"Somewhere in that apartment block," Yuri answered, not pointing.

Another shot rang out and snarled through the rubbish clogging the street. Sure as sure, this one came from the block of flats ahead. It *was* a block: uncompromisingly rectangular, the kind of place to ware-house workers and their families when they weren't at the steel mill or the gypsum plant. He'd seen plenty of apartment blocks like that in the cities of the USSR he'd passed through on his way west. Some of the men called them *Stalin Gothic*. So Poland had them, too? Lucky Po-land, to enjoy the benefits of Soviet civilization!

From a different window in the same building, a machine gun spat death and mutilation down the street. Vasili rolled behind the marble staircase leading up to the church. They saw him do it. A couple of bul-lets smacked off the stone, but they didn't bite him.

Yuri joined him back there after the stream of bullets moved away. "I hate those fucking places," he said. "They might as well be fortresses. You have to clear 'em out stair by stair, room by room, closet by closet. You go in a company, you come out a squad."

Someone hoisted the Polish flag, white over red, above the apart-ment block. In accented, oddly rhythmic Russian, a bandit shouted, "Who do you shitheads keep fighting for a dead man?"

Because they'll kill me if I don't, and you may not if I do, Vasili thought. It might not be the answer the Pole wanted to hear, but it held enough truth to satisfy him.

He knew it also wasn't the answer the Red Army would want to hear. Instead of coming out with it, he asked Yuri, "How come we don't knock the place flat? See how the Poles like 155s and 500-kilo bombs."

"I wouldn't mind. I bet we do, in fact," the veteran said. "But the pussies'll keep fighting in the ruins. Fuck me if they aren't tougher to get rid of than so many bedbugs."

The lieutenant in charge of the company ordered an attack on the block of flats. Some Red Army men dashed forward with cries of "*Urra!*"—mostly, Vasili judged, the ones too young, too stupid, or too drunk to see they didn't have a prayer of a chance. He sat tight himself. Yuri smoked a *papiros* and didn't go anywhere, either. Pretty soon, the handful of soldiers still alive let out different kinds of cries as they writhed in the streets.

After the assault failed—maybe after he showed his own superiors the proper aggressive Soviet spirit—the lieutenant called for a bombardment. Shells slammed into the concrete walls. A good, properly manufactured product might have made them bounce off. But they bit big chunks out of the apartment block. It was built no stronger than it needed to be to keep standing. The Russians and the Poles who'd worked for them had something in common with the Chinese among whom Vasili'd grown up: they cut enough corners to make a whole new street.

Smoke started curling up along with the dust of devastation. "Good!" Yuri said savagely. "If they roast in there, they can't keep shooting at us."

"For Stalin!" the Red Army lieutenant shouted, urging his men on to another rush. "For Stalin and Beria!"

He should have left that alone, Vasili thought. Stalin had inspired people. Vasili didn't understand that, but couldn't deny it. Beria, though? The only thing you wanted to do with Beria was keep him from finding out you'd ever been born. No one loved or even admired Beria.

The lieutenant led from the front. That was always the way to get your men to follow. It was also a pretty good way to get yourself killed. Vasili shouted "For the great Stalin!" as loud as he could and ran forward to a shell hole ten meters farther up. He dove into it as if it were a cool pond on a hot summer day. "Oof!" he said when he hit—the rubble-strewn bottom was a lot harder than any swimming hole.

A moment later, Yuri joined him. Instead of diving, the veteran slid into the crater as if he were a goat hopping off a ledge. And, a moment after he did, the machine gun sent a short, professional burst not nearly far enough over their heads.

"So much for that," Yuri said.

"How much ammo does it take to kill somebody, anyway?" Vasili asked. "How did those cocksuckers live through that?"

"People are tough to kill. It's not like the movies, where they just fall over when you start shooting at 'em," Yuri said seriously. "And even if we did get rid of the shitheads on that machine gun, chances are we didn't wreck the piece. A machine gun's not that hard to serve, and plenty of Poles know how, you bet. Same way with us and the Fritzes and everybody else who paid his dues the last time around."

"Right," Vasili said in a hollow voice.

"Come on, boys!" the lieutenant shouted from up ahead. "For Stalin and for Beria, for the true Communism ahead, we can do it! Forward!" Forward he went again. He sprayed bullets from the muzzle of his submachine gun. Even if they failed to hit anyone, they'd make the Poles keep their thick, rebellious heads down.

Unless, of course, they didn't. The machine gun in the smashed apartment block opened up again. The Red Army lieutenant shrieked like a damned soul. He went on shrieking, too, and howling for his mother. She wouldn't do him any good now, but he didn't know that.

"Poor bastard," Vasili said, wishing he could jam fingers into his ears.

"Uh-huh." Yuri dug out his pack of *papirosi,* stuck a new one in his mouth, and offered them to Vasili. Vasili took one with a grunt of thanks. The lieutenant's animal cries went on and on.

"The struggle continues!" the Red Chinese loudspeakers blared. "That capitalist maggots will be consigned to the ash heap of history, as they deserve to be and as the Marxist-Leninist-Stalinist dialectic demonstrates they must be!"

Cade Curtis' lips moved. He could repeat the propaganda record without making a single mistake—he'd heard it that often. The Chinks just wouldn't leave it alone. Even with Stalin dead, they intended to carry on where he'd left off. The American on the record still had that harsh Midwestern accent Cade was so sick of by now.

Lighting a Camel, he shrugged. The son of a bitch was telling lies. Whether he was telling them because he really believed them or because somebody would do something horrible to him if he didn't, so what? Any American who could think straight would know they were lies right off the bat.

And, evidently, not just any American. Jimmy stood up on a firing step, stuck his head over the parapet, and bellowed "Bullshit! Fucking bullshit!" at the speakers. Then he hopped down before the Red Chinese could plug him for telling the plain truth. Spotting Cade, he saluted and spoke in quieter but more earnest tones: "That number-one fucking bullshit, sir. Number-one fucking annoying bullshit, too, you betcha."

"It sure is." Not for the first time, Cade wondered what to do with Jimmy after the American military bureaucracy had to notice him officially. *I'll manage something,* he told himself. Jimmy might not have been lucky enough to pop out of his mother inside the US of A, but he made a better American than plenty of people who had been.

"I hear bullshit from the Japs when they run Korea," Jimmy said. "I hear more bullshit in Republic of Korea after last war, and in ROK Army. Chinese yell bullshit all over goddamn place now. Only guy I don't hear bullshit from, Captain, is you."

Cade had saved him from the torment his own officers dished out. Like a puppy rescued from a nasty master, Jimmy rewarded his rescuer with loyalty verging on worship. Cade's ears heated. He knew too well he had feet of clay. At the moment, he had feet of muddy clay, because rain had drenched the trenches two days earlier.

Sighing, he said, "Jimmy, for Christ's sake keep your head on straight. I'm full of bullshit, too. I don't think there's ever been anybody who ever lived who wasn't full of it."

He wouldn't have said anything like that when he came to Korea. He'd been nineteen, fresh out of ROTC, a newly minted shavetail greener than paint. He'd been eager to defend democracy, to roll back the Red invaders, and to save freedom from the inroads of tyranny.

All he was eager for now was getting out in one piece. Kim Il-sung and Mao Tse-tung *were* tyrants, no doubt about it. But Syngman Rhee wasn't much better. The war wasn't a fight between good and evil, or even between good and better. It was between bad and worse. As long as he didn't let his men down, that would do for him.

"Can I ask you something else, please, Captain, sir?" Jimmy said.

When you adopted a puppy, you had to take care of it. Cade was discovering that held even more truth when you adopted another human being. He nodded. "Sure, Jimmy. What do you want to know?"

"This stupid goddamn fucking war ever end, what you do then?"

That was a pretty good question, all right. Cade tried *not* to think about picking his life up again in the States. The USA hardly seemed real to him these days. Two years of war and six thousand miles of Pacific had washed that country right out of his hair. He didn't think he belonged there any more. He wondered if he belonged anywhere but in a muddy or dusty trench.

Some people honest to God didn't. To some people, war was the best, the truest, the most exciting thing they ever found. They stayed in a fight, or longed for one, the rest of their lives. Hitler had been like that. There were others, though thank heaven they were rare birds. Cade hoped like anything he could turn back into a civilian again. He hoped he could, but he didn't know if he could.

"Captain? Sir?" Jimmy said.

Cade wondered how long the wheels inside his head had been spinning without gaining any traction. Slowly, he said, "When this war started, I was at the University of Alabama, studying engineering. I wanted to learn how to make better, faster airplanes. I'd like to go back and finish my education. I don't know if I will, but I'd like to."

"Engineer for airplanes!" Jimmy's narrow eyes gleamed. "Can I do something like that, I go to America?"

"There wouldn't be any rules against it or anything," Cade said. "You'd need to learn to read and write English, not just speak it."

"Can do some now," Jimmy answered. "Korean has alphabet, too, you know. English not same, but I learn. But Korean all time one letter, one sound. How come English not all time one letter, one sound?"

As far as Cade was concerned, written Korean was chicken scratches. He'd hardly noticed they were different from Chinese chicken scratches, and he'd had no idea they were built from alphabet blocks. As for English . . . "I don't know why English is the way it is," he said. "Spelling it drives everybody squirrely, not just you."

"Stupid fucking language," Jimmy said without rancor.

"Yeah, I guess maybe it is," Cade said. "But along with learning English—no matter how stupid it is—you're going to have to learn to do mathematics, too."

"You mean like counting? I can do that. I can tell you how much some number and some other number is, too, or how much if you take away." Jimmy spoke proudly now, and well he might. Not many Korean peasants could have matched his claim.

"That's good. That's great." But Cade told him, "There's more to math than that. Not all of it's easy." Trigonometry sure hadn't seemed easy while he was slogging through it, but he'd survived and gone on to analytic geometry and calculus—which also weren't easy. "You have to study a lot."

"I study, then." Jimmy sounded very sure of himself.

I should show him a few things, Cade thought. If you assumed an obligation, shouldn't you fulfill it the best way you knew how? Then he laughed at himself. If Jimmy could add and subtract but could go no further, he'd need more than a few things to turn into an engineer. *And where will you find the time, buddy?* Cade asked himself. *You're running a regiment right now—half the time on Benzedrine. You ain't got the hours to play math tutor, and Jimmy'd get tagged the teacher's pet if you did.*

Every bit of that was the purest Gospel. Cade felt guilty anyhow. Wasn't he letting Jimmy down?

Before he came to any conclusions, three flights of Corsairs zoomed in out of nowhere. The big, beefy Navy fighters—most U.S. air power in Korea came off carrier planes these days—rocketed the Red Chinese lines and dropped napalm on them and shot them up with their heavy machine guns before roaring away. F-4Us were as obsolete as any other prop jobs. Where few jet fighters prowled, they could still bite some nasty chunks out of the enemy.

All the same, Cade rather wished they would have stayed away. The local Chinks had been willing not to shoot if the Americans didn't. Now they came to life with a vengeance. Machine guns spat death across no-man's-land. Mortar bombs started whistling in. The GIs fired back. Things probably wouldn't settle down again for days.

And the stupid flyboys hadn't knocked out the enemy's loudspeakers. If dialectical materialism at top volume wasn't a fate worse than death, Cade hadn't the slightest idea what possibly could be.

ARNSBERG WAS A NO-ACCOUNT TOWN if ever there was one, at least in Rolf Mehlen's imperfectly objective opinion. Why the Red Army wanted to hang on to it tooth and toenail made no sense to him. Odds were most of the Ivans hunkered down against artillery and armor had no idea, either. Their superiors had told them to do it. Somebody from their own side would shoot them if they tried to run away. So they stayed and fought.

Rolf's unit was at the sharp end of the spear. The Americans running the campaign against Russia weren't sorry to spend German lives instead of their own. No doubt they called it a good investment. *They think like Jews,* went through Rolf's mind. You could take the old *Frontschwein* out of the *Waffen*-SS. Taking the SS out of the old *Frontschwein* was harder.

Not even fifty meters separated Rolf from the Slavic *Untermenschen.* Several of them had those damned assault rifles that would shred anything out to four hundred meters. His Springfield didn't seem like much beside them. They would have shredded him if not for the battered stone fence he crouched behind.

The Americans figured he was expendable. He didn't like the idea so much himself. Not showing a centimeter of skin, he shouted, "Hey, you Russian shitheads? You understand German?"

"*Yob tvoyu mat'*, Fritz!" an Ivan yelled back. He repeated the endearment in fair *Deutsch* in case Rolf couldn't follow the original.

But Rolf could. He swore fluently in Russian, and knew some basic battlefield commands, too—*Hands up!* and the like. But he didn't really speak the language. He kept on in German: "You clowns should give it up. What's the point of going on now that the *Scheissekopf* who gave you your marching orders has gone and bought a plot?"

"You sure sound like a Fritz," the German-speaking Russian answered. "Hitler blew out his own brains, and the rest of you pussies couldn't screech '*Kamerad!*' fast enough."

That held just enough truth to sting. The *Reich* had lasted only a little more than a week after Hitler died. Rolf still wanted to believe Hitler'd perished fighting to the last, as German radio claimed at the time. The evidence was against him. He wanted to believe it even so.

He tried again: "We're going to kill your sorry asses. "You know that, right?"

"I think you're trying to bore us to death," the Russian soldier—officer? yeah, probably, Rolf judged—replied.

"Think whatever you want." Rolf hopped up, fired in the direction from which the Russian's voice had come, and ducked before any of the Ivans could ventilate him with those fancy AK-47s. Bullets cracked over his head. Others spanged and whined off the stonework that sheltered him.

He crawled away. He'd been playing soldier a long time. He'd pissed off the Red Army men. If they had anything that could do for a stone wall, they'd use it in the hope that smashing the wall would also mean smashing him.

Not three minutes later, an RPG round pulverized the part of the wall where he wasn't waiting any more. The Russians had borrowed the idea of the RPG from the German *Panzerfaust,* as they'd borrowed the idea of the AK-47 from the *Sturmgewehr*. As with the AK-47, they'd improved the RPG. Its shaped charge could burn through better than twenty centimeters of hardened steel. A stone fence, then, didn't stand a chance. Rolf was glad he'd got too far away for any of the sharp slivers of rock to bite him.

Behind him, somebody said, "Nice to see you still make everyone love you so much wherever you go."

"*Yob tvoyu mat'*, Max," Rolf answered. Yes, he had Russians and Russian on the brain.

Max Bachman only chuckled. He'd spent enough time on the *Ostfront* himself to follow that. But he'd been a conscript in the *Wehrmacht*. When you wore the SS dagger whose blade said *My honor is called loyalty,* you really meant it. You weren't just doing what they told you to do so they wouldn't give you grief.

Rolf was proud of his years in *Leibstandarte Adolf Hitler*. The only thing he regretted was losing. Germany against the whole wide world turned out not to be—quite—an even fight. Max, on the other hand, was a democrat and probably a socialist. But he was also a pretty good man with a rifle, so Rolf cut him some slack.

"Arguing against an RPG is a bad bet," Max said. "Even for a panzer, it's a bad bet."

"Yes, Granny," Rolf said. Max gave back a gesture that, to the Amis, meant everything was perfect. Among Germans, it carried a rather different weight. Rolf returned it.

He kept making allowances for Max. The two of them knew what was what, no matter where Max bought his politics. They'd saved each other's bacon a time or three. The Russians were another story. They'd spent two wars trying to get rid of Rolf. They hadn't done it yet. He'd hurt them, though. He intended to hurt them some more, first chance he got.

First chance he got came that night. He liberated a jerrycan of gasoline, which he slung on his back as if it were a pack. He also festooned himself with a sack of grenades and an American machine pistol: the ugly, functional one the Amis called a grease gun. The heavy pistol cartridges it fired did hellacious damage at close range.

Of course the Ivans had wire and sentries. On a black night, that didn't mean so much, not if the guy doing the sneaking knew what he was up to. Rolf had learned how in the toughest school in the world. The proof of his high marks was that he remained in business.

He had a fair idea where the Red Army men in front of his outfit denned: in the ruins of what had been Ansberg's biggest, or maybe only, furniture store. For all he knew, they were sleeping in the battered beds. He had one bad moment when a soldier back from taking a leak caught a glimpse of him. But the American helmet, unlike a *Stahlhelm*, had about the same shape as a Russian model. The soldier waved vaguely and went back inside.

Rolf waited till his heart stopped thuttering before he moved again. Nerves could kill you. They *would* kill you if you let them. When he was sure everything in the wreckage was quiet, he ghosted forward and set the jerrycan at the front entrance. He slipped the lid off—he'd put Vaseline on it beforehand so it wouldn't squeak. Then, even more carefully, he eased back into a firing position he'd found about twenty meters away.

He squeezed off a short burst with the grease gun. As he'd hoped, one or two slugs slammed into the five-liter can of gasoline. Fire spilled out the holes and burst from the opening at the top.

Well, that got their attention, he thought. Russians inside the furniture store started yelling. As soon as the first one came out, the blazing gasoline gave Rolf plenty of light by which to shoot him. The Ivan fell with a groan. Rolf shot the next one, too. That one squealed like a stuck pig.

But the soldiers couldn't stay in there, not with the fire spreading fast. Just to encourage them, Rolf started chucking grenades. They were American pineapples, not the potato-mashers he'd used the last time around. He liked the German grenades better, but these would do in a pinch. They seemed to pinch the Russians pretty hard, in fact. He fired more bursts from the grease gun.

He threw a couple of grenades in random directions to give his new acquaintances something else to think about. Then he slipped away, suspecting he'd worn out his welcome. No more than a couple of minutes had passed since the fun started.

As he slithered back toward his own lines, a Russian sentry dashed right by him without the slightest idea he was lurking in a gutted doorway. Rolf could have put a burst into the Ivan's back. He refrained. What point to telling the Red Army soldiers which way he'd gone?

They'd used some of their heaviest weapons against him, and hadn't hurt a hair on his head. His own choices had been much simpler, and had worked much better. Simple was great, as long as you knew what to do with it.

Bruce McNulty stared glumly at the cards still in his hand. The contract stood at five diamonds, and he feared he'd bitten off more than he could chew. The dummy laid out on the table in front of him (*like an etherised patient,* he thought, remembering his Eliot: the right thing to do when you were in the UK) wasn't as good as he'd expected it to be.

He played a heart off the dummy to cover the opening lead from his copilot. The queen came out. He used the king from his hand to take the trick. Then he pulled trumps. He got lucky—they split evenly. Then he managed a crossruff between hand and dummy. He took his eleven tricks before he finally had to lead a low spade.

Bam! Down came the ace and king. "Last two are ours," Wally Hickman said.

"They sure are," Bruce agreed. "But I made it."

"Had 'em all the way," Phil Vukovich said. The navigator was his partner. Vukovich rose and stretched. "Hang on for a sec before the next deal, guys. I gotta go take a leak."

That'll be the first time all night when I know what you've got in your hand, Bruce thought unkindly. The line wasn't his; it came from George S. Kaufman. But he'd appreciated it since the first time he heard it. And it fit his current partner only too well. Phil believed in optimism more than he believed in Goren—one of his few, and more expensive, deviations from legal rectitude. If he'd navigated the way he bid, he would have said the bomber was over Moscow before it really got to Berlin.

Ezra Jacobs looked at his watch. "Just about eight o'clock," the radioman remarked. "Shall I turn on the Beeb and see what kind of trouble we're liable to get into next?"

"Sounds good to me," Bruce said. They hadn't flown the B-29 against Russia since the mission where they wiped Petrozavodsk off the map— and that other crew did the same thing with Joe Stalin. Truman kept saying he wanted peace with whoever the new Soviet leaders turned out to be. Keeping the big bombers on the ground for a while was one way to show he meant it.

Bruce didn't mind. He knew how lucky he was to be alive. He knew how many men who'd started the fighting with him weren't alive any more. And neither was Daisy. He tried not to think about that, or to tell himself it was a silly wartime romance that didn't mean anything. The only trouble was, he couldn't make himself believe it. He'd never been any good at lying to himself.

"Good evening. This is the news." The BBC announcer's suave accent and the utter certainty in his voice made you want to believe him. This *was* the news, and in some odd way anything he didn't choose to mention hadn't really happened.

Vukovich came back from the head. He looked at the card table, saw it was still empty, and swung his head toward the radio. When he reached for a pack of Camels, Bruce made a small, beseeching noise. He got a cigarette. After the hand he'd just squeezed out, he thought he deserved one.

"Radio Moscow has announced that Vyacheslav Molotov has replaced Lavrenti Beria as General Secretary of the Communist Party— effectively, as ruler of the USSR," the newsreader said. "No comment was made in the broadcast as to Mr. Beria's whereabouts or safety. Mr. Molotov states that, in principle, he accepts President Truman's terms for peace between the warring sides."

"What does that mean, exactly?" Bruce asked.

As if in conversation with him, the BBC man continued, "The precise meaning of Mr. Molotov's statement remains to be diplomatically explored. Radio Peiping, however, has issued a statement of its own, one furiously denouncing the new Soviet leadership as backsliders and imperialist running dogs. No comment on this statement has yet come out of the USSR."

"Oh, boy," Wally Hickman said. "What fun! Now they're gonna fly us halfway around the world so we can whale the snot out of good old Mao Tse-tung, too. Yeah, I'm really looking forward to that."

"Won't be as rough as what we've been doing up till now." Bruce McNulty spoke with great conviction. "The Russians keep the good stuff for themselves. The Chinks get their sloppy seconds."

"Wet decks, they say over here," Hickman said. "But even a second-line plane can knock us down these days. MiG-15s are real good at it, but a MiG-9 or an La-11 prop night fighter with radar will do the job just fine."

"Maybe we should start playing cards again," Vukovich said. "Give us something to think about besides the goddamn news."

"And it's better than it has been. That's the scary part," Bruce said. "Whose deal is it, anyway?"

"Despite Molotov's tentative agreement to peace terms, fighting goes on in Germany and near the Franco-Italian border," the news-reader said. "No Red Army units have yet received orders to cease fire, much less to withdraw. Rebel radios from within the Communist bloc claim the Russians also continue their efforts to put down local uprisings. And there are unconfirmed reports of serious unrest in the Baltic Soviet Socialist Republics, whose annexation the Western democracies have never recognized."

"Good luck to those poor, brave, sorry sons of bitches," Hickman said. "And they'll need it, too."

"The more troubles the Russians have at home, the less they'll go out and make trouble farther away," Bruce said. "Even now, all bombed to hell and gone, they're still a going concern. Let 'em worry about Estonia and Latvia and Lithuania instead of invading Germany."

Vukovich started shuffling the cards. Bruce didn't think it was his turn, but his partner didn't seem to care. You could argue about politics till the cows came home, but you'd never convince the guy you were arguing with. You'd only piss him off.

In democracies, every so often they saw who'd convinced the most people. Then the ones who disagreed had to sit on the sidelines for a while. Sooner or later, the other side would screw up. Then they'd get their chance.

Hitler and Lenin and Stalin and their chums had other ideas. Instead of taking turns with the people who thought they were wrong, they jailed them or exiled them or just went and killed them. Then they carried out their own programs with no inconvenient opposition.

And how did that work out? Bruce thought sourly. Not so real great, as a matter of fact. Hitler did his level best to drag the whole goddamn world into the fiery abyss. His best barely missed being good enough: his physicists weren't smart enough to make A-bombs. (Some of the men he'd exiled were Jewish physicists who did find out how.)

That gave Stalin his big chance. He did an even better job of smashing everything to hell and gone than Hitler had. *And they said it couldn't be done!* Bruce thought. That only showed what *they* knew. Of course, Stalin had had some excellent help from the USA. Since the USA dropped the first bombs, maybe it had excellent help from Stalin. Any which way, even more of the world was screwed up this time than the last.

As such cheerful thoughts spun through Bruce's head, he automatically sorted his hand into suits, each arranged in rank order. Assessing it came just as automatically. Nine points, no suit longer than five cards . . . Good enough to support with, maybe, but nowhere near strong enough to open the bidding.

"Pass," Phil said.

"Pass," Ezra Jacobs said.

"Pass," Bruce agreed. He glanced over at Hickman. "You got anything worth opening with, Wally?"

"Not even close." The copilot threw his cards on the table, face down. Everybody else did the same. They'd passed out the hand. If that wasn't a fitting metaphor for the wider world, Bruce couldn't guess what would be.

Another tank: a T-54, which warmed Konstantin Morozov's heart. Another new driver. This one was a Jew named Avram Lipshitz. Another new loader, too, a Georgian with a name less pronounceable than Stalin's had been before he took a Russian *nom de guerre*. The bastard knew barely enough Russian to understand the difference between *high-explosive* and *armor-piercing*.

This is how we're supposed to win a war? Morozov wondered as a hand shook him awake. He twisted inside his rolled-up blanket and opened his eyes. There was Lipshitz's thin, beaky, badly shaved face, not fifteen centimeters from his own. Behind steel-framed spectacles, the driver's dark eyes were big and scared.

"What's gone wrong now, Avram Samuelovich?" Konstantin knew only too well that something had.

"Comrade Sergeant, did you send Corporal Eigims anywhere?" Lipshitz asked.

"No, dammit!" Morozov scrambled out of the blanket as fast as he could. "Why? Isn't he here like he's supposed to be?"

"No, Comrade Sergeant." Avram Lipshitz sounded as scared as he looked, which was saying something.

"Oh, fuck his mother up the ass with a board full of nails!" Konstantin exclaimed. "The stupid cunt's liable to have run off to play rebel."

"He's got to be *meshuggeh* if he has," Lipshitz said. "How does he think he'll go across Germany and Poland to wherever he wants to wind up?"

"Good question," the tank commander said. "If you don't have any more good questions, class is dismissed." He had a good question of his own, too. How the devil was he supposed to fight his tank when his gunner'd deserted?

He knew the book answer. Till they gave him a replacement, he'd have to command the tank and lay the gun himself. The tank commander'd had to do that in the early model of the T-34, the one with the 76mm gun. The Germans couldn't come within kilometers of matching its firepower when the Great Patriotic War was young, but they shot three or four times as fast.

And he didn't outgun Yankee and English tanks the way the T-34 had with the Fritzes. The fighting *had* slowed. Maybe it would stop. Maybe.

Avram Lipshitz turned out to have another good question after all: "What do we do now, Comrade Sergeant?"

Morozov lit a *papiros* and sighed out a cloud of smoke. He didn't offer the *Zhid* a cigarette. After another fierce puff and another visible sigh, he said, "I'll go talk to Major Zhuk. He's got to know."

He went with the air of a schoolboy heading to the master's office for a switching. His heart thumped. His feet dragged. If Genrikh Zhuk decided he'd looked the other way while Eigims disappeared, or just decided to make an example of him, he was dead meat.

The regimental CO seemed pretty reasonable. Like so many, he'd been wounded in the last war and brought back to service for this one. He ought to know what was what. Just because he ought to, though, didn't mean he did. And even if he did, he might feel the need to stay safe himself by throwing someone else to the wolves.

He was guddling around in the guts of a T-54's diesel powerplant when Konstantin approached. When he straightened, his right arm was greasy halfway to the elbow. He eyed Morozov. "What is it?" he said sharply. Yes, he could read faces. "It's something, isn't it?"

"I'm afraid so, Comrade Major," Konstantin said. "My gunner, the damned Balt, he's gone and taken a powder."

"Oh, fuck his mother!" Zhuk said. Crucially, he didn't say *Fuck* your *mother!* He wasn't blaming Morozov. Not yet, anyhow. He went on, "You just now found out?"

"That's right, Comrade Major." *I'm not moron enough to sit on news like that.* "My driver woke me up to ask if I'd sent him anywhere. I hadn't, naturally. I've come straight to you. I hope you can get me another gunner with some idea of what he's up to."

"I'll try." Major Zhuk pulled on his lower lip. "But that's the least of your worries, I'm afraid. You're going to have to talk to the MGB. So will I. I'm not looking forward to it."

"Now that Comrade Beria is, ah, indisposed, sir, who's running the MGB?" Morozov asked. That was as close as he could come to asking *Are the Chekists still as horrible as they've always been?* Trusting your life to a man in battle was easier than trusting it to him on account of words.

"I may have heard the new man's name, but damned if I remember it," the major said. "I'm sure they'll still be as strong for security as they have been since the glorious Revolution." That told Konstantin everything he needed to know.

The secret policeman who interviewed Morozov—and, for all he knew, Major Zhuk as well—was a young first lieutenant named Svyatoslav Sverdlovsk. "Did your corporal show signs of disaffection before he deserted?" Sverdlovsk asked.

"Not that I ever saw, sir." Konstantin lied without hesitation. Juris Eigims was already in plenty of trouble. Why pile on more, especially when that meant taking on danger for himself? After a moment, he added, "He's always been a good gunner. If not for him, the imperialists would have killed me a dozen times over."

"A good gunner and a good traitor." Scorn filled Svyatoslav Sverdlovsk's voice. "How many good socialist Soviet citizens will he kill a dozen times over now?"

"Sir, I would have stopped him if I'd had the slightest idea." Konstantin said the kinds of things he had to say to save his skin. This time, he wasn't even exactly lying. He'd had a good deal more than the slightest idea, and he had tried to stop Eigims. It hadn't done any good, but he'd tried.

Sverdlovsk got down to business, saying, "Describe him." Konstantin did, as accurately as he could. Others could contradict him if he lied here. The Chekist asked, "How well does he speak Russian?"

"He's fluent, sir, but he's got that funny Baltic accent, the one that makes him almost sing words," Konstantin said. Sverdlovsk scribbled notes in a little black book.

A buzz overhead interrupted the questioning. It was an American light plane flying along at just above treetop height to get a good look at the Soviet positions. "I could piss that thing out of the sky!" Sverdlovsk burst out. "Why isn't anybody shooting it down? *Bozhemoi!*" He clapped an outraged hand to his forehead.

"I'm just a sergeant, sir. I don't know anything about that." What Konstantin said sounded convincing. What he'd heard was, the Yankees wouldn't fire as long as the Red Army didn't. That helped the Red Army more than it helped the Yankees, or so things seemed to him.

"It's disgraceful." Sverdlovsk was a Chekist. He mostly didn't come so close to the front. He could afford to say such things: his dick wasn't on the block.

"Sir, I didn't tell you how things ought to be. All I do is serve the Soviet Union and fight my tank like I've been trained," Morozov said. "I just told you how things are right now."

"They shouldn't be that way, though." Svyatoslav Sverdlovsk sounded furious. "We should be fighting the enemy, not—not playing games with him."

Konstantin spread his hands. "*Nichevo.*" The Russian word—one of the underpinnings of the Russian soul, really—meant *There's nothing you can do about it* or *It can't be helped.*

"I aim to make sure someone hears about this. It's worse than the shitass Balt's desertion. It's damned close to cowardice in the face of the enemy, is what it is."

Had the Chekist called Juris Eigims a shitass Balt to his face, he would have lost teeth. "Sir, may I go see if I can find someone to handle the gun on my tank?" Konstantin asked, adding, "If the quiet ends, I need to do all I can for the *rodina.*" *And keep my own shitty ass alive,* he finished, but only to himself.

"Yes. Get the devil out of here," Sverdlovsk snapped. Morozov came to attention just short of *rigor mortis* for stiffness, gave a parade-ground salute, and got the devil out of there. The MGB man hadn't shot him or arrested him. That alone made it a pretty fair morning.

Marian Staley cut a bite of roast beef with gravy. The beef sat on the heavy white diner plate with mashed potatoes and the same gravy and some boiled string beans. She looked across the table to Fayvl Tabakman. He was eating fried chicken, a potato baked instead of mashed, and his own helping of green beans.

"Do you think it's really peace?" she asked.

"*Alevai omayn,* it should be peace!" he said. "I hope it's peace. War is terrible thing."

"Oh, is it ever!" Marian said. Her own personal acquaintance with war was brief, but a flash of atomic fire told you everything you ever needed to know in a hurry. And war had robbed her of her husband. Still, she hadn't lived under its bloody thumb for years, the way Fayvl had. That wasn't his first encounter with it, either. He would have been a boy when World War I sent armies back and forth across Poland. Marian tried again: "But do you *think* it is?"

"If the politicians can get it right, yes," he said. "How often do they, though?"

"At least Stalin's dead," Marian said.

"Stalin was very bad man," Fayvl agreed. He paused, took a bite from a drumstick, and went on, "Except next to Hitler."

"Yeah," Marian said quietly. As Stalin had cost her Bill, so Hitler'd cost Fayvl his whole family.

The cobbler didn't want to talk about war. After another bite off the leg, he said, "Fried chicken is so good! In Poland, always we would boil or stew or once in a while bake it. I never eat it fried till I come to United States. You ask me, best way to make it."

"It's pretty tasty, all right." Actually, Marian had had better fried chicken than the guy who ran the diner made. That was why she'd ordered roast beef tonight. The chicken here wasn't terrible; it just wasn't great, or not to her.

"How's it going, guys?" Babs asked, pausing at their table.

"Everything's fine, thanks," Marian told the waitress. "It always is here." If she didn't jump up and down about the chicken, well, that was why the roast beef was on the menu, too.

Babs raised a questioning eyebrow at Fayvl Tabakman. "Me, I can't complain," he said. Then he stopped cold. His face took on a comically astonished expression, as if he couldn't believe what just came out of his mouth. And that must have been it, for he went on, "I don't remember last time I couldn't complain about nothing." With his accent, the last word came out *notting*.

"That's good. That's the way things should oughta work," Babs said.

Neither Marian nor Fayvl said anything. They glanced at each other, though, and understood each other perfectly. As far as Marian knew, Babs had been born and raised in Weed. She'd had the normal sorrows life brought: not enough money, loves that didn't last, people who mattered getting old and dying. She didn't know anything about how bombs and bullets and extermination camps could tear a life to pieces in an instant.

She also didn't know how lucky she was to be so ignorant.

After the two of them finished eating, Fayvl put a five-dollar bill on the table to cover both meals and a nice tip. "With the war, prices have gone through the roof," Marian said sympathetically. "I wish the lumber outfit would give me another raise to help me catch up."

"You should maybe wish for the moon while you're at it?" Fayvl suggested.

She laughed a rueful laugh. "That's about the size of it."

As they went outside, she shrugged on her sweater. Weed was high enough so that, even when the days were hot, it got chilly at night. Off to the east, Mt. Shasta's bulk took a big bite out of the stars. The moon would rise soon, though; its golden glow outlined the mountain.

Fayvl Tabakman looked that way, too. "Pretty," he said. "I never seen mountains so big before I come to America. First Mt. Rainier up in Washington, now Mt. Shasta." After listening to his words in his head, he made a small, annoyed noise. "Should be *I never* saw *mountains*, right?"

"That's right," Marian said.

A man stumbled up to them. "Got any spare change, friends?" he asked.

Marian would have told him to get lost. Eddie was one of the town lushes. He'd drunk himself out of a logging job—not easy in a place like Weed—and out of his family and onto the streets. He'd keep drinking till his liver quit or he walked in front of a car or froze on a frigid winter night.

But Fayvl fished in his pockets and gave him a half-dollar. "Obliged, pal," Eddie said as he lurched away.

"He'll just drink it up," Marian said.

"*Nu?*" Fayvl shrugged. "Giving to them who ain't got is a *mitzvah,* a blessing. He needs the money. He can do what he wants with it. I know he shouldn't oughta be a *shikker,* but how you gonna make him stop?"

"AA might do it." But Marian shook her head even as she spoke. You had to want Alcoholics Anonymous to help before it would. All Eddie wanted was enough antifreeze in his blood to keep him from thinking. You weren't doing him any favors if you helped with that. He would say you weren't doing him any favors if you didn't.

Weed wasn't overflowing with night life. The movie house was showing a Western Marian didn't care about. The bars were full of loggers drinking up their paychecks. Some of them would go the way Eddie had, but what could you do?

The moon climbed over the mountain's shoulder. An owl hooted from a pine near the diner that had somehow escaped the axe and the saw. Headlights flowed by on US 99, an endless stream of them. They hadn't rationed gasoline in this war, the way they did in the last one.

"You want to walk me home?" Marian asked.

"Sure. I do that," Fayvl said. Off they went, not particularly in a hurry. Marian's little rented house was only a few blocks from the diner. They saw an old lady out for a stroll and two men walking dogs. Away from its row of saloons, Weed was a quiet place. Outside Marian's door, Fayvl murmured, "Well, I go back to my place now."

"Come in for a cup of coffee if you want to," Marian said as she turned the doorknob.

"You guys are back sooner than I thought you would be," Betsy the babysitter said. "I just put Linda to bed ten minutes ago." Linda stayed in the bedroom, though. Marian wished she could fall asleep so fast herself. She paid Betsy and watched her head off to her own house.

"Coffee," she said, and put Folger's into the percolator that sat on the stove.

They sat on the secondhand sofa in the living room, their cups on the secondhand table in front of it. Fayvl pulled out a pack of cigarettes. He lit Marian's before his own, and somehow made that feel like Old World courtesy and not just an ordinary piece of politeness.

After he stubbed out his smoke in a glass ashtray, he coughed once or twice and said, "What you suppose Linda think if she come out and find a strange man kissing her mother?"

He was nearly as hesitant as Marian, which helped explain why they'd gone so slowly. After a cough or two of her own, she answered, "Let's find out. I don't think she will, and even if she does you're not a strange man. She's known you longer than anybody else in Weed."

He slid toward her. She slid toward him, not quite so far. The kiss was hesitant, almost as if it were the first for both of them. Fayvl tasted of tobacco and coffee. Marian supposed she did, too. He wasn't as big as Bill had been—not much taller than she was herself. Angles changed oddly.

"Well," she said when their mouths parted, and then, "We ought to try that again."

They did. She might have been—no, she was—ready for more if he pushed it, but he didn't. That was all right, too. In a place like Weed, there was always plenty of time.

MIKLOS WAS SCRATCHING at the Arrow Cross tattooed on the back of his hand when that Magyar-speaking American captain strode into the Hungarian POWs' barracks. The tough guy's head came up and zeroed in on Imre Kovacs the way a hunting dog's head would zero in on a deer.

"Here comes trouble again," Miklos said in a prison-ground whisper without moving his lips.

"Wouldn't be surprised," Istvan Szolovits answered, doing his best to talk the same way. His best wasn't as good as Miklos'; he had less practice.

Up padded Captain Kovacs, as if he had not a care in the world. And why should he? He was an officer. He lived in the United States. He might be a Jew, but he didn't need to fear mobs or government functionaries wanting him dead. He had the world by the short hairs.

He nodded to Miklos as if they were friends. Not so many years earlier, had they met in Budapest, Miklos would have smashed his face with a billy club, shoved him into a cattle car, and sent him off to Auschwitz. They both had to know it. Somehow, it didn't seem to bother either of them.

Or maybe it did bother Miklos. "You're one crazy fucker, you know that?" he told Kovacs.

"Hey, I love you, too," Kovacs said. "And considering the marks you wear, you're the pot calling the kettle black."

"People can know what I am. I don't care. It makes things simple, like," Miklos said. "I don't gotta waste time with bullshit."

Imre Kovacs raised one eyebrow about a millimeter. Istvan wasn't sure Miklos noticed, but *he* did. The tiny gesture said the captain didn't think Miklos had wasted a whole lot of time with bullshit even before he got his decorations. Istvan didn't, either. Miklos slugged first and asked questions later.

Then Kovacs nodded Istvan's way. "Why don't you come along with me?" he said, for all the world as if Istvan could say no if he wanted to.

"Where you taking him this time?" Miklos asked suspiciously.

"Nowhere bad—I promise." Imre Kovacs winked. "You want me to cross my heart?"

Miklos told him what he wanted him to do. Istvan didn't think even an India-rubber man would have been limber enough to manage all of it. Captain Kovacs only laughed. Why not? Who cared what a POW said?

As the captain and Istvan walked out of the building, Istvan asked, "So where am I coming along with you this time?"

Kovacs answered with a different question: "Do you speak Yiddish?" He used that language to ask it.

"I can get by," Istvan said, also more or less in Yiddish. More or less because . . . "We never spoke it a lot at home. Some, but not a lot. My folks mostly used Magyar. But I studied German in school, and they're close. How come you want to know?"

"Because I know you don't speak English yet, and most of the *Yehudim* where you're going won't come from Hungary."

"Oh?" Alarm ran through Istvan. When you were a prisoner, all change seemed bad. "Where am I going?"

"I believe they're sending you to California," Imre Kovacs answered.

For a second, that didn't register. *Where in France is California? Or is it in Spain? With that name, it could be.* Istvan's mind spun its wheels like a car trying to get through deep mud. Then he realized what he'd just heard. His jaw dropped. "California?" he whispered, as if saying it out loud would break the spell. "You mean the one in the United States?"

Kovacs nodded cheerfully. "That's right."

"But why? But how?" Istvan hadn't felt so staggered, so out of his depth, since he was seventeen and a blond girl who lived in the next-door block of flats decided to let him get lucky.

The American officer wagged a finger under his nose. "You don't ask me questions like that. The fairy who handles these things sprinkled you with magic dust, that's how."

So it *was* a spell. Somehow, that surprised Istvan not a bit. He did his best to pull himself together and think straight. Sometimes being too smart for your own good actually did you good. Sometimes. He asked, "Does the fairy with the magic dust look anything like you?"

"Officially, I don't have any idea what the hell you're talking about," Kovacs answered. "But a little bird whispered in my ear that she has my nose. Or maybe I have hers—I dunno." He pointed toward the admin-istration building. "Now come on. We've got about a million forms to fill out so we can get you on a plane to the States."

Like a man in a dream, Istvan came. So the fairy had Imre Kovacs' nose, did she? Istvan had a good notion of why the intelligence officer chose him to go to America and not, say, someone like Miklos. Well, *wasn't* having friends in high places better than having enemies there, the way Jews did most of the time?

"What will they do to me in, uh, California?" Istvan still had trouble bringing out the name.

"They won't do anything *to* you, you goose twit." Kovacs planted a pointy elbow in his ribs. He staggered. He'd got plenty worse on the soccer pitch, but he expected elbows there. This one caught him off guard. The U.S. captain went on, "They'll question you till you're blue in the face. Tell 'em whatever you think you can. Then they'll turn you loose. Somebody will know somebody who can get you a job. How's that sound?"

"Insane," Istvan answered honestly. "Why would anybody do anything like that for me? I'm not anybody. I'm nobody."

"Hey, that fairy liked your looks. You're a smart guy. You get half a chance, who knows what you'll wind up doing? So all right, you've got half a chance. What the Americans say is, when you get a chance like that, you should run with it. How fast can you run, hey?"

"I don't know. I'll find out, though, won't I?" Dizzily, Istvan followed Captain Kovacs into the camp's administrative center. The officer had exaggerated. There couldn't have been more than half a million forms. Some were in French, the large majority in English. Istvan read neither. For a while, Kovacs translated for him. Then Istvan threw his hands in the air. "The hell with it!" he said, and signed and signed without worrying about what he was signing.

"That one you just put your name on says you owe me a hundred thousand dollars," Kovacs said.

"Good luck!" Istvan turned out his pockets. "I've got, uh, fifty francs here, and ten forints from when I was captured. I forgot all about those." He shoved the money at Kovacs. "All yours, if you want it."

"You need it worse than I do," Imre Kovacs said, "not that you'll be able to exchange the forints. Is there anything back at the barracks you have to have?"

"No." Istvan shook his head. He wouldn't have minded grabbing his football boots, but he decided breaking clean was better. He'd have too much explaining to do if he went back in there again.

"Good. Let's get to the bottom of this stack, then."

At last, Istvan did. Kovacs led him to an American truck newer than but otherwise not much different from the ones the Hungarian People's Army used. Already in it were a couple of Poles, a Czech, and an East German. They talked among themselves in variously accented *Deutsch*.

The truck rumbled away. It went . . . in whatever direction it went. After a couple of hours, it stopped at an airfield. A German-speaking American steered the liberated POWs to a beat-up C-54. The only other planes Istvan had seen up close were fighters attacking him. He'd never gone inside one before.

When the engines roared to full throttle, his ears cringed. The transport rumbled down the runway and took off. *I'm going to a whole new world,* he thought, and then, *No. I'm going to the New World.*

Boris Gribkov paced along one of the dirt runways. The airstrip wasn't very far outside of Tula; he could see the town's taller buildings on the northern horizon. His crew's new Tu-4 waited for orders in a netted, camouflaged revetment. Since Stalin's death, no orders had come.

A groundcrew man lurched down the runway toward him. The path had to be seventy meters wide. Tacking like a galleon fighting a strong headwind, the sergeant needed all of that and could have used more. He gave Boris a sozzled grin as they passed.

Drunk on duty? Boris could have placed him under arrest and had him shot. Had the war been alive and not in suspended animation, he might have done it. Then again, had the war been alive, chances were the sergeant wouldn't have gone and grabbed himself a snootful.

He wasn't the first loaded mechanic Boris had seen here lately—nowhere near. Like ice on a lake when spring comes at last, discipline was rotting and starting to melt.

He'd seen drunks aplenty during the Great Patriotic War. He was a Russian, after all. His own people swilled like swine. It wasn't as if he'd never swilled like a swine himself. But, then, he'd never swilled like a swine because the war was going badly. He'd never seen anyone who had, either.

That was partly because he hadn't come into service till 1943. By then, the war against the Nazis was going well. It took two more years of hard fighting to finish, but the result wasn't in doubt. And that was because the USSR didn't dare lose the Great Patriotic War. Lose to Hitler, and the Germans would shoot you or enslave you and rape your sister and experiment on your children. The Nazis made that plain right from the start. You had to win.

It wasn't like that now. The Americans dropped A-bombs on the Soviet Union, but they didn't want to invade it. It wasn't as if the Red

Air Force hadn't A-bombed America, too. The Americans' terms weren't vicious, either. All they insisted on was going back where both sides had started from.

In the last war, Hitler refused to surrender no matter how bad things got. He kept his people fighting, too, for longer than they had any business going on. The way it looked to Boris, things with Stalin worked the same way this time. As long as he lived, nobody dared tell him what a bad idea going on with the war was. But as soon as the Americans finally got him . . .

Muttering and shaking his head, Boris went on walking. He knew he would never fly another mission against the United States or any of the countries in Western Europe. That didn't make him sorry; it made him glad. He didn't want to destroy great and famous cities. It didn't bother him enough to make him put a bullet through his head, the way it had with his navigator after they smashed Paris. But it was nothing he wanted to be remembered for.

He muttered some more. They might fill the Tu-4 with ordinary bombs, or maybe even with an A-bomb, and send it against Prague or Warsaw or Budapest. He'd already bombed Bratislava with conventional weapons—and got shot down for his trouble. He knew he could use conventional bombs if they told him to. Those had been part of warfare since the early days of the century.

What if they tell me to drop another A-bomb? he wondered. He could see why his country wanted to keep its little western neighbors under control. They'd make trouble if it didn't. They always had. Still, weren't A-bombs for the times when you had no other choices?

Boris thought so. Whether his superiors did was liable to be a different question. But they couldn't *make* him fly another mission like that. There was always a way out. Leonid Tsederbaum had shown him that. *I just pull the trigger,* Boris thought. *One second, I'm there. The next, I'm not.* As long as he kept his courage, he had the ultimate defense.

He didn't much fear death. Death was just nothing, or so it seemed to him. Like going under ether and not waking up. Dying? Dying he feared. He'd seen too much of it. Dying was nasty. It hurt like anything.

But if you got it over with all at once, you didn't need to worry about that. Too much.

As long as it didn't come to A-bombs, he could go on doing his job. He hoped it wouldn't. Had he been a praying man, he would have prayed it didn't.

He went up the runway. He went down the runway. He went up the runway again. By that time, he'd walked something close to five kilometers: somewhere close to far enough to work off some of his gloom. Sweatier but easier in his mind, he headed for the field kitchen to get some tea and whatever food the cooks had lying around in the middle of the afternoon.

A samovar bubbled above a spirit lamp that kept the water inside hot. Boris fixed himself a glass of tea with sugar. He would have liked lemon, but none had come up from the southern regions where they grew. The disruption from all the American A-bombs was visible many ways.

"What can you give a hungry man?" Boris asked the cook. The soldier's tunic was unbuttoned. He needed a shave, and had for a couple of days. At a front-line airstrip, none of that would have meant anything. Here in the heartland of the *rodina,* it was another telling sign of decay. Somebody should have told the kid to shape up. No one had bothered.

At least he answered politely enough: "We've got some sausage, sir, and some onions, and black bread, too."

"That'll work." Boris nodded. The cook used a bayonet to cut a couple of slices of bread, a hunk of sausage, and some onion.

Two flyers were playing chess at one of the tables. Boris sat down close enough so he could see the board but not so close as to make them think he was kibitzing. The guy playing black was a pawn up. The older man with the white pieces looked unhappy.

Boris ate. The sausage was full of pepper and dill. It tasted slightly stale anyhow. He didn't much care. It filled his empty. The spices and the onion's bite kept him from paying attention to the gamy flavor. He'd eaten plenty of things a lot worse.

He was almost finished when Faizulla Ikramov came in. The radioman got himself a glass of tea and walked over to Boris. "May I join you, sir?" he asked.

"Please," Gribkov said. Ikramov sat down across the table from him. "They'll feed you if you want."

"That's all right. I was just looking for something with a little kick to it."

"There's always vodka." Boris told him of the groundcrew sergeant who'd staggered down the runway.

"Comrade Pilot, I said a *little* kick." Ikramov's flat Uzbek face twisted into a frown. "Yes, I was raised Muslim, but a shot of vodka every once in a while, that's not so bad. A bottle of vodka every day, that's not so good."

"I can't argue with you, not when I feel the same way," Boris said. "But plenty of people don't."

"Really? I hadn't noticed," Ikramov said, deadpan.

Boris snorted. "You remind me of a navigator I used to fly with. He'd come out with stuff like that, where if you didn't pay attention you wouldn't notice it was funny."

"What's he doing these days?" Ikramov asked.

"He stuck his pistol in his mouth after we bombed Paris." Gribkov lowered his voice so the chess players wouldn't hear.

"Oh." For several seconds, the radioman chewed on that. Then he said, "Now I suppose I know what a sense of humor like that gets me."

"You didn't bomb Paris. You bombed Washington. If any town in the world had it coming, Washington did." Boris grimaced. "And one whole hell of a lot of good bombing it did. We woke the Americans up, and look where we are now."

"About where we would have been if we hadn't bombed Washington, chances are." Ikramov also dropped his voice. "Do you suppose this is really the way to true Communism?"

Now there was a question only a fool would answer! But Boris didn't see how he could ignore it, either. "Well, we'll find out, won't we?" he said after a barely noticeable pause. The radioman beamed at him as if he'd passed a test. And perhaps he had.

. . .

Leon Finch stuck his little finger in his ear and vigorously twisted it. The pediatrician had told Aaron and Ruth never to put anything smaller than an elbow in there, but Leon, unlike his parents, didn't pay any attention to what Dr. Hurst said.

Having twisted, he proceeded to show off the treasure his excavation yielded. "Look, Daddy!" he said proudly. "An earwack!"

"That's earwax, all right." Aaron grabbed a Kleenex and took Leon's booty away from him. "Now go wash you hands."

"What will you do with the earwack?" the three-year-old asked.

"I'm throwing the earwax out." *Just what I want on a lazy Sunday morning, too,* Aaron thought. But he made a point of saying the word the right way so Leon would notice and learn.

Notice Leon did. Learn? Leon's version of logic came at the world from a different angle. "How come it's *earwax*, Daddy? There's only one of it."

Aaron blinked. Leon had taken *wax* to be *wacks*, an obvious plural. Once he'd taken it that way, he'd gone and invented his own singular. Thus *earwack* was born. It made perfect sense . . . if you were three. Aaron said, "After you wash your hands, bring me your alphabet blocks. I'll show you something."

He couldn't have picked a faster way to get Leon to wash. Without more than a token dry, Leon got the box where the blocks lived. "What is it, Daddy?" A puppy waiting for a Dog Yummy couldn't have been more eager. Aaron could all but see his son's tail wagging.

"Here. What does this say?" Aaron used the wooden blocks to spell out WACKS.

That was a lot of letters. Leon had to work hard to get through them. Not many kids his age could have done it at all, but he did. "Wacks!" In his glee, he all but squealed the word.

"Good job!" Aaron told him. "Now, what does *this* say?" This time, he spelled out WAX.

Leon had to work even harder. X didn't show up in many words, and he had trouble remembering which sound it made. But when he did, his grin showed off a mouthful of baby teeth. "That says *wacks*, too!"

"It sure does." Aaron nodded. He knew damn well he hadn't been reading when he was three. He had been read to a lot, though, in English and in Yiddish. He went on, "See, W-A-X is the *wax* in *earwax*." He couldn't spell *earwax* with the blocks; it needed two A's, and the set had only one. *Gotta make some more,* he told himself. "It doesn't mean there's lots of, uh, wackses. It's just a word that happens to end in the *ks* sound."

"Oh." Leon contemplating new information was funny enough to sell tickets for. After a moment, he asked, "Are there other weird words like that?" The word *wax* had to be weird; it broke the rules he thought he knew.

"Yeah, there are." Aaron nodded again.

"Like what?" If Leon asked questions that way after he got bigger, he'd need to be better with his fists than a smart kid was likely to be.

The first word that sprang into Aaron's mind was *sex*. He let that one slide. No matter how smart Leon was, ready for anything that had to do with sex he wasn't. So Aaron took away the W from WAX and replaced it with a T. "What does this spell?"

Leon went through his mental gears, moving his lips as he sounded things out letter by letter. "Tax!" he said loudly.

"You got it. Good for you!" Aaron said.

"What does *tax* mean?" Leon asked. It was a little word, but, like *sex* (though not nearly so much fun), not one likely to show up in a children's book.

"A tax is money people give the government so we have soldiers and roads and things like that," Aaron said. "Not everybody likes to pay a tax, but everybody has to. You get in trouble if you don't."

"Oh," Leon said again. This time, Aaron thought the explanation flew straight over his son's head. But then Leon continued, "If you pay, you can have it. If you don't pay, you can't have it."

"You're a menace, kiddo-shmiddo," Aaron said, but he was laughing as he spoke. He knew where that came from. Ruth had told him how

Leon wanted a plastic horse at a department store and tried to walk off with it. She'd explained how people bought things to the kid. Plainly, the lesson had stuck.

"Menace!" Leon liked the sound of the word, whether he knew what it meant or not.

"That's right. Here, I'll show you something else." Aaron added an E and an S to TAX. "What does this say?"

Leon gave it his best shot. But no matter how smart he was, he wasn't ready for two-syllable words. "You read it, Daddy!" he said.

"It says *taxes*. That's how you show more than one tax," Aaron said. "And if that says *taxes*, what does this say?" Aaron took the T away from the front of TAXES and replaced it with the W.

While Leon was working on that, the phone rang. Ruth answered it. When she responded in Yiddish, Aaron pretty drastically cut the possibilities. A moment later, she called, "Honey, it's Mr. Weissman."

"Coming." Aaron hurried to the telephone. What did his boss need from him on a Sunday morning? He took the handset and said, "*Nu?*"

"Sorry to bother you on Sunday, Aaron, but I've got a question for you," Herschel Weissman said in Yiddish.

"*Nu?*" Aaron repeated on a slightly different note.

Still in the *mamaloshen*, Weissman said, "How do you feel about maybe in a few weeks getting a new partner for the truck?"

"What's going on with Jim?" Aaron asked, also in the Old Country language. "He's not in some kind of *tsuris*, is he?" He didn't particularly like Jim Summers; he never had. Jim was an ignorant bigot. He'd liked Joe McCarthy till the junior Senator from Wisconsin got himself blown to radioactive ash. But that didn't mean Aaron wanted anything to do with costing Summers his job. For anyone who'd gone through the Depression, few sins were blacker.

"Not with me," the boss at Blue Front said. "Not with the cops, either, far as I know. No, I think we'll be getting a new guy in a few weeks, and you're the best man I have to break him in."

"Thanks," Aaron said. "If I'd known I was that great, I would've hit you for a raise a while ago."

Weissman laughed, for all the world as if Aaron were kidding. Then he said, "*Nu,* how does an extra quarter an hour sound, starting when the new guy comes in?"

"Thank you," Aaron said, most sincerely this time. Ten more bucks a week wouldn't put him on Easy Street, but it sure wouldn't hurt. Then he felt he had to add, "You don't have to do that, you know."

"Who said anything about have to?" Herschel Weissman sounded impatient. "People tell me I have to do something, I tell 'em to *geh kak afen yam.* But I can do this and not go broke, so I will."

"Okay." Aaron understood his boss' brand of gruff kindness. It was louder than his own, but otherwise not so very different. He found another question: "Who's the new guy, anyway?"

"He's a *Yehuda* down on his luck, and he doesn't speak a whole lot of English," Weissman answered. "He's supposed to know what's what, though."

"If he works, we'll get on fine," Aaron said. He could see how he'd be better than Jim or most of the other Blue Front men with somebody like that. Yeah, Weissman knew his onions, all right.

Aaron wondered how much Weissman knew that he wasn't telling. He didn't ask. Either it was none of his business or he'd find out soon enough. He said his goodbyes instead. Then he told Ruth, "I just got a quarter raise."

"Good!" Ruth visibly counted the cans and boxes she could buy with the extra cash. "For what?"

"Because I'm cute. Why else?" Aaron said. His wife made a face at him.

Everyone in the gulag was jumpy, *zeks* and guards alike. As long as Stalin lived, tormentors and tormented understood how the system worked. And, as Stalin had seemed likely to live forever, victimizers and victims had looked to see things go on that way, too.

But Stalin was gone. What would the gulags turn into without his strong hand at the controls? And Beria, who'd been Stalin's deputy and head of the security system, was gone, too. Now nobody knew how things were supposed to work.

Luisa Hozzel certainly didn't. All she could do was roll with the punches. And the punches kept coming. Some of the guards were milder with the *zeks* than they had been before. It was as if they thought they needed character witnesses. And they did.

Others, though, got even meaner. They seemed to fear that any loosening up would lead straight to a *zek* uprising. As long as they kept the prisoners afraid, they wouldn't have to worry so much.

That would have been plenty bad by itself. But things got worse, as they so often seemed to when Russians were involved. Some guards couldn't make up their minds whether to be kind or vicious. They'd let you go in sick one day whether you were or not. Two days later, they'd smack you in the face if you asked permission to squat behind a pine and piss.

"All we can do is try to get through it," Trudl Bachman said when Luisa complained. "They have the machine pistols. We don't."

"But it's peace, or almost peace," Luisa protested. "Shouldn't they put us on trains and send us home? They aren't fighting in Germany any more. They won't stay in our part of Germany."

"Almost peace isn't peace," Trudl said. "And what happens after they finally send us home?"

Luisa knew the answer to that. She'd been holding it close to her for a long time, like an extra ace up her sleeve in a card game. "We go to the newspapers, that's what," she said fiercely. "We tell the whole world what filthy animals the Russians are. It's the truth, too."

"Of course it is," Trudl said. "But do you think the Russians don't know it? They hide everything from the outside world, the way the Nazis hid their murder camps. They're uncultured"—she used the Russian *nye kultyurny,* which was much stronger than its German equivalent—"but they know how uncultured they are. They don't want anyone else to find out."

Trudl made much more sense than Luisa wished she did. "By that logic, they'll kill us instead of letting us go," Luisa said.

"I know," Trudl said bleakly. "Have you talked to Maria Grunfeld?"

"Some," Luisa answered. You had to be careful with what you said to anybody who'd got dragged back after an escape. The authorities were too likely to think she was giving you ideas, or that you were looking for them.

"You know what she says about what Russia outside the barbed wire is like, *nicht wahr?*" Trudl said.

"*Ja.*" Luisa had heard Maria go on about that. From what Maria said, Smidovich, the town where she'd been caught, was as full of shabby wooden buildings as this gulag, and not a whole lot better fed. There wasn't any barbed wire around the town, but where could you go if you left? Into the woods, to starve or freeze.

Her story was that she'd stayed with an old Jew in Smidovich, pretending to be his niece. That would have been strange for both of them. Maria hadn't come right out and said how she'd paid for her keep. There was, of course, one obvious answer.

Luisa hadn't used that coin since she got hauled out of Fulda and off to Siberia. Neither, as far as she knew, had Trudl, though she thought her friend had come closer than she had. But both of them would have been better off than they were if they'd used their bodies to their advantage.

When she first got sucked into the gulag, Luisa looked at women who gave themselves to men (or to other women) for their own advantage. They looked like nothing but whores to her. But her own moral perch wasn't so lofty these days. She'd seen too much since she got here.

The rations they gave you were just on or just under what you needed to stay alive. The way they worked you in the endless pine woods showed they didn't care whether you lived or not. If you were on the point of starving or of falling over from exhaustion, why *wouldn't* you lie down with a guard or suck off a kitchen worker so you could keep going a while longer? Wouldn't you be crazy not to?

She'd never quite come to that point herself. She'd dropped ten or fifteen kilos; she was so tired, she always slept like a dead thing. When she dreamt, all she ever dreamt about was food. But she'd never reached the point of desperation that pushed women here into the arms of the guards.

Then again, some women here ended up in the arms of the guards for no better—or worse—reason than that they got so horny, they couldn't stand it any more. When your husband was eight or ten thousand kilometers off to the west, when you had no idea whether you would ever see him again or he was even still alive, shouldn't you take whatever you could get?

Some women thought so. Some simply wanted to be cared for, wanted to be wanted, wanted to know men still hoped to sleep with them. Part of what made Luisa hold back was that she kept hoping she would see her Gustav again. And another part, a large part, was that she was so weary all the time, lust never got the chance to raise its head.

"Trudl," she said.

"*Was ist's?*" her friend asked.

"What do you suppose they'll think of us when we get back to the *Vaterland*?"

"You know what? I don't care," Trudl said. "If I go back to Fulda, I'll eat white bread and boiled pork and roast goose and drink beer till it starts running out my ears."

"That sounds good. That sounds wonderful!" Luisa exclaimed. "I don't care, either, or I hope I won't. Nobody who hasn't been here's got the faintest idea of what this place is like. It's hell on earth, is what it is."

"There are some people who haven't been here who might know what the gulag's all about," Trudl said.

"Who?" Luisa couldn't think of any.

But Trudl answered, "The ones who lived through Dachau and Mauthausen and Bergen-Belsen and the other Nazi camps."

"Oh." The word was only a breath from Luisa's lips. Those people had come back to Fulda, and to other places all over Germany, after the Amis and the Tommies (and even the Ivans) took those places away from the SS men who ran them. The conquerors did their best to fatten them up, but so many of them were still walking skeletons with horror and death in their eyes. Ordinary Germans, people who'd looked the other way while they were rounded up and tormented, did their best not to notice them now. You didn't like to be reminded of what your silence in years gone by had spawned.

The freed prisoners, the surviving Jews and the far more numerous gentiles, often seemed oddly understanding. Some of them had looked the other way, too, till the midnight knock on *their* doors. And then a peculiar thing happened. Most of the prisoners turned back into ordinary Germans themselves. Like everyone else, they got on with the business of putting their shattered country back together again.

Some of them, no doubt, had nightmares where they woke up screaming. But Gustav had had nightmares like that, too. He'd guessed most old *Frontschweine* did. So that bound the prisoners to their neighbors. It didn't separate them.

Luisa expected she would have those nightmares about the gulag. As long as she had them in her warm, soft bed in Fulda, she didn't care a bit.

10

KONSTANTIN MOROZOV SUPPOSED he ought to count himself lucky. The Chekists hadn't arrested him or just eliminated him after his old gunner ran away to be a bandit in the Baltic republics. His T-54 even had a new gunner now. Pyotr Polikarpov was as Russian as a ruble. He wouldn't flee the crew on account of harebrained misplaced patriotism.

The only problem was, he made Konstantin long for Juris Eigims. Eigims might have been—was—a political hothead, but he'd also been a damn good gunner. He knew how to get the best from his piece, and he had a feel for what the enemy might do next that let him anticipate and get off a good first shot.

Polikarpov had none of that. He was fresh out of training, and he hadn't learned his lessons well enough. When they practiced, he was slow. He was careless. Like so many Soviet citizens in so many walks of life, he went through the motions without giving a damn about what lay behind them.

You could get by with that in practice. You shouldn't, but you could. In combat . . . "Listen, pussy, you can't get away with serving your gun while you're playing with your dick," Morozov said. "It's for keeps on the battlefield. The Americans mean it, whether you do or not. I don't care if they kill you, but if you fuck up they'll kill me, too."

"I'm sorry, Comrade Sergeant," Polikarpov whined, which could only mean *Shut up and leave me alone.*

"Listen, peckerhead. You'll be a decent gunner by the time I finish with you if I have to whale the shit out of you to get you that way. Hear me? Get me? You'd better, or your worthless ass is mine."

"I serve the Soviet Union, Comrade Sergeant!" From Polikarpov's lips, that also meant *Shut up and leave me alone.*

Major Zhuk offered Konstantin no sympathy. "He's a gunner, Sergeant," the officer said. "A tank with any gunner functions better than a tank without a gunner. You should be glad I found him for you."

"Plenty of other cowflops in the field, sir," Konstantin said.

He'd pushed it too far. He knew it as soon as the words were out of his mouth. "That will be enough of that," Zhuk said in a cold, dead voice. "You are dismissed."

"I serve the Soviet Union!" Morozov meant *I'm stuck with it, but you're still full of crap.* The major's scowl said he understood the words below the words he heard.

What made things worse for Konstantin was that he had no one with whom he could share his worries. He'd pissed off Major Zhuk. His driver, Avram Lipshitz, was new to him. So was Nodar Gachechiladze, which turned out to be the Georgian loader's handle. And Gachechiladze had more muscle than brains and only the most basic of Russian.

After another horrendous set of gunnery drills, Konstantin drank himself blind. He regretted it the next morning. You always regretted it the next morning. He regretted it all the more because schnapps hurt you worse than vodka did. His head felt as if he had his own gunnery drills going on in there, only with live ammunition.

Pyotr Polikarpov said "Good morning" in his usual, stupidly cheerful way.

"Fuck your mother!" Konstantin snapped.

The gunner looked wounded. He was only a lance-corporal. He couldn't challenge his superior. He couldn't report him, either, not unless he wanted to get in even deeper. All he could do was what he did.

Morozov glumly ate a mess tin full of shchi all greasy with pork fat. That coated his stomach—too late, too late!—but left him wondering whether he'd heave. Then he knocked back one more stiff shot of schnapps: the fang of the snake that bit him. After that, he felt human again, though recorded on a faster speed than the one at which he was playing.

"Comrade Sergeant, are you all right?" Lipshitz asked, watching him down the medicinal dose.

"I'll live. I may regret it, but I will," Konstantin said. "It's all the Americans' fault, anyhow."

"Comrade Sergeant?" The driver didn't get it.

"Never mind." It made perfect sense to Konstantin, even in his fragile state. If the Americans hadn't offered halfway decent peace terms, the fighting would have gone on. In that case, Juris Eigims would have stayed too busy trying to save his own neck to go off and do anything stupid in his worthless homeland. And Konstantin never would have got stuck with Pyotr Mikahilovich Polikarpov.

Two days later, the Georgian sergeant who'd commanded another tank in Konstantin's platoon also disappeared for parts unknown. That made a certain amount of sense to Konstantin, who hoped Nodar Gachechiladze wouldn't follow the man's example. Georgia had got all kinds of preferential treatment while one of its native sons ran the Soviet Union. With Stalin dead and Beria at least out of the picture, the good times would stop. The Russians in charge of things at the moment might even start paying Georgia back.

Which, if you were a proud, headstrong Georgian like Grigol Orbeliani, meant what? To him, it likely meant you headed back to your homeland and tried to pry it loose from the rest of the USSR. Georgia had gone on under its own princes till the early nineteenth century. Nobody now living remembered the days when it hadn't been part of Russia or the Soviet Union. People there still sang songs and told stories about freedom, though. Orbeliani, evidently, still took them seriously. How many other blackasses did?

Not long after Konstantin found out about Orbeliani's desertion, Major Zhuk called on him. "Now I'm going to have to plug in another commander, the way we had to plug in a new gunner for you."

"Yes, sir," Konstantin said, wondering where his superior was going with this.

The major didn't leave him wondering for long: "Whoever I find, whoever they stick me with, odds are he'll be a tub of manure just like the idiot you've got behind your gun."

"Yes, sir," Morozov said again, this time in a different tone of voice. He was amazed. Majors talked with sergeants that way among the Fritzes. Such conversations were much rarer in the Red Army, where most officers were career soldiers and most underofficers just senior conscripts. Zhuk had actually noticed that his tank commander'd been around the block a time or three. Who would have imagined that?

Gesturing impatiently, the regimental commander said, "Yes, I know Polikarpov is a tub of manure. You think I'm blind? But what can we do? The good men are either already serving the Soviet Union somewhere else or they're dead or maimed. Even a tub of manure will plug a hole in a dike."

"Yes, sir," Konstantin said one more time. But it didn't seem enough now, when Major Zhuk was practically apologizing to him. He continued, "If we have to pick up the fight with the Americans, that tub of manure will be dead or maimed pretty damn quick. So will I."

"So will the sorry sons of bitches in what was Orbeliani's tank. He knew what he was doing with it. Fat chance the dickhead we'll get from the replacement depot will." Zhuk couldn't have looked more morose if he'd just watched a T-54 run over his dog. "If we get somebody from the replacement depot. You think the clerks and the mostly better wounded men who go through those places aren't deserting, too?"

"*Bozhemoi!*" Konstantin said. "Comrade Major, I hadn't thought about that at all."

"No reason you should. It's not your worry. It's mine," Zhuk said.

Again, in a lot of armies, the *Wehrmacht* among them, a sergeant might have had to handle such things. Not in the Red Army. Konstantin could read and write, but he knew not a few underofficers who couldn't.

"What are we going to do?" Morozov asked. "How can we keep the rot from spreading?"

"Sergeant, if you find the answer to that one, you'll deserve the Hero of the Soviet Union medal they pin on your chest," Zhuk said. "Right this minute, though, I've got to tell you I don't have any idea. I wish I did."

"I wish you did, too, sir." Morozov was still ready to fight—not eager, but ready. But his readiness didn't do him or his country any good.

Everything in Los Angeles was a fresh marvel to Istvan Szolovits. They told him the city had taken two A-bombs. If they hadn't told him, he wouldn't have known. The city sprawled so, he couldn't see much damage from where he was. They called this district Westwood. They questioned him on a university campus as big as a small town all by itself.

Once in a while, though, when the wind blew out of the southwest, a whiff of barnyard and sewage familiar to him from Europe wafted across the green meadows and red brick buildings of the campus. He asked one of his interrogators about it.

"That's from the refugee camp over in Santa Monica," the man answered in Yiddish—his name was Myron Geller. "It's full of people whose homes got wrecked when the downtown bomb hit. Those people don't have anywhere else to go. Don't you go anywhere near that camp. Some of the *mamzrim* in there, they'll cut your throat for ten cents."

Displaced persons was what they'd called people like that in Europe after the last war. Some were bombed out of their homes, others forced out for political reasons, still others freed from prison camps or concentration camps. Some of them wound up in refugee centers like that. Others avoided them, skulking through the countryside and stealing or robbing as they found the chance.

"This country is so rich, though," Istvan said. "You have refugee camps even here?"

Geller nodded. "Afraid so. One of the things we found out was that A-bombs did more damage than anybody can repair right away."

"If you say so." Istvan had seen more automobiles in Los Angeles in a few days than he had in his whole life before he got here. Drivers were more polite here than in Europe. They often signaled before they turned; horns blared only rarely. All the same, so many cars filled the streets that you took your life in your hands every time you stepped off the curb. Even with the war, the swarms of drivers seemed to have no trouble keeping their machines gassed up. The air had so much car exhaust in it, it smelled bad and burned your eyes.

"Let's get back to you," Geller said, reminding Istvan they'd brought him here to catch questions, not throw them. "How much did you like Matyas Rakosi?"

"I don't think anyone could like him. Do you know what he looks like? Horrible, ugly little man," Istvan answered. "And whenever Stalin coughed, Rakosi caught a cold."

"Heh." Geller gave the small joke a small laugh. "He stayed on the job because he did whatever Stalin told him to?"

"There's no other reason I can think of. The Red Army brought him in. He and his pals were in Moscow before, not in Hungary."

"Yes, we knew that." The American Jew nodded. "What did the native Hungarian Communists think of the newcomers?"

"Not much, from what I hear. I don't know how that is for myself. I wasn't a Communist. I was just a student who got conscripted. But what could the people who stayed in Hungary do after Rakosi came back? Rakosi had all the Russian tanks behind him. He still does."

"There are uprisings against the Russians here and there in Hungary," Myron Geller said. "Some of those Russian tanks have met Molotov cocktails."

"That kind of stuff was just starting to happen when I got captured," Istvan said. "Up at the front, that was the news you whispered to a friend you knew you could trust. Anybody else, forget it. You didn't want the secret police coming down on your head."

"You mean the Russians? The MGB?" Geller asked.

"No, the Hungarian police, the AVO," Istvan answered. "Those guys were meaner, scarier, than the MGB dreamt of being. Some of them really, really believed in what they were doing. And some of them had done dirty work for the Arrow Cross when Szalasi was in power, then just changed uniforms after the Russians brought Rakosi in."

"How many of those were there? Are there?"

Istvan shrugged. "Beats me. All I ever did was hope the AVO never paid any attention to me. But I knew people like that in the Army, too. Bound to be some in the secret police. If you kill everybody who had anything to do with the old government, you have to start over with people who have no idea what the devil they're doing."

"Huh." Geller scribbled in a notebook. "Well, now I understand one of the things Captain Kovacs put in your file."

"What's that?"

"That you're very good at seeing how things work."

"Am I?" Istvan shrugged. "Maybe I am, but what good will it ever do me?"

"Wait till you learn some English. Won't take long—it's an easy language to get the hang of. You'll get your education, and you'll still be on the good side of thirty. A smart guy who doesn't mind working hard can come a long way in America."

"I'll always be a foreigner. They'll be suspicious of me because of how I talk," Istvan said.

"If the USA threw out every smart guy who talked with an accent, they'd have maybe twelve people left," Geller said. "Come on. Let's go over to the Gypsy Wagon and get some lunch."

The Gypsy Wagon was a hut with a corrugated roof that sold cheap food to UCLA students—and to anyone else with money. Istvan looked as if he could be a student. He wore a short-sleeved shirt and pants they called chinos. Geller was older, his brown hair drawing back at the temples. He might have been a graduate assistant or a junior professor.

But he ordered the same hamburger, French fries, and Coca-Cola for himself as he did for Istvan. They ate on the grass. Istvan watched American girls sashay by.

They were all well fed. Most of them had suntans. They wore nice clothes. They put on more makeup than some of them knew what to do with. In spite of it all, they seemed younger than the girls he'd known back in Budapest. Istvan didn't think they were, but they seemed that way.

When he remarked on it to Geller, the American Jew nodded. "In Budapest, the girls you knew lived through the Horthy dictatorship and the war and the Russians and the Hungarian Communists. Here, the war was a voice from another room for these girls. They'd been pretty much at peace their whole lives till the bombs fell on L.A."

"Except for that refugee camp, even those hardly seem to have happened," Istvan said.

"They don't if you're in college here, yeah," Geller replied. "But that's not the only camp. They're scattered across the Los Angeles area, with more up the coast for other places that got hit. Life in them is no fun at all. Then there are the people who got killed and the people who got hurt or poisoned with radiation and the people who lost everything they had but didn't go into the camps. They sleep wherever it's warm and dry and do whatever they have to to get money and food."

"Wherever it's warm and dry . . ." Istvan waved up at the bright sun. "Isn't it always warm and dry?" The air might be foul from too many cars, but Los Angeles, to him, had weather that would make God want to retire here.

"Only most of the time," Myron Geller said. "It gets chilly during the winter, and rainy, too. It even snowed in 1949. January, that was."

Istvan shook his head in wonder. It had snowed . . . three and a half years ago now. That it had snowed at all was remarkable enough to have made Geller mention it. Snow, to Istvan, was an annual nuisance. To Russians, and to the Germans who'd fought in Russia, it had been a fact of life from October into March.

He finished the lunch. He'd discovered he loved fried foods. He hadn't had them very often before Captain Kovacs sent him here. He hadn't known what he was missing, either. He threw his trash in a galvanized sheet-metal can.

Geller threw away his garbage, too, except for a couple of fries he tossed to the pigeons. They were beggar birds; all they needed were sunglasses and tin cups. Then Geller said, "Let's head back."

"Can you question me here?" Istvan asked. "It's nice in the sunshine."

The older man laughed. "You just got to L.A., but you're turning into a Californian, all right."

"Do you think so?" The idea excited Istvan.

Thumping noises said the *Independence* was lowering its landing gear. The DC-6 landed smoothly at Orly. The airport was too far from the center of Paris to have been damaged by the A-bomb that tore the heart out of the French capital.

Peering out the plane's window toward that battered heart, Harry Truman couldn't see much. One of the things he couldn't see was the Eiffel Tower. Some of it had melted and the rest had fallen over, smashing buildings that might otherwise have survived the bomb.

As the *Independence* slowed, Truman slid forward in his seat till the belt held him in place. French airport personnel brought a wheeled stairway to the plane's door. They locked the wheels in place and turned cranks to bring the top of the stairway level with the bottom of the door. A Secret Service man opened the door and stepped out. Another followed him. After the second man was satisfied no assassins lurked nearby, he waved to Truman that it was safe.

French soldiers stood guard on the runway, some carrying rifles, others submachine guns. When the soles of the President's shoes touched French soil, the officer in charge of the men gave the open-palmed salute Truman remembered from World War I. *Well, Lafayette, here I am,* Truman thought.

A moment later, that officer saluted again. Charles de Gaulle came out of the terminal and walked across the tarmac toward the *Indepen-dence*. Though de Gaulle wore a plain gray suit, his straight back re-minded anyone who saw him that he was a career soldier. He headed the French Committee of National Salvation, which had run the coun-try since the A-bomb decapitated the Fourth Republic.

"Hello, Mr. President," he said, extending his hand. "May your com-ing be crowned with success." He spoke good but accented English.

"Thank you, General." Truman shook hands with de Gaulle. He had to look up and up while he did it. Truman was a perfectly ordinary, perfectly respectable five-nine. The big-nosed beanpole who ran France had to be six-three, maybe even six-four.

"Your Soviet opposite number arrived yesterday," de Gaulle said. One of his shaggy eyebrows twitched. "We placed him in a fine Parisian hotel . . . the closest one to the blast zone that still stands. His room has an excellent view of the destruction his bomber created."

"Good," Truman said, and then, "Did you lodge me in the same hotel?"

Charles de Gaulle shook his big head. "*Pas de tout,*" he said, sur-prised back into French. Returning to English, he continued, "Your country has not attacked mine. Through three wars now in this cen-tury, we have fought together. You are at an altogether more enjoyable residence with a much improved vista. Mr. Attlee is staying there as well."

"That all sounds fine." Truman was briefly embarrassed at giving de Gaulle the glove. Only briefly, though. It wasn't as if de Gaulle didn't do everything he could to annoy the United States. He'd grown up in the days when France was a great power and the USA wasn't. He still remembered those days. So did Truman, but he also remembered how times had changed.

A limousine—a Cadillac from Detroit—pulled up to take Truman to the hotel from which he wouldn't see any bomb damage. As soon as he got there, he rang Clement Attlee's room. The hotel operator spoke better English than de Gaulle did.

Truman and the British Prime Minister ate supper together in the hotel restaurant. Attlee, bald and mustached, looked weary unto death. "In normal times, we should have held an election last year," he said. "You might well have been dining with Mr. Churchill here tonight. But all parties agreed to postpone the vote until something like peace returned."

"I think I'm going to have to do something like that, too," Truman said. "It will make people scream at me, but they've been screaming ever since Roosevelt died. You do what you've got to do. Then you make it look legal afterwards."

"Your elections are more regularly scheduled than ours." In Attlee's mouth, the word came out *sheduled*. Truman hid a smile. The Englishman asked the key question: "Can you get away with it?"

"I can ... because I have to. There's just been too much disruption. Unlike our friends on the far side of the Iron Curtain, I don't enjoy ruling by decree, but I haven't had much choice. Congress got smashed to hell and gone."

"Quite." Unlike de Gaulle and Truman, Attlee hadn't had his capital devastated. He'd only—only!—seen some of his provincial cities go up in fire and radioactive smoke.

De Gaulle had arranged for the leaders of the three greatest Western democracies to meet Vyacheslav Molotov at the palace of Versailles. He might have been remembering the peace negotiations at the end of World War I. If he was, he was forgetting how that treaty'd turned out. Or he might have wanted to remind Molotov that France remained a rich country with a rich history.

Molotov was a little chunkier, a little grayer, than Truman remembered him from 1945. They hadn't got on well then; Molotov was reported to have said no one had ever talked to him the way Truman did. Truman's attitude was that somebody should have done it a long time before. One thing hadn't changed: the new Soviet leader's face remained a hard, cold, expressionless mask.

Unlike the others, Molotov didn't speak English. His interpreter's Oxonian accent was even more elegant than Attlee's. Through the worried-looking little man, the Russian said, "Enough is enough. If we return to the prewar situation and the USSR is granted a free hand to set its own house in order, we are happy enough to liquidate this conflict with capitalism."

"No A-bombs on the satellites. No A-bombs on the Baltic republics, either," Truman said. "Otherwise, the USA agrees."

"The Lithuanian, Latvian, and Estonian Soviet Socialist Republics are not within your purview," Molotov said. "They are constituent parts of the USSR."

"We don't recognize their annexation. *De jure,* they remain independent," Truman said. Charles de Gaulle and Clement Attlee nodded. They had diplomats from the Baltic republics in their countries, too. Like the USA, they recognized them more to annoy the Soviet Union than in the belief that they were real nations any more. The President went on, "So no A-bombs there." He didn't say *Don't overrun them with tanks.* He knew Molotov wouldn't have listened if he did.

Still Molotov's face didn't change. The interpreter looked more worried than ever. He wasn't used to anybody save perhaps Stalin laying down the law to his boss. After a pause that lasted half a minute, Molotov shrugged, waggled one hand, and said, "Let it be as you wish." The interpreter let out a loud sigh of relief.

"Don't cheat on this one," Truman said. "You'll be sorry if you do. We'll make you sorry if you do."

"I understand," Molotov said, and not another word. Either he'd listen or he wouldn't. If he didn't . . . *I'll make him sorry,* Truman thought.

"Now, the next thing we have to touch on is the matter of China," Truman said. "Mao's won the war there. We're stuck with him. Chiang has to stay on Formosa. We won't help him if he doesn't. But if Mao doesn't leave South Korea alone, he'll end up envying your country, I promise. We'll knock him flat."

As soon as the interpreter finished translating that, Molotov said, "*Nyet.*" He added detail through the worried little man: "For one thing, Mao is a free agent. I cannot control him. For another, too many A-bombs have already fallen since you started using them. If we are to refrain in the areas you demand, you must refrain in China. Conventional weapons, yes. A-bombs, no. Or you will find out we can still hurt you."

Truman opened his mouth to tell Molotov he was in a lousy position to make demands. But anyone who could manufacture and deliver A-bombs (and, soon, no doubt H-bombs, too) wasn't in such a lousy position as all that. "All right," Truman said. "All right, if you stop sending arms to China and to North Korea. If you don't, all bets are off, and I promise we'll hurt you worse than you hurt us."

"You are a man of no culture," Molotov said. Truman only shrugged. Molotov gnawed on his mustache for a moment, then nodded. "It is agreed."

"Good." Truman had to hope this Treaty of Versailles would turn out better than the one from 1919 did.

Aaron Finch found himself still working with Jim Summers. Something had gone wrong somewhere. The Jew to whom he was supposed to show the ropes hadn't come to work at Blue Front. Herschel Weissman spread his hands to show he didn't know what was going on, either.

Jim was whistling a song as he got ready to go out on deliveries for the last run on a hot July Friday afternoon. "What is that tune?" Aaron asked. Jim wouldn't put a mockingbird out of business any time soon. Since Aaron also frightened notes he couldn't hit, they were well matched in that, anyhow.

"It's 'When Johnny Comes Marching Home Again,' of course," Jim answered. The way he whistled, there was no *of course* about it. He went on, "Seems to fit, don't it, when it looks like the goddamn stupid war's over and done with at last?"

"Boy, I hope you're right," Aaron said. "It is in Europe, anyway. But looks like it's still going on in the Far East, same as the last one did after the Nazis caved in."

"Oughta blow up all them Commie Chinks till they glow in the dark," Jim opined. "Then we won't gotta worry about 'em no more."

Aaron didn't say anything to that. He could see why Jim had liked

Joe McCarthy for President. Well, these days whatever was left of Tail-Gunner Joe was bound to glow in the dark. Aaron didn't miss the Senator from Wisconsin one bit. To him, blowing McCarthy off the map was one of the few good things the Russians had done when they A-bombed Washington.

Off they went, to deliver a stove and a refrigerator to a house in Burbank. Jim went right on dissecting the political scene: "Truman's even more hoity-toity than FDR was. FDR wanted to cancel elections, I betcha, but old Harry's gone and done it."

"They'll come," Aaron said. "We're still picking ourselves up and dusting ourselves off. We're better off than Russia, but we're still pretty beat-up."

He might as well have saved his breath. Jim went ahead as if he hadn't spoken: "Jesus H. Christ, even Abe goddamn Lincoln didn't keep folks from voting. Old Abe was a nigger-loving son of a bitch, but he knew better than to fuck around with elections."

A nigger-loving son of a bitch? At the public schools Aaron went to in Portland, they'd taught him that Lincoln and Washington were the two greatest Presidents. Nothing he'd heard or read since made him disbelieve that, though he thought Franklin D. Roosevelt belonged right up there with them. They must have had other ideas in Alabama or Arkansas or wherever Jim got his sketchy education. Or maybe Jim had picked up that opinion at the same shoddy store where he bought his others.

He went right on venting his spleen while Aaron drove the truck down to Burbank. Then they had to buckle down and get to work. Moving in a refrigerator was always tricky. You couldn't tilt it much. If you didn't keep it close to upright, you'd kill the motor. After they plugged it in, Aaron satisfied himself that it *was* cooling before he got to work on the gas and electrical connections for the stove. He lit the pilot lights for the lady of the house and made sure the oven and all the burners worked.

"Thank you both very much," she said. As they headed back to the truck, she gave them each two dollars.

"Thank you, ma'am. You don't have to do that. We're just doing our jobs," Aaron said. Jim looked daggers at him.

"It's hard work on a hot day," the woman answered. "You deserve a little something extra for it."

"Much obliged, ma'am," Jim said loudly. Aaron let it go. It wasn't as if he couldn't use the money, but tips made him nervous. He was already getting paid to do what he did. He didn't think he deserved to get paid twice. Jim's conscience was more elastic.

Summers drove back to the warehouse in Glendale. He took it slow, to make sure they got back after quitting time. Aaron would have hurried, but he held his peace. After Jim parked the truck behind the warehouse, they clocked out. "See you Monday," Aaron called as he headed for his Chevy. He tried to stay polite. Jim grunted something or other. Aaron got into the car, lit a cigarette to replace the one he'd just stepped on, and headed for home.

He spent a quiet weekend with Ruth and Leon. No annoying relatives from either side of the family visited. Aaron watched a baseball game on TV. The big-leaguers didn't look any better than the hometown heroes from the PCL. He worked on a rocking horse he was making for his son. He had a Burgie with dinner Saturday and another one Sunday.

"See?" he said. "I'm turning into a lush."

"Uh-huh. Sure." Ruth knew better. But she also knew better than to argue with him.

He reread *The Egg and I* for the umpteenth time. He read to Leon. He tried to get Leon to read to him. Leon could manage little words, but he wasn't nearly so good with whole sentences.

At half past seven, Leon went to bed. Aaron found himself yawning, too. "Boy, this is great," he said. "I get sleepy at the same time as my little kid. Is God trying to tell me I'm an *alter kacker*?" Turning fifty still felt very strange to him. It was a marker that showed more lay behind you than ahead.

"You're tired because you work hard, and because you've got to get up early in the morning tomorrow to work some more," Ruth said. "So kindly quit talking like a *shlemiel*."

"Aye aye, ma'am," he said. Till he got married, no one had ever been able to boss him around. Plenty of people had tried, but he had the full measure of Finch stubbornness. Ruth managed, though. Maybe, till he knew her, no one had ever tried to boss him in a pleasant tone of voice.

He went to bed at ten. Before he turned off the lamp on the nightstand, he made sure the alarm clock was set for six. Then he rolled over so he could kiss his wife. Five minutes later, he was snoring.

He woke well before six, and without benefit of the alarm clock. The house was shaking, the walls groaning. Something fell off a shelf in the living room and crashed on the floor. The Venetian blinds beat against the windows.

"Aaron!" Ruth squalled. "What is it?"

"Earthquake. A big one. I'll get Leon." Aaron jumped out of bed. His first automatic motion when he did was to grab for his glasses, but the quake had knocked them away from where he always left them. Well, it was dark. He couldn't see much even with them.

He lurched down the hall to his son's room. The floor shifted under his feet like a Liberty ship's deck in a heavy sea. He grabbed Leon out of bed and carried him back to his own bedroom. The shaking eased just as he got there. "Whee!" Leon said. "Do it again, Daddy!"

"Christ, I hope not," Aaron said. Ruth turned on the light on her side of the bed. Aaron blinked. Since he was specs-less, the room stayed blurry. "Can you find my glasses, honey?"

A shape that was probably his wife leaned toward his side of the bed. She handed him something. "They were next to your pillow," she said.

He put them on. The world came back into focus. "Watch that first step," he said. "It's a dilly. That one just kept going on and on."

The phone rang. He put Leon down and went out to answer it. When he did, his brother Marvin, who also lived in Glendale, laughed a shaky laugh in his ear. "Watch that first step," Marvin said. "It's a doozy."

Aaron laughed, too. "Not half a minute ago, I called it a dilly," he said. "You guys okay?"

"We aren't hurt," Marvin answered. "Olivia's scared like anything, and Caesar's going *meshuggeh*." Olivia was his teenage daughter, Caesar his German shepherd. Aaron liked the dog better than the rug-eating schnauzer that had preceded it. After a beat, Marvin asked, "How about your gang?"

"We're in one piece," Aaron said. "I tell you, though, I won't need coffee before I go in to work this morning." He laughed again, as if he were kidding.

11

JET ENGINES SCREAMED, high overhead. Cade Curtis looked up into the sky. The bombers were barely visible silver points flying from east to west. But the contrails they left behind told where they'd been and suggested where they were going.

"Red China's gonna catch it," Howard Sturgis said happily. "We finally got enough B-47s in Japan to give it to the Chinks but good."

"I bet the guys who've been flying B-29s are just brokenhearted to let somebody else carry the ball for a while," Cade said.

"Yeah, they're crying in their beer, all right," Sturgis agreed. The Superforts had done yeoman duty this time around, as they had in World War II. But things weren't the same now. The B-29s rapidly discovered they couldn't bomb North Korea by day. Even at night, they were vulnerable to radar-guided or -equipped fighters. They'd landed some heavy punches all around the world, but they'd paid a hellacious price.

"We bombed the snot out of the Commies with obsolete planes. And we're fighting 'em on the ground with obsolete men." Sturgis thumped his own chest. He'd slogged his way up the Italian boot the last time around and won a battlefield commission in these other mountains on the far side of the world. "Anybody wants to put me out to pasture or send me home, bet your ass I won't bitch about it."

"Me, neither, but speak for yourself when you talk about obsolete men." Cade had just turned twenty-one. He could legally buy booze now, which hadn't kept him from getting shitfaced before whenever he felt the need. He was a veteran of as much war as anyone was ever likely to want to see. Unlike Sturgis, though, he wasn't a grizzled veteran.

A few Red Chinese antiaircraft guns opened up on the B-47s. Howard Sturgis laughed. "Dumb fuckers're only wasting ammo. Those bombers are way the hell up there. They ain't got a prayer of hitting 'em."

"That's how it looks to me, too." Cade lit a Raleigh. They weren't his brand, but with the supply chain fubar'd the way it was you took whatever you could get when you could get anything. Thoughtfully, he went on, "I wonder if they're up too high for the MiG-15s."

"If they aren't, they'll be sorry pretty damn quick." Sturgis scratched his head. "Or maybe not. They're jets, too. Maybe they can outrun 'em."

"If it's bombers against fighters, always bet the fighters," Cade said. "Bombers are made for load, so they can carry bombs. Fighters have to be fast and twisty enough to run down bombers and shoot 'em out of the sky."

"Makes sense, Captain. But I always knew you were a smart guy," Sturgis said. "Bum a butt off you?"

"Sure." Cade gave him the pack of cigarettes. He knew Sturgis wasn't altogether praising him by calling him smart. The Army didn't want or know what to do with people who stuck out for brains. It needed guys who could get along with other people, follow orders, and not look too far ahead. If you looked ahead, you were too likely to see your own death staring back at you.

Cade tried not to stick out. Sometimes he felt as if he were trying to sneak the sun past a bunch of roosters. Things would have been harder yet for him without the solid reputation he'd earned by coming back from the Chosin Reservoir after the Red Chinese cut off and killed or captured almost the whole UN force up there. They also would have been harder if the Army hadn't needed even halfway capable officers so badly.

When his frozen, frightened platoon was falling back from the reservoir, he'd ordered two soldiers with a light machine gun to cover their retreat for as long as they had to. Basically, he'd ordered the dogfaces to let themselves be killed so the rest of the men had a better chance to get away. He sometimes dreamt about that order, about giving it and about being on the receiving end.

He worried about it, worried over it, while he was awake, too. He suspected he'd go right on doing that if he lived to be eighty. It was the hardest order he'd ever given. None of the others came close.

What did the Bible say? *Greater love hath no man than this, that a man lay down his life for his friends.* But those two scared, grubby guys didn't lay down their lives for love. They did it because he told them to.

He lit another Raleigh and smoked furiously. If the machine gunners hadn't loved their buddies, at least some, wouldn't they have told him to go fuck himself and bugged out? It looked that way to him. That still didn't keep his sleep free from nasty dreams.

Did Howard Sturgis have regrets like that? Did he have dreams like that? He must have given some orders he wished like anything he hadn't had to. How much did they bother him afterwards, though? That was the real question. Cade couldn't ask it. It was too private, too secret, too intimate.

Sturgis had a question of his own: "Sir, you figure bombing the living shit out of the Chinks'll make 'em say uncle?"

"I wouldn't bet on it," Cade said. "If the Russians keep their end of the bargain and quit sending 'em weapons, that would help."

"Don't hold your breath!" Sturgis laughed a scornful laugh.

"Yeah, tell me about it. But if we're not fighting in Europe any more, we can pay some attention to this miserable place. We've had about a hand and a half tied behind our back for a long time. If we show Red China we mean it—"

"If we do mean it." Sturgis had a veteran's cynicism, all right.

"There is that," Cade allowed. "But all we've been fighting for since the end of 1950 is a lousy draw. We ought to be able to get that much, anyway."

"We're the United States, dammit. We're supposed to kick ass all over the place, not settle for a draw. When did we ever settle for a stinking draw?" Sturgis said.

"The War of 1812, I think," Cade answered.

"Christ. They might've taught me about that one in school, but fuck me if I remember anything."

They probably hadn't taught him much about it because it was a draw. It had embarrassed Cade's teachers, too. They went on about American victories on the high seas, and about Andrew Jackson and the Battle of New Orleans. They mentioned the writing of "The Star-Spangled Banner." The burning of Washington and the failed invasion of Canada, by contrast, got short shrift.

In "The Star-Spangled Banner," Francis Scott Key wrote about "the rockets' red glare." The Red Chinese chose that moment to fire a couple of cases of Katyushas at the American lines. The flames that propelled them were yellow, not red. Key didn't say anything about the English rockets' screaming like a pack of banshees, either.

"Hit the dirt!" Cade yelled as soon as he heard those rising screams in the air. He suited action to word.

Down slammed the rocket salvo. Something hard and sharp bit him in the leg. He let out a yowl before he quite knew he'd done it. Then he twisted to try to bandage his wound. His left trouser leg was all over blood from just below the knee on down. He felt woozy and sick.

"Shit! The captain's hit!" Howard Sturgis shouted. "Medic! The captain's down!"

Sturgis cut away the soggy trouser leg and slapped on not one but two wound bandages. *That can't be good,* Cade thought vaguely. Sturgis stuck a morphine syrette in his thigh and pushed the plunger down. The pain started receding.

"Here. I take him back." That was Jimmy. He slung Cade over his shoulder like a sack of rice. He was big for a gook, but Cade was big for an American. It didn't seem to bother Jimmy. He carried Cade as if he came from a long line of stevedores.

Cade grayed out a few times. Next thing he knew, he was back at an aid station. "We'll fix you up, Captain," a doc said through a surgical mask. "You're gonna be just fine."

"You tell him, Hawkeye," another doctor said. Cade grayed out again.

There was a truce in Germany, one that looked to be holding. Ihor Shevchenko watched trains carry troops and tanks and artillery pieces from west to east, out of Germany and back toward the Soviet Union.

Those trains had to cross Poland, of course. There was no truce here. The Americans and Englishmen might not be fighting the Red Army any more, but the Polish bandits sure were. Sometimes, as long as the troop trains looked like they were going through without stopping, they left them alone. They had to figure more Soviet soldiers stopping in their country were the last thing they needed.

Sometimes, though, they fired on them, with rifles or machine guns or whatever light artillery they could get their hands on. To a lot of Poles, killing Russians was an irresistible temptation.

Ihor's section was guarding a stretch of track between Wroclaw and Czestochowa. They had one machine gun and their personal weapons: a motley mix of AK-47s, submachine guns, and bolt-action rifles. They were stretched very thin. Any serious force of Poles would have made them wish they'd never been born.

One of the guys who served that machine gun said, "I was around here in the Great Patriotic War. Only it wasn't Wroclaw then—it was Breslau, and it still belonged to the Hitlerites. We put it under siege, but they didn't surrender till a couple of days before they quit everywhere. The day before they did, the fuckers, I got hit." He held up his left hand, which was missing the little finger and half the ring finger.

"That's the way it goes, Feofan," Ihor said. "Probably everybody in

this outfit who served in the last one has that kind of story. Only difference with me is, I got a leg wound."

"Sure, Comrade Corporal, but if the damn Fritzes in Breslau had
seen the jig was up two days earlier, I'd still be in one piece."

"Uh-huh. And then they would have called you back sooner, and
you might have stopped something bigger this time."

Feofan blinked. "Well, fuck me in the mouth if you're not right.
Y'know, I never thought of that."

The admission didn't exactly take Ihor by surprise. Feofan wasn't
long on brains. He was brave enough, though, and he stuck to any post
you put him in. Plenty of smarter soldiers were trying to melt away
from the Red Army now. Ihor wouldn't have minded melting away
from it himself. He didn't want to be in it to begin with, and he really
didn't want to be in it for no better reason than knocking a bunch of
Poles over the head. Feofan lost no sleep over such things. As far as he
was concerned, an order was an order.

Then one of the pickets Ihor had set farther from the railhead let out
a yell. Somebody yelled back, maybe in Russian, maybe in Polish—the
shout came from too far away to let Ihor be sure. A few minutes later,
the picket came back with a man carrying a flag of truce. That made the
fellow a Pole.

"What do you want?" Ihor called to him.

"A parley," the Pole said. He was in uniform, or pieces of different
uniforms: worn *Feldgrau* pants, a Red Army tunic, and an old Polish
helmet, close to the German *Stahlhelm* but not quite there.

"You've got one," Ihor told him. "If you didn't, you'd be dead by
now."

"Funny man, aren't you?" The Pole spoke fluent Russian with the
rhythmic accent his people gave it. He had a thin, pale face and a blade
of a nose. He looked like an aristocrat, which was plenty to make Ihor
dislike him on sight. He went on, "If you clear out from this stretch of
track, my men won't have to kill all of you when we advance."

"And when's that gonna be?" Ihor asked.

"As soon as I get back to them. If I'm not back in two hours, they'll advance anyway, and avenge me. The other thing is, if they're avenging me they won't bother to take any prisoners."

"Hey, I honored German flags of truce the last time around. I'll honor yours, too," Ihor said.

"Will you let us do what we need to do to set our people free, or will you act like a motherfucking Russian?"

"I'm a motherfucking Ukrainian, dickface, and don't you forget it," Ihor said. "You want to get your chicken thieves shot up, come ahead." He knew how big a bluff he was running. With luck, the Polish aristo didn't.

"That's what you say, Corporal." The fellow had no trouble reading Soviet shoulder boards. He looked to the soldiers with Ihor. "How about the rest of you? Is helping Molotov rape his next-door neighbor worth your necks?"

They could have deserted Ihor. They could have plugged him and then deserted him. That way, he wouldn't rat on them to the Chekists (he wouldn't have anyway, but how could they be sure of that?). They just looked silently back at the Pole till Feofan said, "We're soldiers. We do what we're supposed to do. We'll keep doing it as long as we can. And we'll fucking massacre you pussies." He patted the sheet-metal curve of the machine gun's cooling jacket as if it were his girlfriend's behind.

"All right. You asked for it. Now you'll get it." The Pole turned and stalked away.

As soon as he disappeared behind some bushes, Ihor said, "Quick, guys. Move the machine gun to the second position. Five gets you ten they'll dump as much as they can right here."

"We'll do it, Comrade Corporal," Feofan said. Between them, the Maxim gun and its mount weighed just about fifty kilos. But the mount had two iron wheels. As long as the ground wasn't too rough, you could shift the machine gun without rupturing yourself.

"Dig your foxholes deeper, boys!" Ihor yelled to as many soldiers as could hear him. "The shit'll start any minute."

Sure enough, the first mortar bombs whispered in about fifteen minutes later. The Pole would have got back to his men and told them they had some stubborn Russians to deal with. Ihor had hoped they would just carry small arms, but no such luck. He huddled in his own hole and hoped for the best. With mortars, what else could you do?

The bandits concentrated the vicious little bombs right where the Red Army machine gun had been. Ihor gave himself a small mental pat on the back, but only a small one. They'd still come forward, and they'd still want to kill him. The snooty guy who'd parleyed would want to kill him double for not giving in.

The pickets opened up with their PPSh's within seconds of one another. The incoming fire was mostly Mausers, either captured German weapons or Polish-made copies. But the submachine guns that punctuated the rifles' work were Soviet models, not Schmeissers.

Ihor popped up and down in his hole like a nervous rabbit. When you were up, they could shoot you. But if you stayed down, they could sneak close and then shoot you the next time you did come up. He saw something moving in the weeds, perhaps three hundred meters away. He couldn't have hit it with a PPD or PPSh. He fired a three-round burst from his AK-47. Frantic thrashing told him that was one bandit he didn't need to worry about any more.

Then the Maxim gun opened up. The Poles shouted in dismay. They'd hoped to have knocked out its crew. *No such luck, assholes,* Ihor thought. They concentrated their fire on the machine gun, but the men who served it were well positioned. They'd been through the mill before. They knew how to make fieldworks that gave them the best chance of staying alive.

Advancing against a machine gun was asking to get ventilated, especially if the crew had friends to help protect them. They did here. Had the Poles tried to outflank Ihor's section, they might have managed it. Coming straight at it, they showed how brave they were but played into his hands.

Another white flag came forward. "Can we pick up our wounded?" a bandit shouted—not, Ihor noted, the aristocrat who'd tried to get him to give up.

"Go ahead," he called back. "Twenty minutes—that's it." He liked Poles even less than Russians. That, by God, was saying something!

Rolf Mehlen watched a train flying a flag of truce and a Soviet hammer-and-sickle banner pull into Arnsberg. Soldiers climbed into passenger cars—and into boxcars as well. He watched Red Army panzers mount heavy ramps and fart their way onto flatcars, where their crews chained them in place. Some of the panzers flew white flags from their radio aerials.

"This is what victory looks like," Max Bachman said. "We were all out of those by the time I put on *Feldgrau* last time around. I went out to the front, and it was all falling back toward the *Vaterland* from then on."

"Not all of it," Rolf said. "We drove the Ivans back plenty—we just couldn't make it stick."

"We're saying the same thing two different ways," Max said.

"No, we aren't. We—" Rolf broke off, shaking his head. "Ah, screw it. But if this were the kind of victory it ought to be, we'd be blowing up those dipshits instead of letting them go home."

"I'll take it any way I can get it," Max said. "When I find out the Russians have pulled out of Fulda, I'll see if I can get some leave and go home and find out how my wife's doing."

"Take French leave," Rolf suggested.

"I've thought about it, Lord knows. But I've been away this long. Another week or ten days won't matter."

"If you say so." Rolf had a couple of lady friends in the small town where he'd settled after the last war. As far as he knew, he'd kept them ignorant of each other. He'd sort things out there sooner or later. No hurry, not when getting some while you wore a uniform and carried a rifle was so easy.

The Ivan driving the flag-bedecked locomotive waved in the direction of the German soldiers watching from their side of the barbed wire. Rolf wanted to fire at him, or at least to send back a filthy gesture.

He refrained. Orders were to let the Russians go and not to provoke them as long as they behaved themselves. Here, they seemed to be.

Even mild Max was thinking along with him. "That clown in the engine, he'd be an easy shot," he said.

"Bet your balls he would," Rolf agreed. "Shame we can't knock him over and say it was an accident."

"Naughty, naughty." Max clucked like a mother annoyed at her child. "The bastards *are* actually leaving. Do you want to give them an excuse to stay?"

"I guess not," Rolf said unwillingly. "They should be leaving all of Germany, not just the west, damn them."

"*Ja.* They should. But they're not. You take what you can get. If you grab for it all, you usually wind up with nothing. That's what the *Führer* did. So wave to the nice Russian son of a bitch, Rolf."

Clenching his teeth, Rolf waved to the nice Russian son of a bitch. The Red waved back. He had not a care in the world. For him, the fight was over, and he'd come out of it whole. For Rolf, the fight, the real fight, had been lost in 1945. They might get the Ivans out of West Germany. They might rebuild the place so everybody had a job and food on the table and a nice flat and an automobile. Still, it wouldn't be the kind of Germany he wanted to live in. It wouldn't be the kind of Germany where people were proud to meet a veteran from the *Leibstandarte Adolf Hitler.*

"I don't think you understand what the *Führer* meant to so many Germans," Rolf said, holding his voice down and picking his words with care. "The *Führer* was . . . He was a man in a million. No, a man in a million million."

"That, I won't argue with. He was the best speaker I ever heard. When he talked, you believed him. You couldn't help but believe him. I believed him, too, along with all the other fools," Max said. Rolf bristled. Max held up a hand in a gesture of peace. "Just ask yourself this, Rolf—are we better off or worse off than we would have been if Hitler died when he was two years old?"

"It's better to try grandly and fail than never to try at all," Rolf declared.

"Oh, *Quatsch. Quatsch* with sauce, in fact," Max said. "How many people dead? How many cities smashed in the last war? How many A-bombs this time around because all we are now is a football pitch for the Amis and Ivans to play on?"

"We should have won," Rolf said stubbornly. "It's all England's fault, when you get down to it. If she hadn't made the Yugoslavs betray us, we would have started against Russia six weeks sooner. We'd have made it to Moscow before the mud and the snow could stop us. And the Tommies jumped into bed with Stalin so they wouldn't lose to us. They're still paying the price for that."

"We were fighting England—fighting the whole British Empire. We decided in our infinite wisdom to fight Russia at the same time. Then, because that wasn't enough already, your man in a million million decided to declare war on the United States. Sure, Hitler was the *Gröfaz*, all right." Max used the sardonic German contraction for *greatest general of all time.*

"You don't get it. Hitler made us feel like Germans again. He made us feel like *men* again." Rolf remembered how broke, how hopeless, how far down on his luck he'd been before he joined the Nazis. He remembered how proud he'd been when he got into the SS, and then into the *Führer*'s elite bodyguard. He'd gone to war with a smile on his face and a song in his mouth.

"How many of us feel like dead men thanks to him?" Max returned. "Aren't you sorry about anything?"

"You bet I am. I'm sorry we lost."

"*Himmeldonnerwetter!* You're hopeless, you know that?"

"No, I'm not. I still hope. I just don't expect anything any more. All you want to do is get old and get rich and get fat. I don't give a shit about any of that nonsense."

"Why did you stay in Germany, then? You should have joined the French Foreign Legion or something. I know for a fact they took *Waffen-*

SS men, no questions asked. You could have been fighting Communists in Indochina all these years. See what you missed out on?"

Rolf knew Max was still trying to get under his skin. He answered seriously even so: "You know, I thought about it. You're right—plenty of guys I used to know are wearing the white kepi these days, if they're still alive. But I just couldn't stomach the notion of fighting for France."

"Um, you do know we're on the same side this time, right?" Max said.

"Fuck you," Rolf said mildly. "Of course I know. They're still French, damn them. I'll tell you what they should have done in 1945, them and the English and the Americans."

"I'm all ears," Max said. "What can you see that Churchill and de Gaulle and Roosevelt—no, it would've been Truman—couldn't? Give forth, O great sage of the age."

"It's plain enough. They should have done what the *Führer* wanted. They should have joined up with us and rolled east to put an end to the Russian problem once and for all. I still don't get why they wouldn't do it. Working together, we could have ridden roughshod over the Red Army."

Max made a small production of lighting a cigarette. Then he said, "Well, you were in the LAH. I have to remember that. No wonder you can't see it."

"What are you talking about now?" Rolf demanded, indignant at last.

"Most of us got conscripted and did our bit for the *Vaterland* and hoped we'd come out the other side alive and with our balls still attached. We listened to the Nazi stuff, but most of us didn't pay much attention. You liked it, though. You volunteered. Nobody got into LAH any other way."

"Damn right!" Rolf said proudly. "That's why the *Waffen*-SS was the *Führer*'s fire brigade all over the place. Whenever the *Wehrmacht* weenies got in trouble, we'd go bail them out."

"It's all true." Max made a hash of blowing a smoke ring. "But so what?"

"What do you mean, so what?"

"I mean so what? Look where you are. Look what's happened since you volunteered. Look at everything. Wouldn't we all be better off if we'd stayed home and raised cabbages and left each other and our neighbors alone?" Max said.

For once, Rolf found himself without an answer.

The colonel who commanded the Tula air base was a narrow-eyed Tajik named Aziz Dzhalalov. "I serve the Soviet Union, Comrade Colonel!" Boris Gribkov said as he saluted after coming into Dzhalalov's presence. Asians seldom rose so high in the Soviet military. Either Dzhalalov was a comer or he had good connections.

"Yes. We all serve the Soviet Union, even in these difficult times." The Tajik's Russian was fluent—he spoke with schoolbook purity of grammar, which hardly any real Russians did—but had a throaty accent that showed the influence of his native tongue. "Are you ready to do anything the workers and peasants of the Soviet Union require of you?"

"Comrade Colonel, I would be . . . reluctant to carry another A-bomb," Gribkov said. "I have already delivered more than my share for the *rodina.*"

"Reluctant." Dzhalalov spoke the word as if it left a foul taste in his mouth. "How do you mean, reluctant?"

"In the same way my navigator did, sir."

Had Dzhalalov looked at his dossier? The way his mouth twisted said he had. "You would kill yourself before you obeyed an order?"

"I hope I would have the courage to do that, sir. Leonid Tsederbaum did. Enough is enough. Haven't we had enough?"

Dzhalalov's flat features weren't made for showing emotion, but Boris thought he looked disgusted. "Who gave *you* the power to decide when it was enough? That is for the leaders of the state and the Party."

"Comrade Colonel, how well have they used that power?" Boris asked.

He waited for the Tajik colonel to tell him such questions were no concern of his. Dzhalalov hesitated instead. At last, he said, "Certain mistakes were made. But the man who made them is no longer among the living."

Was that the new line? It would let Stalin's successors steer away from his policies. "I see," Boris said: the most noncommittal noise he could find.

"In any case, no one will ask you to use A-bombs," Dzhalalov said. "Our agreement with the Americans and the other Western powers requires that we hold back. Would your lordship kindly consent to delivering loads of conventional weapons on the bandits in our satellites?"

He didn't use *mat*. That was smart; few who hadn't spoken Russian since they were still in the cradle could hope to do it properly. He used sarcasm instead. Perhaps because the weapon was deployed less often than obscenity, it stung more. "Yes, Comrade Colonel," Boris said. Ten tonnes of explosive delivered devastation on a scale he could understand. Ten thousand tonnes, or whatever the A-bomb was equivalent to? No. If the word *overkill* hadn't already existed, the A-bomb would have birthed it.

"I thank your most gracious lordship." Dzhalalov still wielded that rapier of wit. But he also really did sound grateful. Had some pilots here already told him no? Had despair and indifference reached that far?

Remembering how that groundcrew sergeant had reeled down the runway, Boris asked, "Sir, is maintenance on the bombers adequate? Will they take off fully loaded? That's tight even when everything works well. When it doesn't . . ." He shook his head. "If we do take off, will we fall out of the sky halfway to where we're going, or on the way back?"

"Maintenance will be seen to," Dzhalalov said.

"Sir, do you mind my asking just what that means?" Boris said. Sometimes, when top people in the Soviet Union needed something done, they would tell the people who'd do it that everything was fine.

They would do that regardless of whether it was or not, often regardless of whether they'd look to see if it was fine. And sometimes they got what they wanted, and sometimes the people who tried to do whatever needed doing had unfortunate accidents.

That was known as bad luck.

Colonel Dzhalalov scowled. "Do you doubt my word?"

"Comrade Colonel, you aren't going to be flying the mission. I am. That gives me special interest in making sure it goes as smoothly as it can." Boris spoke as diplomatically as he knew how.

Not diplomatically enough, though, for Dzhalalov's scowl darkened. "Why should I not arrest you for insubordination, disobedience, and obstruction? That would solve my problem in a hurry."

Boris shrugged. "Sir, of course you can do that if you want to. My guess is, you haven't done it because you need this mission flown, you need the guy who flies it not to mess it up, and you figure I'm the one who's most likely to be able to do it for you." Talking to a Russian, he would have said *not to fuck it up,* but the Tajik officer was keeping things clean, so he did the same.

Dzhalalov exhaled through his nose. "Fly the mission, Gribkov. The plane will be airworthy. Fuck your mother if I lie."

So he knew how to use *mat* after all. He just picked his spots. In this context, *Yob tvoyu mat'* meant something like *I really mean it.*

In the same way, Boris' "I serve the Soviet Union!" translated as *You talked me into it.* So much of what went on in the USSR went on between the lines. Then Boris asked a real question: "What's the target?"

"Budapest. The Hungarians are making a nuisance of themselves."

They'd already been making a nuisance of themselves when he got shot down after bombing Bratislava and parachuted into northwestern Hungary. The Red Army convoy that picked him up from the Hungarian secret police and took him back to Budapest had run the gauntlet coming and going. No, the Hungarians didn't love their fraternal socialist allies.

"Budapest it is, then." He saluted and left.

If the rest of the crew for the Tu-4 were thrilled to attack Hungary, they hid it very well. "What kind of airplanes can the Hungarians throw at us?" Anton Presnyakov asked.

"Yaks and Lavochkins, probably," Boris answered: Soviet leftovers from the last war. The copilot nodded. Boris went on, "I don't know if they have radar guidance." If they did, those old fighters would be almost as dangerous as modern jets. If not, then finding the Tu-4 in the black night sky would be a matter of luck.

"Will the plane be fit to fly?" Lev Vaksman asked.

"Comrade Dzhalalov promised it would. I believe him," Boris said. "If you want to ride herd on the groundcrew men while they check out the beast, go ahead."

"I'll do that," the flight engineer said. "It's my dick, too." Off he went, to the revetment that hid the bomber.

Boris didn't see him again till suppertime. "How are they doing?" he asked.

"They're working," Vaksman said, sounding surprised he could tell the pilot that much. "Most of them seem to know what they're doing. We won't fly tonight, though, no matter what the colonel wants. Tomorrow, if we're lucky."

It was the night after. Vaksman got his hands greasy and sported bandages on a cut and a burn. Armorers bombed up the Tu-4. A groundcrew man with lanterns guided Boris out of the revetment. The airstrip wasn't blacked out, which struck him as odd. But the Americans wouldn't come over Tula, and the rebellious Soviet satellites couldn't.

Getting the Tu-4 airborne was always an adventure. Boris did it, as he had so often before. His heart pounded every single time, too. But then the flight turned to routine. He droned southwest, across Russia and the Ukraine. As soon as he crossed into Hungary, antiaircraft fire started coming up. Most of it burst far below the bomber, but the reactionary bandits were very sincere.

Budapest burned below him as the plane delivered its load of death. The Red Army had wrecked the city in 1945. Now the USSR was wrecking it again, or wrecking it some more. Boris wheeled the Tu-4 away. No night fighters came up after him.

"Now," he said, consulting his written orders, "we go back to Mogilev, in Byelorussia."

"Mogilev!" Presnyakov said. "Why not Minsk? It's bigger and closer to the border."

Boris turned his thumb down. Minsk had taken an A-bomb. It wasn't worth landing at any more.

MARIAN STALEY DIDN'T KNOW what she felt about Fayvl Tabakman. She thought it might be love, but she wasn't sure. It wasn't what she'd felt for Bill when they first met. She'd fallen for him hard, head over heels. She would have gone to bed with him the first time they went out, only nice girls didn't do that. It made a man think you were loose. He might have his fun with you then, but he'd never walk down the aisle. You had to make him wait.

Everything with Fayvl was happening in slow motion by comparison. She'd known him for a while before the Russian A-bomb and Russian air defenses turned her life inside out. But then she'd known him as the little refugee man who fixed shoes so well and so cheaply, not as someone she might possibly want to sleep with.

It worked the same way for him. He might have noticed her as a pretty woman while Bill was still alive, but he wouldn't have done anything about it in a million years. She would have sent him packing if he'd tried, and in a hurry, too. He had to know it then.

Not so much now. *Loss draws loss,* Marian thought. The Nazis had robbed him of his wife and children; the Communists had taken her husband. They shared something she'd never wanted to know, but knowing someone else who knew it with her took—a little—pain away.

"Does it bother you that I'm not Jewish?" she asked him one night.

"In the old country, it would. Here . . ." He shrugged. "Less. I like you no matter what religion you got. Does it bother you I *am* a Jew?"

"No," Marian said at once. "You're just you. The Jewish people I've known haven't been any different from anybody else. Not because they were Jewish, anyhow."

"Is funny. I hear lots of Americans say that. Not all Americans, but lots of," Fayvl said. "In Poland, you never hear like that from a *goy.* In Poland, Jews always different. Americans, they don't care so much."

"Why do you suppose that is?" Marian asked.

"I used to think was because American *goyim* all wonderful people and they don't hate nobody," Tabakman said. "Then I'm here a *bissel* longer, and I see is not so. Like Poles and Germans and Russians and Hungarians and everybody else got Jews to beat on, Americans got *shvartzers.*"

"*Shvartzers?*" Marian pronounced the unfamiliar word as well as she could, which wasn't very.

"Negroes," Fayvl said with precision. "Jews got it easy here on account of Americans, they hate somebody else worser."

Marian wanted to tell him that he was wrong, that everybody in America got along with everybody else. She wanted to, but the words stuck in her throat. She remembered the race riots in Detroit during the last war, and the lynchings and segregation that persisted to this day in the South. She didn't think she'd ever said *kike*, but she knew she'd come out with *nigger* a few times.

Quietly, she said, "You haven't been here that long, but you see things about my country I never noticed."

"I don't grow up here. Is to me not like to a fish water. You go to Poland, Poland like it was, Poland before Nazis and Russians, I bet you show me plenty I don't know."

"Maybe," Marian said, in lieu of *I doubt it.* She stood up. "I feel like another cup of coffee. How about you?"

"Please." As usual, he showed off an Old World courtliness. Up till now, she'd found it charming. She'd never wondered how and why he'd had to acquire it. A fussily polite Jew in Poland might have a better chance of keeping his Christian neighbors from deciding to beat him up or burn down his house.

Heating up the coffee and putting in cream and sugar gave her a few minutes away from the problems of Europe and the somewhat—but only somewhat—different problems of the United States. She and Bill hadn't talked about things like this when they were going together. They hadn't talked about things like this after they got married, either.

She wondered why. Her best guess—and it would never be more than a best guess now, because she couldn't ask Bill about it any more— was that he'd wanted to shield her from the dark side of things. He'd seen war; he'd risked his life and had friends lose theirs while she stayed thousands of miles away from danger and death.

I know danger now, by God, she thought, carrying the steaming cups of coffee back to the living room. She'd missed her own death by very little, either from her house crushing her or from radiation sickness. And she knew the death of the one she'd loved best. Fayvl's wound there was older but went even deeper. He'd lost his children along with his wife.

"T'ank you so much," he murmured when she gave him the coffee. He sighed and nodded. "Is good."

"It's coffee." She shrugged. "It's been sitting in the pot too long. It's getting bitter."

"Is good," Fayvl insisted. "Not muddy instant, like in Camp No-where. Not ground acorns and chicory, like in Europe during the war. Coffee."

He had a knack for looking on the bright side of things that Marian wished she could match. She wondered how he did it when he'd seen so much more darkness than she had. Slowly, she set her half-full cup back in its saucer. "Fayvl," she said, and then stopped.

"What is?" he asked when she didn't go on.

"If you want to . . ." She ran down again, then brought the words out in a rush: "If you want to, I guess we can. If you want to." Her face felt on fire. Nice girls didn't talk like that. Well, she hadn't been a nice girl for a long time, and she hadn't liked herself much while she was.

He looked at her. "You sure?" he asked.

She nodded. "It's about time, isn't it? It's past time, really. Let me just make certain Linda's down for the count." She stuck her head into the hall and listened. Only slow, steady breathing floated out of her daughter's bedroom. She nodded again and turned back to Fayvl. "Come on."

After he walked into her bedroom with her, she closed the door behind them. She did it as quietly as she could; her habit was to leave it open. It was very dark in there. "Do you want me to turn on the lamp by the bed?" she whispered.

"Will be fine like it is," he whispered back.

They reached for each other at the same time. They clung to each other, helped each other out of their clothes, then clung to each other again. "It's this way," Marian said, and took the two crabwise steps that guided him to the bed. They lay down together.

First times were always strange. Neither of them was sure of just what the other liked. After a while, Fayvl surprised her by going down on her without being asked (Bill had almost always needed cajoling). She liked that fine, or better than fine. His tongue was warm and quick and knowing. "Oh," she sighed, and "Oh" again. She reached down to hold him there. He wasn't going anywhere, but she did it even so.

When her breathing steadied and her heartbeat slowed, she returned the favor. She'd often needed cajoling herself with Bill. Fayvl didn't have to know that, though. "Easy," he said before too long. "Is something else, too."

He poised himself above her. "Ah," she said when he went in. He'd already brought her joy. She did her best to make sure he got some, too. At the end, he pulled out of her and squirted his hot seed onto her belly and her bush.

"Good. I was able to be careful." He sounded pleased with himself. "Don't want to have to think about a baby."

"No," Marian agreed. Pulling out was less reliable than wearing a rubber, but it was bound to be better than nothing. "Let me up, will you?" When he did, she grabbed a Kleenex from the box on her night-stand and did some quick mopping. "I'm going into the bathroom to clean up. I'll be right back."

She was still naked. If Linda popped out . . . But Linda, bless her, slept like a log. When Marian came back, Fayvl took his turn in the john. He carried his clothes in there and came back dressed. By then, she'd put on a housecoat. *So much for romance,* she thought with a wry smile.

"I should oughta go," he said. She didn't try to tell him no.

Romance briefly returned when he kissed her goodbye. Off he went into the darkness. Marian got ready for sleep. She kept wondering whether guilt would grab hold of her. It didn't. The thought that filled her mind was the same one she'd had before. *We should have done this a while ago.*

Vasili Yasevich squatted in a foxhole. Machine-gun bullets cracked past over his head. Every so often, he'd see a red tracer. The USSR could call the Polish rebels bandits as often and as loudly as it pleased. They were stubborn and brave no matter what it called them.

He'd learned a lot about soldiering the past few weeks. *Baptism by total immersion,* he thought. He wasn't late hitting the dirt any more. He could dig a hole in nothing flat. He could camouflage it once it was dug, too. He read ground as easily as he read a newspaper.

But the most important thing he'd learned was, he didn't want to be a soldier. He especially didn't want to be a Red Army soldier. The idea that the Communist Party of the Soviet Union was using him to help reconquer a country that hated Russia made him want to puke. The only problem was, his comrades or the unsmiling MGB sons of bitches not far behind the line would kill him if he tried to do anything about the way he felt.

There were always angles, though. You just had to find one. Growing up in Harbin made him sure of that. Chinese society was built on angles, on looking for any edge you could find and then riding it for all you were worth. Bribery and favors called in counted for more in China than bullets ever had.

"Fuck your mothers, Russian cunts!" a Russian-speaking Pole shouted. A moment later, half a dozen others took up the call.

"A dog fucked your mothers in the ass!" Yuri yelled back. Vasili clapped both his hands to his mouth to keep from giggling. He ignored the Poles' insults. They threw them out the same way they sprayed ammunition around: in the hope that some would hurt.

Yuri didn't see things that way. To the veteran with the expensive dentistry, you returned fire whenever you got the chance. If he wanted to get excited about it, he could. Vasili didn't see the point.

He might have struck a nerve. The Poles had been content to hose down the Soviet lines with that machine gun and with rifle fire. Now mortar bombs started coming in, too. Mortars were most of what the Poles used for artillery. Vasili stopped wanting to giggle. He folded himself into the smallest ball he could and huddled in the bottom of the hole. The thick mound of dirt in front of it shielded him from bullets. Mortar rounds dropped almost straight down. If one dropped straight down onto you, you had to hope everything ended in a hurry.

Red Army mortars and, a few minutes later, field guns answered the Poles. From what Yuri said, the Russians had been in love with mortars for years. They gave infantry firepower it couldn't get any other way.

After ten or fifteen minutes, the heavy stuff on both sides let up. Small-arms fire went on. From what Vasili had seen, some small-arms fire went on just about all the time when two armies bumped into each other. As long as it wasn't too heavy or too close, you learned not to pay attention to it.

But then a Russian let out a shout of alarm: "Look out! They're coming!" He punctuated it with a long, ripping burst from his submachine gun. Most of those bullets would fly high and wide, but maybe they'd make the Poles keep their heads down.

Vasili popped out of his hole, fired a couple of shots from his rifle, and ducked back down again. He wasn't keen on killing Poles, but he didn't want them killing him, either.

"By the Devil's uncle, how many of those pussies are there?" Yuri shouted. "They'd better get the artillery going again, or we're all in deep shit."

That made Vasili peer over his earthen parapet again and fire at the Poles. He thought he hit one of them, but an enemy round almost hit him, so he disappeared again. If a sniper was drawing a bead on the foxhole . . . *That wouldn't be so good, would it?* he thought unhappily.

Someone yelled, "Back! Back to the far side of the creek!"

Even as Yuri shouted "Don't do it! It's a trick!", quite a few Red Army soldiers, obedient as usual, left their holes and started to retreat . . . whereupon the waiting Poles cut them down. Fighting an enemy who spoke your language had all kinds of horrible complications.

Some of the bandits' bullets were coming from the flanks now, not from in front. That couldn't be good, either. "Hey, Yuri, what do we do now?" Vasili called.

"Save the last bullet for yourself. You don't want to let the bandits capture you," the veteran answered. That was less encouraging than anything Vasili wanted to hear.

The next interesting question was, was Yuri right? Maybe getting captured was exactly what Vasili wanted. He had more sympathy for the Poles than he did for the regime whose uniform he wore. Of course, the bandits didn't know that. To them, he was just another goddamn Russian occupier. Even if he put his hands up, they might kill him for the fun of it. They might do it in some lingering and humorous way, too, rather than with the abrupt simplicity he could use to finish himself.

If he didn't bug out pretty damn quick, he'd find out exactly what they'd do. They'd caught the Red Army with its pants down here, and they were taking advantage of it.

He scrambled out of his foxhole and ran for that creek. He would have given himself up to the Poles if he'd thought they had a prayer of beating the Russians, but he didn't. Spirit and courage took you only so far. The Japanese in Manchukuo had had plenty of spirit and courage in August 1945. The Red Army steamrollered them even so. He guessed it would do the same thing here.

Sometimes all your calculations weren't worth a damn. As Vasili ran, he tripped over a root and fell on his face. He hit hard. He got dirt in his eyes and dirt in his mouth. When he brushed at his face, his fingers came away bloody—he'd smashed his nose, too.

He was rubbing at his eyes and groping for his PPD when somebody screamed, "*Rukhi verkh, Russki metyeryebyets!*" It wasn't very good Russian, but he understood it. *Hands up, Russian motherfucker!* was hard to get wrong.

Nerves thrilling with fear, he raised his hands. Two Poles grabbed him and jerked him to his feet. Another covered him with a PPSh. One of the two frisked him. He didn't have much worth stealing. What he had, they stole. The man with the submachine gun asked, "Holdout weapon? You don't tell us and we find it anyway, you're dead meat."

"Right boot," Vasili answered dully. They relieved him of the little knife he carried there.

"Well, come on," the Pole with the submachine gun said. Vasili lurched away from his former comrades. The Polish rebels hadn't killed him out of hand, anyhow. The fellow with the PPSh asked, "You fight to liberate us before you fight now to enslave us?"

"No." Vasili wanted to laugh. "I was in Harbin through the last war."

"Where in Russia is Harbin? I never heard of it."

"Not in Russia. In China."

"Tell me another one," the Pole scoffed. "If you were in China, you'd speak Chinese, right?"

"Of course I speak Chinese, you stupid turtle," Vasili snapped in that language. If anything, he spoke it better than Russian. He thought in it more than half the time, though less often lately.

"Fuck me. Sounds like you do." The bandit sounded astonished. "But if you were in China, how'd you end up a Red Army asshole?"

"It's a long story. The short part is, Mao's men were so nasty, I hoped

Stalin's would be better. So I went from Manchuria to Siberia. It was about as bad—not quite the same, but nothing great. Then the Russians drafted me. They would have thrown me in the gulag if I said no. That's how I wound up here."

"Fuck me," the Pole repeated. "I'll take you to the major, let him figure you out. Get moving, prick." Vasili got moving. Anything that kept him alive a while longer sounded good to him.

After the wretched breakfast, after the hurried and stinking latrine call, Luisa Hozzel joined her work gang. Aside from the guards' new uncertainty, nothing much had changed in the gulag after Stalin's death. Luisa suspected the authorities in Moscow, or wherever Soviet authorities worked from these days, had long since forgotten they'd ever set up this camp.

She looked around for Trudl Bachman so she could share the conceit. They'd stood side by side in the early-morning lineup. She knew Trudl hadn't reported to sick call or anything—sick call might have been the biggest waste of time in the history of the world. Going to the camp infirmary was more likely to make you worse than better, and everybody knew it.

They started out toward the taiga, carrying the axes and saws they'd use to knock down pines. The guards were alert: axes and saws could turn into weapons in the blink of an eye. Luisa'd daydreamed of smashing in a guard's head if she ever got the chance. She didn't have the nerve, but what were daydreams for but thinking about things you dared not do?

She casually found a place near an Asiatic guard who was more easygoing than most of the bastards with machine pistols. "How it goes, Mogamed?" she asked in her bad Russian.

"It goes," he answered. His Russian wasn't a whole lot more fluent than hers. "How is with you, German lady?"

"It goes," Luisa echoed. "I don't see Trudl. You know where she is?"

"She your friend, yes? She your work partner, yes? Or she was. How come you not know where she is?" Mogamed said.

"I don't know why I don't know where." Luisa listened to that after she said it, to make sure it meant what she wanted. Satisfied that it did, she went on, "You know where?"

"*Da.*" What could only be a smirk crossed Mogamed's flattish face. "Her back inside camp."

"Is she sick? Not at sick call."

"No, not sick." Mogamed smirked some more. "Her back in camp with friend."

"With friend?" Luisa didn't like repeating his words over and over, but she found she couldn't help herself. What he said made no sense for a few seconds. Then, when she noticed the masculine ending on *friend,* it did. Luisa gasped in horror. "You mean she —?" She broke off. She couldn't make herself go on.

"She fucking him, *da,*" Mogamed said matter-of-factly. "He have pull to keep her out of work gang."

"*Der Herr Gott im Himmel!*" Luisa burst out—Russian wasn't enough to satisfy her. Trudl'd wavered more than she had herself when it came to rejecting advances from the guards and trusties. She'd wavered, but she hadn't fallen. Not till now she hadn't, that was.

It couldn't have been love. Both male *zeks* and guards were among the least lovable men Luisa had ever imagined, much less met. But when you were half starved all the time, when you were more than half exhausted all the time, lying down with somebody in exchange for more food or for work inside the barbed wire might not seem such a bad bargain.

Trudl must have decided she'd never see Germany again. If you thought that way, making the best of the gulag had to seem more sensible. Luisa still clung to hope. Here, as in the Nazi concentration camps, they did their best to take it away from you. Their best was mighty good, too.

But Luisa knew how stubborn she was. If she'd had any doubts, things Gustav said would have removed them. But she had none. She understood herself pretty well. Dying seemed better to her than giving a guard any satisfaction—and you could take that however you pleased.

She'd thought Trudl felt the same way. Finding out she didn't made the axe on Luisa's shoulder seem fifty kilos. She trudged out to the stretch of forest the work gang was systematically denuding. Then she had fresh trouble—there she was, without her work partner.

Some of the female *zeks* in the gang smirked the way Mogamed had. They knew why Trudl wasn't there. How many of them were close to making the same choice she had?

Finally, Luisa hooked on as a helper with two other German women. Their names were Elena and Susanna. They had her do the hard, rough work, cutting a trunk into manageable lengths and trimming branches from those lengths while they started felling another pine. She was a spare wheel and a labor-saving device for them, nothing more.

The day seemed to go on forever. Days in the taiga often did, especially when summer stretched them like elastic. This was worse than usual. She felt more dead than alive by the time the guards finally marched the gang back to the camp. Her progress was more shamble than march, but she liked the direction in which she was going.

When they got back, the guards counted the tools of the lumberjack's trade as carefully as they would soon count the *zeks*. Worries over weapons, again. If the women managed to hide some, they might rise up against their oppressors. Luisa thought that a forlorn hope, but the guards didn't.

Once the axes and saws were seen to be all present and accounted for, the prisoners took their places for the evening lineup and count. Luisa saw Trudl up near the front of the square. She couldn't get near her. She had to stand where she was while the guards tried to get the camp to come out straight. They had to do it twice before they got an answer they liked. Since that happened almost as often as not, Luisa could only tiredly fume.

Then it was supper. As always, she emptied her bowl in nothing flat and wolfed down her chunk of husk-filled black bread. The noisome latrines again after that, and back to the barracks. The *zeks* had a little time to themselves after that, till lights-out forced quiet on them.

Trudl's bunk wasn't far from Luisa's. Luisa went over to her and said, "I missed you in the woods today."

"I don't want to talk about it." Trudl's chin rose.

"Is it worth it?" Luisa asked.

"I'm not hungry. Do you hear me? I'm not hungry," Trudl said. "For the very first time since they hauled us out of Fulda, I'm not hungry. I didn't remember what it was like to have enough to eat. I'm not dead-tired, either. Can you believe that?"

Luisa had trouble recalling what a full belly and a little extra energy felt like. She hadn't known such luxuries since they got taken out of Germany, either. But she said, "One of these days, we'll go home again. What will you do then?"

"Home?" Trudl laughed raucously. "We're never going home. We'll be in Siberia till they throw us into a hole in the ground."

"I don't believe that. I *won't* believe that," Luisa said.

"Believe whatever you want. But believe *this,* too." Trudl grabbed Luisa's arm and pulled back the sleeve of her quilted tunic. Beneath dirt and mosquito bites, the skin stretched tight over tendons and bones. The arm looked hardly thicker than a broomstick. "How much longer can you last?"

"You're as skinny as I am," Luisa said.

"I am *now.* I won't be for much longer. That's why I'm doing . . . what I'm doing. If I die tomorrow and they throw out my carcass, the wolves will leave it alone—not enough meat on it to be worth eating," Trudl said. "I don't want to starve to death or get worked to death. I don't want you dying like that either, Luisa."

"If living means fucking one of these filthy pigdogs, I'd sooner die," Luisa said.

Her husband's boss' wife—how strange to recall that that was what Trudl had been back in far-off, longed-for Fulda—only sighed. "Well, I can't make you," she said. "But we aren't going home. That's the long and short of it. We aren't. We've got to make the best of things here."

Luisa shook her head. She turned and walked back to her own bunk, not looking over her shoulder even once.

Bruce McNulty had leave. Getting a weekend pass was the easiest thing in the world for B-29 pilots these days. They weren't flying missions against the Russians now that this uneasy peace seemed to have taken hold. That being so, they were about as useful around the base as baby buggies in a steel mill.

He took the train down to London. His neat blue U.S. Air Force uniform made him stand out among the Englishmen with whom he rode. That wasn't because it was American; it was because it was nearly new. The limeys wore a motley assortment of threadbare tweeds and houndstooths and checks, many carefully patched and darned. Hardly any of their clothes dated from after 1939: cut and wear testified to that. They hadn't eased up on rationing after the last war ended. They hadn't been able to. They'd bankrupted themselves beating Hitler. Afterwards, they'd stayed busy trying to hold on to their empire. They hadn't had much luck there.

A tall, skinny fellow with bad teeth sitting across the compartment nodded to Bruce and said, "'Ere, Yank, are those a pilot's wings you've got on?"

"That's right." Bruce nodded.

"What d'you fly, you don't mind my asking?"

"Superfort." Bruce wondered if the Englishman would lay into him as a wholesaler of death. He laid into himself that way sometimes, usually after he'd had a pint or two too many.

But the fellow grinned, showing off more brown and pitted enamel. "Ah, one o' the big 'uns," he said. Bruce had to work to follow his northern accent. "Last go, I were a Lanc mechanic meself."

"They were good planes." Bruce meant it. Lancashires had carried the load for the RAF's night-bombing campaign against Germany. But they were even more comprehensively obsolete than B-29s these days. So were the Lincolns that had succeeded them.

When Bruce got off the train, he went to the tube station that was part of the same building. He was no Londoner, to know which route he needed before he stepped into the Underground. But he had a map of the system. It was a hell of a lot simpler than the maps he'd read planning flights over Germany in the last war and Russia and the satellites this time again.

Twenty minutes later, he walked into the British Museum. London had been basically the capital of the world for a couple of hundred years; its greatness was only just now passing. British explorers and archeologists and collectors of all sorts had brought back the best of what they found. And here it was, on organized display.

Sumerian, Babylonian, Assyrian, and Egyptian art from the dawn of civilization. Greek pots with shapes of breathtaking purity. The Elgin Marbles, taken from the Parthenon (Greece wanted them back, but the British Museum didn't have to pay any attention to Greece). Roman statues that had inspired countless inept imitations back in the States. Coins and helmets and swords and even a ship from the Dark Ages. He wandered and stared and wandered and stared some more. You could lose yourself, or lose days, here.

He wound up in the Reading Room. Scholars and crackpots studied one volume or another at the polished tables. How were you supposed to tell which was which, though? Karl Marx did a lot of his research in this domed chamber. Which had he been? Opinions varied to this day. They'd fought over the variation with atom bombs, too.

Bruce shivered, though the Reading Room was warm by English standards. He'd brooded now and again about all the human lives he'd blown to radioactive dust. But here he was imagining some Soviet counterpart of his destroying, disintegrating, the Elgin Marbles and everything else this miracle of a building held. That would have been a bigger crime against humanity than taking out a whole ordinary city, wouldn't it?

He shivered again. What treasures had he blasted to hell and gone himself? He had no idea. Till this moment, the question had never once crossed his mind. Now it would haunt him along with all the unquiet ghosts of those he'd killed. He wondered how he ever got to sleep without phenobarbital.

If you took enough of that crap, of course, or if you took it after you'd done some heavy drinking, you might not wake up the next morning. *And would that be such a bad thing?* he wondered. Unless you owned a mechanism that let you turn off your conscience, did you have any business dropping A-bombs?

Daisy'd known what he did, but she hadn't *known* what he did till the Russians leveled Fakenham when they took out the air base at nearby Sculthorpe. After that, she understood because she was holding on to the shitty end of the stick. And Bruce understood because he saw how the kind of thing he did made someone he loved suffer.

Where ignorance is bliss, 'tis folly to be wise. Somewhere not far from here, Shakespeare had inked a goose-quill pen and put those words on paper. Or was it Shakespeare? Somebody more recent? Bruce couldn't bring up enough English Lit to remember. Whoever it was, he'd had a pretty good notion of what he was talking about, all right, and a Russian bomb would have sent wherever he'd written up in fire and smoke along with the museum.

Right around the corner from the British Museum stood a fish-and-chips shop, as homely as the museum was grand. The place might have been homely, but it was good. Bruce doused his food in malt vinegar and dug in. "Wasn't sure if you'd know to do that, you bein' from the States an' all," the counterman said.

"Oh, yeah. I've been here a while," Bruce answered with his mouth full. A couple of the chips had ink stains from their newspaper wrapping. He ate them anyway. The English did it all the time. If it didn't hurt them, chances were he'd also live through it.

He looked at his map again. The Tower of London wasn't far away—only a few tube stops. Off he went. When he emerged from the Underground and walked into the Tower, he felt as if he'd fallen back into the sixteenth century. Gaudily uniformed Beefeaters carrying halberds patrolled the grounds.

Bruce was tempted to laugh at their ridiculous getup. A second glance made him change his mind. The men in those silly clothes looked hard and capable; several of them wore nasty scars along with their silks and brocade. They were combat veterans for sure. He wouldn't have been surprised if they came out of the elite SAS. If they did, they would be very bad news even with only those overgrown tin openers in their hands.

One of their number fed some of the half-tame ravens that strutted and flapped as if they owned the place. They probably thought they did. A raven with a bit of meat still dangling from its big, sharp beak cocked its head to one side and stared at Bruce with a disconcertingly knowing black eye. The beak opened and closed. The scrap of meat disappeared.

When Bruce looked at his wristwatch, he muttered under his breath. How had it got to be three o'clock already? He headed back to the tube station. The hotel where he'd booked a room for the night was close to Piccadilly Circus. He wanted to make sure everything was okay there before he figured out where to eat and what to do tonight.

If he wanted company for the evening, he wouldn't have any trouble finding it. Piccadilly Circus swarmed with women of easy virtue. Some were bold as brass; others, you had to look at two or three times to be sure. His American uniform drew them the way a magnet drew iron filings. During the last war, Englishmen had complained that Yanks were overpaid, oversexed, and over here. It was only too plainly the *overpaid* part that drew the girls now.

He said "No thanks" several times. Then he shortened it to "No." Pretty soon, it was "Go away." By the time he found the hotel, he was yelling "Get lost!" One gal tried to follow him into the lobby anyway.

The doorman discouraged her. She swore at him. He made as if to swat her on the backside. She flounced off. The doorman touched the brim of his cap to Bruce. "Popular, sir, are you?"

"Christ, I hope not!" Bruce blurted. The doorman laughed. Bruce wasn't so sure it was funny.

MARIAN STALEY DUMPED CHEERIOS into a bowl. She poured in milk. It was real milk, straight from the cow (well, pasteurized, but that made it safer), not the horrible powdered crap they'd used all the time at Camp Nowhere. Slices of bananas finished breakfast.

"Come on, eat up," she told Linda. "I've got to take you over to Betsy's and then head for work." Having Betsy watch Linda all day during summer ate up too much of her paycheck, but her daughter was too little to leave her in the house by herself.

Linda spooned up a couple of bites. Then she stopped and said, "Mommy?"

"What is it?" Marian asked impatiently. "Why are you wasting time?"

"Mommy, is Mr. Tabakman gonna be my new daddy?"

Whatever Marian expected, that wasn't it. "Where did you get that idea?" she asked after a pause longer than she would have liked.

"Betsy asked me about it," Linda said as she started to eat again. "Is he gonna be, Mommy? I'd like to have a daddy again, and Mr. Tabakman's a nice man, isn't he?"

"He *is* a nice man," Marian agreed. "I like him very much. He likes me, too—"

"I know *that*," Linda broke in, as if her mother had lost points for coming out with the obvious.

Bravely, Marian went on, "And he likes you, too."

"Well, then." By the way Linda said it, nothing else needed saying. Things looked real simple when you were six.

But Marian wasn't six any more. Neither was Fayvl Tabakman. Marian picked her words with care: "Fayvl and I, we'll see how much we like each other, and we'll see how we get along, and then we'll decide if we want to get married. And if we do, he will be your new daddy. Okay?"

"Okay." Linda dug into her Cheerios again, this time in earnest. She stopped only once, to say, "I hope so."

Well, I hope so, too, Marian thought. She'd hoped so for a while now, or she wouldn't have slept with Fayvl. She'd hardly admitted it to herself, though. *And I hope Betsy just shuts the hell up from here on out.* The teenage babysitter couldn't very well not see that she and the cobbler were going together. She couldn't very well keep from jumping to conclusions about what that meant, either. But did she have to start grilling Linda to see if she was right?

Marian sighed. Betsy probably did. Weed wasn't the kind of place where a lot of big things happened. The campaign to get an ambulance for the town had gone on for years, not months. When little things were all you had to wonder and gossip about, of course you made the most of them.

She took Linda over to the babysitter's house. She didn't say anything to Betsy about keeping quiet. She knew too well that would only make Betsy jump to more conclusions and blab more. Sometimes the best thing you could do was pretend you hadn't had a nerve hit.

Linda gave Marian a dutiful kiss. Marian walked back to her yellow Studebaker. She slid in, pulled out the choke, and started the engine. Then it was off to another exciting, fun-filled day at the Shasta Lumber Company.

Typing, filing, preparing invoices, answering the telephone, gabbing with the other clerks in the office . . . None of it, except the gabbing, was anything Marian would have done for fun. But she wasn't doing it for fun. She was getting paid. Now that she'd been there a while, they'd bumped her up to a buck and a half an hour. All of the raise, of course, went straight into Betsy's pocket.

Thanks to Betsy, Marian brought her lunch more often and ate at the diner less. Sometimes she would take her brown bag over to Fayvl's shop and eat with him. That made the other girls—one of them had to be sixty, but they were all girls—smile and even giggle. It doubtless made them gossip about her while she wasn't there, but she couldn't do anything about that.

She hadn't planned to have lunch with Fayvl today, but she decided to a few minutes before noon rolled around. His face lit up when she walked in. She liked that. He turned the sign in the window from OPEN to CLOSED. "What's new with you?" he asked. His own lunch was a salami-and-pickle sandwich on rye bread, an orange, and a banana. Hers was ham-and-cheese on the Wonder Bread Linda liked, with a banana and an apple.

She didn't beat around the bush: "This morning, Linda asked me if you were going to be her new daddy."

"Did she?" Tabakman said. Marian nodded. He took a bite from his sandwich. After he swallowed, he asked, "*Nu?* What you told her?"

"I said we hadn't decided yet, but that if we kept on liking each other the way we have so far, you might. You probably would, in fact."

"Thanks. That sounds pretty good." He nodded.

"She likes you. She said so. But you already knew that, right?"

Fayvl nodded again. "Oh, yes. I always like her, even before the bomb falls. She has—what you say?—she has grit, that one."

Marian just thought of Linda as her little girl. But maybe Fayvl saw something she hadn't. Linda had come through the horror of the A-bomb attack and the different, slower horror of Camp Nowhere and the loss of a father, and here she was, a reasonably happy little girl in spite of it all. If that didn't take grit, Marian couldn't see what would.

She wondered if Linda reminded Fayvl of one his own murdered children. He'd hinted at that once or twice back at the camp. She didn't ask him. It wasn't so much that she didn't want to know as that she didn't want to hurt him by making him remember what he'd gone through in Poland.

He said, "I would be proud to be the daddy of a little one like that."

"Well, mister, I'd say your chances are getting better by the day," Marian answered. "Can I scrounge a cigarette from you?" She was only a sometime smoker, but this seemed like a pretty good sometime.

"Sure." He gave her his pack of Old Golds, then took one himself after she returned it. He lit hers and his with a Zippo. "This is a fine tool," he said as he put it back in his pocket. "It does what they say it does. You want a light, you got a light. Every time."

"That's good." Marian took a drag and coughed. No, she didn't have the habit the way somebody who went through a pack or two a day did.

Fayvl smoked with sober intensity. It gave him an excuse for not doing anything else for a little while. When he stubbed out the cigarette, he looked down at his scarred hands. Still eyeing them and not her, he said, "You know—you got to know—I'm going to ask you sooner or later if you want to marry me."

"Yes, I know that," Marian said in a low voice.

"Didn't want to be too quick," Tabakman said. "I know you got *tsuris* of your own, your poor husband not coming back. You need time to take care of that inside yourself."

"Thank you," she said, more softly still.

Fayvl shrugged. "You got to understand, I know how this is. If I don't know, we couldn't put up with each other, I think."

"I think you're right."

"Yeah," he said. "But now Linda wants to know what's what, and it ain't like we haven't, well, you know." His Old Country reticence about such things made him sound downright Victorian. "So, *nu*, I guess I should ought to ask you now, *eppis*. You want you should marry me, Marian?"

As he said, the question wasn't exactly a surprise. It made her gasp just the same. "Yes, I'll marry you," she said. "Linda needs a father, and you'll be a good one." She realized she needed more than that. "And I love you. You're a rock of a man, you know?"

"Some rock!" He snorted. "Smashed to pieces, rolled around, washed up half the world from where I started."

"Grit," Marian said. "That's what you called it with Linda. Takes one to know one, is what people say in English."

"Huh!" He didn't sound as if he believed that. "I do best I can for you and the girl. I love you, too, you know." Marian nodded, because she did know it. It was the biggest reason she'd said yes.

When Cade Curtis woke up from his latest operation, he thought for a woozy moment that he'd died and gone to heaven. That wasn't a muddy, smelly, unshaven dogface looking down at him. It was one of the prettier girls he'd ever seen. Only the surgical mask covering her mouth and nose made him realize she was a nurse, not an angel.

"How'd it go?" he rasped—his throat seemed surfaced with sandpaper.

"Here." She put a paper cup to his lips. He opened his mouth. Ice chips spilled into it. They didn't want to give you water right after you shook off the ether. You might drown or something. But ice chips were okay. He sucked on them and swallowed the melt.

When he said "How'd it go?" again, his voice was no worse than a ragged parody of the one he usually used.

"Captain, I wasn't in the OR," she said. Her sky-blue eyes went from warm to wary. "Dr. Eckhardt will have to tell you about what they did this time."

"My leg feels funny," Cade said.

"Where?" she asked.

"Down by the toes," Cade answered. "They itch. I can't feel anything up above them, but they itch." He tried to wiggle them. He couldn't tell whether he did or not. *You* are *groggy,* he thought . . . groggily.

"I'll get Dr. Eckhardt. He can explain everything to you." The nurse wheeled and hurried away.

Dr. Eckhardt came over to the bedside a few minutes later, tailed by the nurse. He didn't look like a doctor. Had Cade tried to guess what he did for a living, defensive tackle would have come a long way ahead of surgeon. He was big as an ox, broad-shouldered and slow-moving. "How are you doing?" he asked.

"My toes itch," Cade said. "What did you do to me this time?" He'd had four or five operations; he couldn't remember which. *Time flies when you're having fun* ran through his mind.

Like the nurse, Eckhardt was still wearing a mask. He sighed, which made the cotton gauze whuffle out. "Son, I'm sorry as hell, but we had to take the leg off below the knee," he said. "We pumped all the penicillin and erythromycin we could into you, but the circulation from the wound down was just too lousy to let 'em do everything they should. If we didn't amputate, you would've been dead in a week."

Cade heard the words. He understood them, after a fashion. But it seemed as if the doctor had to be talking about someone else. "You must have the wrong patient, Doc," he said. "I've still got my leg. How can my toes itch if I don't have my leg?"

"That's called phantom pain," Dr. Eckhardt answered. "Sometimes it goes away pretty soon; sometimes it lasts for years. But we gave you a good stump, with plenty of flesh. Once you heal and you get your prosthetic fitted, you should be able to move around almost as well as you did before you got hit."

"You're crazy," Cade said. It wasn't just coming out from under the anesthetic that made him so loopy. He realized they'd pumped even more morphine than usual into him after surgery. The dope made everything distant and unimportant, including the fine philosophical point of whether you needed to own real toes to have them itch.

"We'll get you back to the ward," Eckhardt told him. "Maybe you'll go back down into sleep. That may do you some good. And when you wake up again, you'll be a little more with it."

"I'm just fine," Cade protested, but his eyelids were sliding shut. He remembered the doctor and the nurse starting to move his bed. He even remembered realizing it must have wheels and feeling very clever. But he never remembered getting to the ward.

He came back to himself some indeterminate time later. Not just his toes hurt then. The whole leg seemed to have been hit by napalm. He must have made some kind of noise because a nurse—not such a pretty one—came over and asked, "You in pain, soldier?"

"Yes," Cade whispered. And an A-bomb blast was warm, and the ocean was moist, and. . . .

She gave him a shot. The pain didn't disappear, but it drew back to a place where he could deal with it. That seemed miracle enough for the moment. Cade didn't care if he turned into an addict who prowled the streets looking for a pusher to sell him his next shot. Without morphine, the next shot he would have asked for was one right between the eyes.

Wait, he said to himself. The doctor—Eckhardt, that was his name— had told him they'd amputated his leg. How was he supposed to prowl around looking for his next fix if he had only one leg?

Slowly (he couldn't think any other way with the drug in his veins), he began to wonder about everything else the amputation would do to his life. *Call me Stumpy,* he thought, but it wasn't funny. What kind of girl would want to go out with a cripple, much less marry one? The worry felt less urgent than it would have if he weren't full of morphine, but it was still there.

And I'm never going to be a general, he realized. It wasn't likely that an ROTC kid would ever wear stars on his shoulders, but it sure wouldn't happen now. In spite of everything, it might have if he'd stayed whole. The past two years, war had been all he knew, and he'd shown the brass he was good at it. (He'd also shown them he was a loose cannon, but he didn't dwell on that.) If he'd stayed in, he could have kept rising.

Not without half his leg, though. They'd pin a Purple Heart on him to go with his Bronze Star, and then they'd hand him an honorable discharge. They might even promote him to major while they were at it: a pat on the ass to go with the kick out the door. He'd just been demobilized in more ways than one.

The nurse came back with a glass full of golden liquid and a straw. "Can you drink some apple juice?" she asked.

"Yes, please," he said. She cranked up the front end of his bed. The straw had a corrugated section up above the juice line that let it bend without closing up. Cade had never seen one like it before. He marveled at how clever it was. He also marveled at how good the cold apple juice tasted. If the nurse hadn't told him what it was, he might have taken it for the nectar of the gods.

Now that he'd been elevated, he could look down at himself and see what was what . . . and what wasn't. Sure as hell, the shapes of his two legs—or rather, his leg and a half—under the sheets didn't match. The morphine kept him from getting too upset about it.

"They really took it off," he said, more wonder than distress in his voice.

"I'm afraid so, yes," the nurse said. "I'm sorry."

"Me, too," Cade said. Then something else crossed his mind. "Hey, what happened to Jimmy? Uh, the Korean soldier who brought me back to the aid station?" He'd had too many worries of his own lately even to think about Jimmy. That shamed him, but there it was.

Her nostrils flared. "You can't expect me to know anything about one gook or another," Her expression showed that, if she hadn't been brought up so well, she would have said *one goddamn gook or another.*

"Jimmy's no gook!" Even doped silly, Cade was sure of that. "He's a better American than most of the Americans I know. Can you find out what's up with him? Please?"

"Don't worry about it right now. Just worry about getting better." The nurse might have been soothing a six-year-old with a cold.

Trouble was, it worked, at least for the moment. Cade didn't have the energy to keep up the argument. He was both too fresh from the operating room and too doped up to have the energy for much of anything. Holding his eyes open seemed as hard as lifting heavy barbells.

But he didn't forget. Jimmy was his obligation. He wouldn't have abandoned a kitten he rescued from a cruel master. He owed Jimmy at least that much. The powers that be wouldn't think so. Cade didn't give a damn about the powers that be.

Casimir the Polish bandit chieftain—he called himself a major, but he wasn't exactly, not in the military sense—scowled at Vasili Yasevich. "Yes, you've persuaded me," he said in his odd Russian. Every so often, when he couldn't find the word he wanted, he'd drop in the Polish equivalent. Sometimes Vasili would get it, sometimes not. He went on, "You really talk Chinese, and read it, and write it."

"Yes, sir," Vasili said. Casimir had only to say the word and his men would kill Vasili. Getting in bad with him was idiotic.

"Now," Casimir said, "what the fuck can you do that might actually be worth something to us?"

"I've told you before, sir—I'm a druggist, or trained as one, anyway," Vasili answered. "I know the Chinese style, but I know the Western one, too. My father made sure I did."

"That would be great if we had any drugs," Casimir said. "What we get, though, we have to take from the Red Army."

"You ought to see if you can hit an aid station, then. Good medicines will keep your men going when they fall over without 'em."

"I know that," Casimir said impatiently. "What I really want is ether or chloroform. We have doctors, but there's so much shit they can't do if they can't knock out somebody who's hurt. Do you know how to make anesthetics?"

"No. Sorry, sir." Vasili would have said yes if he'd thought he had the least chance of succeeding. But he knew he didn't have enough chemistry.

Casimir's grunt made ice run up his back. It was the kind of grunt that preceded orders like *Knock him over the head—he's useless.* But Casimir tried a different kind of question: "What would you do if you could do anything you wanted?"

"Settle down somewhere. Be a druggist or do odd jobs. Try like hell to stay out of trouble." Vasili meant it. The way things looked to him, trouble had found him in Harbin and then in Smidovich. He hadn't gone looking for it. Grigory Papanin might have had a different opinion, but Papanin was still back in Smidovich . . . if the Red Army hadn't conscripted him by now, too.

"Odd jobs? What kind?"

"Carpentry. Masonry. You name it, pretty much."

Casimir grunted again, this time on a different note: one that showed interest. "How are you with field fortifications? Russians are usually good at that kind of shit, aren't they?"

"I know how to dig foxholes and trenches. The way things worked was, they conscripted me, stuck a uniform on me and gave me a machine pistol, and then they put me on the train for Poland. As soon as I got here, they dropped me into the line against you guys."

"They really are scraping the bottom of the barrel, then," Casimir said. Vasili didn't try to argue with him. The Pole went on, "Either you've got some idea of what you're doing or you're lucky. Otherwise, you would have got killed by now. So let's see what you can manage. You see that stretch of high ground over there?"

Vasili hadn't paid much attention to it, but it was there, all right. He wasn't quite a field engineer, but yes, he could read ground. It was a knack whose acquisition helped keep him alive.

"I see it," he answered.

"Get us dug in just at the crest, so we can hit the Russians and then slip back when they hit us. You know the kind of thing I mean, right? You'll have seen it in the Red Army."

"Oh, sure." Vasili nodded, as if in wisdom. If the Pole was trusting him to have superior military knowledge . . . it meant Poland had lost a lot of wars to Russia. Russians had that same nervous regard for Germans. Vasili asked, "The men will do what I tell them?"

"Bet your balls they will," Casimir said. "They want to keep breathing like anybody else. Most of 'em know enough Russian so that shouldn't be a problem. Point if you have to, or get one of the fluent guys to translate for you."

"I'll do it." In his Red Army uniform, Vasili felt like a Nazi in *Feldgrau* working with a bunch of Russians. But, here, he was just uncommonly consistent. The bandits wore a motley mix of Soviet, Polish, and old German uniforms, along with civilian dungarees, wool shirts, jackets, boots, and hats. One of them called the band *a carnival from Vienna.* Vasili didn't know exactly what that meant, but it sounded good.

And Casimir had it right: they did what he told them to do. It wasn't the slavish obedience the Red Army demanded, but it turned the trick. They dug in along the swell of ground, and used bushes and junk to conceal their foxholes and entrenchments. Zigzag trenches ran back from the main position, so they could get away if they had to.

Surveying the half-kilometer of work from the front as the sun sank in the west, Casimir nodded. "That's not half bad," he said. "Better than I expected, to tell you the truth."

"I want the line to be good," Vasili answered. "I'm going to be in it, aren't I? I want the Reds to have trouble blowing me up."

Casimir chuckled. "The Reds, huh? What does that make you?"

"A conscript—I already told you that. My folks were Whites. Why do you think they wound up in Harbin?"

"Why does anybody do anything?" Casimir returned.

Vasili found no ready answer for that. A bandit leader with a taste for philosophy? What could be stranger than that? Instead of an answer, Vasili came out with a question of his own: "You don't mind my asking, what did you do before you picked up a rifle?"

"I studied for the priesthood till I decided I wouldn't make a good one. That didn't take as long as I wish it would have. Then I taught Latin and Greek, mostly to kids who didn't want to learn them. But I've been carrying a gun for a long time now. An awful lot of people in Europe have."

"I guess so." Vasili hadn't thought about it much. But plenty of the people who hadn't wanted Hitler running their country for them wouldn't have wanted Stalin running it for them, either. The Red Army would have seemed too big and too strong to take on for a while, and the governments Russia imposed would have featured a string of baby

Stalins. But when the satellites saw that the USSR had taken a beating . . .

A scout came back to Casimir and said something in Polish. Vasili could make out words here and there, but not sentences. Casimir spelled out what he'd suspected: "The Russians are on the way. Now you get to find out how good your fieldworks are."

"Do I get a piece of my own?" Vasili asked.

"If you do, there's no going back. If they catch you in arms against them, they'll kill you as soon as they hear you speaking Russian," Casimir warned.

"I understand that," Vasili said. "I'm a Russian. I can't help being a Russian. But I'm not a Soviet Russian, and I don't want to be one."

"The oath we swear is to the Black Virgin of Czestochowa. That wouldn't mean much to you, would it?"

"Afraid not." Vasili thought of himself as indifferently Orthodox. Catholic rites didn't matter to him. "But I'll fight for you any which way."

He got a Mauser. It could reach farther than his lost PPD, but not nearly so fast. He practiced working the bolt a few times without a magazine on the rifle. It wasn't hard. They put him in the trenches with a minder. The big guy didn't speak much Russian, or need it to make clear to Vasili what would happen to him if he tried to take a powder.

He didn't mind shooting at men he might have served with. What the hell? The Red Army soldiers were shooting at him. They tapped at the defenses he'd designed, then pulled back when they saw the Poles wouldn't flee in terror. They might have been ready to fight for the *rodina* against the Americans. But what Russian wanted to get killed by a bunch of Poles? Vasili sure hadn't, and the way his ex-buddies made that halfhearted poke at his line said they didn't, either.

Rolf Mehlen advanced into the portion of West Germany the Ivans had occupied armed with a rifle and a mine detector. The rifle stayed slung on his shoulder; the ceasefire seemed to be holding. He'd got the mine detector because . . . He supposed he'd got it because his superiors understood perfectly well that he didn't give a shit.

He remembered when mine detectors were brand new and wonderful, halfway through the last war. Before that, the pioneers found mines by crawling up to and through the minefields, probing with bayonets or sharp sticks. When you went after mines like that, sooner or later one of them would find you first.

With a detector, you didn't have to probe. When the gadget found a mine's metal case, it would play a tone in your earphones. You could dig the mine out yourself or mark it for later disposal. It was great.

In theory, it was great. The Russians didn't take long to figure out that the detectors searched for metal in the ground. They started manufacturing mines where the explosive charge lived in a varnished wooden box. The only metal those had was in the fuse mechanism. Sometimes, if you were lucky, the detector would pick that up. More often than not, it wouldn't, and you got a pioneer splashed all over the landscape. The survivors went back to hunting with sticks and bayonets.

Rolf had a new-model American detector. It was said to pick up the wooden-cased mines the Ivans still used better than the old German marks had. Whether what was said had anything to do with what was true . . . Rolf was out there to find out for himself.

There was a tone, from a third of a meter in front of his right boot. He didn't take the next step, the one his brain had already started to order. Instead, he crouched very carefully. He dug toward the mine with his bayonet. After he found the edge of it, he could also locate the center. He tied a strip of red cloth to a little bush growing above it so the people behind him could get rid of it. Then he rose, moved around the place the detector had warned him of, and went on.

He found two more mines in quick succession, one of them a sneaky wooden job. Maybe the American detector lived up to what they claimed for it after all. He could hope so.

He wished he had the Russian who'd come up with the wooden mine in front of him. That was what a rifle was for, by God! The evil bastard was probably a Jew, too. (That Germany had quickly adopted wooden mines itself never entered his thoughts.) Rolf hated Russians and Jews in more or less equal measure. They'd combined to brew up Bolshevism, hadn't they? They'd combined to rob good, decent Aryans of the *Lebensraum* they deserved, too.

Had things gone the way they should have, he would have been raising a family on a farm in the Ukraine somewhere. The only Slavs within kilometers would be a few slave laborers. Jews? There wouldn't be any Jews at all, not above the ground.

But things hadn't gone that way. Instead, here he was, hunting for Russian mines deep inside his own country. God must have been looking the other way when the *Reich* had to lay down its arms in 1945. If the Amis and Tommies had only followed Germany east against the hordes of *Untermenschen* . . .

They were too stupid. They paid for their foolishness. They paid for it, yes, but how much more did the *Vaterland* pay? Who could calculate that? Rolf knew how far beyond him it was.

Something moved, out beyond the edge of the minefield. Rolf flopped flat before he was consciously aware he'd done it. His Springfield got off his back and into his hands the same way. He already had a round chambered. He flicked off the safety. If he needed to fight, he was ready.

He didn't think he'd need to. Reflex responded to anything that made its alarms jangle. The motion of a stray cat or a farm dog or a cow tripped his circuits the same way a man's movement would. You stayed alive by responding even when you didn't have to. Not responding when you should have was what cost you your neck.

But that was a man out there, a man in Red Army khaki. Rolf drew a bead on him. He wasn't supposed to be there. The Ivans had pulled out of these parts—except this Ivan hadn't. If Rolf potted him, nobody would say boo.

He didn't fire right away. The enemy soldier had no idea he was there. After a moment, Rolf realized the Russian wasn't a soldier, not in the strict sense of the word. He was a deserter, a very different beast.

After watching him a little while longer, Rolf realized he was also drunk as a lord. He lurched. He staggered. He wobbled along like a crumpled-up sheet of wastepaper blowing on the breeze. His irregular progress took him closer and closer to the mines.

Rolf thought about shouting a warning. Max Bachman surely would have. But Rolf had thought Max was a sponge-soft pussy from the moment he'd met him. Max wasn't yellow; in a fight, he was fine. But as far as Rolf was concerned, the printer was damn lucky he'd gone into the *Wehrmacht* and not into one of the SS's concentration camps.

On came the toasted Ivan. Wherever he'd found his schnapps, he'd got himself a royal snootful. *I'll warn him if he gets too close,* Rolf thought. By *too close,* he meant *close enough so that if he blows himself up, some of the fragments may bite me, too.*

Bismarck had said something about God loving children, drunks, and the United States. Children made sense to Rolf; children were the future. He couldn't see why God would love the Jew-and-nigger-ridden USA. But God plainly did. The Americans couldn't have succeeded on the scale they had without something that sure looked like divine help.

Drunks, though . . . No, that wasn't nearly so obvious. Rolf had been drunk lots of times. All he'd ever got for it were some horrible hangovers and, once, a dose of the clap.

That damned Russian was singing some fierce-sounding song. It made the hair rise on the back of Rolf's neck. He'd heard Red Army men singing that song in the Ukraine and Romania and Hungary. They used it to nerve themselves to attack. Most of the time, they came in drunk, roaring like animals and spraying bullets in front of them. They died like flies, of course, but, however many the Germans killed, there were always more. The Ivans bred like flies, too.

The bastard was getting close. God had kept him from stepping on anything so far. If God happened to change His mind, he might endanger Rolf was well as the Russian. "Hey, Ivan!" Rolf bawled. *"Achtung! Minen!"* He didn't care whether the Russian knew much German or not. If he understood any at all, he'd get that.

And he did. He recoiled in a panic that would have been funny on the stage, but wasn't what you wanted to do when you were staggering around in the middle of a minefield. His right foot came down all right. His left foot came down, too—and then he wasn't there any more.

Rolf had heard that exact explosion too many times, in the last war and this one. Fire and smoke and dirt flew up and out. So did chunks of the Ivan God had suddenly stopped loving. He didn't even last long enough for a final shriek. In an odd way, Rolf almost envied him. The poor, luckless so-and-so went out without ever knowing what hit him. In wartime, most soldiers who got killed weren't so lucky.

There's one mine I won't have to hope the detector finds, Rolf thought. Had he had any comrades along, he would have said it out loud. Somebody like Max could be relied upon to cluck about what a callous SS *Arschloch* he was. Annoying Germans of Max's stripe was almost as much fun as watching drunk Russians blow themselves to smithereens.

Somebody came to see what had made the boom: a farmer in overalls. "Watch yourself! There are mines!" Rolf called to him. "That damnfool Russian just stepped on one."

"Oh. A Russian," the farmer said. "Too many of those fuckers anyway." Rolf snickered. Evidently he wasn't the only callous *Arschloch* running around loose.

MYRON GELLER NODDED to Istvan Szolovits. "Well, kid, that's about it. Looks like we've got everything out of you we're going to get."

"All right," said Istvan, who seriously doubted it was. "But what happens to me now?" What did you do with an apple core once you'd eaten the apple? You tossed it in the trash, that was what.

"Now? Now you get your graduation present, of course. You're at UCLA, so that fits." Geller reached into his pocket and pulled out a piece of thin green cardboard. "This is what they call a green card. It shows you're an alien legally in the United States. You'll have to register at a post office once a year in January, but that's a formality as long as you don't get in trouble for forgetting." He held out the card.

Istvan took it. It had his name and date of birth, a couple of official stamps, and some English text he couldn't make much sense of. He was learning the language, but he wasn't anywhere near fluent yet.

"Thank you," he said. "Will this let me look for work?"

"Yes. It's legal for people to hire you. But wait. I'm not finished yet. Here's this." He took a small, folded piece of paper from that same pocket. Istvan unfolded it. It bore a neatly printed name—HERSCHEL

WEISSMAN—and a telephone number. "Call him. He knows Yiddish—and he knows about this program. He'll help you with a job."

"Thank you very much!" Istvan exclaimed. Captain Kovacs had said they'd treat him all right, but Captain Kovacs was a continent and an ocean away from Los Angeles. He'd known what he was talking about, though.

"Hang on. We're still not done." Myron Geller reached into that pocket once more. This time, he pulled out a roll of American paper money. Istvan found it boring: all the bills were the same size and the same darkish green. Geller tossed him the roll. "This is five hundred bucks, courtesy of Uncle Sam. It'll keep you housed and fed for a couple of months. You won't have to sweat till Weissman starts paying you."

Istvan wondered how many forints went into five hundred dollars. A pretty thick stack of them; he was sure of that. Of course, after the last war Hungary had gone through a hyperinflation balloonish enough to put Weimar Germany's more famous one to shame. That hadn't hurt the Communists' rise to power, though with the Red Army sitting on the whole country that likely would have happened anyhow.

He felt he had to say, "I don't think anything I've given you is worth this much money."

"Uncle Sam didn't ask what you thought. He asked what you knew. You told him, and the stuff you told him checked out. He decided what it was worth." Geller lit one of the little plastic-tipped cigars he affected. After blowing out smoke, he went on, "A little bird happened to tell me that one of the fellows you named as knowing things is part of this operation, too. You had it straight, all right—he does know things."

That could only mean one man. Istvan started to laugh. "My God!" he exclaimed. "If Sergeant Gergely slipped on shit, he'd still manage to fall into a vat of cream. Is he in Los Angeles, too?"

"That I can't tell you." Did Geller mean that he didn't know or that he wasn't allowed to answer? It hardly mattered. Sergeant Gergely had served in the Hungarian Army when it fought side by side with the Nazis against the USSR. He'd served in the Hungarian People's Army after Hungary had to change alignment. And now he was serving the Americans? Istvan laughed some more. That sounded like Gergely, damned if it didn't.

"I'll tell you something about him, then. A friend of mine—Tibor's dead now, dammit—said a German called guys like the sergeant sock people, because they'd fit on either foot."

"Not bad, not bad. I'll pass that on, in fact," Geller said. "Now I'll let you make your phone call. Whether you know it or not, you're on your way to turning into an American, same as I was not so long ago. Luck to you."

He spoke Yiddish better than English, though his English was way better than Istvan's. He might think of himself as an American. Did people for whom English was a native language, not one learned in adulthood, feel the same way about him? It was a far less mocking question than it would have been in Hungary. Americans really did let other people join their ranks.

Istvan didn't need to go far to find a telephone booth. They were all over the place in the USA. The country seemed awash in phones, as it did in automobiles. In Hungary, only fancy shops and rich people—or, in the brave new Marxist-Leninist-Stalinist world, well-connected people—had them.

He put in a dime. American coins impressed him far more than U.S. paper money. All but the two least valuable had silver in them. No brass or aluminum or stainless steel or zinc or pot metal here. American coins really were worth something. When he got a dial tone (also not guaranteed in Hungary), he called the number Geller had given him.

The pay phone spat out the dime. "Please deposit twenty-five cents for three minutes," an operator said primly. "Please deposit—" He followed well enough to feed the phone a quarter. "Thank you," the operator said. Clicks and pops told him the call was going through. One ring, two rings . . .

"Blue Front Appliances. How may I help you?" another woman's voice said.

"Herschel Weissman, please." Istvan knew his bad English made the last word sound like *pliz*. Nothing he could do about it but try to get better.

"Who shall I say is calling?"

"My name Szolovits Istvan." He was so rattled, he gave it Hungarian style, with his family name ahead of his own.

"One moment, please."

More clicks and pops. Then a man said, "This is Herschel Weissman"—in English.

"Mr. Weissman, this is Istvan Szolovits," Istvan said in a mix of Yiddish and German. "Myron Geller gave me your name and number. He said you might possibly have work for me." He didn't want to make it sound any more certain than that. If Weissman told him no, he'd go looking elsewhere. He had some money in his pocket now to cushion him, thanks to Geller.

But Weissman switched to Yiddish himself: "Oh, sure! You're that guy! I've been waiting to hear from you. Can you be here at half past seven tomorrow morning? I have a man here who'll break you in. He knows the *mamaloshen,* too—that won't be a problem."

"Thank you! I will be there. Where do I need to be?"

"We're in Glendale. You have a pencil? I'll give you the address."

Istvan did have a pencil. He wrote the address on the paper that already held Weissman's name and number. "Thank you. I'll be there," Istvan repeated. He said his goodbyes and hung up before the operator could hound him for more money. Then he went to the UCLA library to find out where Glendale was. Los Angeles and its suburbs sprawled across what would have been a Hungarian county. Glendale was about fifteen miles away. When he translated that to twenty-five kilometers, it made more sense to him.

If you didn't have a car, getting around here wasn't so easy. Buses and trams didn't run all the time or go everywhere, the way they would have in Budapest. He'd have to leave his digs very early if he wanted to get there on time. Very early it would be—he didn't dare *not* get there on time.

He made it. He got there early, in fact, and had a cup of coffee at a diner around the corner. American coffee seemed like bathwater to him, but it was caffeinated bathwater. Thus fortified, he walked back to the Blue Front warehouse.

A stocky man in his early sixties stood in the parking lot. "Are you Mr. Weissman?" Istvan asked.

"That's me. Only call me Herschel." Weissman stuck out his hand. Istvan shook it. The older man had a grip like a pliers. He went on, "Welcome to Blue Front. Work hard and we'll both be happy. Let me call Aaron. He'll show you what's what." He raised his voice and switched to English: "Hey, Aaron! C'mere a second, will you?"

Aaron Finch had just poured himself a cup of coffee. This early, the joe in the big percolator wouldn't have had time to turn to battery acid. He didn't have a delivery till half past eight. He was going to catch up on some paperwork till he had to take that washer and dryer over to Van Nuys.

But then Herschel Weissman called from out front: "Hey, Aaron! C'mere a second, will you?"

"On my way." Aaron gulped as much coffee as he could and tossed the half-filled paper cup into the trash can. The boss didn't exactly mind when people drank coffee on the job, but he didn't like to see them doing it. He thought it made them look as if they were goofing off even when they weren't.

Weissman stood in the parking lot with a young guy Aaron had never seen before: right around six feet, sandy-brown hair cut short, pale skin, alert hazel eyes. Something about his mouth and chin made Aaron tag him for a member of the tribe. That let him make a pretty fair guess about who the kid was.

He wasn't startled, then, when Weissman spoke in Yiddish: "Aaron, this is Istvan Szolovits, the fellow I've been telling you about. Istvan, this is Aaron Finch. Work the way he does and I'll never have a bad word to say about you."

That was nice. *How come you never tell me that straight out?* Aaron wondered. Weissman was probably afraid he'd get a swelled head and slack off, which only proved his boss didn't know him as well as he thought he did.

But such worries could wait. Aaron held out his hand. "Good to meet you," he said to Szolovits.

"Good to meet you, too. Good to be here," the kid said. His Yiddish had an odd intonation, at least to Aaron's ear. His own family came from Romania, Ruth's from the Ukraine, and Herschel Weissman's from Poland.

"You'll show him what needs doing, right?" Weissman said.

"Sure. Whatever you want," Aaron answered. What else would he say? "It's not complicated. You've just got to do it." He turned to the youngster. "Do you drive a truck, uh, Istvan?" He tried to pronounce the name the way Weissman had, and guessed the boss was trying to imitate the newcomer.

Looking worried, Istvan shook his head. "I am sorry, but no. In Hungary, only rich people had motorcars, and only rich people and chauffeurs and truck drivers learned how."

Hungary? That explained the funny accent. "Don't worry," Aaron said. "Are you learning English, too?" He asked the question in the language he used more often than not.

"Oh, yes," Istvan said. Aaron worked hard to keep his face straight. Istvan's Yiddish accent sounded strange to him. In English, the kid was a ringer for Bela Lugosi in *Dracula.*

Aaron's father had come to America at about Istvan's age. Here sixty years later, he still spoke English with a strong accent. But he had a large vocabulary and wrote his adopted language well enough to have had several long letters published in Portland papers.

"Good," Aaron said, still in English. Dropping back into Yiddish, he went on, "Come with me. You can help load the truck in a little bit." By the way Istvan's eyebrow twitched, he suspected that meant he'd do all the hard work. With Jim Summers, he would have. Aaron meant the words as he'd said them.

"Do you want me to tell Jim you'll be showing the new guy what's up?" Weissman asked. Summers was on his mind, too.

"I'll owe you a favor if you do," Aaron said gratefully. The boss nodded and went off to tend to it.

Aaron led Istvan into the warehouse. He showed him the Maytag washer and dryer they'd be taking over to the San Fernando Valley. He covered the washer with a padded moving blanket and secured the blanket with masking tape so the machine's enamel finish wouldn't get dinged on the way.

That done, he tossed Istvan another blanket and the roll of tape. He expected the kid to be clumsy the first time, but Istvan made perfect mitered corners with the blanket and taped it into place on the dryer. "You were in the Army—somebody's army," Aaron said.

"Hungary's," Istvan agreed. "I am—how do you say it?—a paroled prisoner of war. You also served?"

"Not in the Army. My eyes were too bad. They wouldn't take me." Aaron tapped the frames of his thick glasses. "I was a merchant seaman on the Murmansk run, in the Mediterranean, and in the Pacific."

"The Murmansk run?" By the way Istvan said it, he understood what it meant. "Yes, you went into danger. But you could have stayed at home?"

Aaron shrugged. "I wanted to do my bit. I *needed* to do my bit. I didn't want Hitler winning. We didn't know everything the Nazis were doing, but we knew they were pretty horrible."

"Yes." Istvan said that in English, and then not another word. What had he gone through in Hungary when it was a German puppet? He'd lived, anyway, when so many hadn't. And then he'd watched his country go from aping the Nazis to aping the Reds. Talk about the school of hard knocks!

Aaron set a hand on the new arrival's shoulder. "That kind of shit doesn't happen here," he said. *Not when Joe McCarthy's dead, it doesn't,* he thought. But Istvan might never have heard of Tail-Gunner Joe. He was lucky if he hadn't.

"I hope you're right," Istvan said. "This country is too big for others to push it around. Hungary isn't."

"I guess not." Aaron changed the subject. "Let me show you something else." He slid a dolly under the washing machine and leaned it back so the washer's weight came onto the wheels. "This is how you move 'em so you don't bust your *kishkes* so hard. Try it with the dryer, why don't you?"

He spoke as if that were a question. Istvan took it as an order, which Aaron was glad to see. Well, if the kid had been a soldier, he'd have had people telling him what to do in a pleasant tone of voice.

Aaron also showed Istvan how to lower the steel ramp at the back of the truck's cargo bay. He didn't want the kid to mash his fingers because he didn't know what he was doing. Before they loaded the appliance, Aaron stuck yet another Chesterfield in his mouth. He held out the pack to Istvan. "Want one?"

"Yes, thank you." Istvan used what English he had.

They got the washer and dryer into the truck. Aaron secured the washer with ropes; he had Istvan do the dryer. The Hungarian Jew might never have gone to sea, but he knew how to tie knots.

Then it was off to Van Nuys Boulevard. Aaron knew where he was going. He told Istvan to navigate with the Thomas Brothers street atlas just the same. That seemed a good way for the youngster to start learning how to get around in L.A. Istvan had no trouble. He might not be able to drive yet, but he could read a map and give accurate directions.

Mrs. Rubin's house stood in a new tract sandwiched between groves of oranges and figs. She spoke English with a heavy accent. "Would you sooner talk Yiddish?" Aaron asked. She nodded eagerly, which also let Istvan join the conversation.

Aaron showed him how to hook up the washer to the pipes and the dryer to the gas lines. Istvan wouldn't need long before he knew as much about it as Jim Summers, not that that was saying anything special.

Mrs. Rubin fed them both cheese blintzes she'd just fried up. She cried when she found out Istvan had gone through the war in Budapest. "So many cousins in Europe I lost!" she said. "We tried to get them to come, my Benny and me, but they said everything was fine. Some fine! *Vey iz mir!*" She gave Istvan five bucks and Aaron only two. Aaron thought that was funny.

"*Nu?*" he asked Istvan on the way back.

"I can do the work. I have to learn to drive," Istvan answered. "It's not . . . real exciting, is it?"

He was less than half Aaron's age. "You wanted excitement, you should have stayed a soldier," Aaron said. Istvan shut up.

Dwight D. Eisenhower walked into the Philadelphia office that made do for the White House. Harry Truman rose to greet him. "Good to see you, General," Truman said, though Ike had retired from the Army. "Thanks for coming."

"It's my privilege, Mr. President," Eisenhower answered. He'd been born in the Midwest—Kansas, if Truman remembered straight—and his accent wasn't too far from the President's.

"Have a seat," Truman urged, and sank back into his own chair. When his visitor was also comfortable, he went on, "I'm grateful that you understand I haven't postponed the Presidential election because I'm all sweaty to keep running the country."

"Yes, I do understand that, but you also have to understand how I feel about it," Eisenhower said. "You have been running things since 1945, and I—"

"Almost certainly would be running for the Republicans right now, especially since Senator Taft and Senator McCarthy aren't with us any more," Truman finished for him. "Between you, me, and the wall, I don't miss Senator McCarthy even one goddamn little bit, but that's neither here nor there. Nixon's trying to carry on for the SOB, but I don't think he can derail you."

"Between you, me, and the wall, I don't miss McCarthy, either. And Richard Nixon is a nasty little piece of work in his own right, but I also don't think he'll derail me," Eisenhower replied. "As you say, none of that has anything to do with it. If the election came around in the usual way, I'm pretty sure I'd win it. I'd like to hear you tell me I'm wrong."

"I'd like to hear me tell you you're wrong, too. I don't think I can do it, though." Truman didn't love Eisenhower. The general had been more a military executive than a field commander. Truman could see him heading one big company or another. The United States? That, to him, was different. Still, Eisenhower had it straight. He would have been odds-on in November. But . . . "Let's get Congress back in one piece first. Governors are still appointing replacement Representatives, and they'll all have to run again this fall. They can't appoint replacement Senators. They have to hold a special election for each one. And some of those guys will have to run in November, too. Remember, Congress has to certify the votes from the Electoral College to make a Presidential election official. Popular vote doesn't cut it."

Eisenhower made a face. "That hadn't occurred to me, though I'm sure it has to some of my associates more familiar with the Constitution's fine print."

"I won't drag my feet on this, I promise. I was thinking of delaying the election for a year," Truman said. "If Congress wants to say the new term will only be three years, and the following election will come in 1956 and get us back on the regular cycle, I won't say boo. A year, I hope, will be long enough, especially since the—armistice, I guess you'd call it—seems to be holding."

"We won't be back to where we were in a year's time," Eisenhower said.

"Of course we won't." As he had to Vyacheslav Molotov, Truman quoted Mother Goose to the loyal opposition's leader:

All the king's horses and all the king's men
Couldn't put Humpty together again.

We won't get back to where we were for years and years, if we ever do. But we will be back in something like working order, or I hope we will."

" 'All the king's horses and all the king's men,' " Eisenhower echoed sadly. "Yes, that's about the size of things, isn't it? I hope we've learned our lesson and we never do anything like this again."

"So do I. The United States knows better now. I daresay Russia does, too," Truman said. "But England's working on the A-bomb. She's very close to having one. France will want one, too. With de Gaulle running things there, you can bank on that."

Eisenhower pulled another face. "He thinks too much of himself. He thinks too much of his country, too—when he can tell the difference between himself and France, I mean."

Truman laughed. "Good one, by God! He'll pretend he's running a great power, and all the people in France will love him till something rubs their noses in the truth that they aren't big enough to play those games any more. Then they'll turn on him and throw him out."

"They've already done it once," Eisenhower said. The President nodded. De Gaulle wouldn't have survived to head the French Committee of National Salvation if he hadn't been writing his memoirs out in the provinces because the Fourth Republic's politicians wanted nothing to do with him.

"So is it a bargain, then?" Truman said. "Congressional elections on schedule. We'll get the House and Senate up and running again, and then in a year we'll get a new President. I said before that I wouldn't run again no matter what, and I mean it more than ever now."

"Well, I understand that," Eisenhower said. He could have meant it several ways. Maybe it was *You're not young, and you've had a bellyful of politics.* Maybe it was *You lost your family, so you're ready to give someone else the ball.* And maybe it was *You screwed up this war so hard, you know nobody will ever want to vote for you again.*

Truman could have got huffy. He didn't see the point. He'd been beating himself up with the third one since Stalin answered A-bomb with A-bomb instead of blinking. The second one had hit him like an avalanche when one of Stalin's A-bombs fried Bess and Margaret in Washington.

"And yes, Mr. President, it is a bargain," Eisenhower continued while Truman's thoughts went on the unhappy journey they took too often these days. The Republican leader held out his hand. The Demo-cratic President took it.

"You know what else we're going to have to keep an eye on one of these days?" Truman said.

"Tell me," Eisenhower replied. He thought he'd be doing this job after the next Presidential vote, whenever the next Presidential vote happened to come along. If Truman wanted to talk, he'd listen. Then he'd ignore what he'd heard if he felt like it.

"Red China." Truman held up a hand. "I know, I know—not for a while. They aren't within miles of building an A-bomb yet. They're years away. But there are a hell of a lot of 'em and they've got a big coun-try. It could be rich if they quit messing it up. And they're sore at us on account of what we did in Manchuria, and they're scared of us for the same reason. It's a lousy combination, if you want to know what I think."

"Will you drop more A-bombs on them if they don't cut a deal in Korea?" Eisenhower asked. "I know you told Molotov you wouldn't, but—"

"I won't do it unless the Russians use A-bombs on the satellites or the Baltic republics," Truman said. "That was the deal. The Russians can still hurt us if we renege on it. If they go back on it, we have a free hand. But I don't think they will. We have an armistice, not a surrender. I can't get too pushy. They're still a nation under arms."

"Okay. I see your point." Eisenhower nodded, with luck in wisdom. "This is Germany after Armistice Day in 1918. It isn't Germany after V-E Day in 1945."

"That's it exactly!" Truman exclaimed. Eisenhower looked so per-fectly corn-fed, he surprised you when he came out with anything as-tute. He wasn't a dope; he just looked and sounded as if he ought to be one. The President went on, "I don't want to stick the Russians with a Treaty of Versailles they'll resent, either. Whoever comes after me will have the last word on that, but I hope he'll follow through, whoever he turns out to be." *Yeah, Ike, I'm talking to you.*

"We don't want to be too hard on the Soviet Union, no," Eisenhower said. "But do we want to be so soft, we make it easy for them to rebuild and think about trying again?"

"This map is secret," Truman said as he pulled it out of his desk. "Red stars show Russian cities we hit with A-bombs. Yellow stars show the ones that only got conventional weapons dumped on them."

Eisenhower studied the map. He knew, of course, what the USSR had done to the USA. This was . . . a good deal worse. "They won't start up at the same old stand any time soon," he said at last.

"No. They won't. I don't take much satisfaction from this war. What little I do take, I take from that," Truman said.

Ihor Shevchenko fastened new shoulder boards to his uniform tunic. These had three red stripes, not one. The authorities liked his defense of the railway line so much, they skipped junior sergeant and promoted him straight to sergeant.

There were things the authorities didn't know, of course. One of those things was that he'd shot a particularly obnoxious Red Army sergeant in the back. The late underofficer had taught him all the lessons he needed in how not to do the job.

A good thing they didn't know, too, because along with the new shoulder boards they'd given him a company to command. "We may have to take it back in a while," the earnest captain in charge of the regiment said apologetically. "If the replacement depot coughs up some more officers, I mean. The bandits' snipers concentrate on people with officers' shoulder boards." He shrugged a fatalistic shrug. "*Nichevo.*"

In the last war, Red Army snipers had concentrated on Fritzes with fancy shoulder straps the same way. The Hitlerite officers quickly learned to turn the straps upside down so the snipers wouldn't spot pips and silver or gold braid.

The company's junior sergeant was a swarthy, mustached Azerbaijani named Safir Safarli. Anatoly Prishvin, the pussy Ihor had scragged, would have given him endless grief about his looks and his accented

Russian. Ihor treated him the way he would have treated a man from Leningrad.

Safarli didn't need long to notice. "How come you no call me black-ass or nothing?" he asked, sounding more suspicious than pleased.

"Hey, I'm a Ukrainian. Russians come down on me, too," Ihor answered with a shrug.

Safarli scratched his head. To him, the difference between Ukrainians and Russians was as incomprehensible as the difference between an Azerbaijani and a Turkoman was to a Slav. He asked, "What we do now?"

"Whatever the captain tells us to, for the big stuff. We're stuck with that," Ihor said. The junior sergeant nodded. Ihor went on, "For the small stuff, sit tight as much as we can get away with. I don't want people killed for no good reason. Make damn sure our sentries don't fall asleep or get snookered when they're out there. *Damn* sure, you hear?"

"I hear, yes." Safarli touched his ear with his index finger. As if admitting something he half felt he ought to keep to himself, he added, "Serving under you maybe not so bad."

"Wait till you get to know me. You'll really hate my guts," Ihor said.

Safarli looked puzzled, then realized it was a joke and laughed. "You not like a lot of sergeants," he remarked.

"A lot of sergeants are drippy dicks. I've served under too many like that myself, thank you very much," Ihor said. "Me, I don't give a shit about the little crap. As long as the guys clean their weapons and they're ready to fight when they need to be, the hell with the rest. I treat 'em the way I'd wanted a sergeant to treat me."

He thought of the Golden Rule. He didn't know where or how Jesus had talked about it; when he was growing up, nothing got you in trouble faster than teaching your children religion. Safir Safarli wouldn't know, either. Muslims had a whole different set of teachings, though a lot of their moral rules weren't far from what he was used to.

The Polish bandits didn't seem eager to prod his company. He must have taught them a lesson when he chewed up that aristo's band of rebels. Instead, they went after outfits that hadn't proved themselves.

Sometimes Red Army squads or platoons would surrender en masse to the Poles. Ihor kept hearing that, but had trouble believing it. It turned out to be true, though. Captain Pavlov sought him out to pick his brains. "You've been around the block a few times, haven't you, Shevchenko?" he said.

"Comrade Captain, I fought in the last war till I got a leg wound," Ihor answered honestly. "You know I still limp. For a while, it kept them from conscripting me this time. Then it didn't, because they needed more men. So I went back to it again." He didn't say *They would have shot me if I'd told them no.* Pavlov had to understand that already.

"Most of the, ah, weak units had a majority of men who weren't Slavs," the captain said. "Sometimes that's the luck of the draw, but we have to keep an eye on it."

"My junior sergeant's a good, solid soldier, sir, and he's a blackass," Ihor said. "They aren't all bad apples. And—forgive me, 'cause I don't mean you—I've heard Russians giving Byelorussians and Ukrainians a hard time like they were a bunch of Kalmuks."

"I've heard it, too. It stinks," Pavlov said. "It disgraces the Soviet Union."

"Yes, sir." Ihor hadn't realized he was poking one of his superior's buttons.

"Well, it does, dammit," Captain Pavlov said. "Russians still give Jews grief, too, same as they did in Tsarist times. No wonder so many of the Bolsheviks who made the October Revolution were Jews. They wanted a better place for themselves and their children."

"Yes, sir," Ihor repeated. He'd known that a lot of the Old Bolsheviks were Jews, even if many of them took Russian-sounding names. And he knew what had happened to those Jewish Old Bolsheviks. Kaganovich still survived, but he was almost the only one. Some made the mistake of backing Trotsky against Stalin, and got read of out the Communist Party in the 1920s. The rest lingered on into the next decade, only to perish in the show trials and purges before the Great Patriotic War.

They could have been Ukrainians, he thought somberly. Whatever else you said about Stalin, he didn't believe in half measures. His methods were brutal, but no one in the whole Soviet Union mounted a successful challenge against him as long as he lived.

And, now that he was dead, everybody else had to pay the piper. All the resentments nobody dared let out for fear of his monstrous strength came bubbling up like swamp gas. The Poles, the Czechoslovakians, the Hungarians, even the Bulgarians! The Bulgarians, more than any other satellite nation, had actually liked Russia. Things inside the USSR were starting to boil, too.

"Comrade Captain," Ihor said, not quite out of the blue, "have you heard of any troubles in the Ukraine?" He wondered what the Banderists were up to these days. A few of them had lurked in the woods even before those MGB men dragged him back into the Red Army. They'd wanted an independent homeland, a lot of them had been willing to collaborate with the Nazis to get one (thought the Hitlerites were none too eager to collaborate with them), and some hadn't given up even after the Red Army threw the Germans out.

"By all I know, things are pretty quiet there." Captain Pavlov eyed Ihor. *"Et tu, Brute?"*

"Comrade Captain?" Latin was Greek to Ihor.

"Never mind," Pavlov said. "We've had too many desertions, though, even from units where the men don't give themselves up to the bandits."

"I know, sir." Ihor knew why, too. Those guys mostly headed east, back toward their homelands, to help them throw off the Soviet yoke—which all too often seemed to them the same as the Russian yoke had. He suddenly understood the captain's measuring stare. "You don't got to worry about me, sir. I'm not going over the hill."

"That's good." Pavlov's voice sounded desert-dry. How many men had told him the same thing just before they bugged out? He might be a kid, but he'd likely heard enough bullshit by now to turn a saint cynical. He went on, "The *rodina* needs good men to hold things together when times get tough. I want you to be one of them now."

"Yes, sir," Ihor said yet again. But Captain Pavlov's motherland wasn't his and had done horrible things to his. How much loyalty did he owe it?

"Everything will work out for the best. You'll see," Pavlov said. "We'll whip the Poles into line here, and then we'll clean up the Soviet Union. We'll all be better for it." No more than a second after he finished, something blew up with a rending crash. It wasn't close enough to be dangerous—it had to be a kilometer off—but it did remind Ihor how far the Poles still were from getting whipped into line.

ANOTHER MORNING OF WAKING UP to a guard banging a hammer on a shell casing hanging from a rope. Another morning of taking your boots out from under your head and putting them on your feet. Another morning of rushing out to roll call as fast as you could so the guards wouldn't have the excuse to beat you. Sometimes they'd beat you without any excuse, but they were worse when they had one.

Luisa Hozzel took a place in the roll-call grid without having anything uncommonly horrible happen to her. She hated the gulag with a bitter, implacable hatred made worse because so much of the bitterness sprang from hopelessness. She had been here, she was here, she would be here. World without end, dammit.

Trudl Bachman stood a few meters away. Luisa eyed her without seeming to. Did Trudl look sleeker, pinker, better fleshed? Luisa thought so. *Whore. Russian's whore.* The words resounded inside her head.

But so what? What difference did words like that make? Not much, not in a place like this. What made a difference was that Trudl had more to eat and did easier work than most *zeks*. She was dying more slowly than Luisa. She fucked? She sucked the Ivan's dick? Again, so what?

It's only so what? *here,* Luisa reminded herself as a guard stumped by, his brow furrowed in concentration as he worked on the count. When they got out of Siberia, when they went back to the *Vaterland,* what would Max say when he found out his wife prostituted herself for extra helpings of black bread and stew? What would Gustav say if Luisa did the same?

When they went back to the *Vaterland . . .* But what if, as seemed all too likely, this *was* world without end, amen? What if they never went back? Didn't doing everything you could to stay alive longer make perfect sense then?

Luisa refused to believe any such thing. If that made her a stiff-necked, priggish fool, then it did, that was all. If it made her a *dead,* stiff-necked, priggish fool, well, was life in the gulag worth living?

The count was taking longer than usual. Were the guards dumber than usual? Or had there been an escape during the night? Luisa didn't miss anybody's face from her barracks or her work gang, but no telling how much that meant.

At last, the MGB lieutenant nodded and said, "*Khorosho.*" They'd just had trouble counting on their fingers. Again. He turned—awkwardly, because one of his legs didn't work well—and waved toward the mess hall.

Along with the rest of the women lined up out there, Luisa rushed toward the door. She threw a few elbows to get inside fast. One of them would have earned her a stern talking-to from a referee on the football pitch. No referees here. She also caught a couple of elbows like that.

Bread. The chunk she got was bigger than most, and less full of husks and grit. They'd thrown a little salt pork in the stew pot. She could smell it in the broth, and saw, or thought she saw, a few shards in among the cabbage and turnips and nettles and whatever else they'd boiled up. A glass of weak sweet tea. No coffee white with milk, not here. You grabbed what they gave you, and you were glad you got even so much.

Latrine call was as filthy and noxious as always. Luisa fled as fast as she could. Then she lined up again, this time with her work gang. As she shouldered an axe, a mosquito whined around her head. They infested the taiga as long as the mercury stayed above freezing.

Trudl, of course, wasn't with the work gang any more. She stayed inside the barbed wire, counting paper clips or polishing doorknobs or doing whatever she got to do in exchange for putting out.

"Come on, you cunts!" a guard sergeant bellowed in bad Russian. "Out to forest to do real workings!"

Whatever Trudl did wasn't real workings. Luisa was sure of that. Whenever she thought about it, it infuriated her and made her jealous at the same time. All Trudl had to do was lie down or get on her knees, and. . . .

Stop that, Luisa told herself as she trudged past logged-off stumps and out to the current work area. But, for once, she couldn't stop it. That camp barber had had the hots for her since he first cropped her head—and her armpits and crotch. He probably wouldn't last long or want it very often. If giving it to him kept her from working herself to death here, why not?

Because he's a filthy animal, Luisa answered herself. *Because Gustav will find out if you do. You may think you'll get away with it, but if you get back to Germany word will, too.* She knew what would happen then. Her husband would beat her up and throw her out, and she'd never be able to hold her head up in public again. If she moved away, gossip would follow wherever she went.

If she got back to Germany. If she didn't go back, if she wouldn't or couldn't ever go back, weren't things different? Trudl thought so. Luisa might have, if the idea of having that barber touch her didn't make her want to hurl.

"Now, pussies, hard workings!" the sergeant shouted.

Another way to get things over with in a hurry would be to go after him with the axe. She might even kill him before he or his pals leveled their machine pistols and filled her full of holes. That would be worth something. Not enough, though. Coward that she was, she still wanted to live.

Despite yells and threats from the guards, she worked no harder than she had to. Nobody in the gang did. The Russians called people who worked hard for the sake of the state shock workers or Stakhano-vites. They were rare among the *zeks,* and seldom lasted long. You had to guard your strength, what there was of it.

The day was warm and muggy. It felt like summer, in other words—till an hour or two before sunset, when a breeze from out of the north-west reminded everybody how young summer died in this godforsaken part of the world. In a couple of months, maybe sooner, breezes like that would carry snow on them.

She shambled back to the camp, gave up her axe inside the barbed-wire perimeter, and lined up for the evening count. Before the guards let the *zeks* go to supper, the camp commandant came out to speak to them. With his eye patch, his hideously scarred face, and his hook, he held a post like this so someone with all his working parts could go off to fight foreign foes.

By the look in his one good eye, he hated all the prisoners for whom his word was law. "I have an announcement," he said, first in Russian and then, to Luisa's surprise, in German as well. "We are going to begin a repatriation program for female prisoners from Germany sentenced to corrective labor. I do not know when the program will commence. I have not yet received any orders on that subject. When I do receive them, I will follow them. In the meantime, camp administration and routine will continue unchanged. That is all."

He turned and limped away. He had a damaged leg, too. He didn't wait for questions. To him, questions would have been an affront. He did what he was told when he was told to do it. He told the *zeks* what to do, and he expected them to obey him the way he obeyed his superiors. If they didn't, he would make them sorry. It was that simple. It was to him, anyhow.

No one in the prisoners' ranks said anything. No one even moved. Luisa wanted to scream and dance and carry on. Fear of the guards and of the grim commandant held her where she was. Fear held all the women where they were.

Luisa glanced around to see where Trudl Bachman stood. Trudl's face was a study. She looked as if someone had smacked her in the chops with a large, dead fish.

The wages of sin seemed pretty good till you discovered you might have to pay them back after all. What was going through Trudl's mind right now? Was she hoping Max had caught one fighting the Russians? Even that wouldn't help her much. Her reputation would still go up in smoke, only as a widow rather than a wife.

"Dismissed to supper!" a guard sergeant shouted.

Russian *zeks* ran to the mess hall the way *zeks* usually ran. The German women moved more slowly. Luisa knew she could hardly believe what she'd just heard. Why should she be the only one? For the first time since she'd got here, she didn't care at all what kind of supper she got.

Boris Gribkov spooned up borscht in the dining hall outside of Mogilev. He didn't know what kind of meat had gone in with the beets and other vegetables, and he didn't much care. He'd found out in the last war that not knowing was often better. Cook it long enough and it all tasted tolerable. As long as there was plenty of it, who cared?

"Moscow speaking," came from the radio that ran off a truck battery. Radio Moscow went right on pretending it still emanated from the Soviet capital. Boris didn't know where Roman Amfiteatrov was reading the Party's version of the news. Moscow, though, struck him as one of the less probable places.

"What's gone wrong now?" somebody behind Boris said. All things considered, it was a reasonable question.

"Soviet naval infantry have landed unopposed on the Black Sea coast of Bulgaria," Amfiteatrov intoned in his bovine southern accent. "Their mission, to help restore the full control of the lawful socialist government in that country, is expected to be quickly and victoriously accomplished."

"Bulgaria? *Bozhemoi!*" No, it wasn't the voice that asked what had gone wrong. Whoever it was, he had a mouth that ran kilometers ahead of anything resembling good sense. If you said something like that where people you didn't know well and trust could hear you, you were just asking to get to know the Chekists.

Or you would have been, while Stalin ran the USSR and Beria the MGB. Now? Who could tell now? Molotov was a hardliner—no doubt about that. But how hard a line could the new Soviet leader take with his country in ruins and the satellites in revolt? If he did try to take a hard one, how many people (assuming secret policemen *were* people) would follow him?

"I regret to have to inform the Soviet people that our ambassador in Prague, Yuri Vladimirovich Andropov, was assassinated last night by reactionary Czechoslovak elements. Despite this atrocity, the USSR is doing everything in its power to cooperate with the progressive socialist government in place there. Czechoslovakian leaders have pledged that their nation remains firmly within the Soviet camp."

Two or three people in the dining hall coughed. Boris didn't, but he felt like it. The last time he'd personally cooperated with the progressive socialist government of Czechoslovakia, insurgents shot down his Tu-4 over Bratislava. As far as he knew, he was the only one who'd got out and hadn't got captured or killed on the ground.

"In Poland, Defense Minister Rokossovsky has announced his resignation because he has been unable fully to suppress banditry within his country's borders," Roman Amfiteatrov continued. "The government of the Polish People's Republic is expected to name a replacement within twenty-four hours."

"All kinds of good news today!" Boris thought that *was* the fellow who'd wondered what had gone wrong. By the sound of the news, everything had.

Many people inside the Soviet Union would take the last squib as a time-waster, a space-filler. If you knew more, as Boris Gribkov did, you also tried to read between the lines. Polish Defense Minister Rokossovsky was also Soviet Marshal Rokossovsky: a Pole gone gray in service to Moscow. Had Molotov sacked him because he couldn't stifle the uprisings in Poland? Or were the Polish Communists who'd had to flee

Warsaw getting frisky and ousting someone they knew they couldn't trust?

Boris didn't know enough to guess which. Neither would help the *rodina*. As for the Soviet marshal who'd doubled in brass as the Polish minister, his long career was probably over.

"The Trans-Siberian Railway now passes through Moscow once more, with no unfortunate stoppages and reroutings," Amfiteatrov said proudly. Boris couldn't imagine a more bloodless way to talk about A-bomb damage. The newsreader continued, "Shock brigades drove tracks through the heart of the city two weeks ahead of schedule."

"And now they glow in the dark!" a mess-hall comedian put in.

"Fuck 'em! What difference does it make? They're just *zeks* anyway," someone else rationalized.

It really is falling apart. No one would talk that way if it weren't, Boris thought. Had people joked about the Tsars like this before Lenin tossed Nicholas onto the ash-heap of history? They probably had. When you started laughing at a regime, it wouldn't last long.

The base commandant got to his feet. Colonel Volodymyr Petlyura was Ukrainian by blood, but, like Colonel Dzhalalov back at Tula, acted more Russian than the Russians. Boris hadn't even noticed him up till now; he'd been shoveling borscht into his gob like everybody else. He noticed him now. So did everyone else in the dining hall. It got very quiet. Even Roman Amfiteatrov's moos seemed to recede.

"That will be enough of that," Petlyura said in a harsh, flat voice. "That is too much of that, in fact. We serve the Soviet Union. We had better remember that we serve the Soviet Union. Do you understand me?"

"Yes, Comrade Colonel!" the assembled flyers chorused.

Boris added his voice to the rest. You couldn't fail to acknowledge a challenge like Petlyura's. The regime might be falling apart, but it hadn't completely broken down. A determined loyalist with connections could make mockers very unhappy. The commandant struck Boris as such a man.

Amfiteatrov returned to the foreground of his attention. The newsreader was bragging about industrial and agricultural norms being shattered through Stakhanovite exertions. Propaganda as blatant as that would have spawned smiles even when the USSR seemed sure to go on for the next thousand years. Now, though, no one said a word. No one looked anything but respectfully attentive.

Maskirovka, Boris thought. If you lived in the Soviet Union, if you lived through a purge or two, you learned how to hide what went on behind your eyes. If you couldn't learn, they'd get you. It was that simple.

"And in sporting news, Dinamo Kiev defeated Lokomotiv Moscow by a score of three goals to two," Amfiteatrov continued. "The match was played before a capacity crowd in Polotsk."

He didn't say why the match was played in Polotsk. The Americans had hammered both Kiev and Moscow. Chance were neither club had a home stadium worth playing in, or supporters who felt like watching a match. A provincial town like Polotsk wasn't worth incinerating with A-bombs. People there got to see a fancy football game . . . if the first-stringers hadn't got roasted and replaced by stumblebums wearing shirts they didn't come close to deserving.

Boris remembered the smashed groundcrew sergeant reeling along the airstrip runway at the Tula base. So many first-stringers from every branch of the Soviet armed forces were roasted now. So many of the people wearing those shirts didn't come close to deserving them.

He suddenly felt more sympathy for men like Petlyura and Dzhalalov. The base commandants had been fighting the rot longer and harder than he had. They hadn't given up. They were still in there battling. The Romans had given one of their generals a commemoration after Hannibal slaughtered the legions at Cannae. Why? Because he hadn't despaired of the republic. The Ukrainian and Tajik deserved awards like that. They were still trying to bring their people with them, too.

It was noble. Boris feared it was hopeless. Petlyura and Dzhalalov didn't care. The USSR had been good to them. They were doing their best to be good to it.

There would be people like that from one end of the vast country to the other. They'd run this way and that, plugging a hole here, patching a rip there. They'd be Stakhanovites in the cause of holding things together. Tsar Nicholas would have had men like that, too. Much good it did him.

Polotsk! These days, Polotsk counted for a metropolis, a place where top-division football clubs could square off. *If Polotsk is a metropolis, I'm a hippopotamus,* Boris thought. He almost wished he were a hippo. Then all he'd have to worry about would be crocodiles. Compared to Soviet predators, they were nothing much.

Bruce McNulty pulled back on the stick. The plane, which had been taxiing sedately down the runway, lifted its nose and hopped into the air. "Christ, I wish it was this easy all the goddamn time!" he exclaimed.

Of course, he wasn't in a B-29. He didn't have to worry about trying to make an emergency landing if one of his overstrained, chronically overheating engines quit just when he was getting off the ground. This was a Piper Grasshopper, the Army version of the good old Piper Cub. It was made to be forgiving.

He smiled at the instrument panel. The only way it could have been more basic was not to be there at all. Altimeter, airspeed indicator, fuel gauge, revs, oil pressure, ammeter, artificial horizon, turn-and-bank indicator, compass . . . What more did you need? Not a thing, not in a Grasshopper. Again, a Superfort was a different bird.

There was the Channel, dead ahead. He droned on to the southeast. The Grasshopper bounced in the choppy air. He remembered the Kaydet biplane in which he'd learned to fly, and how it had shivered with every air current. In a B-29, you hardly noticed them.

Once, he'd talked with a Navy guy who'd flown a blimp on antisubmarine patrols out over the Atlantic. From what the gasbag pilot said, those babies were way more sensitive to weather than any plane. No surprise if you thought about it—a blimp gave the wind a hell of a lot of surface area to play with.

"Land ho!" he said when France—or would it be Belgium?—emerged from the mist ahead. He steered east along the coast. Pretty soon, he found what he was looking for. There was Antwerp, with the heart torn out of the great harbor as if it were an Aztec sacrifice.

The area where everything had been smashed flat was about a mile across. Beyond that, the damage looked more like the kind he'd seen in the last war: buildings that leaned drunkenly away from the blast center or had chunks bitten out of them or had burned down. He circled above the wreckage at 8,000 feet, getting an eyeful.

This is what I do for a living, he thought. *This is what I owe Daisy, to see it with my own eyes.* He could have flown to Paris instead, but this was easier. The Grasshopper didn't have the range to reach the German cities that got leveled to stop the Red Army.

He wondered how much fallout he was breathing. Enough to notice, was his guess, but not enough to hurt him if he didn't stick around too long. That being so, it behooved him *not* to stick around too long. He swung the light plane away from ravaged Antwerp and back towards England.

Flying a B-29 was work. Even with the hydraulics, hauling the big bomber around the sky involved hard physical labor. No hydraulics here, just wires leading from the controls to the surfaces they moved. This was flying as God meant flying to be. It was simple, easy, direct.

The only way it could have been any simpler would have been for Bruce to grow wings on his back like an angel and do his own flapping. The limeys called each thousand feet of altitude an Angel. Right now, he was at Angels Eight.

He wondered what he'd do now that the war seemed over. When you were flying at right around a mile a minute, nothing happened fast. It was almost like crossing the ocean on a sailing ship. You had time to think.

One thing was too obvious to need much thought: he wouldn't keep flying a B-29. The big bombers had been obsolete when this war started. They soldiered on because the USA could bring a lot of them back into service in a hurry. Except for the asshole-puckering takeoff at full combat weight, the bugs had been worked out of the aircraft, too. Neither of those things held true for the B-36 or the B-47.

They were the coming thing, though. The B-36 was a hybrid, with a couple of little jet engines helping its props push it along. It was bigger and faster and could carry more bombs than a B-29, but prop jobs, like Kansas City, had gone about as far as they could go. In the B-47, the future was now. The jet bomber flew high enough and fast enough to give it a decent chance against even the hottest new fighters.

So he could stay in the Air Force and train up on one of the new planes. *But haven't I already killed upwards of a million people? Isn't that enough?* he thought. If he did leave the service, what would he do then?

"I'll keep flying, one way or another," he said, there in the solitude of the little cockpit. Didn't airlines grab pilots with Air Force experience? The pay would be a hell of a lot better. He wouldn't have to drop any more bombs, thank God.

He wouldn't have to retrain so hard, either, at least not right away. The old workhorses like the DC-3 and DC-4 were simpler than the Superfortress. Even the DC-6 wasn't any more advanced.

Yes, Air Forces were converting from piston-engined planes to jets. How long till airlines started doing the same? A few years, but probably not much longer than that. How slick would it be to fly from New York to London or Los Angeles in six or seven hours, not ten or twelve?

That might be worth doing. It would certainly keep money in his pocket. But wouldn't it be about as exciting as driving a bus? The Grasshopper reminded him how much fun flying could be. What if he hopped in a cropduster, an open-cockpit biplane that sprayed DDT on melons or corn to make the bugs leave them alone?

He imagined himself zooming along thirty feet off the ground, the wind blasting in his face, maybe with a pair of World War I-style goggles so his eyes wouldn't tear up. That was the real deal! Helping farmers at the same time seemed pretty good, too.

Then again, what did cropdusters make? He didn't know for sure, but *nowhere near as much as airline pilots* seemed a good guess. What would Daisy have said if he'd brought her back to the States and gone to work dusting crops in California's Central Valley? Once more, he didn't know for sure, but *goodbye* looked like the most probable answer.

"Fucking Russians," he muttered. If they hadn't sent that Beagle bomber over Norfolk, if the night fighter hadn't shot it down so a chunk of blazing wreckage landed on her . . .

Then it might have landed on my head, he thought with a different kind of shiver. *She'd be mourning me, not the other way around.*

What made that chunk of wreckage fall the way it did? Luck? Wind currents? The way it flew off the rest of the stricken Russian jet? If it had fallen in an ever so slightly different way, no one would have got hurt.

The whole world was made up of chains and webs of might-have-beens like that. It was the way it was, but was it the way it had to be? *If that aluminum had come down only a few feet from where it did, Daisy would still be alive and I'd be a happy man today.*

On the world's scale, that was a small thing. If the chains and webs of cause and chance could change small things, though, why not large things with them? What would the world look like if the Nazis had won the last war? If the South had won the Civil War? If the American Revolution had failed? Or the French? Or the Russian? One thing sure—it wouldn't look the same.

"Hell, why think small?" Bruce said, there in the solitude of the cockpit. Why indeed? No one else had to pay any attention to his mental maunderings. If his imagination wanted to run wild, all he had to do was let it.

What if the Roman Empire never fell? What if Jesus never lived? Or Moses? Or Mohammed? What if Alexander the Great didn't die in his early thirties, but lived out his threescore and ten? What would the present world look like after any of *those* might-have-beens?

Was that more mist over the channel, or did thinking about all the myriad ways the world might change stretch the fabric of what was "really" here too tight? Could the Grasshopper squirt out of this world and try to land in one where nobody'd ever dreamt of airplanes? Would they burn him for a wizard as soon as he stepped out of the cockpit?

Out of the mist came the English coast. Bruce flew low: lower than he'd planned to. Yes, there were roads with cars on them. There were railroad tracks. There was a train, the locomotive sending up a plume of coal smoke. There was a town, and there was an airstrip—not the one he'd set out from, but a promise he'd find it soon. He flew on.

Konstantin Morozov and his tank crew rode their T-54 back to the east. The tank didn't make the trip under its own power. It was a rugged, reliable vehicle . . . as far as tanks went. Tanks, unfortunately, didn't go very far in that direction. He couldn't guess how many breakdowns he would have had on the road from West Germany to the *rodina*. He could be sure the number wouldn't have been small.

And so the T-54 was chained to a freight car, one piece of a long train bringing this chunk of the Red Army home. As long as the train stayed in the Soviet occupation zone, everything was fine. Well, the landscape through which it passed wasn't. Much of the damage from the last war had yet to be repaired. Air strikes had added more. Konstantin, however, didn't waste much sympathy on Germans.

The train stopped just west of the Polish border. "Take the tarp off your tank," Major Zhuk told Konstantin. "Put HE in your main armament and have your machine gun ready to fire at anything that looks like trouble. We'll try to pass through Poland peacefully, but the Poles may not let us."

"You want me to run the motor, then, sir, so we can traverse the turret in a hurry if we have to?" Morozov asked.

"*Da.* Do it," the officer said. "The bandits are supposed to know we're on our way back to the motherland and won't come off the train to fight them unless we're fired upon. What they're supposed to know, though . . . Who the devil knows if they really do?"

"I understand," Konstantin said. "I serve the Soviet Union!"

"I believe you. Nice to know someone still does," Zhuk said, and went on to the next flatcar-mounted tank.

Konstantin told Pyotr Polikarpov, "Have the machine gun ready. Load the main armament with high explosive. Don't open fire without my order or you'll bring a world of hurt down on us from the Poles. Have you got that?"

"Naturally, Comrade Sergeant." The new gunner sounded offended at the question.

"Repeat it back, then." Morozov's distrust for his reluctant crewmate knew no bounds.

Polikarpov made a hash of it the first time he tried. Konstantin swore at him in weary disgust. He repeated the orders twice more, then told the gunner again to give them back. Polikarpov got them more or less right this time.

Slowly, slowly, the train started rolling forward once more. Something that big and heavy—*about the size of Pyotr's stupidity,* Morozov thought sourly—needed a while to build momentum. Western Poland looked the same as eastern Germany. And well it might. Up till 1945, what was now western Poland had been eastern Germany.

They'd gone no farther than a few kilometers when a rifle bullet clattered off the T-54's side armor. "Anybody see where that came from?" Konstantin asked.

No one said anything for a few seconds. Then Polikarpov asked, "Can I fire, Comrade Sergeant?"

"Have you got a target?"

"No, but if I smash up the landscape those fuckers'll think twice before they try shitting on us again."

"If you fire without an order, I'll tear off your stupid, worthless, empty head and piss down the hole in your neck," Konstantin said. "Do you need me to explain that to you again, or was it plain enough the first time?"

"You don't want me to shoot, Comrade Sergeant." Polikarpov sounded sulky, even wounded. Konstantin couldn't have cared less.

On they rolled, there in their buttoned-up tank. Every so often, Morozov stuck his head out of the cupola and looked around. There wasn't much to see. Most of the Polish countryside was as flat as if a steamroller had leveled it for a football pitch. A lot of the buildings had been leveled, too, in the last war or this one. A lot that hadn't been leveled had been smashed.

Not much traffic used the roads: horse-drawn wagons, a tractor or two, and military vehicles. Konstantin made sure those wore his country's red star, not the two-by-two red-and-white checkerboard the Poles used.

Poles hidden where he couldn't spot them kept taking potshots at the train full of Soviet armor. Nobody shot back, though Pyotr Polikarpov got gloomier than ever. You couldn't say the train was under anything like an organized attack. The Poles were just giving the Russians passing through their unhappy land some harassing fire.

They halted for the evening somewhere north of Warsaw. Konstantin didn't know why they weren't passing through the Polish capital. Maybe the populace there was even more hostile than it was in the countryside. Or maybe an A-bomb made the direct route impassable. Morozov couldn't remember whether the Americans had dropped one there.

He did ask Major Zhuk, "Sir, why are we stopping at all? Why not run on through the night?"

"The engine driver says in the dark he can't spot a mine on the tracks in time to stop," Zhuk answered.

"Oh." Konstantin chewed on that for a while. He found he didn't care for the taste. "No wonder we weren't going very fast, then, even in the daytime."

"No wonder at all," the regimental commander agreed. "We just want to get back inside the Soviet Union, that's all. And then—" He broke off, shaking his head like a bear bedeviled by bees.

"What, sir?" Morozov asked.

"Then they'll probably send us into action against bandits," Zhuk said. "We'll be doing the same things inside the Soviet Union we'd be doing here if we'd got different orders."

"Well, sir, remember Eigims. Remember Gamsakhurdia. They aren't the only ones who bailed out, either, are they?"

"There are only a couple more in my regiment. I've worked my balls off trying to stop that kind of assholery. But the division's lost a lot of tankmen, yes." The major looked troubled. "Odds are we'll be facing some of them when we get to wherever they send us."

"That crossed my mind, too. We trained them, and now they use the training to try and kill us. Doesn't seem right." Konstantin muttered darkly to himself. Juris Eigims had been a fine gunner—a hell of a lot better than the lazy son of a bitch warming that seat now, no matter how Russian Polikarpov was. And, if the bandits up by the Baltic had managed to get their hands on a few runners, he'd be in the turret of one, doing his best to give the Red Army an armor-piercing shot in the teeth.

His best wouldn't be good enough. Or rather, there weren't enough Balts to stop the Red Army once it got going. Lithuania, Latvia, and Estonia would fly the hammer and sickle for as long as the Soviet Union wanted them to fly it. If they didn't understand that, the hammer and sickle would fly over piles of ruins. The USSR had incorporated the Baltic Soviet Socialist Republics in 1940. The Nazis overran them the next year. Stalin's men reclaimed them in 1944. Whatever still stood after all that would get wrecked now.

"Sir," Konstantin asked, "do we know we're ordered north? Or will they send us down to the Caucasus to give the blackasses what-for?"

"Nobody's told me yet," Zhuk said. "I'd guess we're heading for the Baltics. We're a lot closer to them. But that's only a guess. Whatever they tell us to do, we'll do it, that's all. We serve the Soviet Union!"

All along the fringes of the USSR, people didn't want to serve the Soviet Union any more. They wanted their own leaders to tell them what to do, not gray apparatchiks from Moscow or wherever the USSR's apparatchiks based themselves these days.

Some of the bandits were ready to die for the sake of that vision. For his part, Konstantin Morozov was ready to kill them.

16

WHEN FAYVL TABAKMAN SET ABOUT doing something, he didn't do it by halves. The engagement ring he got Marian Staley was of eighteen-carat gold, and sparkled with diamonds. "I think it is from Old Country," Fayvl told her. "Americans, you mostly use fourteen-carat."

"It's beautiful." Marian spread her fingers and moved her hand a little. The diamonds in the setting caught the light and threw it back in flashes of coruscating flame.

"That is important thing," Fayvl said. "Maybe next weekend we go over to justice of peace, get license, and make things official?"

"If that's what you want to do, we'll do it." Marian had had something more elaborate in mind, with Linda costarring in the role of the flower girl.

Fayvl only shrugged. "A big wedding first time around, that's nice, long as someone's got *gelt* to pay for it. But this? This is first time for neither one of us. We had what we had. It was good, but it got busted up. Now we try and pick up pieces from two broken lives and see if we can make 'em fit."

"'All the king's horses and all the king's men—'" Marian began. The phrase had been in the news lately.

Fayvl waved it away. "I hear that too much. Maybe is true for country. Can't fix country up like before. But for us? Why not? Plenty people, they lose somebody, they end up happy with somebody else. Why *not* us?"

"When you put it like that, I can't think of any reason," Marian said. Linda liked him and respected him. Marian herself liked him and admired him. She'd already found out he made her happy in bed. And if she didn't please him, his acting deserved an Oscar. Maybe not a movie definition of love, but it worked for her.

"Hokay," Fayvl said, as if it were all very simple. "Then we do."

It wasn't quite that simple. He'd forgotten or hadn't known that getting a California marriage license required both people involved to have a negative Wassermann. Fayvl and Marian went to Doc Toohey's on her lunch hour to get stuck. "Congratulations to you both," the doctor said. "*Mazel tov!* Is that how you say it?"

"That's how you say it," Tabakman agreed.

"I'd rather do something like this than patch up loggers and drunks, which is where I get a big part of my business. It reminds me life has a good side, too," Toohey said.

"How soon till we get the results?" Marian asked.

"First part of next week, chances are," Toohey said. "Thing is, I can't do the test myself. I don't have the reagents I'd need. I have to take the samples down to the hospital lab in Redding. I'll do it after I close up shop tonight."

"But it's eighty miles to Redding! I'm so sorry to have to put you to the trouble," Marian said.

"Me, too," Fayvl Tabakman said gravely.

Doc Toohey shrugged. "A lot of ways, living in a little town like this wallops the kapok out of city life. You've got to take the bad with the good, though. Some things that'd be easy in a city, you can't hardly do at all here. You never can tell, folks. Maybe this afternoon a tree'll try and drive a logger into the ground. Then I'll get to hop in the ambulance and haul him down to Redding to see what they can do for him there. If I do, I promise I'll take your test tubes along, too."

"Nobody should ought to get hurt to make things easy on us," Fayvl said. Marian nodded.

"I didn't say anyone should," Toohey replied. "But it happens every couple of weeks. Loggers do work that's dangerous to begin with, and a lot of them aren't the most careful people the good Lord ever put on earth."

Marian found herself nodding again. Loggers had accidents because the work was hard and rough, as Toohey said. And they had accidents because they often drove like maniacs, both in their own cars and in the big, snorting company trucks that brought timber down to Weed for processing and distribution. *And* they had accidents because they weren't always sober on the job.

They were often drunk when off work. Then they brawled in Weed's bars. Taking care of those battle wounds kept Doc Toohey hopping, too.

Tuesday morning, the good doctor called Marian at Shasta Lumber. "Everything's the way it's supposed to be," he said. "You can go ahead with the Health Department's blessing."

"Did you think there was any doubt?" Marian asked indignantly.

"Ma'am, a positive would have surprised me, but it wouldn't have amazed me, if you know what I mean," the doctor said. "You spend some time dealing with people, after a while you get to where nothing amazes you. So long." He hung up.

If you poured a few stiff bourbons down his throat, what kind of stories could he tell? Juicy ones, for sure. What kind *would* he tell, though? She'd never known him to get drunk. Unlike so much of his clientele, he was a cautious, sensible soul.

"You're supposed to have the certificates with you," the town clerk complained when Marian and Fayvl appeared before him again.

"Call Doc Toohey," Marian answered. "I'll bet you the fee, double or nothing, he calls you eighteen different kinds of idiot. Go on, call him." The clerk didn't bet. He also didn't call. He issued the license for the customary fee.

When Marian walked down Mahogany Row and asked her boss for the following afternoon off, Carl Cummings frowned. "Why do you need it?"

"I want to get married then, sir," she said.

His face cleared. "Oh, that's right. You and the fellow with the shoe-repair shop. Well, all right, go ahead. Can't very well say no to anything like that, can I? We'll pay you for the time, too."

"Thank you very much, Mr. Cummings!" Marian said in glad surprise. She hadn't intended to ask for that; she hadn't thought she had a chance of getting it.

But Cummings actually smiled. "The company won't go broke. We don't have people getting married every afternoon." Marian thanked him again and got out of there while the getting was good. The rest of the office girls out front were as amazed as she'd been at the boss' generosity.

For the afternoon the next day, she put on a gray silk dress and had Linda wear a pink one good enough for church. They met Fayvl at the little city hall. He wore baggy tweeds that were plenty formal enough but seemed to belong more to 1932 Warsaw than 1952 Weed. Marian said not a word. That might have been where and when he got married the first time.

The justice of the peace (who made most of his money as a real-estate agent) was a bulky fellow named Harlow Foote. "Good to see you, good to see you," he wheezed. Several chins wobbled as he spoke. He peered over his half-glasses at Linda. "Whose little girl are you?"

"Theirs," she answered.

That warmed Marian's heart—Fayvl's, too, by his shy grin—but could leave the wrong impression. "My first husband was killed in combat over Russia last year," she said quickly.

"I see," Foote said. "Good she seems to care for your fiancé, then."

"Is very good," Fayvl said.

"Um, yes. Shall we get on with things?" Without waiting for an answer, the justice of the peace flipped open his book to a dog-eared page and began the ceremony. Marian and Fayvl both said their *I do*s. A few seconds later, Harlow Foote declared, "Under the authority vested in me by the state of California, I now pronounce you man and wife." He nodded to Fayvl. "You may kiss the bride."

"I love you, Mrs. Tabakman," Fayvl said, and he did.

"I love you, too, Mr. Tabakman." Marian kissed him back. She'd already started practicing her new signature. She didn't want to slip and write *Staley* by mistake.

"Kiss me, too!" Linda said. Laughing, her mother and new stepfather did.

Trucks came up the dirt road through the taiga to the gulag. Like all the ones Luisa Hozzel had seen bringing *zeks* to the camp, they were old, worn-out American models. Like the guards here, they weren't good enough to be worth anything in war any more. They could still do the job, though, when it came to things like hauling prisoners around.

The German women lined up in their camp clothes. They remained under guard. The MGB men with machine pistols looked eager for an excuse to open up on them, in fact. A man with a clipboard came down the line. "What your name is?" he asked Luisa in Russian not much better than hers.

"Hozzel, Luisa. Г963," she said, family name before personal name, with camp number at the end. That was the way you did it here. They hurt you enough so you learned in a hurry

"Hozzel, Luisa." He ran a stubby finger along the list of names on the clipboard till he found hers. "Г963." He checked the number she'd given him against the one stenciled on her jacket and trousers. When he saw they matched, he ran a line through her name on the paper, as if to deny she'd ever been here at all. She wished to God she hadn't.

There were a couple of delays because the guards were morons or because a *zek* was wearing clothes with the wrong number on them. The women stood there, waiting. No one complained loud enough to annoy the MGB men. No one dreamt of throwing away the chance to get out of this place.

At last, after what seemed forever, the outer gate opened. The guards gestured with their weapons, urging the *zeks* toward the trucks. One of the men stood right next to Luisa. She risked asking him, "Where are we going?"

He stared at her. "You go home to Germany, you dumb cunt."

"*Da.*" She nodded. "Where are we going now? Where are the trucks taking us?" Not in her worst nightmares in Fulda would she have been able to ask those questions in Russian. For her sins—and they must have been bad and numerous—now she could do it with ease.

"Oh. The trucks. They take you to Birobidzhan. You get on train there."

She'd never heard of Birobidzhan before the MGB men grabbed her in Germany. Now she knew it was the capital of the Jewish Autonomous Region. The Nazis had murdered their Jews. The Russians sent theirs to Siberia and bragged about it afterwards.

The guards packed the women into the truck like sardines. Again, no one grumbled. Birobidzhan sounded more wonderful than Paris, London, or New York could have right then. Birobidzhan was where they would board the train west, the train taking them home.

They'd each got a chunk of black bread, the size of a morning or evening ration, to take with them. Luisa was always hungry. She'd have to figure out what to do with the bounty. Eat it now or save it for later? She didn't worry about anyone using the latrine. They'd all got used to the morning and evening rushes, to occasional leaks behind a tree out in the woods, and to holding and holding and holding.

"We're moving!" someone exclaimed when the truck started along the rough road. She couldn't have sounded any more thrilled in her lover's arms. Luisa knew just how she felt.

Jounce, rattle, bang—Luisa wondered if she'd bite her lip or break a tooth before she made it to Birobidzhan. The truck's springs and shocks were only a memory. Well, if she did break a tooth here, she could have a good German dentist put a crown on it, not some Russian butcher.

They took three or four hours to reach the Siberian town. That was as close as Luisa could put it. The place didn't look like much. Most of the buildings were log cabins out of the American Wild West. Maria Grunfeld, who'd escaped for a while, said the smaller town of Smido-vich looked like that, too.

More guards waited at the railway depot. "Out!" they shouted, and then, "This way! This way!" This way the women went. They stood by the track for the next hour or two. A man who looked like a *zek* but had probably served his term came by with a bucket of water and a dipper. Luisa got a sip. The lukewarm water tasted of rust. It went down her throat like champagne even so.

Up chugged the train. The guards squeezed all the women into three cars. They were crowded, but not nearly so crowded as Luisa had been on the way to Siberia. She couldn't move much, but she could breathe.

Everything seemed simple when the train rolled out of Birobid-zhan. It would keep going for several days, maybe for a week or longer. Luisa knew she could endure that. The reward at the other end of the tracks made it all worthwhile. Fulda. *Home.*

She looked around to see if Trudl Bachman was in this car. If she was, she wasn't in this compartment. How did she look forward to her homecoming? What would she have to say to Max?

What will I have to say to Gustav? Luisa wondered. He'd woken up screaming time after time from nightmares about his stretch on the Eastern Front, but he'd never said much to her. His attitude seemed to be that anyone who hadn't gone through it wouldn't understand.

Luisa hadn't pushed him about it then. Now   Now she'd been through some things he hadn't. Maybe the gulag wasn't as bad as com-bat. Maybe. But it had horrors of its own, horrors that were liable to wake her in the middle of the night for years to come.

She began to realize things wouldn't be so easy as she'd hoped when the train stopped on a siding for a couple of hours in the middle of the night. Several trains went by while it waited there. The bread was only a memory.

Maria said, "I don't think we'll be getting back to the *Vaterland* as soon as we hoped." The only thing that made her sound different from Dorothy going *I don't think we're in Kansas any more* was that Dorothy sounded excited about the world turning Technicolor once she got to Oz. Maria sounded glum at having to linger in grim, gray Russia.

Luisa closed her eyes, stretched out in her seat as much as she could—which wasn't much—and tried to sleep. She'd just gone under and drifted into a blissful dream about roast goose and rhubarb pie slathered with whipped cream when the train jerked forward and back onto the main track again. The lost rest was bad enough. The lost feast seemed ten times worse.

The sun was coming up when they stopped in Kubychevka-Vostochnaya. Luisa had no trouble reading the name on the badly painted sign at the train station. By now, she took the Cyrillic alphabet almost as much for granted as the one she'd grown up using. She even guessed the name meant something like *Eastern Kubychevka;* the Russian word for east was *vostok.*

Three men in shabby clothes, like the fellow at Birobidzhan probably released *zeks* still subject to internal exile, brought the German women food. The bread was the same nasty black stuff they'd endured in the gulag. But with it everyone got fifteen centimeters of sausage. The stuff was stale and stretched out with bread crumbs, but it still tasted of pork and pepper and dill and caraway seeds. Luisa had no idea when she'd last eaten anything so delicious. By the ecstatic sighs from the other women—sighs more joyful than some other kind of sausage seemed likely to give them—no one else in the car did, either.

When the women asked for water, the men brought them two full buckets and a dipper with which to drink. They asked to be paid in the only coin women were likely to have on their persons at all times. Then they laughed to show they were kidding. If they hadn't laughed, they might have got what they asked for. So many female *zeks* got used to opening their legs to thank men for favors.

By the time the train pulled out of Kubychevka-Vostochnaya, the car's toilet started backing up. "Nothing but the best for us, hey?" Luisa said. The stink was bound to get worse, and they still had a long way to go. She told herself she didn't care, and almost made herself believe it.

. . .

Vasili Yasevich didn't have too much trouble learning to speak and understand Polish. A lot of the vocabulary was similar to Russian, though the Poles always put the stress on the next-to-last syllable of words with more than one. He spoke with an accent, but he could get them to follow him.

Reading the language, though . . . The Poles didn't use Cyrillic, the alphabet he knew best. And they had a variety of lines and hooks and accents to modify the sounds of the Roman letters they did write. Also, because the Roman alphabet had fewer characters than the Cyrillic, they used odd combinations of letters. Russian needed only a single letter, Щ, for the sneezing sound of *shch*. Polish had that sound, too, but wrote it *szcz*.

"This is made to drive people crazy," Vasili said.

Major Casimir scowled at him. "I don't know what you're grousing about. Every sound has a letter or set of letters that matches it. This isn't English, by the Virgin. English spelling is all one big lie."

Since Vasili spoke and read no English, he couldn't say much to that. He did say, "Russian uses one letter where you use four sometimes."

"You Russians as schismatics, though," Casimir said with what sounded like exaggerated patience. "You've been schismatics for nine hundred years. No wonder you use a stupid schismatic alphabet. We use the same one the holy Pope does, God bless him."

"If ours is better than yours, what difference does being schismatic make?" Vasili said. "Besides, our church says we're the ones with the orthodox doctrines and you Catholics are the miserable schismatics."

"Schismatics always think they're orthodox. That's part of what's wrong with them," Casimir declared loftily.

Before Vasili argued more theology with the bandit chieftain, he recalled that Casimir could still order him shot with a wave of the hand. Changing the subject seemed the better part of valor. "What do you suppose the Red Army will try against us next?" he asked.

The Pole leered. "You were in it. You tell me."

"Way it looks to me is, if they don't knock something out of the way the first time they try, they keep banging away till they do," Vasili answered. "They don't fight cute."

He got a smile and a chuckle from the major. "Cute, huh? No Pole would use that word with fighting. But you're probably right. They're stupid and they're stubborn and they have soldiers falling out of their asshole. They like to keep butting till they smash something down. What shape are your fieldworks in?"

"They could be better," Vasili said. "Your men don't like shoring them up after they get knocked around."

"And this surprises you because . . . ?" Casimir said. "Patriots don't pick up a rifle and risk their lives to play with shovels and dirt and sandbags. They do it so they can kill the invaders who want to take their country away from them."

"I understand that." Now Vasili was the one who let his patience show. "But do they want the invaders killing them because they'd sooner knock pears out of trees with their dicks than work?" The Russian *mat* for *screw around* sounded silly in Polish, even if the languages were close cousins.

"Because they'd sooner *what*?" Casimir laughed out loud this time, which told Vasili just how silly the *mat* sounded in Polish. The major went on, "Never mind. Don't explain it. I get you, I think. I'll tell them to get off their lazy asses."

And maybe that would do some good, and maybe it wouldn't. The bandits didn't follow orders for no better reason than that they were orders. If the Poles thought your orders were stupid, or that following them took too much work, they'd just ignore you. They didn't have the Red Army's solid chain of command backed up, at need, by the secret police.

Major Casimir scratched his chin in thought. His face stayed smooth all the time; he had a bone-handled straight razor he stropped against a square of leather he carried in his pocket. "You know, I'm going to move a few guys with PPDs up in front of our line tonight and tell them to dig in so the Russians don't spot them. That'll make the bastards shit when they start taking flanking fire."

"*Tak.*" Vasili remembered to say *yes* in Polish. "The Red Army doesn't like surprises. I saw that."

"The Germans saw it, too. But knowing something is true doesn't always mean you can do anything about it," Casimir said. "We'll just hope we'll be able to."

Vasili didn't think the bandits put in much work on the field fortifications he'd designed. He didn't push them. He was still more a useful POW than a fellow fighter. The proud Poles disliked obeying orders from somebody like him. The way things looked to him, if they hadn't had Russians to squabble with, they would have fought among themselves.

Of course, the Red Army had its own problems. Few of the soldiers it sent to Poland wanted to be there. They didn't fight the way they had against Hitler's men or the Americans. Their officers might order them to keep coming no matter what, but they didn't care to get killed for what looked to them to be no good purpose.

And, with Stalin dead, it was as if a huge, strong hand had come off the Soviet throttle. Soldiers didn't fear Molotov the way they'd feared his Georgian predecessor. That also left them less eager about fighting.

Which didn't mean they wouldn't. They started their latest assault on Major Casimir's position with an artillery bombardment that might have readied them for the final move against Berlin. Vasili huddled in a hole, praying nothing would come down on him and that blast wouldn't rip up his lungs from the inside out.

Katyushas rained down along with the 105s and 155s. Vasili hated being on the receiving end of the Stalin organs. Were his erstwhile comrades calling them Molotov organs now? He didn't believe it. He did hate the way the rockets screamed in before they burst.

No sooner had all that let up than the Red Army infantry came forward. Vasili had heard those drunken "*Urra!*"s before, from the middle of a swarm of foot soldiers. As a matter of fact, he'd let out some of them himself. Now, as with the Katyushas, they were coming at him.

Given the chance, he would have run away. He wasn't given the chance. He popped up from his hole, fired once or twice, and ducked down again. Just in time, too, since a tracer drew a line of fire through the place where his head had been a second or two earlier.

Casimir's men fought hard. They didn't run. The Russian had to clear them from the forward foxholes with machine pistols and entrenching tools. If you knew how, you could do some horrible things with an entrenching tool. Some of the Red Army veterans knew how.

Then the Poles with machine pistols Casimir had sent out ahead of time opened up on the Russians from the flank and rear. Even Vasili, in his scanty experience as a Red Army soldier, had seen how well the Soviet Union's soldiers did when they executed a fixed plan. They would carry it out come hell or high water, caring no more about casualties than about worn boots. Such indifference to damage was daunting and admirable at the same time.

But when it went wrong, when the officers and men suddenly had to think for themselves, most of them weren't up to it. They'd grown up in a system where blind obedience to superiors was the only thing that counted. When it didn't count any more, when blind obedience would obviously get you killed . . . They had no idea what to do. Some froze. Others panicked and ran away.

So it happened here. The Russians had been driving all before them. But, when they took fire from behind and from the side, they realized things weren't as they'd been told. To them, unexpected meant disastrous. They ran like rabbits. Some of them threw away their weapons to run faster. They'd been on the point of winning. They weren't any more. Vasili laughed and laughed, not least in relief.

Konstantin Morozov swigged vodka from his canteen to celebrate when the troop train rolled out of Poland and into the USSR. It even entered the Russian Soviet Federated Socialist Republic, of which Kaliningrad Oblast was a small, noncontiguous part. Kaliningrad—

named for a Finnish henchman of Stalin's—still didn't seem to wear its new handle well.

Up until 1945, it had been East Prussian Königsberg, a great German bastion against Russia. As the Great Patriotic War swirled towards an end, Königsberg stood siege and held out longer than it had any business doing. Wounded soldiers, nervous Nazis, and terrified civilians had taken ship out of there by the tens of thousands.

The city still lay shattered. The Soviet Union had expelled all the Fritzes who hadn't shipped out and whom the fighting hadn't killed. Loyal Russians skulked through the ruins. One day, maybe, Kaliningrad would turn into a real Soviet city. It hadn't begun to yet.

"We stay here, maybe, Comrade Sergeant?" Nodar Gachechiladze asked.

"I've heard ideas I liked less—I'll tell you that," Morozov answered. The stocky Georgian didn't speak much Russian, so Konstantin often thought he was on the dull side.

But the question held bite. As long as they stayed in the Kaliningrad Oblast, they were among Russians who (mostly) didn't hate the Soviet Union and everything it stood for. The next border, though, would take them into the Lithuanian Soviet Socialist Republic. The Lithuanians had thought Hitler made a better overlord than Stalin. They'd slaughtered their Jews, who knew damn well Hitler didn't and favored Stalin accordingly. Then the Red Army drove the *Wehrmacht* out again, and the Lithuanians got it in the neck one more time.

Gachechiladze chuckled harshly. "We go long enough, maybeso we see your Eigims again, hey?"

"I've heard ideas I liked more—I'll tell you that," Konstantin said.

The loader needed a moment to realize the tank commander hadn't gone and repeated himself. When he did, he chuckled again. "Me, too, specially we still gots dumb *metyeryebyets* at our gun," he said.

Pyotr Polikarpov was sitting right next to him in the turret. He paid no attention to anything Gachechiladze said. Maybe he thought listening to a loader was beneath a gunner's dignity. Or maybe he just didn't make the effort to penetrate Gachechiladze's thick Georgian accent. Either of those, to Konstantin's way of thinking, did indeed make him a dumb motherfucker.

Before sunrise the next morning, the troop train moved east again. It hadn't even got to the border between Kaliningrad Oblast and the Lithuanian SSR before bandits started shooting at it. These guys weren't fooling around the way the Poles had been. They knew the Red Army men weren't just going to pass through their shitty little country. The Russians were coming to Lithuania to do a job of work, work the Lithuanians didn't want done.

They had rifles, machine pistols, and machine guns. None of those would do much to a tank. But things stopped being funny when they started lobbing mortar bombs at the train. A hit from one of those could wreck a tank if it came down on the engine louvers. It could wreck the locomotive. Or it could tear up the tracks and force a derailment.

Ignoring the nuisance fire, Major Zhuk went from flatcar to flatcar and tank to tank of his command. "The gloves are off," he told Konstantin. "You see anybody shooting or getting ready to shoot at us, ventilate the pussies. You got that?"

"I serve the Soviet Union, Comrade Major!" Morozov said. After Zhuk went on to the next tank, Konstantin thumped Polikarpov on the shoulder. "You heard the boss man. Anything that looks like trouble, blow holes in it. How's that sound?"

"It's all right with me," Polikarpov said. Here, where he could actually be useful, he sounded as bloodthirsty as a tulip.

He did do some firing with the machine gun, though, not long after daybreak. Konstantin looked out through the periscopes built into the T-54's cupola. He saw the enemy machine gun spitting bullets at the train. He saw Polikarpov's tracers reaching out for it.

"By the Devil's granny's stinking old cunt, can't you shoot straighter than that?" he howled.

"Sorry, Comrade Sergeant. I've never fired at a stationary target from a moving gun platform before."

"How is that different from firing at a moving target from a station-ary tank?" Morozov demanded.

"I don't know, Comrade Sergeant. It just is." Polikarpov sounded offended that anyone should question his idiotic explanation.

Things didn't get better when they rolled into Lithuania. They'd just passed through the town of Taurage, a few kilometers inside the bor-der, when the train stopped. Konstantin didn't hear any crashes or booms that made him think the engine had been hit or had gone off the tracks. That was about the only good news he could find.

Genrikh Zhuk pounded on the turret roof a few minutes later. "Un-chain the tank," he said. "As soon as they position the ramp, dismount. We'll go into action as soon as enough of us get down. This is real war. They have *Panzerfausts* and old tanks. They're bastards, they're bandits, but they mean it. Be careful. Don't do anything stupid." He moved on.

Can I throw Polikarpov out? Konstantin wondered. He passed the word to his crew. "*Panzerfausts* are bad news. They were the Nazis' RPGs at the end of the Great Patriotic War. They don't have much range, but they can kill a tank. Pyotr, you see a guy with a stovepipe, kill him fast, you hear?"

"I'll do it, Comrade Sergeant," the gunner said, which was at least the right answer. He added, "Bandits must be Nazis themselves if they saved that shit all these years."

He might have been right. It didn't matter now, though. And, if the Lithuanians had tanks, those wouldn't be German leftovers. No, they'd be looted from Soviet armories. How much treason had gone into that? *Not a little bit, or I'm a virgin,* Morozov thought.

Out of the cupola went his head. You had to be able to see. If that gave snipers a better shot at you, then it did. Life was full of chances.

Here came a tank, from the direction of Taurage. It was one of the original T-34s, the ones with the 76mm gun and the small, two-man turret. At first, Konstantin just accepted that. Then, even before he saw the yellow-green-red flag painted on the turret, he realized such an ob-solete machine was exactly the kind the bandits were likeliest to be able to steal. "Kill it, Pyotr!" he screamed into the intercom.

Pyotr fired the T-54's main armament—and missed. The T-34 fired back. It missed, too. The commander in there was his own gunner. The Fritzes had shot rings around those T-34s, but with their puny guns it did them less good than they wanted. Pyotr took another shot, and missed again. A third, and another miss. Konstantin swore horribly. The T-34 hit his tank then, but the undersized round didn't get through.

One more try from the worthless Polikarpov. This time, the Lithuanian tank started to burn. "Took you fucking long enough," Konstantin snarled.

Then, too late, he saw a lance of fire flying straight at his tank. The *Panzerfaust* might have been old, but it still worked. The shaped charge slammed into the engine compartment. Fire and smoke erupted. The T-54 stopped.

"Out!" Morozov screamed. "Out! Out!" The hatches were narrow, but everybody made it. Konstantin had a pistol. Nodar Gachechiladze had a PPSh. That was it, against a country full of bandits who hated every Red Army man ever born.

ROLF MEHLEN OPENED his tin of American rations and eyed
the canned scrambled eggs and ham with resignation. "This isn't what
anybody would call good, but it keeps you going, I guess," he said.

"It's better if you heat it up first," Max Bachman said.

"Better isn't good. Besides, I haven't got the patience." As if to prove
as much, Rolf spooned the glop into his mouth.

Max had some different ration—Rolf thought it was beef stew. He
also shoveled it straight into his gob. Rolf didn't blame him; the stew
was just as bad warm. After Max swallowed, he said, "No, this isn't
great, either. But you know what?"

"No. What?" Rolf said obligingly.

"It beats the hell out of half-rotten horsemeat stewed with turnip
tops."

"Well, yeah. Those were the days, by God. Christ, there were plenty
of times when we wanted to jump up and down and dance because we
had horsemeat, even if it was off. How much fighting did you do on an
empty belly?"

"Too much, same as you." Max's spoon scraped the bottom of the tin. "Haven't had to do much of it this time around, though. Nice being on the end of the Amis' supply chain, isn't it?"

"It's a miracle the Americans aren't all too fat to walk, let alone fight," Rolf said. If he mocked them, he didn't have to think about how much they had. Last time around, they'd supplied big chunks of the Russian and English armies along with their own, and they'd been fighting Japan at the same time as Germany. They sure weren't any poorer this time around. It was daunting, if you let it be.

Max lit a Lucky Strike—more bounty from the rations. He blew out smoke. "How's the javelin-catching going?"

"The what?" Rolf knew he sounded irritated. He hated it when he didn't get a joke, and Max's were more obscure than most.

"Mine-clearing duty." The printer condescended to explain. "You know what they call somebody who does that long enough?"

"As a matter of fact, I don't, but what difference does it make? You're going to tell me anyway, right?"

Instead of telling him right away, Max blew him a kiss. "You're cute when you're mad," he said. "And I am going to tell you, because you're obviously too dumb to figure it out for yourself. They call him a casualty, that's what."

"*Yob tvoyu mat',*" Rolf said—it sounded filthier in Russian. "Besides, that's rubbish. Some of those guys made it all the way through the last war. They were good."

"They were good and lucky," Max said. "And they had the fancy training. What do you have besides a detector and a probe?"

"Enough sense to be careful," Rolf retorted. "I didn't blow myself up like that stupid Ivan."

"You know, it's peace now, or pretty close. They'll be mustering us out. We can go home, maybe even in one piece. If I'd been able to get leave, I'd've done it already."

"I guess so." Rolf knew he should have sounded enthusiastic. He didn't, not even to himself.

Max blew a stream of smoke at him. "I know what's wrong with you."

"Nothing's wrong with me!" Rolf said hotly.

"Like hell. I'll tell you what it is, too. You don't want peace to break out. You want to go right on shooting Russians."

"That's—" Rolf broke off. He wanted to say it was all a load of trash. But he couldn't, not without having both Max and himself know what a liar he was. He'd never felt more alive, more real, than when the *Leibstandarte Adolf Hitler* roared into action against the *Reich*'s enemies. He'd thanked God when this new war broke out. He could open up his business again at the same old stand and go back to doing what he did best in all the world: killing Communists.

Oh, it wasn't the same as it had been in the good old days. Some swishy queers had rewritten the rule book. People had kittens if you shot prisoners now, for instance. But it was still war, the best thing there was, maybe including pussy.

"You see?" Max said with a knowing chuckle.

"Oh, shut up," Rolf told him. He tried a new tack: "The *Führer* was the same way, you know. The fighting he did in Flanders in the first war, that was the high point of his life."

"He was a runner then, wasn't he?" Max said.

Rolf nodded. "That's right."

"From what my pa and his *Bierstube* buddies said, most of those guys got killed in a few weeks. Except for the time he caught some gas, Adolf went through that whole war with hardly a scratch. Talk about lucky!"

"God looked out for him." Rolf meant it.

But Max just rolled his eyes. "If God looked out for Germany, Hitler would've caught a fragment between the eyes in 1914. We'd all be better off if he had."

Rolf turned away in disgust. "Why do I waste my time talking with you?"

"You don't like it, go out to the minefields and talk with the mines," Max said. "Half the time in the last war, I thought you SS clowns fought so you could die for the *Vaterland* instead of making the Russians die for the *rodina*."

"Like anybody could expect a conscript to understand honor." Rolf got to his feet and stalked off. Behind him, Max laughed out loud. That only stiffened his back—and his resolve.

Out he went, with his fancy new American mine detector . . . and with his rifle, just in case. The grassland he stomped through wasn't marked or mapped as a minefield, but he hadn't gone more than thirty meters or so before he heard a loud buzz in his earphones.

"What the devil?" he said. His first guess was that the gadget had found a buried tomato tin or something. But you didn't get to be an old soldier by assuming your first guess was right. If you got a signal, especially a strong one like that, you had to proceed as if it were the real thing.

He flattened out on the ground, careful to go no farther. Then, cautiously, he probed with his bayonet. The steel met more metal. He withdrew it and began to dig. Without noticing he was doing it, he whistled tunelessly between his teeth.

Before long, the curved metal of the mine casing made him mutter "Well, fuck me" under his breath. He knew that shape, all right. He should have. He'd laid enough of them. It was a Tellermine, a German antipanzer mine from the last war. This had to be a *Wehrmacht* minefield everybody'd forgotten about.

The Tellermine wasn't dangerous to people; its tripping pressure was too heavy. It wasn't dangerous unless the firing mechanism had been booby-trapped, anyhow. Then the guy defusing it would get the last nasty surprise he ever needed.

That wasn't what made the fear sweat drip from Rolf's armpits. You didn't plant Tellermines by themselves. No—you laid a bunch of S-mines and wooden-cased *Schü Minen* with them, to maim the enemy foot soldiers who'd be loping along with the panzers. The antipersonnel mines made clearing the field one of those interesting bits of business, too.

Rolf wondered why sheep or cows or herders hadn't blown themselves to sausage meat around here. Somebody would have got rid of this minefield if they had. But no. He was stuck with it. He was, in fact, stuck in the middle of it.

Better to go back than forward, he decided. He didn't have—he didn't think he had—far to go before he got back to safe ground. Then he'd report to an officer and let the officious son of a bitch figure it out.

He stepped very carefully. One mistake, and . . . If he was diligent with the detector . . . He made it to the edge of the overgrown bare ground and relaxed. Out of the worst of it now. One more step and . . .

Pop! It didn't really sound like an explosion. The S-mine had sat there since 1945, but it still worked fine. German engineering. The Amis called them Bouncing Bettys. It jumped to about waist-high, then blew up for real, spraying shrapnel balls every which way. Rolf looked down in amazement at what was left of him. He screamed. He screamed and screamed and screamed, until he finally stopped.

A nurse came up to Cade Curtis' bed. She wasn't bad, but he still had enough morphine in him to make his interest purely academic. *I'll be a junkie, a one-legged junkie,* he thought. He couldn't get very worried about it: one more side effect of the drug.

"A couple of men here to see you, Captain," she said.

Doped as he was, Cade couldn't miss the disapproval that stuck out all over her like a porcupine's spines. He didn't get it. Nobody'd come to see him since he'd been wounded. Visitors would be something different, anyhow. "Okay," he said.

She sniffed and seemed to gather those affronted prickles around her before she flounced off. When she came back, she was leading two soldiers in American uniform. One was Howard Sturgis. The other, Cade saw with delighted surprise, was Jimmy. The nurse didn't scream *Gook!* at him, but that was what was eating her, all right.

Seeing Jimmy, though, was the best thing that had happened to Cade since he got hit. Morphine or not, he grinned from ear to ear. "Hey, what are you doing here?" he exclaimed.

"He made me bring him," Sturgis said dryly. "I figured he'd roll a grenade into my dugout if I didn't, so here we are."

"He should be under arrest!" the nurse said.

"It's a joke, honest," Cade said. Howard Sturgis nodded. The nurse relaxed—by some small fraction.

"Captain Curtis, he like father to me," Jimmy said, missing the by-play. "Before I meet him, I nothing. I never be nothing, neither. Now I am man. Now I am *American* man." He couldn't have sounded prouder.

By the expression on her face, the nurse wanted to tell him he was no such thing and never could be any such thing. The expressions on Cade's face, and on Sturgis', made her keep her mouth shut.

"Have to pay respects to father. Have to help take care of father." Jimmy used English to voice a very Korean sentiment.

And Cade suddenly murmured, "Holy cow!"

"What's cooking, Captain?" Sturgis said. "You okay?"

"Except for missing a leg, I'm great," Cade answered, and for once he meant it. "Know how we've been trying to finagle a way to get Jimmy back to the States?" He waited for Sturgis to nod, then hurried on: "How about if I adopt him? They can't keep him out if he's my kid, right?"

"You're out of your mind, and that's fraud against the government!" The nurse's voice went high and shrill.

"Oh, baloney," Cade said. "He's fought for the USA. Heck, he saved my life—I wouldn't be here if he didn't haul me to an aid station. He works like a son of a gun."

"That's all true—every word of it," Howard Sturgis affirmed.

"You're still crazy," the nurse said.

"Why?" Cade asked. "He'd make a better American than an awful lot of people born in Alabama or Wisconsin."

"He's a gook, that's why," the nurse said.

Jimmy swung toward her. He was a medium-sized, smooth-cheeked man, but the rage in his eyes made him seem eight feet tall and completely covered with hair. "You don't call me that," he said in a soft, low, deadly voice. "You don't never call me that, you hear?"

Howard Sturgis held out an arm in front of Jimmy to bar his path if he lost his temper. "Easy, boy," Sturgis said. "She's a dumb bitch, but she's an officer."

The nurse squeaked in fury. "How dare you talk about me that way?"

"You brung it on yourself, that's how." Sturgis didn't care if she didn't like what she heard. He'd won his battlefield commission for bravery. If they busted him back to sergeant, or even down to private, because he was insubordinate, he'd probably kiss them on both cheeks.

"I know guys have adopted Korean kids." Once Cade got an idea, he ran with it—which was more than he could do in the flesh right now.

"This is not a kid." The nurse pointed at Jimmy. In his much-worn U.S. uniform, he sure didn't look like a kid.

"Maybe he's just a big kid." Cade knew damn well there was more than one way to skin a cat. He'd never been a barracks lawyer before, but he was ready to start. "How old are you, Jimmy?"

Jimmy shrugged. "I don't know, Captain Cade, sir. Maybe nineteen, maybe twenty. Something like that."

"See?" Cade told the nurse. "He's still a minor."

"And you're still a nut job." She rounded on Sturgis and Jimmy. "Get out! All you've done is upset him."

"I'm not upset," Cade said. The nurse turned hard of listening. She shooed the men from his unit out of the ward.

An hour or so later, one of the doctors at the military hospital showed up at Cade's bedside. "Vera tells me you've gone round the bend," Lieutenant Colonel Nathan Marcus remarked.

"Sir, if you ask me, Vera's the one who's gone Asiatic," Cade said.

Marcus studied him with dark, pouchy, mournful eyes. "Well, you don't look like I need to send for the guys with the butterfly nets."

"No, not much need for that," Cade said bitterly. "I'm not flying anywhere real fast."

"Asiatic gets us back to where she was going," the doctor said. "She told me you were talking about legally adopting a Korean soldier and taking him back to the States. Why would you want to do that, son?"

Cade told him why, starting with how he'd liberated Jimmy from his own brutal captain—"Ever take in a puppy, sir?"—and ending with the mortar attack and Jimmy lugging him to the aid station. "I probably wouldn't be here if he hadn't," he said. "I expect I would've bled out pretty damn quick."

"I expect you're right." Dr. Marcus pinched his chin between his thumb and bunched fingers. "Well, you've got your reasons, sure as hell, and if you ask me they're good ones. I've seen a couple of these requests before, and. . . ." He shook his head.

"What do you mean, sir?" Cade was in many ways still an innocent young man. To be fair, he was also a long way from at his best.

"Let's put it like this—the Americans who wanted to adopt those Koreans liked them for different reasons than yours."

"Huh? Oh!" Even with morphine in him, Cade's cheeks heated. "That's disgusting!"

"The people in charge of such things agree with you. Those requests were rejected. I think yours could go forward. The paperwork is a bitch, though. Would you like some help with it?"

Which could only mean *I want to give you a hand*. How much clout did Marcus have? More than a little, for sure. "Thank you very much, sir. Anything you can do, I'd be grateful for." Cade added, "Can you tell Vera to go fly a kite, too?"

"As a matter of fact, it would be a pleasure," Dr. Marcus said. "You have kind of a drawl—you must be a Southern gentleman. I would have found something hotter than that to tell her to do."

"My father always told me to be polite to ladies," Cade said. His father had also backed up the telling with his hard hand, and sometimes with his belt.

"Nice to hear you listened to him. My old man told me all kinds of things, too. He told me I was a natural for the used-clothes business, which was the line he was in. But I quit listening to him when I was eleven, twelve years old. I'm better off for it, too."

Since Cade had never stopped listening to his father, he could only shrug. But he didn't think Nathan Marcus was wrong.

. . .

A car door slammed, out on Irving Street. Aaron Finch grinned a sharklike grin. "Somebody's here," he called to Ruth, who was working in the kitchen.

"Who is it?" she asked.

He looked out the living-room window. "Marvin," he answered.

"Uncle Marvin!" Leon squeaked. He liked Aaron's younger brother. That sometimes made Aaron wonder if something was wrong with the kid.

Aaron opened the front door. Marvin came in, along with his wife, Sarah, and their teenage daughter, Olivia. Leon liked Olivia, too. That was good, because she babysat him fairly often. Marvin and Aaron shook hands. Marvin had an odd grip; Aaron had cut off his little finger with a hatchet while chopping wood when they were kids. Marvin rarely let him forget it, even more than forty years after the fact.

"You told me Roxane and Howard were coming," Marvin said.

Another couple of car doors closed. Aaron looked out the window again. "Here they are now, in fact. And I hope you don't mind, but I invited a young guy who started working with me at Blue Front. He came over from Europe not too long ago, and Mr. Weissman gave him a job."

"A *Yehuda*?" Sarah inquired.

"*Fraygst nokh?*" Aaron answered. *Do you need to ask?* He went on, still in Yiddish, "His name's Istvan Szolovits." He pronounced the Hungarian handle as best he could, adding, "He hasn't learned much English yet, so we all get to trot out the *mamaloshen*."

Olivia looked pained. "I can mostly understand you—Mom and Dad talk Yiddish when they don't want me to know what's going on, so of course I learned to follow—but I don't speak it for beans." By the way she said it, she didn't want to, either. To the second generation born in America, Old Country ways flew out the window.

As Howard and Roxane walked in, Marvin told Olivia, "Don't worry, kid. Children should be seen but not heard, anyway." She made a horrible face at him. Marvin would have done the same thing or worse had anyone said that to him when he was Olivia's age.

Istvan arrived a couple of minutes later. He was driving a Hudson from before the war that smoked more than Aaron did. The way he ground the gears didn't do the transmission any good, either; he was still learning how. But he'd bought it for a hundred bucks. It got him back and forth to Blue Front. With luck, it would keep running till he could afford something better.

He was wearing a short-sleeved cotton shirt and Levi's, but he bowed over women's hands like a count from the vanished Austro-Hungarian Empire. Olivia was visibly smitten. Istvan said, "So good of you to invite me to meet your charming family, Aaron. I thank you so much."

"My pleasure, believe me," Aaron said, which was true in ways the kid from Hungary didn't begin to understand. "Can I get you something to drink? Can I get everybody something to drink?"

Requests were about evenly split between beer and scotch. Marvin asked for a martini: "Just wave the vermouth over it. Can't get too dry for me."

Istvan asked for a brew. When Aaron gave him a Burgie, he swigged and then made a face. "America is the richest country in the world. Why is the beer so much worse here than in Europe?"

If Aaron hadn't drunk beer in European ports during his hitch in the merchant marine, he might have been offended. As things were, he knew Istvan was right. He said about the only thing he could: "Any beer is better than no beer at all."

"What smells good?" Howard asked. He was beginning to get a lean and hungry look. Being out of work would do that to you. Roxane brought in some money typing and clerking, but not a lot.

"*Holuptzas,*" Ruth answered. That sparked some interesting talk. There were almost as many version of the Yiddish name for stuffed cabbage as people in the house. Aaron heard *holishkas* and *golubtsy* and a couple of others.

Howard said, "During the war, I knew a gal from Chicago who called 'em pigs in blankets—in English, I mean. She was Jewish, too."

"Crazy." Aaron turned to Istvan. "How do you say it in Hungarian?"

"*Töltött káposzta,*" he said, which was way out in left field.

Or Aaron thought so, anyhow. Ruth said, "*Cabbage* is *kapusta* in Russian, too. My mother and father would call it that sometimes, along with *kroyt.*" The common Yiddish word was German *kraut*'s half-brother.

They sat down to dinner in a little while. Everybody devastated the stuffed cabbage. Howard Bauman ate as if they'd outlaw the stuff at midnight. He kept saying "Boy, this is good!" to soften the gluttony. It did help, some.

"How did you come to America, Istvan?" Roxane asked when people had slowed down enough to talk as well as eat.

"I was in the Hungarian People's Army. I got sent to Germany—I was fighting there when I got captured. They questioned me at a POW camp in France, then sent me here for more," he said. "When they finished with me, they told me to keep my nose clean and fixed up the job at Blue Front."

"What did you think of the progressive government in Hungary?" By the way Roxane asked the question, she was sure she already knew the answer.

"Well . . ." Istvan *was* a polite young man. He did hesitate. But he answered with the truth as he saw it: "Rakosi is a Russian puppet, of course. The Communists are better than the Arrow Cross, I will say. The Arrow Cross killed everybody they didn't like. The Communists just kill the ones they *really* don't like. The rest, they send to prison or a lunatic asylum or a labor camp. Admiral Horthy was better than the Communists *or* the Arrow Cross, way better."

That a country without a coastline should have been ruled by an admiral said something about Hungary. Aaron was damned if he could see what, though.

As for Roxane, she looked as if she'd just walked into a straight right from Joe Louis. Here was somebody from an actual Communist country—maybe the first somebody from an actual Communist country she'd ever met—and he didn't like the workers' paradise? Aaron, who'd already heard what Istvan thought of the current rulers in Budapest, had invited him with malice aforethought.

"But . . . wasn't Horthy a Fascist dictator?" That was Marvin. His politics didn't lean as far to the left as Roxane's and Howard's, but lean they did.

"He was a dictator, yes. More nationalist than Fascist, I think," Istvan said. "The Arrow Cross, now . . . *They* were Fascists. They made the Nazis proud of them. And Rakosi, he made Stalin proud of him the same way. He acted just like the people who told him what to do."

"But didn't he break up the landed estates and give the peasants farms of their own?" Howard asked.

"He broke up the estates, yes. But most of the land went to collective farms, and people didn't like them," Istvan answered. "The peasants didn't get rich, or even middle-class. Now that I've seen America . . . I'm not sure even Rakosi has as many good things as this house does. Telephone, TV set, radio, books, all with no censor, terrific food—this is wonderful!"

"Who wants dessert?" Ruth asked quickly. Unlike a lot of her relatives and even more of Aaron's, she didn't relish argument for its own sake. She went on, "They're cherry pies from Van de Kamp's bakery."

She was a good cook most ways. She'd done her own baking once, not long after she and Aaron got married. The result showed why bakeries made money. After that, she'd bought baked goods.

For some reason, conversation languished even though the pies were good. People went home early. To his credit, Marvin told Istvan he was glad to have met him. Roxane and Howard didn't.

"You did that on purpose," Ruth said after everybody was gone.

"Who, me?" Aaron tried for innocence, but felt himself failing. He changed the subject: "The *holuptzas* will be even better tomorrow after they've sat in the icebox all day. The flavors blend."

"You aren't fooling me one bit, Buster," Ruth said, and Aaron felt like a chess player who'd just watched a gambit fail.

Boris Gribkov minded bombing Budapest less than he would have with, say, Warsaw. He'd been through Hungary. He knew damn well that the country was chock full of bandits. They'd taken shots at the Soviet convoy that brought him back to the capital.

Matyas Rakosi and his pro-Soviet faction were supposed to be in charge in Budapest. Theory was wonderful. Boris hoped the people throwing antiaircraft fire at his Tu-4 weren't committed Communists. If they were, they needed to be committed, all right—to the loony bin.

"Can we unload?" he shouted to the bombardier.

"Another fifteen seconds, Comrade Pilot, and we'll be over the rebellious area," Fyodor Ostrovsky said.

Anther fifteen seconds flying straight like this and they were liable to be dead. That was one of the chances you took when you flew bombing runs. Boris had lived through all of them so far. It only took one, of course. The heavy bomber bucked in the air from the turbulence near misses kicked up.

"Bombing the target!" Ostrovsky said. The bombs fell free. The bomb bay hissed closed. Boris jammed the throttles on all four engines to the red line. He wanted to get the hell out of there as fast as he could.

Intelligence types had assured him that the Hungarian People's Air Force remained loyal and that no warplanes had gone over to the reactionary counterrevolution. Unfortunately, Soviet intelligence types had assured him of any number of things that later turned out not to be true. He hoped the radar operator wouldn't suddenly start screaming about bogies. Even obsolescent fighters could outperform the still more obsolescent Tu-4.

Boris patted the yoke. Tu-4s might be obsolescent, but they'd visited enormous destruction on the USA and its allies. The B-29s after which they were modeled had visited even more on the Soviet Union, though. That he wouldn't be landing in Minsk—that he couldn't be landing in Minsk—proved the point.

How would the *rodina* get back on its feet after two devastating wars in the course of a decade? The Soviet Union had just started recovering from the last war when this one broke out. And Truman had done to Soviet cities what Hitler only dreamt of doing.

They came down at the airstrip outside of Mogilev. No A-bombs had hit Mogilev, which only proved what a miserable little town it was. Now towns like Mogilev were the centers from which the USSR would have to pull itself back together.

After the landing, Boris reported on the attack to Colonel Petlyura. The Ukrainian officer went on as if obedience to Soviet central authority were the only possible course. For him, it was. That made him admirable. Whether it also left him out of touch with reality was a different question.

"How heavy was the flak?" he asked.

"I've seen worse," Boris said, "but it shouldn't have been there at all, should it?"

"Traitors everywhere," the colonel said. "Once we have things under control again, they'll get what they deserve." If he had any doubts about whether that would happen, he didn't show them.

"I hope you're right, Comrade Colonel," Boris said.

"Once we put enough soldiers on the ground there, and once the fence-sitters in the satellites see which side their bread is buttered on, things will be all right," Petlyura said. "Some of the fools there think the Americans will come to their rescue, but that isn't going to happen."

"I hope you're right," Boris repeated.

Petlyura nodded. "I *am* right," he said, sounding as certain as Stalin ever had. He had his reasons, too: "The armistice lets us do what we have to do with those people, as long as we don't drop any more A-bombs on them. The Americans don't like that any better than you did." He'd talked with Dzhalalov back at Tula, then, or the information had gone into Boris' file. His scowl said Boris' reluctance to have anything more to do with atomic weapons should have been a firing-squad offense.

Were the war against the USA still going on, it might have been. Of course, were the war against the USA still going on, Boris might not have been so reluctant. As things were, with the situation less urgent and with the Soviet government less sure of itself, he had a little more leeway to act like a human being.

Poor Leonid Tsederbaum hadn't had that kind of leeway. And he'd been issued or acquired a soul more finely grained than Boris'. Tearing the heart out of Paris was more than he could stand. He hadn't waited for a firing squad or even done anything to deserve one: the *rodina* called him a Hero of the Soviet Union. He used his service pistol to show what he thought of his own wartime exploits.

"Comrade Colonel, may I ask you something?" Boris said.

Volodymyr Petlyura's pale eyes narrowed further. "Go ahead," he said. *Go ahead if you dare* was what he meant.

But Boris said, "Thank you, sir. After we finish putting down the bandits in the satellites, how much good will we be able to get out of them?"

"Quite a bit," Petlyura said implacably. "The Americans didn't hit them nearly so hard as they hit the Soviet Union. More of their facto-ries and farms are intact than ours. Their economies can be the starter motors that help our larger one get moving again. And, of course, they are still our shield against aggression from the west."

The worst of it was, he might have been right. The Hungarians, the Czechoslovakians, the Poles, and the East Germans would certainly welcome American invaders with open arms—their women with open legs. But Soviet troops garrisoning the satellites would have hundreds of kilometers of non-Soviet soil to fight on. And those countries hadn't taken so many A-bombs as the USSR.

"With everything going on in the Baltics and the Caucasus, can we keep the satellites under control?" Boris asked.

"Oh, absolutely," the air base commandant said. "My people resisted the Russians, but in the end there are always too many Russians to fight. The Nazis found out the same thing. There are just too many Rus-sians. You're one yourself, Gribkov, so you don't think about that. But all the neighbors do. We have to."

Under the law, everyone in the Soviet Union was the same as every-body else. In practice, things ran pretty much as they had back in the days of the Russian Empire. Russians ruled the roost. Byelorussians and (despite what Petlyura said) Ukrainians were all right, too, as long as they forgot where they came from and acted as Russian as they could.

The same held true for small, clever groups like Armenians, Georgians, and Jews—though they had a harder time making Russians forget their origins. Jews, without a state of their own till Israel was born again, couldn't do much about that. Armenians and Georgians longed to get out from under the Russians' muscular thumb.

For their part, the Balts looked down their noses at Russians. They might almost have been Germans, as far as that went. Back in the day, a lot of their nobles *had* been German.

As for the Asians—the Kazakhs and Tajiks and Uzbeks and Turkmens and all the rest—they had to be twice as good as Russians to get half as far. Russians didn't take them seriously. When you thought ahead of time that someone would be ignorant and superstitious, chances were you'd see him that way regardless of whether he really was.

Colonel Dzhalalov, back in Tula, had beaten those odds. Colonel Petlyura here certainly showed he was aware of them. And what did he think of Russians? He'd given Boris a hint. Pushing for more wouldn't be smart. Boris said, "Comrade Colonel, we need to make sure this is a country worth living in. All of us do."

"Yes, that would be good. That has always been the goal. How we manage it . . ." Petlyura shrugged. "It's not for soldiers to decide. Our leaders will tell us what to do, and we'll do it." Boris nodded, even while wondering whether blind reliance on leaders wasn't part of the problem.

18

HARRY TRUMAN NODDED to the Yugoslav foreign minister as that worthy—and his interpreter—walked into the President's office. "Good morning, your Excellency," Truman said, extending his hand.

Edvard Kardelj had a smooth, firm grip. He was in his mid-forties, with a neat mustache and dark hair that drew back at the temples. After he said something in his harsh, consonant-filled native tongue, the interpreter told Truman, "He apologizes for not speaking English. He knows Italian, French, and German, but never had the chance to learn your tongue."

"I haven't studied German or French since my school days," Truman said. "I'm sure we'll do better through you." The interpreter spoke like an Englishman who rolled his r's.

Kardelj said, "It is strange I am here at all. To the People's Republic of China, Yugoslavia is a deviationist socialist state. But it is one of the few to have relations with both China and the United States, so the Chinese government approached our embassy in Peking, asking for our good offices."

"I'll listen to what you have to say for them. Will they listen to what you have to say for me?" Truman asked.

"I think so. Why would they have gone to the trouble of arranging this if they then ignored the return step?" Edvard Kardelj returned.

"Okay, fair enough. That's a good point. Well, what's the message they want you to deliver?"

"They will agree to an armistice based on the *status quo ante bellum* if you leave off your bombing campaign against their cities and railroads."

"Will they?" Truman breathed. That was what he'd been hoping for since MacArthur's offensive into North Korea and the A-bombs falling on Manchuria hadn't persuaded either Mao or Kim Il-sung to pack it in.

"So they assure our people in Peking, at any rate," Kardelj said.

"Do they mean it? Do your people in Peking judge that they mean it?" Truman asked. "And if they do mean it, can they bring Kim along and make North Korea stop fighting, too?"

"The ambassador judged they were serious, yes." Kardelj pulled a gold cigarette case out of his inside coat pocket. For a Communist, he was doing pretty well for himself. He gave a smoke to his interpreter and held the case out to Truman. The President shook his head. Shrugging, Kardelj lit up. He went on, "I would not have come to Philadelphia if he had judged them to be playing games."

"That makes sense," Truman agreed. "But making sense doesn't prove anything, either. And what about Kim? If he tries to keep fighting after the Red Chinese leave, I'll knock North Korea even flatter than it is already. Make that very clear to Peking, your Excellency."

"I will do so," Edvard Kardelj replied. "Chou En-lai, the Chinese foreign-affairs minister, seems to be capable. He says his country is able to ensure that the People's Democratic Republic of Korea will abide by the armistice."

"Okay," Truman said. "But we will have reconnaissance planes over the Yalu day and night. If Mao starts sending Kim little presents, we'll make them both sorry. Make sure Peking gets *that*, too."

"I am sure, sir, that the Chinese authorities have taken it into account," Kardelj said. That could mean anything or nothing. Maybe they thought the USA wouldn't go back to war once it had made something close to peace. *And maybe they're right, too,* Truman thought. Everybody from Maine to California had had a bellyful of fighting.

The interpreter opened his attaché case and took out a small, squat bottle. "Slivovitz. Plum brandy. Good Yugoslavian slivovitz, not the paint thinner the Hungarians brew. It is to toast what we have done today." Like a conjurer, he produced three shot glasses from the case. He handed Truman the cork as he poured from the bottle.

Truman sniffed. It smelled of plums and alcohol. Kardelj raised his little glass. "*Zhiveli!*" he said.

"To life!" the interpreter glossed. They both knocked back their shots. Truman followed suit. The plum brandy scorched its way down to his stomach, where it exploded like a grenade. If this was good Yugoslavian slivovitz, he hoped to God never to try the bad stuff.

"Is there enough in that bottle for another toast?" the President asked. "If there isn't, I'll have them bring up some bourbon."

"I think we have sufficient," the interpreter said. He poured. They did.

"Good. To peace!" Truman said. "May it last longer than the last one did." Everyone drank again. It hurt less this time. Truman guessed his nerve endings were stunned.

"I hope the fighting is over," Edvard Kardelj said. "Sometimes fighting is necessary. No one can say otherwise. But in my life I have seen too much."

"So have I, starting with the First World War. You would have been a little boy then," Truman said. The foreign minister nodded. Truman continued, "Everyone has seen too much by now."

"I am a Slovenian. I joined the partisans when the Nazis invaded Yugoslavia," Kardelj said. "I was a Communist before that, you understand, opposing the Yugoslavian monarchy. It was really a Serbian monarchy, and oppressed Slovenians and Croats and Bosnians and Macedonians."

Truman remembered that the Croats had enthusiastically sided with the Nazis after the invasion. The Fascist Independent State of Croatia (so-called—it was always Hitler's puppet, always on strings) had been nasty enough to horrify even the SS. It spent its four years of existence paying back the Serbs in blood. Up till now, Truman had hardly thought to wonder whether the Croats had grievances of their own.

"Marshal Tito doesn't discriminate among the nationalities in Yugoslavia?" the President asked.

"No, sir. You understand, after the Federal Socialist Republic of Yugoslavia was established, he naturally punished criminals and traitors," Kardelj said. By *punished,* he meant *killed* or *jailed* or *sent to a labor camp.* Tito hadn't been as vicious as the Croats before him, but he hadn't been Mr. Softy, either. Kardelj went on, "Now all positions are given in proportion to the number of people each nationality has. If the Serbs still get more than any other group, it is only because they have the largest population. They get no excess above that. Thus no one is in any position to complain."

"Of course." Truman's voice was dry enough to make the interpreter raise a bushy eyebrow. *Well, too bad,* Truman thought. Nobody in Yugoslavia was likely to complain about anything Tito did. People who tried that tended to be bad insurance risks.

Maybe Truman's tone got through to Edvard Kardelj. Or maybe he followed more English than he let on. He said something in . . . Serbo-Croatian? Slovenian? Were they different? Truman didn't know. The translator rendered it as, "You must remember, Mr. President, we are in a revolutionary situation. We have no time for kindness or gentleness."

"Back before I was born, we fought a civil war, too. At the end of it, we hanged the people who plotted to kill President Lincoln and some of the men who ran an especially bad prisoner-of-war camp, but that was all. No one thinks the South will ever try to leave the United States again."

Not unless we try to make Negroes really equal to whites and give them all the vote, Truman thought. *Or maybe not even then.* After World War II, he'd ordered the armed forces desegregated. People had said the sky would fall. No matter what they'd said, it was still up there.

That would be something for his successor to worry about. No one except Richard Nixon was screaming too loudly about his extra year. He was bending the Constitution by staying on. Wartime Presidents often did that. FDR had, with his internment camps for Japanese-Americans. Lincoln had, suspending *habeas corpus* during the Civil War. Truman didn't think he was breaking the Constitution. Once peace settled in, the old rules would come back.

And the Red Chinese had had enough! That was worth toasting, even with a plum-flavored Bunsen burner.

Everyone at the air base near Dundee celebrated, Bruce McNulty as eagerly as the rest of the flyers and groundcrew men. The B-29s wouldn't redeploy to the Far East. The Red Chinese wouldn't get the chance to shoot them down in bunches.

A very drunk groundcrew sergeant—a senior mechanic—said, "This has to be how the leathernecks felt when they found out they wouldn't need to invade Japan after all."

Bruce didn't know how to answer that. For one thing, what made the invasion of Japan unnecessary was the A-bomb. He'd already dropped too goddamn many of those. For another . . .

"Christ on the crapper, Andy, you didn't have anything to worry about anyway," a tail gunner said. "You'd stay back at the airstrip and stuff your face at the mess hall all the time. It's us guys who go up in the air, we're the ones sweating bullets."

Andy looked comically amazed. "Oh, yeah," he said. "I forgot about that." He put his head down on the table and started to snore.

Raising his own pint mug, Bruce said, "Here's to unemployment!"

"I've never been so glad to get put outa work," another pilot said.

And that was about the size of it. When your job was destroying cities, you were a lot happier if you didn't have to do it. Bruce had heard of pilots and navigators and bombardiers who couldn't stop brooding about the hell on earth they'd delivered during the war. A couple had got Section 8's—psychiatric discharges. A couple of others had made sure they stopped brooding for good, one with a .45, the other with a noose.

The scary thing was, it wasn't as if the notion hadn't crossed Bruce's mind. He wished he hadn't taken the Grasshopper across the channel. He'd seen Fakenham laid waste. Why did he need to see Antwerp, too? What was the difference but a matter of scale?

But wasn't scale the point? Sure it was. Over almost half a century, conventional bombs had come to seem like an extension of ordinary artillery. A-bombs were either on or just over the edge of what warfare could bear and still go on. The next stop up, H-bombs . . . One had killed Stalin, and everybody else for miles around him. Three or four could murder everybody in a New England state or a smallish European country.

Why have them, then? Because if you didn't and the other bastard did, he could use them on you and you couldn't hit back. If he knew you had them and would use them, he wouldn't dare trot his out. It would be like fighting a duel with flamethrowers at two paces.

Truman, of course, hadn't thought Stalin would use his A-bombs. Along with Hitler's invasion of Russia, that had to count as one of the biggest military miscalculations in the history of military miscalculations. As with a lot of such things, it was much too late now to brood about might-have-beens.

And yet, as Bruce had that thought, he also wondered how he and Daisy would have wound up getting along. He feared they wouldn't have done very well. She'd been A-bombed. She'd barely pulled through her bout of radiation sickness. Could she have spent the rest of her life with someone who'd brought death or that kind of anguish to so many people who'd done nothing to deserve it except be born in the wrong country?

It seemed unlikely, to say the least. He would have gambled all the same. He thought she would have, too. You couldn't win if you didn't bet. But you didn't win just because you bet, either. Any number of people coming home from Nevada broke would testify to that.

He started to get up and go to the bar for another pint of bitter. Then he realized he'd already had plenty. As the sozzled sergeant named

Andy had, he put his head down on the table and went to sleep—or passed out, depending on how you looked at things.

He woke with the sense that a good deal of time had passed and with the overwhelming urge to piss. He staggered to the jakes, almost as unstable as a B-29 with its tail shot away. The reek in there did more to wake him all the way than his bladder could. He fought not to puke while he did what needed doing. Someone, or several someones, hadn't managed not to.

Daisy'd cleaned her pub every night after closing time. As far as Bruce knew, she'd done it all by herself. The Owl and Unicorn was always spotless, the john always clean when it opened. Daisy'd never bitched about the work, not where he could hear her do it. To her, it was just part of the job.

Outside the pub sat the bicycle he'd bought for getting around off the base. He mounted it and pedaled back toward his barracks. He had trouble remembering to stay on the left and trouble doing it even after he remembered. The blackout had been lifted, but street lights were few and far between. Luckily, no cars came along the road.

The bicycle found the right building almost the way a horse with a dozing rider found the barn. Bruce lurched inside and found his cot the same way.

When he came to the next morning, he discovered he hadn't even taken off his shoes. Since he was an officer and presumed to be a gentleman, everyone assumed he knew his own business and nobody did it for him. He had a thick head, but not a horrible hangover. Some cold water on his face and a couple of aspirins down the hatch and he felt close to human, in a mournful way.

Breakfast was coffee and burnt toast without butter. Quite a few of the young presumed gentlemen ate lightly and moved carefully, as if afraid their noggins would fall into their coffee cups if they weren't wary.

Caffeine helped the aspirins do whatever they did. Bruce went to the Quonset hut where Colonel Frank Pagliarone, the base commander, did his duty. Pagliarone was one of those Italians who got five o'clock shadow at eight in the morning. He eyed Bruce. "Have a good time last night?" he asked with a knowing smirk.

"I got drunk, sir, if that's what you mean," Bruce answered. "It isn't the same thing."

"No, hey? Plenty of people would tell you different," Colonel Pagliarone said. "But what are you doing here if you tied one on? You don't need me to read the riot act. I know you better than that."

"No, sir," Bruce admitted. He would have been laughing behind a wooden façade if Pagliarone had told him off. But the base CO was smart enough to know as much. Taking a deep breath, Bruce went on, "Now that peace looks like it's here worldwide, I want to start the paperwork that will separate me from the Air Force."

"Okay. That's serious business." Pagliarone lit a Camel and held out the pack to Bruce. He took one with a word of thanks. After a puff or two, the colonel went on, "You sure you want out, son? You stay with it, you'll make bird colonel for sure, likely wind up with stars on your shoulders."

Bruce shrugged. "None of that matters to me any more. Permission to speak frankly, sir?"

"How am I gonna stop you? You leave the Air Force, it won't matter. You change your mind and stay in, you'll never see another promotion, but you say you don't give a shit. So go ahead and talk."

"Thank you, Colonel. Way it looks to me is, I've blown up too many cities. I've dropped too many A-bombs on men, women, and children, and most of them would never have done me any harm in a thousand years. If I do any more of it, I'll shoot myself next time I get as drunk as I was last night."

"You aren't the only flyer who feels that way." Pagliarone's voice went from rasping to surprisingly gentle. "Some of them get over it, you know."

"Uh-huh. And some of them don't. Everybody knows suicides are way up. Everybody with an eye to see knows why, too. If you ask more from a man than he can possibly give and he gives it anyway, how surprised are you gonna be when he discovers he's got nothing left inside afterwards?"

Pagliarone looked at the short butt on his Camel. He stubbed it out in an ashtray made from a brass shell casing. He started to say something, stopped, and then tried again. This time, he came straight to the point: "Okay, McNulty, you sold me. I'll get those papers rolling. Won't be long, promise."

"Thank you very much, sir," Bruce said. *I may live. I just may.*

"Here. Want a cigarette?" Aaron Finch asked the question in English. He held out the pack so Istvan Szolovits could have no doubt what he meant.

"Thank you." Istvan knew he was a smart kid. He still had an accent when he used English, but he was getting good at small talk. One step led to the next, almost as if in a dance. For more complicated things, or things where he didn't know in which direction the conversation would go, he stuck to Yiddish. Behind that, he longed for Magyar. His thoughts still came first in it, and had to be translated into other, less satisfactory tongues.

"Any time." Aaron flicked his lighter. Istvan leaned close to start his cigarette. Aaron went on, "I had a good time when you came to dinner a couple of weeks ago, just so you know. You're welcome any time."

"Am I really?" Istvan fought to hide his surprise. "I've kept meaning to tell you how sorry I am that I upset your relatives. The only thing that stopped me was, I was too embarrassed."

"Don't worry about it," Aaron said. "You told 'em the truth, and they didn't like it. Is that your fault or theirs?"

"What is truth?" Istvan returned.

Aaron pushed his glasses farther up on his nose. "Thank you, Pontius Pilate," he said. In America, a Jew could come out with a crack like that without worrying who might overhear. It was exhilarating, as if water had turned to wine. For Istvan, freedom took getting used to. Aaron went on, "You told 'em what the truth looked like from your point of view, anyway. They needed to hear it."

"Did they?" Istvan knew he sounded doubtful.

"Damn right they did." Aaron sounded very sure of himself. From what Istvan had seen, he always did. He wasn't always right—who was?—but he was always sure. He added, "It's easy being a Jew in the USA. It's easy being a Red in the USA, too. You really have to work to get thrown in jail for it here. And you're never going to grab power, not in a million years. So you sit on the sidelines and you make noise and you drink. You might as well be at a football game."

He didn't mean what Istvan meant by football. Americans called that soccer, and ignored it almost completely. American football was something like rugby and something like war. They played it in helmets and body armor. They needed the protection; it was the kind of game that broke unprotected people to pieces.

"How come you are not like them?" Istvan asked.

"I had to work harder," Aaron answered without hesitation. "Marvin does public relations and makes deals and shoots himself in the foot. Howard's an actor who can't get parts these days. They don't get their hands dirty. I've been a delivery driver, a streetcar motorman, a mechanic, a cowboy, part of the black gang in the tubs I sailed in during the war."

"You are a genuine proletarian," Istvan said. "The Hungarian government would have . . . said it loved you."

"But proletarians are supposed to be ignorant, right? My old man taught me to read before I started school, same as he did with all his kids. I never quit, either. So I maybe have a suspicion the stories the Reds tell about pie in the sky by and by are just that—stories."

"That's how it looked to me." Before Istvan said so, he looked over his shoulder. No, no AVO or MGB men lurking just within earshot and waiting to pounce like a cat at a mousehole.

Aaron not only saw that glance, he recognized it for what it was, which most Americans might not have. "You're okay here, kid," he said.

"They won't haul you away for anything you say. You have to do something. Even then, you get a lawyer."

That impressed Istvan less than Aaron might have hoped. You could usually get a lawyer in Hungary, too. But he wouldn't do you any good once you got him. He was just another way for you to waste your money.

"I am glad you aren't angry at me." Istvan meant that in more ways than one. If Aaron were to whisper a bad word about him to Herschel Weissman, how long would he keep his Blue Front job? How much trouble would he have landing another if he lost this one? In Communist Hungary, not having a job was a criminal offense. Was it here, too? Would they use it as an excuse to ship him back to the POW camp in France? Were they turning people loose from that camp yet? If they were, would he have to go back to Matyas Rakosi's workers' paradise and explain what he'd been doing in the United States?

Those were a lot of worries to pack into a brief expression of relief. Though he didn't realize it, he was wasting his time on every single one of them. Aaron would never have reported him for anything short of high treason or sabotage. Aaron would rather have gone to the rack than squeal on a fellow worker. He'd put up with Jim Summers for years rather than reporting him to the boss. Even if no Marxist-Leninist, he was fiercely loyal to his own class.

All he said now was, "Don't get yourself in an uproar about it. C'mon. We've got a TV and an icebox to take to Pasadena."

What he called an icebox—probably because that was the name he'd used as a kid for the cases that kept food cold—was a refrigerator fancier than any in Budapest. It had its own freezer compartment where you could keep meat fresh for weeks, not just days.

As for television . . . Istvan had heard of it while he was still in Europe. He'd seen a couple of dead sets in German houses where his unit of the Hungarian People's Army had camped. But he'd never seen TV in action till he came to the States. More than the abundant food, the cars and the roads and the phones and the radios (some of them in the cars!), television made him think he'd taken a ride on H. G. Wells' time machine (he'd read the book over and over in Hungarian). If TV wasn't something out of the future, he didn't know what would be.

"It seems very strange to me that, if you have the money, you can put it on the counter and buy a television," he said as he dollied it up the ramp into the Blue Front truck.

"How come? I did. I needed to save for a while so I wouldn't have to make time payments, but I'm glad I did." Aaron handled the refrigerator. Those, Istvan had learned, were surprisingly delicate. You had to keep them upright. If you didn't, you'd kill the motor and be left with a several-hundred-dollar piece of junk.

The refrigerator was bigger and heavier than the TV. Istvan was bigger and heavier than Aaron, and felt guilty when someone more than twice his age handled something that size while he just watched. But Aaron knew the business better than he did. The older man had whip-cord muscles, and understood lifting and hauling and securing cargo from long experience.

Even by American standards, Pasadena had money. The woman who accepted delivery was polite to Aaron and Istvan, but in a distant way. A colored housekeeper was sweeping and dusting. Istvan tried not to seem to stare. She was the first Negro he'd ever seen close up.

Setting up the TV meant hauling it into the front room where Mrs. Blankenship wanted it, hooking up the wires that led to the antenna on the roof, and plugging it in. Aaron took care of the refrigerator. He made sure it had survived the trip from the warehouse and talked with the lady of the house about the temperature control. Istvan followed maybe one word in four.

Mrs. Blankenship didn't seem to follow much more. "Lucille!" she called sharply. "Come in here and get the low-down on how this thing works."

"Comin', ma'am," Lucille said. Aaron went through it again. He sounded the same talking to Lucille as he had to Mrs. Blankenship. Istvan thought better of him for that.

Mrs. Blankenship signed the paperwork acknowledging receipt in good working order and gave Aaron a check. He stuck it in his breast pocket. "Thank you very much, ma'am," he said.

Istvan tried out some English once they were driving away: "She is—how you say?—not too smart."

"More likely, she just doesn't want to listen to the hired help," Aaron said. "It isn't hard. Lucille picked it up easy as you please. She'd get in trouble if she didn't. Not Mrs. Blankenship, though. She thinks angels come out when she takes a crap."

"Maybe American needs revolution after all," Istvan said.

Aaron gave him a peculiar look. "Yeah," he said after a pause. "Maybe it does."

A couple of Ihor Shevchenko's men used their entrenching tools to deepen a hole at the bottom of a 155mm shell crater. After a while, one of them looked up and said, "Think that's deep enough, Comrade Sergeant?"

Ihor studied the grave. "Give it another half a meter, Misha," he said. "We don't want the dogs digging up poor Volodya, right?"

What a sergeant said was right by definition, at least if you were a private. Misha and the other Red Army man dug some more. Volodya's body, wrapped in bloody burlap sacking, lay by the edge of the crater. He was dead because he'd been greedy and stupid. He'd grabbed a bottle of vodka without noticing the wire attached to it. That had to be one of the oldest booby traps in the world. The charge had blown Volodya, the booby, to bits.

Those bits, or most of them, went into the grave. The soldiers shoveled dirt over their late comrade. "Put some paving stones and bricks on top of all that," Ihor said. "Gotta keep the scavengers away." They both sighed heavily, but did as they were told.

And that was the only monument Volodya would ever get. It might have been just as well; a proper headstone would have read *Died of stupidity*. Back in the USSR, they'd built all sorts of fancy memorials to soldiers who gave their lives in the Great Patriotic War. And how many of those memorials still stood? How many had gone up in atomic hellfire?

Come to that, how many memorials would go up to all the people who'd died in this war? Not very many, not unless Ihor missed his guess. The survivors would be too busy trying to put the country back together again to care about everyone the A-bombs had rubbed out.

A machine gun chattered to life. Ihor's head went up as if he were a hunting dog taking a scent. "Fucking bandits," he muttered—that was a German MG-42, as unmistakable as any weapon ever made. The Poles had salted it away in 1944 or 1945, then hauled it out when they thought it would do them some good.

"I hope they run low on ammo for the damn thing," Misha said.

"Hope all you want, but don't bet on it," Ihor said. No one nowadays made the 7.92mm cartridges that had been the German standard till Hitler blew his brains out. But it had also been the Polish standard, so the bandits probably had all they needed.

Ihor knew what *he* needed. He needed to go home, even if home was only a collective farm a little too far outside of Kiev to have been smashed by an American A-bomb in the early days of the war. He needed Anya, too. When you marched off to war, you couldn't afford to let yourself think. If you did start thinking, you'd realize how completely insane you'd gone.

He did the things you did when you were trying not to think. He made a production of rolling a cigarette with *makhorka* and a scrap of newspaper. He gauged the distance and direction of the machine gun. It wasn't close enough to be dangerous, even if it was close enough to make his hackles rise.

But thought wouldn't go away. Even as he sucked in smoke, he wondered what his chances of getting back to the Ukraine were if he deserted. Regretfully, he decided the odds were slim and none. An officer might have pulled it off. Even in the classless society the USSR extolled, people were reluctant to question officers without some pressing reason. Sergeants? No. Sergeants were conscripts who hadn't got shot right away. Anybody could bark *Show your papers!* at a sergeant. If you didn't have papers . . . Well, in that case your destination would suddenly change.

"Comrade Sergeant . . . ?" Misha said hesitantly.

"What?" Ihor tried not to sound too gruff.

"What are we doing here?"

Had Ihor been a different kind of sergeant, the soldier would have found himself in the MGB's claws in short order. Had he been another different kind of sergeant, he would have answered that that was a question for a priest, not for an underofficer. But he knew what Misha meant. In the Great Patriotic War, the whole country had been fighting for its survival. Here . . .

"We're trying to stay alive. If we have to kill some Poles to do it, that's all right," Ihor said. "Sooner or later, we'll knock 'em around enough to make 'em quit. Then we'll go home and pick up our lives again."

As if to underscore that, Red Air Force bombers unloaded on the Polish positions a few kilometers away. The planes with the red stars could do as they pleased. As far as Ihor knew, the bandits didn't have anything that flew.

Their MG-42 snarled again, doing its best against the bombers. They flew low; Ihor didn't think they flew *that* low. But he understood why the gunners wasted a belt or two of cartridges. You liked to hope you were doing something to hurt the guy who was hurting you, even when part of you knew better.

Soviet artillery opened up, raining more tonnes of high explosive down on the bandits' heads. With all that descending on them, someone who knew little of war would have guessed the Poles had no chance to live. Ihor knew better. He'd been shelled and bombed too often by the Nazis, who knew exactly what they were doing, and by the Americans, who had less expertise but more ordnance to throw around.

When you got down to it, human beings were damned hard to kill. They dug in. They could take surprising wounds and come back to the fight. Ihor had only to look down at the scars on his own leg to know the truth of that. Only A-bombs reliably did for everyone in a given area.

Pretty soon, some bored Soviet brigadier general would order the division forward to clean out what he imagined to be the handful of Polish survivors. He would be positive the planes and big guns had smashed them all to sausage meat.

And the bombardment would ease off, and the Poles would come out of their dugouts and onto their trenches' firing steps. They'd come up from their cellars and into their sandbagged firing positions on the ground floor of apartment blocks and pharmacies and tailors' shops. And they would chew up the oncoming Red Army men, and everyone ranked higher than captain would be astonished. Never mind that the Fritzes had done it a hundred times in the last go-round. Never mind that the ordinary veterans had often done it, too. The officers would be astonished even so.

Captain Pavlov sent a runner to Ihor with the message he expected: "Get your section ready. We move up in fifteen minutes. Our signal is a red flare and then a green one."

"A red flare and then a green one." Ihor nodded. "I serve the Soviet Union!"

He had no watch. The flares did go up after what felt like a quarter of an hour. Like many of his men, Ihor used the time to gulp his vodka ration. A hundred grams went a long way toward smothering the fear that scraped along his nerves.

"*Urra!*" he yelled. "*Urra! Urra!*" The rest of the Red Army soldiers were shouting their heads off with him. When you sounded like a savage, you had an easier time believing you were one.

Muzzle flashes ahead. Bullets cracking past. Ihor hunched lower. He fired a burst from his Kalashnikov. If the bandits had to duck, they wouldn't shoot straight. He could hope not, anyhow.

A moving shape ahead—a careless Pole. Ihor fired with serious intent this time. The man crumpled. *He would have shot me* ran through Ihor's mind.

The Poles left behind a rear guard and skedaddled. They would make a serious fight of it some other day, when their chances looked better. The rear guard was well hidden and stubborn. The ones who didn't get away had to be finished off with grenades and entrenching tools.

Ihor slumped against the side of a metal trash bin. He noticed his ear hurt. When he touched it, his hand came away bloody. "Fuck me," he said to no one in particular. "I got wounded and I didn't even know it."

Strength dribbled out of him. So did the artificial rage from the vodka. He was all at once just a man who'd swallowed another heaping spoonful of hell. He wanted to retch it up, but he couldn't. Like all the ones he'd swallowed before, it was part of him now.

VASILI YASEVICH STARED from the outskirts of Warsaw toward the half-built pile of Stalin Gothic that dominated the skyline—that practically *was* the skyline. "*Bozhemoi!*" he said. "It's hideous. It's only half done, but it's already hideous. What's it going to be, anyhow?"

"Why, it'll be the Palace of Culture and Science, of course." Casimir raised a cynical eyebrow. "A gift to celebrate the lasting friendship between the Soviet and Polish peoples."

"Let me guess—a gift inflicted on the Polish people by the Soviet Union."

"Right the first time." Casimir hoisted that eyebrow again. "And do you know what they say? They say the view from the top of the Palace of Culture and Science will be the best in Warsaw after the building gets done. Do you know why they say that?"

"Hmm." Vasili considered, but not for long. The answer was as obvious as . . . "Because it'll be the only place in town you can't see the goddamn Palace of Culture and Science from."

"Right the first time," Casimir repeated, but this time on a disappointed note. He studied Vasili. "People who are too smart for their own good don't always have happy endings."

"Is that what happened to Warsaw?" Vasili asked, as innocently as he could.

Casimir gave him a dirty look. Except for the hideous palace that was going up and a handful of other new buildings, Warsaw was rubble and shanties built from rubble. Hitler's men had blown up and bulldozed the city after the Polish Home Army's uprising failed in 1944.

With a sigh, Casimir said, "In a way, we *were* too smart for our own good. When we rose up against the Nazis, we expected the Red Army would help us liberate our own capital. But it sat on the far side of the Vistula while Hitler solved Stalin's Polish problem for him."

That sounded reasonable. But Vasili, who kept his ear to the ground, had heard some other stories, too. Still sounding innocent, he said, "You mean, the same way the Polish Home Army let Hitler solve Poland's Jewish problem for it by sitting on its hands when the Warsaw Ghetto rebelled the year before?"

Casimir started to answer, then stopped. At last, he said, "You want to be careful to whom you say that. Otherwise, you're liable to open your big mouth a little too wide, fall right in, and never be seen again."

"Which means it's true, but it embarrasses you," Vasili said.

"I should have given you a noodle as soon as they captured you. My life would have been simpler," Casimir said. *Noodle* was what both the SS and the MGB called a bullet in the back of the neck. Vasili didn't know who'd borrowed it from whom, or from which secret police force Casimir had taken it. That didn't seem the kind of question one asked.

He found what he hoped to be a safer query: "How many really committed, pro-Soviet Communists in the Polish government these days?"

"Fewer than the motherfucking Russians wish there were." Casimir gnawed on the inside of his lower lip. "More than we freedom fighters wish there were. Some of those people, they're almost Catholics, the way they believe."

"Even after the Molotov-Ribbentrop treaty?" Vasili asked.

"You're no ordinary Russian, that's plain," Casimir said. "Any ordinary Russian would tell you Stalin bought two years to get ready for

Hitler with his treaty. Of course, your ordinary Russian wouldn't tell you he stuck those two years up his ass. And your ordinary Russian wouldn't say a word about what the treaty did to Poland. He wouldn't care, either."

"Do the Polish Reds care?"

"They . . . look the other way. Some of the police in Warsaw will look the other way at us. Some will, but not all, so keep your eyes open, you hear? This city isn't all free yet, even if it's on the way there. If we get separated, find your way to a druggist's shop named Witold's after the guy who runs it."

"I'll do that," Vasili said. "Maybe we can talk business."

"Hope you don't have to. Come on," Casimir said.

Warsaw was livelier than its battered appearance suggested. People scavenged through the ruins. Old women selling things they'd found sat next to farmers' wives selling produce and cheese and sausages. The policemen going this way and that looked nervous and hangdog, as if they weren't sure whose orders to follow. Japanese soldiers in Harbin had looked the same way on the few days after the Russians invaded Manchukuo but before they reached the city.

Casimir had a grand duke's arrogance to go with his narrow, blade-like face. He strode along as if he owned the narrow, dusty streets and expected every pretty girl to grant him the *droit du seigneur*. Vasili clumped behind him like a weary retainer, which was how he felt.

A couple of tough guys with machine pistols made as if to block Casimir's path. He wasn't visibly armed, but he walked up to them and then past them as if they weren't there. They fell back in disorder. One of them crossed himself. The other made a sign to avert the evil eye. Casimir impressed them so much, they didn't even bother Vasili.

But just when Vasili began to think they'd get in, do their business, and get out again, a Russian soldier—or maybe he was an MGB man—recognized Casimir. He yelled "Hold it!" and reached for the Tokarev automatic on his belt.

Casimir had his own pistol hidden under his shirt. He fired first. The Russian went down with a howl, but he shot back. "My God! I am hit!" Casimir shouted, and fell over with a look of intense surprise on his face. By the spreading red spot on the left side of his chest, he wouldn't get up again, either.

The Russian had friends. Vasili heard them running up. He didn't wait around to meet them. He fled instead. He went left and right at random till he was sure no one was on his heels.

He was also in a big city, and quite lost. He waited till he saw a man with a halfway friendly face and asked him, "How do I get to Witold's drugstore? The Russians are after me!"

Too late, he realized his mouth gave him away as a Russian himself. That didn't faze the Pole, who gave quick, precise directions. The idea of Russians chasing other Russians, he took for granted.

Two blocks up, three blocks over, two more blocks up, one to the left . . . The Roman alphabet still didn't come naturally to Vasili, but he saw an amateurish sign with Witold's name on it fronting a building plainly made from mismatched pieces of older construction. He went inside.

The smell was instantly, achingly, familiar. Vasili's nostrils twitched at the odors of camphor and mustard and camomile and all the other things that went into medicines. He figured he'd see a skinny bald man hunched over a brass mortar and pestle, grinding dust into finer dust.

But the person who looked up from the porcelain mortar and pestle was a blond girl a bit younger than he was. "*Tak?*" she said. In Russian, *tak* meant *you know* or *that is* or *well*. He had to remind himself it was *yes?* in Polish.

"I'm looking for Witold," he said.

His accent made her frown, but she said, "He isn't here right now. I'm his daughter. Can I help you?"

He didn't know if she knew what all her father was involved in. He didn't know what all Witold was involved in himself. He didn't know if either one of them was to be trusted. But, unless you were Robinson Crusoe, you had to trust somebody. "I started to come here with Casimir," he said. "A Russian shot him. He's *kaputt*." He turned a thumb down.

"Good God!" She crossed herself—the horizontal stroke went left to right, not right to left in Orthodox fashion. "That's awful news! What do we do now?"

"I was hoping you'd tell me. I have no idea. Uh, I'm Vasili, by the way."

"I'm Ewa." She eyed him. "Why do you talk like a Russian?"

"I *am* a Russian. A White Russian—I mean, a Russian White." Vasili explained how he'd started in Harbin and wound up in Warsaw. He didn't fail to mention being a druggist's son.

"I believe you," Ewa said when he finished. "I have to believe you. No Chekist or spy would ever dream up such a stupid, unlikely story."

"Thanks." Vasili sounded hurt.

"Don't mention it," Ewa said absently. She thrust the mortar across the high counter at him. His hands knew what to do. The rye-bread odor of crushed caraway seeds floated up to his nose. Ewa nodded. "The way you use the pestle, you're a druggist's son, all right. I'll get my father. Maybe he'll have some idea of what we can do without Casimir." She hurried out the back of the shop. Vasili went on grinding the caraway seeds. He wasn't—he hoped he wasn't—altogether alone.

Everyone said the knock on the door always came at midnight. You staggered out of bed and opened up. The lumpy-faced men in the ill-fitting suits or the sharp, dark uniforms hauled you away, and your life changed forever. Istvan Szolovits had lived under tyrannies of both the right and the left. They all worked the same way.

Now he was living in America, in a cheap flat somewhere near where Glendale turned into Pasadena. It might be cheap, but it had electricity, gas, and hot and cold water. It boasted a toilet and tub, as well as two sinks. It would have been an important man's place in Budapest.

His alarm clock had hands that glowed in the dark. They showed him it was half past one, not midnight. But somebody was knocking on the door just the same—not loudly, but insistently. Ice ran up his back, as it would have at a bullet cracking past his head. *They've come for me!* he thought, long before *But I didn't do anything!* crossed his mind.

The sofa in the front room unfolded to make a bed when you shoved aside the low table in front of it. The mattress wasn't wonderful, but he'd slept on plenty worse: during basic training in the Hungarian People's Army, for instance. He slid out of bed and went to the door in his undershirt and boxers.

"Who is?" he asked in English. Were burglars here so polite that they'd knock?

To his shock, the low-voiced answer came back in Hungarian: "Open up, you little rat, in the name of the people's justice!"

They can't know I'm here! was his first panicked thought. Then he realized, *Even if they do know, they can't get me here.* Only after that did he recognize the voice. His fingers had already closed on the doorknob of their own accord and started to turn it. He finished opening the door with his will fully engaged.

There in the dimly lit hallway stood Sergeant Gergely, laughing as hard as a man could laugh while making a very little noise. As far as Istvan could recall, he'd never seen Gergely in civilian clothes before. Fury replaced both sleepiness and fear. "You goddamn son of a bitch!" he hissed. "A horse's cock up your ass!"

Gergely didn't quit laughing. "Christ on His cross, your expression was worth ten thousand dollars," he wheezed, wiping tears away from his eyes with his sleeve. He pointed at Istvan's skivvies. "You're out of uniform, soldier."

"Fuck you! Fuck your maggoty old whore of a granny and her clapped-out, stinking cunt," Istvan said. "What are you doing here, anyway?"

"You aren't going to invite me to come in?"

"I'll invite you to take a long walk off a short pier, you shitstick. I have to go to work in the morning."

"All right, all right. Keep your clothes on, kid, what you've got of them. Besides, I owe you one, don't I? I was sitting in a POW camp outside of Strasbourg with nothing to do but play with myself till they sent me back to Hungary, and then this wiseass American Jew, Hungarian Jew, whatever the hell he is, he pulled me out of there and grilled me for a while. Next thing I knew, I was on a fucking airplane heading over here. You must have fed the Yankees my name, hey?"

"Was he a U.S. captain? Fellow named Kovacs?"

"That's him, all right. Too fucking smart for his own good."

"Oh, I don't know. I told him they should shoot you out of hand if they caught you. If you didn't commit war crimes this time around, you must have when you fought for Horthy and the Arrow Cross."

Just for a second, Gergely rocked back on his heels. "Kid, everybody who fought the Russians last time committed war crimes. So did they," he said quickly. Then he took another look at Istvan. "Ah, you little prick! You set me up for that. You really did tell the Kovacs item about me?"

"Yeah." Istvan nodded. "If anybody knows who the Hungarian army's worked for the last twenty years, you're the guy."

"I know it like a tapeworm knows a gut just before he gets shit out," Gergely said. "But thanks, I guess. Jesus, Stalin must've been as crazy as Hitler to take on a country as rich as this!"

"Tell me about it!" Istvan said. "Are they taking care of you? You have work and money and a place to stay and everything?"

"I'm fine. They treat me almost as good as if I were circumcised." Gergely's grin showed his bad teeth. He went on, "They're still raking me over the coals. You were just a dumb fucking conscript. Me, though, I know how things went back in the day and how they are now—or at least till Rakosi gets strung up. You're right about that. So I've got a flat and cash, and they say they'll get me a job when my English is up to snuff. After German, it isn't that hard, is it?"

"Not too bad, no." Hungarians had to learn other languages if they were going to get a window on the wider world. Istvan said, "Ask you something?"

"Why not? I'm the one who came to you."

"Boy, did you ever! What I want to know is, what's your name? I don't think any of us ever knew it. You were always just Sergeant Gergely to us."

"That's how it's supposed to work." Gergely bared his teeth again. "But I'm in civvies now, huh?" He wore a loud sport shirt and pale gray slacks—civvies indeed. "I'm Erno, just like Gero."

"Lucky you," Istvan said. Hungary's foreign minister was cold and bloodless, a baby Molotov where his boss was a baby Stalin. Like Matyas Rakosi, he was also a Jew. Neither of them was even slightly observant, but that didn't do anything to lessen ordinary Hungarians' anti-Semitism.

"Lucky me is right. I fell in shit and got up smelling like a rose." Erno Gergely reached out and patted Istvan on the cheek. "Go back to bed, darling. God knows you need all the beauty sleep you can get." He slipped away, as silently as if he were on night patrol.

Shaking his head, Istvan took a leak and slid under the sheet again. He didn't think he would get any more sleep, but he did. The alarm clock bombed him awake. For a few seconds, he wasn't sure his encounter with the sergeant hadn't been a dream. But he realized his imagination wasn't that good. He couldn't have made up the run-in with Gergely.

He threw two sausages in a skillet. They weren't spicy enough to suit him, but they were what the market had. He fried three eggs in the grease. Washed down by a big cup of coffee white with cream, they'd keep him going till lunchtime.

When he got to Blue Front, he told Aaron Finch about the strange meeting. "This guy was a friend of yours?" Finch asked.

"Not exactly. I don't know if he had any friends. As a person, he's a *shmuck*," Istvan said. "But he's the best sergeant a sergeant could be, if you know what I mean."

"I think so. I've known a few people like that." The older man smiled crookedly. "You may find some who say I am a people like that. Lord knows my old man is."

"You've been great with me." Istvan meant it.

"Good. Here in a funny new country, you've got enough to worry about. Maybe that's part of why my father is the way he is, too. But mostly I just don't care. My wife likes me, my kid likes me, my boss puts up with me. What else do I need?"

"You make yourself out to be less than you are," Istvan said.

Aaron only shrugged. "So maybe every once in a while I surprise somebody. But not too often. The less people have to say about you, the less trouble you wind up in." He lit one of his ever-present Chesterfields. "Mr. Weissman'll have something to say about me, and about you, too, if we don't get cracking. C'mon."

Come Istvan did. If he wasn't wild about the work, he didn't mind it, either. He wondered how small a *shtetl* Aaron's folks came from. Aaron's attitude certainly reflected parents who'd taught him to keep his head down because anything else was dangerous for Jews. Istvan's parents, Budapest sophisticates, hadn't thought that way. Then Hitler and Szalasi came along. All they proved was, everything could be dangerous for Jews.

Konstantin Morozov had never been in Lithuania before. The first thing he saw was that it was richer than Russia. People had nicer houses, better furniture, and more things generally than they did in the small town west of Moscow where he'd grown to manhood. The Lithuanians had them in spite of being annexed to the Soviet Union in 1940, overrun by the Nazis the next year, and going through more fierce fighting when the Red Army came back to liberate the Baltic republics in 1944.

The second thing he saw, right after the first, was that the people wanted to be liberated *from* the Red Army and the Soviet Union. Not to put too fine a point on it, they hated Russians and fought them tooth and nail. Konstantin had got some hint of what folk in the Baltic republics felt from serving with Juris Eigims. Seeing it with his own eyes made him realize how much Eigims had soft-pedaled it till he finally deserted.

For that matter, Konstantin counted himself lucky to be able to go on observing such things. After he and his crew bailed out of their wrecked tank, a Red Army patrol found them before the Lithuanian bandits did.

They had one more new tank. Actually, they had one more old tank:

a T-34/85, a veteran of the Great Patriotic War. Konstantin didn't scream the way he had in Germany. He wouldn't, or he hoped like blazes he wouldn't, be facing anything more modern here. The T-34/85, unlike his dead T-54, had a bow machine gun. The bow gunner who got added to the crew was a fresh-faced kid named Alexei Yakovlev.

"How old are you, anyway?" Konstantin asked him.

"Comrade Sergeant, I'm seventeen," he answered proudly.

"*Bozehmoi!*" Konstantin covered his eyes with his hand. "Nobody's seventeen. Nobody."

That wasn't true, of course. Plenty of fifteen- and sixteen- and seventeen-year-olds had served the Soviet Union in the Great Patriotic War. When you'd used up everybody older, you started going through your seed corn. Some of that got used up, too. And some of the children who'd lived were back in uniform this time around, now in their twenties. They'd earned a second chance to get killed.

"Can you shoot anybody who gives us trouble?" Konstantin asked.

"I sure can, Comrade Sergeant," Yakovlev said. Seventeen wasn't an age that came equipped with doubts. "If some bandit motherfucker's trying to kill me, I'll fix him, you bet."

"*Khorosho. Ochen khorosho,*" Morozov said. How that would work once they went back into action was anyone's guess. But Alexei seemed willing, anyhow.

It was an odd kind of warfare. The Red Army sat on all the major towns in Lithuania—and, Konstantin assumed, in Latvia and Estonia as well. Soviet troop convoys could go from one major town to another—as long as they were well protected. Soviet supply columns from Russia and Byelorussia could bring in food and munitions—as long as they were well protected, too.

The countryside belonged to the bandits. To a certain extent, it had for a long time. The group that called itself the Forest Brothers had stayed in the field since 1944. Convoys along the roads had to move slowly. So did trains. Land mines and derailments waited for the unwary.

And a stopped column was an invitation to bandits, the way a dead cow in a field was to vultures spiraling down out of the sky. The Lithuanians had rifles, pistols, submachine guns, a few machine guns and mortars. Against tanks, they should have been defenseless.

But anywhere the tanks didn't go, the bandits roamed freely. They pushed back Red Army foot patrols with what seemed like contemptuous ease. Most of the men in Soviet service had had a bellyful of war. They went through the motions, no more. The Lithuanians showed both courage and initiative. If Konstantin stuck his head out of his tank's turret for a better look around, some bandit would try to blow it off.

"Comrade Major, I can't stay all buttoned up," he complained to his regimental CO. "If I do, I'm like a turtle with its head pulled into its shell. I can't see what I've got to do next. But if I keep coming out, those motherfuckets will kill me for sure unless the infantry keeps them farther away."

Major Zhuk scowled. "You aren't the first tank commander to report this problem to me. I've discussed it with the infantry officers."

Konstantin waited for him to say what the infantry officers had promised to do about it. Instead, Genrikh Zhuk just stood there, still scowling. "Well?" Konstantin said at last. "Uh, sir?"

"Well, Sergeant, the reassurances they gave me are shit, pure shit, nothing but shit," Zhuk ground out. "Their men have no interest in fighting. They don't want to fight. The officers have no idea how to make them fight. They're more afraid the Red Army men will desert to the bandits and fight hard for them. Things are much worse among the foot than for tankmen. *Much* worse."

"Maybe the Chekists can put the fear of God in those worthless pussies." Konstantin had never imagined a sentence like that coming out of his mouth, but there you were. Desperate times demanded desperate measures.

"It's not that simple," Major Zhuk said. "Three MGB men—two officers and a corporal—have been shot in the back since this division came to Lithuania. Two are dead; the other will be months getting over his wound. They aren't so eager about pushing soldiers forward now."

"No, eh?" Morozov's voice was dry, not least to disguise the shock he felt. If the ordinary soldiers were losing their fear of the MGB, what would hold the Red Army together? Anything?

In the last war, knowing Hitler was even worse than Stalin had done the job. There was no foreign bogeyman like that now.

But if slacking off could get you killed, wouldn't you at least pay enough attention to keep breathing? The Lithuanians lured a squad down an alley where a rusty old car sat. The car was packed with explosives, with wires leading from a house behind a stout stone wall. The Red Army men didn't notice the cunningly hidden wires. When the bastard with the detonator got the signal, he let it rip. The blast took out the whole squad. As far as anyone could tell, not a single bandit got scratched.

Things turned uglier after that. Red Army men started shooting at any Lithuanians they saw. The Lithuanians started not just murdering but also mutilating any Soviet soldiers they caught alive.

Nodar Gachechiladze glumly shook his head. "Is bad. Is very bad," he said. "Is as worse as fighting Hitlerites." His Russian was shaky, but nothing was wrong with his judgment.

"Fucking Lithuanians fought alongside the Hitlerites. I learned that in school," Alexei Yakovlev said. "Same with these other Baltic cocksuckers."

It wasn't even that he was wrong. Unlike most of the Soviet Union, the Baltic republics had indeed preferred the Nazis to the Communists. But *I learned that in school* made Konstantin flinch. Alexei would have been a short-pants kid during the Great Patriotic War. Time marched on . . . everybody.

Pyotr Polikarpov said, "Comrade Sergeant, shall we take out any locals we happen to run across?"

"If you see men with rifles—hell, if you see women with rifles— that's why you've got your machine gun." Konstantin's gaze slid to Yakovlev. "That's why you've got yours, too. But don't go killing people for the fun of killing people. The ones who keep living won't give up because you do. They'll just cut your balls off and stick your dick in your mouth if they get hold of you."

The kid gulped. Maybe he hadn't learned about that kind of thing in school. Konstantin knew damn well it had happened often enough during the last war. Plenty of Germans had saved a last cartridge for themselves to keep Soviet soldiers from capturing them and having fun with them before they died. And it wasn't as if the Nazis gave Red Army men great big kisses and bowls of borscht when they caught them, either.

This war in Germany had been cleaner . . . A-bombs aside, of course. Remembering how flat radiation sickness had left him, Morozov knew that was a large aside. Without A-bombs, the bandits here couldn't kill in carload lots. But knives and hammers and hot iron— those, they had and used.

In the middle of the night, mortar bombs hissed down and burst not far from the T-34/85. Konstantin and his crewmates were sleeping in holes dug under the old tank. Sharp steel fragments clattered off its road wheels and side. The beast couldn't take on a modern battle tank, but it was plenty good enough to stop such nuisances cold. Konstantin woke up, swore, wiggled, and went back to sleep.

"Are you sure you want to proceed with this . . . adoption? Absolutely sure?" By the way the judge advocate sounded, he'd just found Cade Curtis in his apple.

Cade was used to those tones by now. "Yes, sir," he said, and left it right there. The less you said, the smaller the handle you gave them.

Major Horatio Bowers shuffled papers. "We cannot find anything suggestive of moral turpitude in your application." He seemed disappointed, even devastated, that they couldn't.

"Yes, sir," Cade repeated. They thought he was a fairy or Jimmy was a fairy or they were both fairies who'd spend their time in the States playing filthy games with each other. Cade wanted to rise up from his bed and punch Horatio Bowers square in the snoot. He couldn't, of course. This was the first time losing his leg had ever done him any good.

"Your colleagues speak well of your relationship with this young Korean."

"I'm glad, sir."

"His home town has been under Communist rule. With the armistice, it returns to the jurisdiction of the Republic of Korea. Unfortunately, it has seen no small amount of fighting. Full recovery of Chun Won-ung's birth records and other information may not be possible."

"I see, sir," Cade said. *Why don't you go ahead and believe what he tells you?* But if he said that, he'd shock the bureaucratic Bowers to the depths of his little shriveled-up mule turd of a soul. If it wasn't on paper, preferably with three carbons, it didn't exist.

Bowers examined a sheet he took from one of the three manila folders he carried. Whatever was on it made him look as if his stomach pained him. Coughing, he said, "Due to your outstanding combat record, Captain, and due to the wounds you suffered in the service of the United States and the United Nations, and due to your longstanding association with the aforesaid Chun Won-ung, the authorities have chosen to grant your petition and have approved not only the adoption but also transportation to the USA for this individual."

"Thank you very much, sir!" Cade felt as happy as he did right after a big slug of morphine. Man had bitten dog! He'd got one past the American military higher-ups in spite of everything! Another thought occurred to him. Whatever connections Dr. Nathan Marcus had, they were pretty goddamn good.

"Don't thank me." Major Bowers made a pushing motion with both hands, denying everything. "I'm only the messenger here. If it were up to me, I would be delivering a different message. I don't approve of letting more Asiatics into the United States. If you ask me, we've got too many already. But the decision wasn't mine. I'm here to tell you what it was."

"Yes, sir." Cade bit back everything else. It wasn't easy, but he did it. By the way Horatio Bowers talked, if Jimmy wasn't the mysterious Dr. Fu Manchu with his mustache shaved off, he surely was the evil doctor's number one henchman. Jimmy had about as much Fu Manchu in him as your average cocker spaniel puppy. Cade knew that, but Major Bowers would never believe it if he lived to be 190.

"I hope your recovery continues to progress," the major said stiffly. With a brusque nod, he went off to inflict his charm and warmth on someone else.

The guy in the next bed leaned toward Cade. "They're no-shit gonna let you take your buddy back to the States?"

"Yeah." Cade nodded. The guy didn't say *gook buddy,* as a lot of men would have. He didn't when he was talking about Jimmy, anyhow. He'd seen how it pissed Cade off. He still let fly with it for other Koreans, though.

"That's pretty neat," the other wounded man said. His left arm and upper torso were encased in enough plaster to stucco a couple of houses. "When'll they let you go?"

"Beats me. Whenever they do," Cade answered. "Longer I stay here, the more practice on crutches I get." His arm and underarm muscles were starting to get used to them. They didn't make him hurt the way they had when he first started stumping around on them.

"They're not gonna fit you with a peg leg while you're here?"

"Nah. They want the stump to heal some more. I'll have to wait till I get back." Cade didn't say *get home.* He always had a place to stay as long as his folks lived. But Tennessee didn't feel like home any more. Korea did. Especially, trenches in Korea did. Hot and dusty in the summer, muddy during spring and fall, frozen iron-hard and half the time full of snow during winter, the enemy no more than a few hundred yards away, your own guys always in your pocket . . . That was the life he'd known most of the past two years. As a young man will, he'd adapted to it and made it his own.

But he couldn't have gone back to it now even if the war had continued. The English let Tin Legs Bader keep on flying fighter planes, but they'd been desperate—and you didn't run around a hell of a lot in the cockpit. Tin Leg Curtis wouldn't help his own side in an infantry action.

A couple of days later, Dr. Marcus paused to watch him making his slow way along a hospital corridor. "How are you doing there?" the surgeon asked.

"I'm doing," Cade said. "I won't ever make the Olympics, but I'll get where I'm going. Eventually."

"The Olympics." Nathan Marcus rubbed his chin. "We missed 1940 and 1944. They would've been in Helsinki this year, but we missed that, too. Maybe we'll make it in '56. That'd be the second one since Hitler's Games. Not such a hot track record, y'know?"

"I guess not." Cade hadn't given it much thought.

"If I get you and your adopted son on a ship in a couple of weeks, will you be ready to go?" the surgeon asked.

His voice had changed. This was business, not small talk. "I think so, sir." Cade returned to military formality. "I can't thank you enough for everything you've done."

Marcus waved that aside. "Get well. Find a pretty girl. Settle down. Raise some kids who aren't Korean. Have a good life. You can do it, you know."

Cade aimed his chin at his stump. "You think any girl will look at me twice when she sees this?"

"Some will," the doctor said. "I guarantee it. And most of the ones who let that bother them aren't worth much to begin with."

"I wish I could believe that. I'm gonna try real hard, I tell you."

"You'll find out." With a friendly nod, Nathan Marcus went on his way. Neither of his legs stopped a little below the knee, but maybe he knew what he was talking about anyway. Cade hoped so.

At least when it came to travel arrangements, Dr. Marcus did. Cade had the feeling he usually did. A halftrack took Jimmy and him and four other soldiers discharged from the military hospital over a horrible road (Korea had no good ones) to the port at Masan. Everything there was new and hectic. The Russians had bombed Korea's main port, Pusan, the year before.

"The ocean! The ocean! Never see before! The ocean!" Jimmy said over and over. Cade thought of Xenophon's Greeks shouting *Thalassa! Thalassa!* after they fought their way across the Persian Empire to the Black Sea.

He'd wondered if he would go back to America in a hospital ship, all gleaming white with red crosses everywhere. No such vessel was tied up at any of the piers. The halftrack unloaded its passengers at the harbormaster's office. They didn't see the harbormaster, only a petty officer. He examined their hospital papers and gave Cade an honorable discharge from the Army. Cade had to look twice to notice that they *had* promoted him to major before they turned him loose. The promotion officially dated from the day he was wounded, so he got a little extra cash to go with it.

Then the petty officer said, "Youse guys is all on the SS *Joe Harris.* Pier Four—it's the closest one." He eyed Cade's crutches and pinned-up trouser leg. "You don't got far to go, sir."

"Thanks," Cade said.

The SS *Joe Harris* was a Liberty ship that had seen a lot of hard use. Instead of white paint everywhere, she was streaked with rust. Cade needed Jimmy's help getting down the steep stairway to the cabin they shared with two other men. It was cramped and airless. A Liberty ship would take a month waddling across the Pacific. This would be no luxury cruise.

All the same, Jimmy started to cry when the freighter pulled away from the pier. "America! I go America!" he said. Cade wished he could get even a fraction that excited himself.

20

LUISA HOZZEL LOOKED UP and to her left at the neat bullet hole in the passenger-car window. It was thirty centimeters above the top of her head. The bullet hadn't hurt anybody. Even the little sprays of glass it had blown out hadn't caused anything worse than a couple of scratches on the women who shared her compartment.

They couldn't have gone ten kilometers inside Poland before they got that greeting. They'd had to change cars at the border between the USSR and Poland. The Soviet Union used a broad rail gauge, not the one standard farther west. The Ivans did that on purpose, to make it harder for invading Germans to exploit their railroads.

Whether the whole train had got shot up or only this car, Luisa didn't know. She did know the train hadn't stopped to let off any wounded. She also knew the stories that had been whispered through the camp at the other end of the USSR were true. The Poles were in revolt against their Russian overlords.

Maybe the Russians had a way of letting the rebels know the train carried only returning *zeks*. The Poles didn't fire at it after that once. Once was at least twice too often. How many bullets had come that close to Gustav? Luisa didn't want to know the answer.

No one opened up on the train after it pushed through Poland and into the Soviet zone of Germany. Even though it *was* the Soviet zone, with slapdash Russians and humorless German Reds running things, it seemed much cleaner and more orderly than Poland did . . . at least to her eye.

They passed south of Berlin. Whether that meant the Americans had incinerated the city was one more thing she didn't know.

On the border between the Soviet zone—the so-called German Democratic Republic—and the American zone—the biggest part of the Federal Republic of Germany—the train halted once more. Germans in Soviet-style greatcoats shouted, "Out! Everybody out now!"

"What's the matter?" Luisa asked as she stumbled onto the platform. She never would have dared to question a Russian. Asking something of one of her own folk, though, seemed possible. "Why aren't they taking us all the way home?"

He looked at her like an attendant eyeing an inmate in a home for the feeble-minded. "The Soviet Union's responsibility ends the moment you leave the DDR," he said, as if she should have known that for years. "How you proceed from then on is your worry. The capitalist authorities have established a control point on their side of the frontier. They will process your entry into the American zone."

Guards with machine pistols and fierce, barking dogs herded the women towards a gateway festooned with barbed wire. The gateway stood open, though. On the far side flew the West German flag, without the hammer-and-compass-flanked central shield the East Germans used. The soldiers on that side wore American uniforms, but they were also Germans.

At the control point, Luisa gave her name and home town to a military clerk, who checked a register. He ran his finger down the typewritten list. The moving finger stopped. The clerk nodded. "*Ja, Frau* Hozzel," he said. "We have a report of your arrest and deportation. Welcome back to freedom."

"*Danke.* Can you tell me if my husband is well, please?" Luisa said. "His name is Gustav, Gustav Hozzel."

"One moment, *bitte*." The clerk reached behind him to pull out a different register. He flipped through it, then went down another list. His index finger stopped again, more abruptly than it had before. Something in his face tightened. He tried not to change expression, but he couldn't help it. Luisa knew what he was going to say before he came out with it: "I am more sorry than I can tell you, *Frau* Hozzel, but Gustav Hozzel was killed in combat not quite a year ago."

"Are you sure?" Luisa understood how hopeless the question was even as she asked it.

"I am sorry," the clerk repeated, "but there can be no possible doubt. You will receive a payment from the Federal government to compensate in some small way for your loss. . . ."

The words seemed to come from a billion kilometers away. "I don't care a fart for any of that," Luisa said. "What am I going to do without my Gustav?" The pain hadn't hit yet—only the loss.

Sensibly, the military clerk didn't try to answer that. "If you go to Stop Four, *Frau* Hozzel, you will find there a bus that goes through Fulda. Let me give you this first." He handed her five hundred-Deutschmark bills. "This has nothing to do with your husband's loss. This is a welcoming payment to all returning from Soviet captivity. It will keep you going for a little while."

This was the first money Luisa had handled since the Russians seized her. Numbly, she tucked it into a pocket on her camp jacket. Like a sleepwalker, she stumbled toward Bus Stop Four.

Trudl was already on the bus. Without thinking, Luisa sat down next to her. Trudl beamed from ear to ear. "So wonderful!" she said. "We're going home! Home! At last! We'll be able to put our lives back together again."

"Yes," Luisa muttered in a voice like ashes.

For the first time, Trudl looked at her face. "*Der Herr Gott im Himmel!*" she exclaimed. "What happened? What's wrong?"

"Gustav . . . isn't coming home." Luisa had thought her husband was a damn fool for going off and playing soldier again. Hadn't he got all that out of his system forever in the last war? Did he want new nightmares to wake him up screaming when the old nightmares didn't?

Well, no nightmares would wake him now. He'd never scream again. He hadn't been playing soldiers after all. When you played, you could walk away from the game and start over. This was real. When you got killed, you stayed dead. Forever.

"Oh, no!" Trudl folded Luisa into a hug she didn't want. "Oh, you poor thing! I'm so sorry. I'll help you any way I can."

"Thanks." The word felt meaningless in Luisa's mouth. Everything felt meaningless to her, meaningless or worse. All the meanings she could tease out of the past couple of years were bad. She needed a couple of seconds before realizing she ought to ask, "Did you hear . . . ? Is Max . . . ?"

"I did hear, *ja*. He's all right, *danken Gott dafür*." Trudl worked to sound more serious with her good news than she would have if she hadn't just heard her friend's husband was dead. As far as Luisa was concerned, that was wasted effort. She hated Trudl anyway, for her good luck.

And how ironic was it that she'd got skinnier and skinnier in the gulag, not taking easier work and better rations in exchange for lying down with a guard or a clerk or a barber? She'd kept herself for Gustav long after Gustav wasn't there to be kept for. Trudl, who did have a husband to come home to, had ended up screwing somebody so she could eat better. Why hadn't Max got killed, so he wouldn't find out about her shame?

She won't tell him, never in a million years, Luisa thought. *So how will he find out?* But that was one of those questions that answered itself, wasn't it? Why should Trudl, who'd done wrong, get to enjoy life when Luisa couldn't even though she hadn't? How was that fair or right?

More women were climbing onto the bus. Some lived in Fulda, others in towns not far away. Some of the German women who'd vanished into the vast reaches of the USSR wouldn't be coming home. The war had killed them no less than it killed Gustav.

The driver, who wore a gray uniform that looked more American than German, started the engine. With a hiss of compressed air, the doors closed. Gears ground as the bald, grizzled man started driving.

East Germany had been bombed but not fought over. This side of the border, everything that could be shattered was. *Including my life,* Luisa thought. No one had let the Russians take anything. Whatever they'd grabbed, they'd paid for. Even the road was cratered. The bus dodged holes as best it could. More than once, it had to go off onto the shoulder.

What with all that and with stops to let women off, it took two hours to get to Fulda. Luisa and Trudl and the other locals stepped out onto the street. Luisa stared. The Americans had bombed the town again and again after she was taken to Russia. She walked to her block of flats. It was nothing but more burnt-out wreckage. She stood in the street and started crying again.

Somewhere out beyond the air base's perimeter, a machine gun let loose with a long, ripping burst. Boris Gribkov looked up from his shchi and his fried pork cutlet. So did half the other Red Air Force men stuffing their faces in the mess hall.

"What *is* the world coming to?" a major exclaimed in disbelief. By his ruddy cheeks and double chin, he liked the world just fine as it was. "This is Beylorussia! There aren't any stinking bandits in Beylorussia."

Another burst from the gun said he didn't know everything there was to know. Some rifle shots followed, perhaps aimed at the machine gun, perhaps to clean up whatever it hadn't. Boris glanced down to the automatic pistol on his hip. It wasn't the kind of weapon a flyer often thought about using. Things weren't the way they often were, though.

No bandits tried to waylay him when he went back to his quarters. Twenty minutes later, though, a private who looked about fourteen hurried in and said, "Excuse me, sir, but Colonel Petlyura wants to talk with you right away."

"I serve the Soviet Union!" Boris said, and then, as he followed the kid to the base commandant's office, "Did he tell you what it was about?"

"No, sir. He called me and he said, 'Go get Gribkov. Quick, you hear?' So I did," the private replied. Boris realized he'd asked a stupid question; a colonel wouldn't tell an enlisted man one word more than he had to.

When he walked into the office, he got a surprise: Volodymyr Petlyura had a liter of vodka and two glasses sitting on the card table that did duty for his desk. Pretending he didn't see the bottle, Boris said, "Reporting as ordered, Comrade Colonel."

By the way Petlyura returned the salute, he hadn't started drinking yet. He waved Boris to a folding chair. Then he asked, "Do you speak English, Gribkov?"

"No, Comrade Colonel. I'm sorry. Some German, but no English. May I ask why, sir?"

"I started learning during the Great Patriotic War. The Americans and English were our allies, and it was useful to the state to have men who could follow what they said. Then they became our enemies, and that grew more useful yet. There is a poem in English called 'The Second Coming.'"

"A religious poem, sir?" Boris asked. How did the state gain from religious poetry?

"No, or not exactly—and I have never been a believing Christian. But religious or not, it is a striking poem. It is about ends and beginnings, you might say, and two lines are 'Things fall apart./ The center cannot hold.' I have been thinking about that poem a lot lately." Volodymyr Petlyura opened the liter of vodka and filled the glasses. He shoved one toward Boris.

Boris lifted it. He knew without a doubt the toast he needed to make: "Comrade Colonel, I serve the Soviet Union!" He knocked back the vodka. It was so smooth, he barely felt it going down.

Petlyura drank with him, with the wrist snap of a practiced toper. "Ah!" he said. "That's the straight goods!" He poured two more shots.

"To the Communist Party of the Soviet Union!" Up went his glass, and Boris'. Down the hatch went the vodka.

After that, Boris toasted the USSR's workers and peasants. And after *that,* he started noticing he was getting toasted himself. Supper slowed things, but you couldn't drop three depth charges like that without feeling the blast.

The colonel raised a glass to the Red Air Force, the Red Army, and the Red Fleet. Boris gulped that one down, too. By then, they'd put a considerable dent in the bottle. "Don't worry about it," Petlyura said. "I've got more."

"Sir, I wasn't worried," Boris said truthfully. The only thing that worried him was how thick his head would be come morning.

"Good, good." The more the colonel drank, the less Russian and more Ukrainian he sounded. "'Things fall apart./ The center cannot hold,'" he repeated. Then he said something in what might have been English—perhaps words with the same meaning. He said, "You know what the spring *rasputitsa* is like."

"Oh, yes, Comrade Colonel. Who doesn't?" Boris said.

As if he hadn't spoken, Volodymyr Petlyura went on, "All winter long, it's ice and snow. Everything is frozen hard. Then spring comes, and the ice and snow melt, and it all turns to mud for six weeks, and nothing moves. Am I wrong or am I right?"

"You're right, sir. You're so very right." Boris would have agreed to anything just then.

Petlyura's thoughts took a turn he hadn't expected: "And that's what's happening to the Soviet Union right now, dammit. We've been hard and strong and frozen for years and years. Now we're in the *rasputitsa,* and the whole country is flailing around in the mud. The center can't move to bring the outer parts back into line."

"I never looked at it that way before, Comrade Colonel." Again, Boris told the truth. Stalin's iron hand hadn't let anyone get even a centimeter out of line. The longtime ruler had killed or sent to the gulag those bold enough to disagree with him. But now the iron hand was gone. All the restlessness that had been frozen in place was bubbling up at once.

And Petlyura had managed to get that across without once mentioning Stalin's name. He seemed very clever to Boris, especially after almost half a liter of vodka.

He filled the glasses again, and threw the dead bottle in the trash can. Boris said, "To victory over the bandits!"

"*Tak!*" Volodymyr Petlyura said. The commandant went on, "The Soviet Union means everything to me. It educated me. It gave me something bigger than my village to care about. Why do people want to destroy it? It is great. It is glorious." He reached behind him and produced another liter of antifreeze. "Marx! Lenin! Stalin! Molotov!"

As with the others, that was a toast that had to be drunk. Though his head was seriously spinning, Boris thought he understood what the Hammer and Sickle meant to Volodymyr Petlyura. Without it, he would have been just another Ukrainian peasant with cowshit on his boots. Under it, he'd become a New Soviet Man, as good as any other New Soviet Man, regardless of whether his Russian had an accent. No wonder he thought the state Lenin and Stalin had built was worth preserving.

But old prejudices kept more life than the base commandant wanted to see. Most citizens of the Soviet Union, like most citizens of the Russian Empire before it, disliked and distrusted Jews. Most of them thought people who came out of the Turkic republics in the East didn't deserve to be anything more than second-class citizens. They called people from the Caucasus blackasses and were sure snooty Balts walked around with their noses stuck high in the air.

So was it any wonder the Georgians and the Armenians and the Balts and the Kazakhs had had a bellyful of the USSR? Was it any wonder so many Ukrainians had sided with Hitler against Stalin and still resented their Great Russian neighbors? Was it any wonder there'd been machine-gun fire even here in placid Byelorussia?

Petlyura looked expectantly at Boris. The pilot realized he had to offer the next toast. He did: "To peace in the Soviet Union and peace in the world!"

"To peace!" the commandant echoed, and drank. But then he shook his head and sighed like a man mourning a lost love. "Why don't the Poles and the Hungarians and the Czechoslovakians show us thanks for setting them free? No wonder we drop bombs on the ungrateful sons of bitches!"

Since the end of the Great Patriotic War, they'd done what Stalin told them to do almost as if they were republics of the USSR themselves. Not everyone in them could have been happy about that. Unfortunate things happened to people who let their unhappiness show, though. Both the MGB and the Red Army made sure of that.

Now the USSR was badly battered from its war against America. Now Stalin's strong hand was off the wheel. No wonder the satellites were tying to spin out of the Soviet orbit.

Boris knew he couldn't explain that to Volodymyr Petlyura. As a matter of fact, he couldn't explain anything to Petlyura. The colonel had passed out, slumped down onto the card table. *Dumb* muzhik *can't hold it*, Boris thought, a moment before he slumped down unconscious himself.

Ihor Shevchenko listened to Radio Moscow with a radio hooked up to a truck battery. Roman Amfiteatrov reeled off a stream of Soviet successes in the Baltics, in the Caucasus, and in Czechoslovakia. He didn't say anything about Hungary or Poland. Ihor had a pretty good idea why, at least when it came to Poland: Red Army propagandists couldn't even invent successes here.

"And furthermore, Fascist broadcasters abroad are reporting significant unrest in the Ukraine," Amfiteatrov said indignantly. "General Secretary Molotov has directed me to inform the nation and the world that these are shameless lies, and that the Ukrainian SSR remains as loyal to the Soviet Union as it has always been."

As loyal as always? Where a Russian wouldn't, Ihor heard the irony there. When he was a boy, Stalin had starved the Ukraine into submission and collectivization. Was it any wonder, then, that some Ukrainians greeted the invading Nazis with bread and salt and flowers? After what Stalin had done, Hitler looked like a liberator.

The Ukrainians rapidly discovered the cure was worse than the disease. Stalin killed till he broke the survivors to his will. Hitler killed till he couldn't kill any more. Some Ukrainians didn't care. With German encouragement, they hunted and slaughtered Russians and Jews. Some went right on fighting the Red Army after it rolled the *Wehrmacht* out of the Ukraine in late 1943. A few skulkers still raided and stole and sometimes fought even as the new war broke out.

Now Radio Moscow was denying that the Ukraine held any unrest? Were the men trying to run things now that Stalin was gone really so stupid? Didn't they understand that the quickest way to confirm a rumor was to deny it?

Up till this moment, Ihor hadn't wanted to get back to the Ukraine till the powers that be released him from Soviet service. But now, he judged, they might not do that till the Ukraine, or big chunks of it, had broken away from the central government's control. Where would that leave him? Could he even get home if he was discharged? Would people at the border think he was some kind of Russified foreigner?

He'd told Captain Pavlov he wouldn't desert. Pavlov was one of the better officers he'd served under. He decided he owed the man at least a glimpse of what was on his mind. Pavlov could give him to the MGB as soon as he finished talking, of course. Had he thought Pavlov would do that, he wouldn't have wanted to give him that glimpse to begin with.

He hunted up the captain—which, given how thin-spread the Red Army was here, took a while. Then he had to wait while Pavlov waded through a squabble between two corporals. Pavlov settled it: sensibly, or so Ihor thought. As the corporals ambled off, the captain said, "And what's on *your* mind, Sergeant?"

"Talk to you for a few minutes, sir?" Ihor said.

Pavlov caught his tone, one of the things that marked him as a good officer. He started walking across the field in which his tent was pitched. Ihor followed at his heels like a well-trained hound. After they'd gone a couple of hundred meters, the captain said, "All right, nobody'll eavesdrop on us here. *Now* what's on your mind?"

"Comrade Captain, d'you know how bad it really is in the Ukraine?" Ihor spoke Russian, not his birthspeech. But he could hear himself using his native *h* for *g* and putting more Ukrainian endings on Russian verbs than usual.

"Why would you ask me that right now?" Captain Pavlov sounded as if he really wanted to know.

"When Radio Moscow goes out of its way to say there's no trouble . . ." Ihor didn't go on, or think he needed to.

He proved right. Pavlov looked disgusted. He sounded disgusted, too, as he answered, "You heard the news, did you? What I've heard is, it's not as bad as Latvia or Lithuania or Georgia. It's not an all-out war, not most places. The west isn't so good, but everything else could be worse."

What was now the western Ukraine had been part of southeastern Poland until 1939. The people there had lived under Soviet rule for only a few years, not since the Russian Revolution. They were still getting used to their new masters. Resistance to Soviet authority had always been strongest there. The Nazis had recruited an SS infantry division there, too. Life was rarely as simple as you wished it would be.

Ihor said, "Sir . . ." He had trouble getting the words out.

"You want to head east and see what's going on wherever it is you call home." He didn't need to say anything. Pavlov already knew.

"Comrade Captain, I do." Ihor let out a wry chuckle. "I don't want to catch a noodle in the neck while I'm doing it, though."

"Funny how that works," the captain said dryly. "And why should I give you an authorization to leave the war?"

"Because I caught a shell fragment for the Soviet Union, sir. Because I got radiation sickness for the Red Army. Because I haven't seen my wife in years."

"Do you suppose you're the only soldier who can say things like that?" Pavlov asked after a moment's thought.

"Of course not, Comrade Captain. All the men my age can. But you asked why, and I tried to tell you."

Captain Pavlov thought some more. At last, he said, "I can't do it on my own. They wouldn't pay any attention to a captain's order, not for something like that. Let me talk to the colonel commanding the division."

"Sir?" Ihor said in alarm. He hadn't set eyes on the colonel more than twice. "He won't give me to the Chekists?"

"*Yob tvoyu mat'*, Shevchenko, he won't," Pavlov said. As it could with *mat*, obscenity turned to promise. "He'll have to give me to them, too. But he's a human being, so he won't."

"Maybe you should just forget the whole thing," Ihor said.

"I'll make it work," Pavlov told him. Ihor nodded. What else could a sergeant do when a captain said something like that? But was Pavlov giving him a promise or a threat?

Action picked up over the next couple of days, and Ihor almost forgot what he'd asked the captain. Then Pavlov came to him the way he'd gone looking for the battalion CO. Pavlov held out a folded sheet of paper. Ihor opened it. It was divisional stationery, something of whose existence he'd been ignorant till that moment. It was festooned with official, or at least official-looking, stamps.

A strong hand had written *The bearer, Sergeant Ihor Semyonovich Shevchenko, is ordered to report to Kiev Military District headquarters to instruct raw troops in weapons and tactics, as directed by the KMD chief of staff. Express transport is authorized.* The signature, in the same bright blue ink as the order, read *V. I. Rogozin, division commander.*

"*Bozhemoi!*" Ihor whispered. "You did it! How did you do it, uh, sir?"

"I got lucky," Pavlov said. "It turns out that the assistant chief of staff in the Kiev Military District is Vsevolod Ivanovich's brother-in-law."

"How about that?" Ihor said. Even in the classless, rational Soviet Union, whom you knew counted for more than what you knew.

"A car should be here—had better be here—in a few minutes. It'll take you to the airstrip," Pavlov told him. "When Colonel Rogozin says express transport, he means it."

"He must, sir." Ihor felt dizzy. He'd never flown in his life, or expected to. There was a first time for everything.

The car was an old, wheezing Mercedes someone must have commandeered for the Red Army, likely at gunpoint. The driver seemed astonished he'd been sent out for a sergeant. The pilot of the *Kukuruznik* at the airstrip seemed even more astonished he was supposed to fly a sergeant to Kiev. But Colonel Rogozin's orders had the power to bind and to loose. The little Po-2 biplane buzzed into the air with Ihor in the front cockpit and the man who could actually fly the plane behind him.

They had to stop for fuel twice along the way. The flight took all day; it was about a thousand kilometers to Kiev, and the trainer only made 150 going flat out. Ihor didn't care. They never went very high—he didn't think the Po-2 *could* go very high—and the view was fascinating.

He reached an airstrip outside of Kiev as it was getting dark. The plane bounced hard when it landed. Ihor was glad to make it in one piece. No one on the ground seemed to have any idea what to do with him. "Nothing will happen till tomorrow anyway," another sergeant said. They fed him borscht and black bread. Somebody gave him a pack of Belomors.

He got a blanket and some tent floor to sleep on. The other sergeant apologized. Ihor took it all in stride. He heard no gunfire anywhere. That put this tent way ahead of where he'd slept the night before.

A German underofficer sat behind a card table that housed a typewriter. He gave Max Bachman a weary nod. You couldn't just release people from the armed forces. You had to collect information from them first. You did if you were German, anyhow. Max wondered whether the Americans wasted time with such foolishness. For their sakes, he hoped not.

This fellow took his name, birthdate, and home town. He took his rank. He took his blood group. Then he asked, "And did you serve in the last war?"

"What business of yours is that?" Max said. "What difference does it make now?"

"It's on the form," the underofficer said. "I'm required to enquire."

"Look at me. Do I look like a virgin?" Max said.

"I'll take that for a yes." The military bureaucrat hit the space bar several times so the X he typed would go into the right box. Then he asked, "And where did you serve in the last war?"

"Where do you think, sonny?" Max said—the underofficer might have been too young to go through the last grinder. Something like three-quarters of the *Wehrmacht* had fought in the east. Russia was the main event, everything else just a sideshow. However many men Hitler sent to the *Ostfront,* though, he never had enough, not after the first year. He should have seen that sooner. He should have seen a lot of things sooner.

"You were never affiliated with any organizations now illegal?"

"*Nein.* I was *Wehrmacht.*" Max could say that and mean it. Rolf would have said it, too, and banked on records being too badly damaged to make a liar of him—or banked on no one's ever checking. Rolf wouldn't have to tell any more lies, though. Ironic that one of his own country's old mines got him . . . ironic and a nasty way to go. What would he have to say to St. Peter? Or would someone else, at a warmer entranceway, ask the questions?

Clack! Another X went into the right box. "*Sehr gut,*" the clerk said. "Now I need your signature on this affirmation that all your statements are true and correct, and then you may go on to the paymaster, collect the money due you and the mustering-out bonus, and proceed from there to a transportation manager, who will arrange your journey to, uh"—he checked the form—"to Fulda, *ja.*"

Max signed without even looking at what the form said. His name would have gone on the dotted line even had the paperwork insisted he was a blue baboon with bad morals. On to the paymaster, who doled out Deutschmarks with as much eagerness as if they came from his own billfold. The mustering-out bonus was three hundred Deutsch-marks.

"That's generous," Max said. "Just about fifty pfennigs a day. Nice to know the *Bundesrepublik* thinks so much of me."

He couldn't have been the first discharged soldier to complain to the paymaster. By the man's martyred expression, he couldn't have been the three hundredth, either. "If you don't want it, you don't have to take it," the fellow snapped.

"Oh, I want it. I want about ten times this much."

"So does everybody who was in the *Bundeswehr*. And if they pay out that kind of money, they'll start another Weimar inflation."

"I'd take the chance," Max said. He'd been born around the time the mark zoomed into the ionosphere. By the time that inflation got done, it took a wheelbarrow full of paper money to buy half a wheelbarrow of food. A dollar or a pound brought billions of marks. He didn't believe for a second the government feared that would happen again. He believed the burghers who ran the government were a bunch of damn skinflints.

"Go on to the transportation section." The paymaster didn't say *and get out of my hair,* but Max needed no magnifying lenses to read between the lines.

"Fulda . . ." said the corporal he eventually saw. "Well, I'll try. It will take some work. The road network is pretty chewed up around there."

"How about a train ticket?" Max said. "You think a train ticket on top of my great big bonus here would bankrupt the state?"

"You've been listening to your paymaster too much," the transportation manager said. "I'd give you a train ticket in a second if we had trains that could get there. The Russians' *Jabos* and the ones from our side have chewed up the railway lines like you wouldn't believe."

Since Max had seen some of that destruction, he did believe it. "Maybe I should just hitchhike," he said.

"Drivers who'll pick you up and take you where you want to go don't fall under the federal assistance program," the corporal said.

"What does, then?"

"Let me see what I can do." The corporal flipped schedules and muttered to himself. He went off to commune with an officer. When he came back, he gave Max not one but two travel vouchers. "The first one is for a bus ride as far as Kassel," he explained. "The second one will— eventually—put you on a four-wheel-drive vehicle that should get you to Fulda. Maybe a jeep, maybe a truck, maybe a halftrack. I don't know. You've got food and lodging vouchers to go with that one. You may have to stay in Kassel a while."

"As long as I'm going the right way, I don't care." Max stuck the travel vouchers in an outside pocket on his jacket. The cash was stowed in an inside pocket, to make it harder for ambitious optimists to separate him from it. He wished the powers that be would have let him keep his Russian machine pistol. He could see why they didn't want civilians armed with military weapons, but made his wish even so.

The bus left the demobilization center in Paderborn that afternoon. It was full of German veterans in full American kit. "Back in '45, I killed anybody I saw who looked like me now," one of them said in broad Bavarian dialect. He'd be going farther than Fulda.

Max had seen plenty of smashed country during the last war. As the Germans retreated, they wrecked all they could so the Red Army couldn't use it. Scorched earth, the generals called it. Some of those generals went to prison for war crimes because of it. Several towns had been fought over four different times as the winds of war blew back and forth.

And now the same thing was visited on West Germany. Americans had dynamited roads and bridges as they fell back. Scorched earth? Close enough. Land mines, fighter-bombers, and Russian occupation finished the job of wrecking the countryside.

Most of the roads down from Paderborn were bad. The rest were worse. The corporal who'd arranged Max's travel knew what he was talking about, all right. And Kassel was nothing but a sea of rubble. An A-bomb would have had a tough time leveling it any more completely. Olive-green tents housed men waiting to go farther south and the ones who fed them and eventually sent them on their way. People who actually came from Kassel lived in huts made from wreckage and caves dug into it. Women offered themselves for ration tins or cigarettes, the way they had after Hitler stuck the pistol in his mouth and pulled the trigger.

Max stayed there four days before he finally climbed aboard a half-track that stopped at Fulda. It was an American model, a little roomier and more comfortable than the ones he'd ridden on the *Ostfront*. The alleged roads were all craters and shell holes and chunks of asphalt and concrete sometimes mounded in near-barricades. Towns and villages were almost as flat as Kassel. Not all the burnt-out hulks of enemy fighting vehicles had been cleared yet. Once, skirting a killed tank, the halftrack nearly bogged down in the mud. Passengers had to jump out to lighten the load. Engine roaring, the halftrack pulled itself free.

Fulda didn't look as bad as Kassel, but it came close. Max had to remember that he'd come down from the north to get his bearings. As he got nearer to where he'd lived and worked, he began to see people—mostly women—he'd known. He asked one of them about Trudl.

"*Ach, ja*, she got back a few days ago," the mechanic's wife told him.

"Back? Back from where?"

"Why, from Siberia, *aber natürlich*."

It wasn't *of course* to Max. He found his shop and his apartment block had both been flattened. A few minutes later, he found Trudl in a crude lean-to that would have embarrassed a Red Indian. She was as skinny as if she'd just come out of Dachau. "I'm better than I used to be, too," she said. The scary thing was, he believed her without hesitation.

21

THE AIR FORCE didn't set up its C-54 Skymasters for comfort. They were the military version of the Douglas DC-4, but you wouldn't have known it from looking inside the passenger compartment. You could jam fifty men inside a Skymaster. They'd almost be sitting in one another's laps, but the Air Force didn't care. It just wanted to haul as many troops in one plane as it could.

Bruce McNulty didn't care, either. Cramped seating he could handle. To get back to the States, to cut his last ties with the service, he would have hung by his heels like a bat if he had to. Scrunching up his knees so he wouldn't give the dogface in front of him a back massage? Piece of cake.

On one side of him sat an Air Force sergeant who tugged his service cap down over his eyes and started to snore even before they took off. On the other was a kid with his right arm in a plaster cast. "How'd you do that?" Bruce asked, raising his voice as the engines roared to life.

"Car accident. Jeep accident, I mean," the kid said sheepishly. "I had me a couple-three beers and I forgot they drive on the wrong side of the road over here. Hit a car comin' the other way. Got thrown out and landed on my shoulder. Broke my arm. Doc says the bone's called the humerus, but the way the son of a bitch hurt, that wasn't funny one bit."

"I know," Bruce said. "Busted my collarbone falling out of a tree when I was twelve. I howled like a coyote—you bet I did."

"Oh, yeah," the kid said. The C-54 began taxiing toward the runway. "Sure will be good to get back to the US of A. This here is the biggest airplane I ever seen, let alone rode on."

"How about that?" Bruce had been thinking how small it was. He'd also been thinking how old-fashioned it seemed next to a B-29. And a B-29 was yesterday's engineering. The Skymaster came from day before yesterday.

But it could cross the Atlantic. As long as it landed safely outside of Portland, Maine (Bangor, having been A-bombed early in the war, was no longer preferred), he wouldn't fuss.

Behind him, somebody went through Our Fathers and Hail Marys as the plane lumbered down the runway and into the air. Bruce hid a smile. When you were a pilot, you forgot how flying scared some people out of their skins.

"Thank you, Jesus!" the prayerful fellow said loudly.

The kid with the cast turned his head to stare out of one of the transport's small windows. "Ain't that somethin'?" he said. "There it is, all spread down there like a map."

"How about that?" Bruce repeated. He took such views, and better ones, for granted. You saw more from the cockpit than any mere passenger ever could. But passengers saw things with fresh, unjaded eyes. They didn't take looking down at the world from a mile or two above it for granted. It was something, all right, when you let it be something.

Then the plane seemed to lurch in the sky. The Catholic started praying again. Bruce hoped it wouldn't be too bad. When you flew against the prevailing winds, things could get rough. And the DC-4 wasn't pressurized, so it couldn't fly above the nasty weather. He shrugged. The Skymaster was as reliable as any machinery could be, no matter what the man gabbling Latin thought.

By the time they landed in Portland, Bruce felt ready to do some praying of his own. He'd bounced as if he were on a carnival roller coaster. He hadn't been airsick himself, but several other travelers had. The aroma did nothing to improve the trip.

It was dark when the plane touched down. People stumbled off onto the tarmac. Signs by the runway guided them to different doors in the terminal prefab. One said MUSTERING OUT. Bruce went that way, along with half a dozen other men.

Customs inspectors searched them and their duffels. One guy had a .45 confiscated. He squawked, but the inspector wouldn't bend. "That's Uncle Sam's piece, not yours," he said. "I could jug you for smuggling."

The man called him a piece of something. Bruce wouldn't have done that, not to someone who could land him in hot water. But the customs inspector had the air of someone who'd already heard everything twice; it rolled off him.

A yawning sergeant dealt with people one by one. Bruce gave him his paperwork. "Here you go, sir," the noncom said after he'd been through everything and filled out some more forms. "This shows you aren't in the Air Force any more—we'll put you up for a night at the barracks here, but after that you're on your own."

"Can I get a taxi to the train station in the morning?" Bruce asked.

"Ayuh," the sergeant said. Bruce looked at him. He chuckled. "Sorry. I mean *uh-huh*. I really am from Maine."

"How do I find these barracks? I could use some shuteye after that bronco ride across the ocean. Some chow, too, if the mess hall's still open."

It was. Greasy fried chicken and lukewarm baked potatoes didn't fill Bruce with delight, but they kept his boiler fueled. His cot was . . . a cot. He'd long since lost track of how many of them he'd slept in. Breakfast, being fresher, was better than supper had been. After Bruce finished, he flagged a cab. It was a big Buick with portholes on either side of the front end. After jeeps and the one-lung English cars he'd driven, it seemed as roomy as a house.

He bought a ticket to San Francisco at the station. The train that would get him to Boston didn't go out for an hour and a half. He went to a newsstand to buy some magazines to kill time with, but found it almost empty. "How come this is all you've got?" he asked the white-mustached man who ran the stand.

"'Cause they're mostly put together and printed in Noo Yahk," the newsstand man answered in a Down East accent thick enough to slice. "And Noo Yahk, it went up in smoke, hear what I'm sayin'?"

"Yeah." Bruce had heard about the A-bomb that hit Manhattan, but he hadn't thought of everything it might mean. Boston had got hit, too, of course. He asked the local how things went there.

"Fubar," the guy said. At Bruce's sandbagged expression, he chuckled and added, "My boy, he was in the Marines. But the train goes through, even if it don't stop there no more. You do your switching in Worcester now." The town's name came out as *Wustah*.

Bruce checked his ticket. Damned if the newsstand man wasn't right. He hadn't even noticed. He bought a Portland newspaper and read every word of it, including a recipe for roast duck with a cranberry glaze.

He was on his second reading when the train finally came in. He found a seat and watched the countryside roll by. Maine gave way to New Hampshire. New Hampshire yielded to Massachusetts. Boston was another example of what he'd been doing for a living. The train crossed the Charles River on a bridge thrown up by the Army Corps of Engineers to replace the slagged, melted mess that had been there before. The field of wreckage stretched as far as the eye could see. Bulldozers and steam shovels labored to clear paths through it. They looked as puny and hopeless as ants struggling to move the carcass of a dead hippo.

"Wonder if the air around here is good to breathe," a woman said, puffing on a cigarette.

His voice boneyard-dry, an unmistakable New Englander responded, "Try not breathin' for ten or twelve minutes an' see if you like that bettah."

Since the bomb had fallen half a year earlier, it probably was safe enough, at least if you were only passing through. Bruce wasn't so sure about the men operating the heavy machinery and stirring up the dust. Were they wearing gauze masks? If they were, would those be enough? Wouldn't real gas masks protect better?

Poetry from high-school English ran through his head:

> *My name is Ozymandias, King of Kings:*
> *Look on my Works, ye Mighty, and despair!*
> *Nothing beside remains. Round the decay*
> *Of that colossal Wreck, boundless and bare,*
> *The lone and level sands stretch far away.*

And what did Robert Oppenheimer say after the first A-bomb blew up in the New Mexico desert? *I am become death, the destroyer of worlds*—that was it. Looking at the ruins of what had been a great city, Bruce understood the verse from the *Bhagadvad Gita* better than he ever had before. Boston vanished behind the train, but stayed in his memory.

Was love easier the second time around? Marian Tabakman—she still had to concentrate every time she signed her new last name—hadn't thought so before she tried it. But now she felt as if they'd been married for years, not weeks. They fit together more naturally than she and Bill had. Bill had had to learn how to live with a woman, and then how to be a father. Fayvl already knew. He'd done it before, for longer than Marian had.

They'd also both had brushes with death. After you came through something like that, you didn't get so excited about the little things. You forgot to defrost some hamburger? One of the Studebaker's headlights burned out? Linda was being impossible? You dealt with everything as best you could. Not perfect? Okay, not perfect. Good enough, and on to whatever came next.

And she and Fayvl got along. They didn't yell at each other. Fayvl hardly ever raised his voice. He worked hard to make her happy, in bed and out of it. She tried to do the same for him. They were comfortable with each other.

And Linda blossomed like a flower when the sun came up. She liked having a man in her life again, maybe even more than Marian did. She called him Papa Fayvl, which made him smile and which also suited Marian. Bill would always be Linda's daddy, but Bill wasn't here. Fayvl was.

Some stepfathers turned into ogres with their new wives' children by old husbands. Fayvl seemed just the opposite. He was gentler with Linda than he would have been with his own flesh and blood. A couple of times, when she drove him crazy, he said he'd give her a *potch in tukhus*. Marian needed some work to find out that that meant *a swat on the behind*. But his bark was worse than his bite. He never lifted his hand against her.

Little by little, his things came out of the room above his shop and into the house. He had not much in the way of clothes or furniture or kitchen goods, but several boxes of books in English and Polish and German and Yiddish—or was it Hebrew? Whatever it was, its alphabet meant nothing to Marian.

He also brought a chess set: a nice one, with pieces carved from ivory and ebony. He'd made some of the stake he needed to come down to Weed by playing chess in Camp Nowhere. He knew what he was doing, in other words. Marian knew how the pieces moved, but hardly more than that.

"I can teach you more, if you want," he said.

She shrugged. "It's not my game," she said honestly. "I'm halfway decent at bridge, if we can find people to play against. Maybe Linda will be more interested."

Linda was interested in doing anything with Fayvl. He taught her with the same care and precision he used to put a new heel on a logging boot. She soon picked up the rules. Before long, she was better than Marian had ever dreamt of being.

Seeing that, Marian asked, "How good can she be?"

"Pretty good," Fayvl said. "She sees the board. She remembers mistakes. She don't too often make them twice." He nodded. "Yes, she can be a good player. Samuel Reshevsky, she'll never put out of business."

Who? Marian wondered. She supposed he was a chess champion. "Did you ever play, uh, Reshevsky?" she asked.

"One time," he said. "In Latvia, in 1937. He beat me. I thought I could maybe get a draw, but he beat me." He sounded prouder of his defeat than he would have over a victory against lesser competition. "He tied for first at that tournament. Me, I came in twenty-third. Best I ever done." He sounded proud of that, too.

"You were working then, right? And you had your family?" Marian said. Fayvl nodded. Marian stared at him. "How did you find time to practice?"

"You don't find time. You make time," Fayvl said. "Or else you don't, and then you don't play so good." Now he sounded stern. People who didn't know him well might not think he looked like much, but there was iron in him. If there weren't, he wouldn't have survived Auschwitz. He would wear the number on his arm for the rest of his life.

They said two could live cheaper than one. Three together could definitely live cheaper than three apart. They began saving a little money—not a lot, but Marian liked that. Like so many others who'd gone through the Depression, she thought highly of money in the bank. She didn't know what the Depression was like in Poland. Fayvl salted money away whenever he got the chance, though.

"Is better when you can," he said. "Tomorrow don't take care of it-self. You got to take care today of tomorrow."

"I'm not arguing," Marian said. Even if she hadn't been that way on her own, living with Bill would have brought her around. He was a bookkeeper when he wasn't blowing cities off the map: a suspenders-and-belt man if ever there was one.

And she and Fayvl didn't argue much anyway. Oh, they snapped at each other every now and then. They were human beings. But they didn't have the kind of quarrels that festered for days or weeks. Neither of them worked to get under the other's skin. They did fit together well.

One night (perhaps not so coincidentally, it was after a week when they'd been able to bank more money than usual), Marian asked, "Have you ever thought about a little brother or sister for Linda?"

Fayvl had been reading the *Weed Press-Herald*. He looked up with an expression of pleased surprise. "Of course I think it," he said. "I don't want to say nothing about it so soon, though. I wonder if is maybe too quick for you. But yes, I would like a little child. Maybe a boy, to say *kaddish* for me after I'm gone. But a girl is fine, too."

"Well, then, we won't worry about rubbers for a while," Marian said. Fayvl was as wryly resigned to them as Bill had been. But if you wanted to fool around and you didn't feel like knitting little booties, what else were you going to do?

Fayvl coughed. "We have a child, you and I, I would like to raise it Jewish, you don't mind too much."

"I don't mind at all!" Marian was glad she was able to say that quickly. She'd thought about it before she mentioned anything to Fayvl. She'd been brought up a Methodist, but she hadn't been to church for years. Her religion, such as it was, meant little to her. The Nazis had almost killed Fayvl on account of his. No wonder he wanted to see it go on for another generation.

"T'ank you," he said. Before she could wave that aside, he went on, "Not so easy here. We don't even got enough *Yehudim* in Weed for a minyan, I don't t'ink. But I do what I can."

"For a . . . ?"

"A minyan. Ten grown men to worship together." He shrugged. "In Poland now, not hardly enough for a minyan in the whole country."

Marian didn't know how many Jews had lived in Poland before Hitler overran it. Lots—she knew that. Millions, probably. No more. Never again. Many of those who hadn't died had got out, as Fayvl had. "Everything will be fine," she said.

"*Alevai omayn,*" her husband answered. "May it be so."

She turned the subject a little: "Linda will be glad to have a brother or a sister. She'll be big enough to help take care of the baby, too, at least some."

"You have a baby, you go *meshuggeh*," Fayvl said. "Is what babies is for, to make the mother and father *meshuggeh*."

That was a Yiddish word Marian had learned. She nodded rueful agreement. Even one baby outnumbered both parents. She couldn't imagine how people with twins or triplets coped. Odds were they didn't.

When Marian was pregnant with Linda, she'd had what they called morning sickness. Only she hadn't just had it in the morning. Any time at all, any reason at all or none . . . She'd made it to the toilet every single time, but she'd sure had a couple of close calls. She hoped she would have a nice, quiet pregnancy with the second baby.

Of course, what you hoped for didn't always match what you got. If it had, she wouldn't have been sitting here in Weed with Fayvl. Not that this was bad. It was better than she'd thought it would be, in fact. But it wasn't what she'd hoped for up in Everett. All you could do was go on.

The *Independence* landed at O'Hare and taxied to a stop. Its four big props windmilled down toward stillness. A Cadillac limousine rolled across the runway to take Harry Truman into Chicago.

"Nice to be in a part of the country where everything's still standing," the President said.

"Everything's still standing in Philly, too," Joseph Short said.

Truman eyed his press secretary over the tops of his glasses. "Fool luck, and you know it as well as I do. If that Bull hadn't clipped something on the ground and crashed, Philadelphia would have gone up in smoke along with Boston and New York and Washington." The Russian bomber's tail still stood in that field in New Jersey. Truman was thinking about ordering it preserved as a monument to a war whose major monuments were mostly detectable by Geiger counter.

Secret Service men preceded the President out of the DC-6. They worried about assassins more than he did. If somebody wanted to bump him off, he just hoped the son of a bitch could shoot straight. But you couldn't stop Secret Service men from guarding, any more than you could stop pointers from pointing.

When they got to the bottom of the wheeled staircase, they waved to show it was safe for him to descend. Down he went, Short behind him. Mayor Martin Kennelly stepped out of the limousine, his white hair gleaming in the afternoon sunshine. "Welcome to Chicago, sir," he said, extending his hand.

"Thanks." Truman shook it. They were both professional politicians with polished grips. The clasp was so smooth, it hardly seemed there at all. "I was just telling Joe it was nice to be in a part of the country where it's all still in working order."

"Chicago's called itself the Second City for a long time," Mayor Kennelly said. "Maybe we're the first one now. I don't know."

"I don't, either. Just between you, me, and the wall, Mr. Mayor, I don't think I know much any more," Truman said.

Martin Kennelly's smile slipped. "Well, let's take you to the hotel and let you relax till the dinner tonight."

"Okay by me." Truman and his press secretary got into the limo with the mayor. The big black Caddy had plenty of room for all. The driver put it in gear. The Secret Service had men in lesser vehicles ahead of it and behind. Flanking those, in turn, were cars full of Chicago's finest, their red lights flashing and their sirens wailing like damned souls. The motorcade streamed into town. More cops stood at intersections on the route to block cross traffic and make sure its progress stayed smooth.

Watching those upstretched arms in police blue, watching stopped motorists swear and shake their fists at the cops, Truman chuckled and said, "Nice to see you know how to make the voters love me."

"Don't worry about it, Mr. President," Kennelly said. "They won't blame you one bit. They'll go, *What's that damn fool in City Hall got his flatfoots doing now, and how late is it gonna make me?*"

Truman laughed. Laugh or not, he knew the mayor had it right. Politics was local. You blamed the guy you could reach with your vote.

If Kennelly tried to run again—not obvious, not when he was already in his mid-sixties—some challenger would throw this motorcade in his face.

However it might play out in Chicago politics, the traffic control made the trip to the Loop quick and easy. The limo pulled up in front of the Blackstone Hotel, at the corner of Michigan and Balbo. Truman had stayed at the Blackstone before. It was a landmark of sorts, with red and white walls and a green roof.

The Secret Service men piled out of their cars to cordon off the vehicle that carried the President. Truman disliked having so much security around; it put him in mind of Hitler and Stalin. But the times were what they were. He didn't see how he could do without his human hunting dogs.

He walked in, got his key from the manager—no standing in line at the front desk—and took the elevator up to his room to shower and to relax till he came down to eat rubber chicken and make his speech to well-heeled Democratic contributors in the Grand Ballroom. The whole ritual was as stylized as a Catholic Mass. The only differences were, most of the drinks wouldn't be wine and he wouldn't have to make the speech in Latin. With so many Irish and Italian movers and shakers here, they might have understood it if he did.

The mattress was too soft. Hotel mattresses almost always were. He turned on the radio to drown out the noise from the hallway and dozed for forty-five minutes. When he woke, he splashed cold water on his face, combed his hair, and put on his shoes. Then he stepped out. He was ready for action.

One of the Secret Service men rapped on Joseph Short's door when Truman emerged. Short popped out like a jack-in-the-box. "I'll take you down to the banquet room, sir," he said.

"How can I say no?" Truman murmured.

The banquet room was an enormous sea of tables, white linen, and uncomfortable chairs. Truman had seen a million like it, in other words. The platform against the wall held the high table where he and the other big, big shots would sit. The carpet, a horror of crimson and gold, was ugly even by hotel banquet-room standards, but he'd seen worse.

Waiters and cleaners were still getting things into shape. A colored sweeper came up to Truman and said, "My brother Louie, he's in the Army. He jus' made staff sergeant, suh, an' he says he never coulda done that without you killin' segregation in the service."

"Thank you." Truman held out his hand, and the janitor shook it. The President went on, "When I hear something like that, it makes me surer than ever that I did the right thing."

"Yes, suh," the Negro said. "Should oughta do it all over everywhere." He went back to work without waiting for a reply. On the whole, Truman agreed with him. Only the enormous row the South would kick up continued to hold him back.

Chicago being a cow town (Truman tried not to remember *The Jungle*), dinner proved to be overdone steak in place of rubber chicken. Mayor Kennelly introduced Truman as the man who'd won two World Wars. It wasn't a title Truman wanted, but he could see he'd be stuck with it. He waved to the applauding Democrats as he walked over to the lectern.

"I hope no one else ever has to fight a world war. With all my heart, I do," he said. "That's what makes the Republicans, especially the Nixon-McCarthy wing of the Republicans, so dangerous. Their symbol should be the ostrich, not the elephant. They want to stick their heads in the sand and pretend the rest of the world isn't there.

"I'm going to mangle John Donne to show what jackasses the elephants are. No nation is an island, entire of itself; every nation is a piece of a continent, a part of the main. Any nation's trouble diminishes me, because I am involved in mankind. And therefore never send to know for whom the air-raid siren tolls; it tolls for thee."

He got several seconds of the thoughtful silence that is a higher compliment than any applause. Then he got the hand, too. "Thank you," he said. "Thank you very much. The other thing I need to tell you is, we still have a ton of work to do, around the world and here at home. And we have to keep working for engagement and involvement no matter who's President after me. I hope and expect that will be Governor Stevenson." More applause, loud and fierce. Truman held up a hand to quiet it. "Even if we aren't lucky, even if the Republicans bamboozle America, we still have to keep working for what we believe in. The country can survive a Republican. It can't survive forgetting what makes us great."

He wasn't surprised at a knock on his door later that evening. There stood Adlai Stevenson. His bald head and glasses made him look like an intelligent, amiable egg. Truman waved him in and closed the door behind him.

"So you don't think I can win, either," Stevenson said.

"It's not your fault, Adlai," Truman said, busying himself with a bottle of bourbon for both of them. As they clinked, he continued, "The people are sick of the party that got them kicked in the face. They're sick of me, but I'm afraid they'll take it out on you."

"Losing to Eisenhower . . . I can deal with that," Stevenson said. "If it's Nixon and I lose, though, I want to jump off a tall building. Before him, no one ever campaigned on the slogan 'Throw the rascals *in*.' The man is a disaster."

"So is a hurricane. We get over them. I do think it'll be Ike," Truman said. "Here's hoping, anyway." They drained their glasses. He poured them full again.

Aaron Finch slid two cartons of Chesterfields and a five-dollar bill across the counter at the Rexall near his house. The checkout girl rang him up, put the cigarettes in a bag, and gave him his change, then asked, "Anything else?"

He snapped his fingers. "Darned if there isn't. Be right back." Luckily, no one was in line behind him. He went to the aisle full of medicines, pulled a bottle of Cheracol off the shelf, and brought it back to the counter. "Need something with codeine in it. My little boy's got a nasty cough."

"I hope he gets better," the girl said. "That'll be another dollar and nine cents." He paid her and put the cough medicine in the sack with the cigarettes.

It had warmed up while he was in the drugstore. The Los Angeles area could get into the upper eighties any month of the year. This was one of those days in October. The bag would have sweat stains on it by the time he finished the fifteen-minute walk home.

Ruth greeted him with, "You have the Cheracol, right?"

"I almost forgot it, but I didn't," Aaron answered. "How's Leon doing?"

"He's coughing like he's been smoking longer than you have," his wife answered. As if to confirm that, Leon barked from his bedroom. When he was willing to stay in bed during the day, you knew he felt rotten.

"C'mere, Leon!" Aaron called. "Daddy brought home cough medicine for you."

Leon came, but paused at the kitchen door like a nervous wild animal on the point of bolting. "Does it taste yucky?"

"Lemme see." Aaron poured a couple of drops into the bowl of a teaspoon, then stuck the spoon in his mouth. A demon made him want to froth and fall down. He suppressed it. "Nah, not too bad. Kinda like cherries."

Leon let himself be dosed. "Waddaya think, kiddo?" Ruth asked him.

"It's not *too* bad." Leon had the air of a man who'd just heard they'd only have to pull two teeth, not four. He went back to the bedroom, probably to tell his Teddy bear how his father and mother mistreated him.

"Codeine makes most people sleepy, too," Ruth said. "Maybe he'll take a nap."

"*Alevai!*" Aaron exclaimed. Leon hadn't slept much the night before, and his coughing woke Aaron up several times. He turned on the fire under the coffee pot, waited till it got perking hard, and poured himself a new cup. After adulterating it with sugar and Pet condensed milk, he sipped.

"Turn it back on," Ruth said. "That's a good idea."

They gravely touched cups when hers was ready. Aaron said, "Darned if I know what parents did before people found out about this stuff."

"They went bonkers, same as they do now, only they were sleepy all the time while they did it," Ruth answered.

The phone rang. Aaron picked up the handset. "Hello?"

"Hello, trouble." That tenor belonged to Marvin. The tenor of his younger brother's voice had always graveled Aaron. Marvin went on, "How about you guys come over here for the afternoon?"

"No can do—sorry." Aaron got to beg off without even lying, an unexpected bonus. "Leon's sick. He's barking louder than Caesar." Marvin's German shepherd was wolfy enough to leave Leon scared that he'd get eaten when they visited.

"Ah, that's too bad. Tell him I hope he feels better." Marvin sounded as if he meant it. He and Leon did get on well. Aaron wondered whether that was a judgment on his brother or his son.

"I'll do it," Aaron said. "How's by you? What's up with your gang?"

"We're fine," Marvin answered. "I'm doing my due diligence on what may be *the* way to do business for the next fifty years."

"What is it this time?" Aaron asked. Marvin had been through more fly-by-night schemes than Charles Lindbergh. He got enthusiastic. He worked like blazes for a couple of weeks, sometimes even for a couple of months. Then, when he failed to set the world on fire, he went back to doing very little till the lightning struck again. He was the hare in the family, Aaron the tortoise.

"Franchising," Marvin said now, in portentous tones. "Say you've got a hot-dog stand. No, say you've got the *idea* for a hot-dog stand."

"Okay, I've got the idea for a hot-dog stand," Aaron said agreeably. "I go out and I get a hot-dog stand. I sell hot dogs, maybe chili on the side. I hope I make enough money to live."

"That's the old-fashioned way to do it." Marvin's voice dripped scorn. "With franchising, I get a chain of hot-dog stands. They all look the same. They all sell the same stuff. The help all wears the same clothes, even. The managers get the stuff and the uniforms and all from me, and they pay me a chunk of the profits. It's like a license to coin money, I swear to God it is."

"If there are any profits, yeah," Aaron said. "What happens if your managers fleece you or if they lose *gelt* from the start?"

"You know, Aaron, that's what's always been wrong with you. You won't think big," Marvin said.

"*Nu?* I'm still here. I'm not broke. My wife loves me. What more do I need?"

"I was going to ask if you were interested in investing with me, but I can see I'd be wasting my breath."

"You can ask. How much would I have to sink into this scheme?"

"Two, three thousand *taler* would be good."

"I bet it would," Aaron said. He had that much in the bank, and a bit more besides. He was patiently saving up for the down payment on a house, so he could own instead of renting. He wanted a little more besides before he did any serious shopping. That way, he'd still have some cushion if anything went wrong.

"I told you you didn't have the smarts to come in with me," Marvin said.

"Save the *I-told-you-sos* for when you hit it big and you come by in your fancy-shmancy Rolls-Royce to look down your nose at the peasants, okay? Listen, I gotta go. Say hi to Sarah and Olivia for me, will you? 'Bye." Aaron hung up.

"What is it this time?" Ruth asked.

"A chain of hot-dog stands," Aaron answered. "By the way Marvin talks, he does none of the work and gets all of the rakeoff. How many times have I heard that song before?"

"Oh, maybe two or three," his wife said.

"Two or three dozen, you mean."

"You didn't let me finish."

"If he worked as hard on working hard as he does on the stupid get-rich-quick ideas, I bet he really would be rich by now," Aaron said, lighting a cigarette. "But no. It has to be the pot of gold at the end of the rainbow."

"He's not even Irish," Ruth said.

"I know, but that's how—" Aaron broke off. He sneezed, wetly, and coughed several times. When he blew his nose, he was snottier than he should have been.

"*Gesundheit,*" Ruth said at the sneeze, and then, "Oh, no! I hope you're not coming down with whatever Leon's got."

"So do I," Aaron said. "I've got to go to work any which way, but working while you're sick's no fun."

He kept telling himself he was fine the rest of the day. When he got up Monday morning, he couldn't lie to himself any more. His throat wasn't just scratchy; it hurt. His head felt like a balloon. He took a couple of aspirins, and moved more from the bottle into a little pressed-tin pill case he stuck in his pocket. Just before he went out the door, he swallowed some of the Cheracol he'd bought for his son.

"You all right?" Herschel Weissman asked when he got to the Blue Front warehouse.

"I'll live," Aaron said. His boss nodded and patted him on the back.

Istvan was more direct: "You're sick! Why didn't you stay home?"

"Because nobody will pay me if I do," Aaron told him.

"No sick leave?" Istvan asked in surprise. Aaron shook his head— and coughed again. Istvan went on, "So the Communists weren't telling *all* lies about capitalism, then?"

"Maybe not all. But a lot of them," Aaron said. "Come on. We've got a lot of stuff to take care of today."

CADE CURTIS HAD TAKEN more than a month to cross the
Pacific in a westbound troopship. He didn't remember being bored
then. He'd been too eager and too excited, or he thought now that he
had been then. But he couldn't say for sure. He'd been different so many
ways. He'd believed he was protecting democracy. He'd had two legs.
Details, details . . .

Coming back took just as long as going over had. Aboard the SS *Joe
Harris*, Cade knew damn well he was bored. The only time he wasn't
bored was when he was going to and from the galley, which was a deck
up from his cabin. Then he was scared. Jimmy saved him from breaking his neck on the steep steel stairs more than once—they weren't
made for a man with crutches.

Jimmy also saved him from going completely out of his skull with
boredom. In the trenches, teaching Jimmy as much math as the Korean
kid could soak up had been just a daydream. On the wallowing Liberty
ship, it was a godsend: it helped make time go by.

And Jimmy learned way more than Cade thought he would. Multi-
plication and division naturally followed the addition and subtraction
he already had. Fractions were harder. Jimmy's face lit up like a star

shell when he figured out how they worked. Square roots . . . Cade was mildly surprised he still remembered how to extract them himself. His own trouble made it easier for him to help Jimmy over the rough spots.

Then they reached negative numbers. "What do you get when you take five away from three?" Cade asked.

"You mean take three away from five, right?" Jimmy returned.

"Nope. What do you get when you take five away from three?"

"You get nothing. Is nothing left. Less than nothing." Jimmy laughed to show how ridiculous the idea was.

But it was less ridiculous than he thought. Cade drew a number line on a sheet of paper. He numbered backwards from ten down to one. Then he added zero. He looked at Jimmy. Jimmy nodded—okay so far. Cade put another mark to the left of the zero. Above it, he wrote *-1*. Then he wrote *-2*, *-3*, and so on down to *-10*. "You see? You get it?" he asked. He touched his pencil point to the three on the number line, then moved it five spaces to the left. "So three minus five is . . . ?"

Jimmy put his finger on the *-2*. "How you say it?"

"Minus two or negative two," Cade answered. Jimmy exclaimed in Korean. He'd just seen something he'd never dreamt of before, and it excited him.

He was doing simple algebra by the time the *Joe Harris* neared the San Francisco Bay. A small boat came out to guide the freighter into the bay. Jimmy helped Cade up on deck so he could watch the ship enter the famous harbor. He'd been a little boy when the Golden Gate Bridge opened. Now . . .

Now he knew that the Russians had A-bombed San Francisco, but he hadn't thought about what that meant. They'd collapsed the bridge, making it impossible for ships to get in or out. Engineers had finally opened a narrow path through the wreckage. The little boat led the *Joe Harris* through the cleared channel.

Staring at the countless tons of steel all melted and knocked askew, Cade felt tears sting his eyes. One flash, and the Golden Gate Bridge went from wonder of the world to scrap metal. And how many cars, how many people, had been on it when the bomb went off?

Of course, the bridge was far from the only thing the A-bomb had wrecked. The northern rim of the city of San Francisco was all ruin and devastation, too. The smashed cityscape seemed to impress Jimmy even more than the toppled bridge did. "This is what happens with A-bomb?" he asked Cade.

"This is what happens, all right," Cade said somberly. He was a little better prepared for the sight than Jimmy was. He'd seen the burning outskirts of Pusan right after the Russians hit it. But Pusan was a foreign place, a city he'd never heard of till the Korean War broke out. Everybody in America knew about San Francisco and the Golden Gate Bridge. The difference was between a murdered stranger and a murdered loved one.

"They should never use those things," Jimmy declared.

"If you think I'm gonna argue with you, you got another think coming," Cade said.

His eye went to the little island in the bay, not far east of the ravaged bridge. That had to be Alcatraz, he realized. The worst bad guys went to prison there. Or they had gone to prison there. By the way the place looked, none of those bad guys remained among the living.

The Bay Bridge that linked San Francisco and Oakland still stood. The A-bomb hadn't been strong enough to take it down with the Golden Gate Bridge. *Need an H-bomb to get both at once,* Cade thought. His shiver had nothing to do with the wet, chilly air. An H-bomb would have incinerated the whole city, not just the part near the sea.

The *Joe Harris* docked at Pier 46, on one side of what a sign called China Basin. Gulls wheeled overhead, hoping for garbage. Plump seals swimming in the basin and lolling on the pier said the gulls didn't get it all. Jimmy's face was a study. "America," he whispered, more to himself than to anyone else. "I am in America."

A handful of people waited at the landward end of the dock to meet the passengers the Liberty ship carried. Cade paid no attention to them till somebody down there called his name. Since he wore an uncommon one, he didn't doubt the call was aimed at him. There were his father and mother and older brother, all waving as if they were practicing semaphore.

He waved back with more restraint. If you started flailing around while you were using crutches, you'd land on your butt. "Who they?" Jimmy asked.

"My mom. My dad. My brother Jerry."

"Ah. Mother and father." Jimmy sounded very serious. Koreans had an almost reflexive respect for their elders.

Before Cade could meet his family, he and Jimmy had to go through customs. Their worldly goods were not a problem; they had next to none. The paperwork that let Jimmy enter the United States, though . . . There was a lot of it, and it was complicated. Patiently, Cade said, "This is my adopted son. His Korean name is Chun Won-ung. His American name is Jimmy Curtis." He said it several times.

"Jimmy Curtis—that's me," Jimmy agreed.

"I've never seen papers like these before," the inspector said doubtfully. "I don't know if you can do that. I better get Mr. Ledesma."

When Mr. Ledesma—a plump little man with a lounge-lizard mustache—arrived, Cade went through the whole rigmarole again. The inspector's boss scratched his jowls with carefully manicured fingernails. "I've never seen an arrangement like this before," he said. "Usually, our policy is to exclude Asiatics, not invite them in."

Jimmy bristled. "Easy," Cade murmured. To Mr. Ledesma, he said, "Jimmy's no Asiatic now. He's my kid. That's what the paperwork is all about."

"Yes, so I see," the senior customs man replied. "Everything looks to be in order, and it's backed up by the signatures and stamps of some mighty high-ranking people. I don't know how you did it." He eyed the service ribbons and medals on Cade's chest, and his pinned-up trouser leg. "Mm, maybe I do. You did your country some favors. So what if you got one back?" He plied his rubber stamp with might and main. "Welcome to the USA, Mr. Curtis . . . both Mr. Curtises, I should say."

"Thank you," Cade and Jimmy said together.

Out they went, into the cool, watery San Francisco sunshine. Ralph, Myrna, and Jerry Curtis greeted them with whoops. Like their father, Jerry Curtis was shorter and stockier than Cade. He'd fought in France in the last war. He was an engineer himself, and hadn't got Uncle Sam's *Greetings!* letter this time around. Everybody was polite to Jimmy, though Jerry said, "Usually it's the girls who have a child out of wedlock."

"Oh, shut up," Cade answered sweetly.

Jimmy couldn't have been more formal with Cade's folks if he were playing a butler in an English movie. "My grandfather. My grandmother," he said. They might not have looked exactly thrilled about that, but they didn't call him on it. Cade was relieved. What he'd told them had been brief.

"Let's get something to eat," Ralph said. "Long as we're here on the coast, we can eat seafood." He grinned crookedly. "Bound to be fresher here than it is in Knoxville. And then we'll see about getting us all home and about what we can do for that leg of yours."

"Okay, Dad." Cade nodded. His father wasn't a man who beat around the bush. He wouldn't pretend nothing had happened to Cade. And his *all* plainly included Jimmy. A weight of worry dropped from Cade's shoulders.

Konstantin Morozov wished he had eyes in the back of his head. In Lithuania, the enemy was all around him. Anyone at all might pull out a machine pistol and bang away at him when his tank went by. That was the chance he took, sticking his head out of the cupola for a better view. Man? Woman? Child? It didn't matter. You couldn't trust anybody. And if you stayed buttoned up inside the turret, you might not spot the mine waiting to blow off a track.

All things considered, Konstantin would rather have been fighting the Americans back in Germany. They had better weapons than the bandits here, but you never had any doubts about who was a soldier and who a civilian. For that matter, Konstantin would sooner have gone up against the *Wehrmacht* than the Lithuanians. The Germans had been tough, but their hatred for the Red Army was different from the locals'. They fought like devils, but they didn't want to die. The Lithuanians didn't seem to care, as long as they could take Russians with them.

The other thing that bothered him was, he had no one in the crew with whom he could share his worries. He'd been able to talk with Juris Eigims. The gunner had been able to talk with him, too, but that hadn't stopped Eigims from going over the hill the second he saw the chance. Maybe he was in a T-34/85 himself. Maybe he was even commanding one at last, and rolling into action against the Red Army.

These guys, though . . . Konstantin still loathed Pyotr Polikarpov, Eigims' replacement. Maybe Nodar Gachechiladze was smart, maybe not. He still didn't know enough Russian for Morozov to tell, let alone to talk with him. Alexei Yakovlev was too young to have any idea what was what.

That left Avram Lipshitz. The driver was no dope; Konstantin hadn't needed long to see that. But he had his own worries, which seemed worse than the tank commander's. Pretty plainly, he was scared all the time. It didn't keep him from doing whatever Konstantin told him to do. Konstantin gave him credit for coping, but not for having the fear in the first place. It didn't help. You could get killed just as easily with it as without it.

And he was a Jew. How loyal was he? Would he bail out the way Eigims had? Probably not—he had nowhere to go. But he wasn't someone Morozov wanted to open up to. So he didn't open up to anyone. If his stomach sometimes pained him, that was part of the price he paid for leading the tank crew. So he kept telling himself, anyhow.

A truck convoy full of munitions and spare parts reached Vilnius from Byelorussia, which was, if not quiet, a lot quieter than Lithuania. Had the convoy stayed in Vilnius, everything would have been fine— and the people who needed the supplies wouldn't have got them. The long column of trucks had to get to Ukmerge, in central Lithuania. The roads were bad, though few roads outside the USSR's big cities were good.

Trucks couldn't get to Ukmerge by themselves. The Lithuanian bandits would have had themselves a field day, sitting in the bushes with their rifles and machine guns and shooting up the column at their leisure. Red Army brass, in their infinite wisdom, decided a few tanks would be just what the convoy needed to keep the trucks safe.

Konstantin didn't believe it even before his T-34/85 got tapped for escort duty. The tanks would give the column more firepower, true. But the bandits had already proved they didn't worry about such things . . . hadn't they? The brass didn't think so. Nobody asked Konstantin what he thought. Nobody cared. He was a sergeant, there to do what he was told.

He did make sure his tank had its full load of ammunition. He went heavy on HE, light on AP. He didn't expect to be fighting many Lithuanian tanks. Tanks weren't the problem. Stubborn men with small arms and grudges were.

As they set out, he said, "Polikarpov, don't fuck off on this one or it's your nuts. You hear me?"

"I serve the Soviet Union, Comrade Sergeant!" the gunner replied. That should have meant *Of course I hear you*. Morozov had the bad feeling it was more on the order of *Shut up and leave me alone*.

The wind was wet and chilly. The fall *rasputitsa* was on the way. Roads would turn to muck till they froze solid again a few weeks later. The spring mud time was worse, but the fall *rasputitsa* caught the Germans by surprise and probably kept them from taking Moscow in 1941.

Vilnius had lain under the Red Army's steel fist. So would Ukmerge, fifty or sixty kilometers to the north. In between . . . In between was bandit country. The bandits swam among the rest of the Lithuanians like fish in a school. Rooting them out was next to impossible. No one gave them away. When they weren't raising hell, they cached their rifles and machine guns in the woods or in a hole in the ground or in a shack wrecked in one war or another.

Russian soldiers couldn't prove who took potshots at them and who didn't. Sometimes, following German practice, they seized hostages when they were fired on, and shot them after no one admitted guilt. That, of course, endeared them even more to the Lithuanians.

A kilometer and a half outside of Vilnius, a bullet clanged off the T-34/85's turret a meter below the cupola. It whined away. Konstantin let himself drop down into the fighting compartment. The next one might be aimed better.

"Anybody see where that came from?" he asked—a hopeless question. Lipshitz and Yakovlev could see straight ahead through their vision slits. So could Polikarpov, with his gunsight. Nodar Gachechiladze couldn't see out at all.

"Shall I drop some shells on the countryside?" Polikarpov asked.

Konstantin surprised himself by answering, "Sure, give 'em a couple of rounds. Won't hurt."

The gun roared. Cordite fumes filled the compartment. Dirt fountained up outside. Whether the shelling did any good, Konstantin doubted. Maybe it would make the bandits thoughtful, anyhow.

Along with the tanks, a few armored personnel carriers full of soldiers rolled north with the convoy. Their machine guns hosed down the bushes. The infantrymen didn't get out and attack, though. One carrier came too close to a bandit's foxhole, as lovingly camouflaged as if the man inside still served in the Red Army. The driver had no idea the bandit was there till he fired his rocket-propelled grenade. The carrier went up in smoke and flame. Konstantin didn't think anyone got out.

It was a running fight all the way up to Ukmerge. The bandits had plainly known the truck column was on its way. How? They might just have kept their eyes open and guessed well. They might have intercepted Red Army radio messages; Soviet signals security rarely was what it should have been. Or there might have been spies or traitors inside Vilnius.

They put several trucks out of action. A couple caught fire. The rest, with flat tires or shot-up engines, unloaded their cargo. It wasn't easy, since all the trucks were fully laden. The journey should have taken no longer than a couple of hours. It went on and on and. . . .

Pabaiskas was the last village in front of Ukmerge. The lead tank had almost got through when it hit a mine that blew off a track. That made the rest of the column stop. Bandits in the village opened up with everything they had.

"Christ have mercy! We're fucked!" Pyotr Polikarpov shouted.

Konstantin only wished the gunner were wrong. "Keep shooting! Give 'em hell!" he said. "Cannon and machine gun both!" He yelled into the intercom: "Avram! Knock down the houses in your way! We've got to get forward!"

"I'll do it, Comrade Sergeant!" Lipshitz answered. He might be scared, but he followed orders.

As the tank turned bulldozer, though, a bandit scrambled up onto its rear decking and smashed two Molotov cocktails on the engine louvers. Blazing gasoline knocked out the diesel. "Now what?" Polikarpov howled when the T-34/85 quit.

Grabbing a PPSh from a rack inside the turret, Konstantin said, "Now we bail out. We'll start roasting if we don't."

He yanked the hatch open. When he popped out, he found himself staring at a tall, blond Balt who looked much too much like his old gunner for comfort. The bandit had a machine pistol, too. They both fired at the same time, from a range of no more than five meters. Konstantin saw the Lithuanian fall, but he got sledgehammered in the chest himself. He tried to keep moving, but the world went red, then gray, then black.

Ihor Shevchenko watched *zeks* rebuild Kiev. Everyone assured him it was safe to go into the city for a while. Whether what the workmen were doing was also safe, he had no idea. He didn't think the commissars who put them to work gave a damn one way or the other. They were only *zeks*. If you used them up, you could always get more.

Colonel Rogozin's brother-in-law was a lieutenant colonel named Nikita Azarov. If Ihor's division commander had thought well of him, Azarov wasn't inclined to worry about it. And the staff officer used him exactly as Rogozin suggested: as a weapons and tactics instructor.

That worked better than Ihor had thought it would. He'd figured the

soldiers in the Kiev Military District would be men like the ones alongside whom he'd fought: retreads, most of them, who know as much
about the art of organized murder as he did. What could he teach soldiers like that?

But these guys were almost all kids, fresh conscripts, whose only
fighting expertise came from the schoolyard or the playground. Quite
a few of them looked to have been drafted a year or two early, too. The
veterans, the men who'd been through the grinder against the Nazis,
were committed in the satellites or the seriously rebellious regions of
the USSR. This was what the Soviet Union had left to hold down more
quiet regions and to begin to rebuild the Red Army.

So Ihor showed them what he'd learned in two wars. He showed
them how to cut a man's throat without letting him get out a squawk
while you were doing it. He showed them how to sharpen the blade on
their entrenching tool, and how to use it to ruin an enemy's face or ribs.

"If you know what to do with it, this thing beats the shit out of a
bayonet on the end of a rifle," he told them. "In the trenches, you want
one of these babies, some grenades, and a submachine gun or a Kalashnikov."

They listened hard, their smooth faces serious. They practiced with
that same air of doing it because they had to, not because they understood it would help keep them alive. They'd find out. Or, if things settled down, they'd be lucky enough not to.

He gave them one other piece of advice: "Always clean your weapon
whenever you get the chance. I know we make 'em tough. I know a
PPD or a PPSh or a Kalashnikov will probably work no matter how
filthy you let it get. But do you want to feel like a stupid pussy—a stupid
dead pussy—on account of it jams just when you need it worst? Clean
the fucker!"

He showed them how to read the little swells of ground any field or
plain had, and how to camouflage a foxhole so it disappeared into the
landscape. "This is a lot more work than digging and hopping in," one
of them grumbled.

Ihor shrugged. "You want to do that, be my guest. You might as well put up a sign that says CHUCK YOUR GRENADE IN HERE while you're at it." The youngster who'd complained turned red as hot iron.

After he'd been at it for a week or so, Lieutenant Colonel Azarov summoned him and said, "I'm getting good reports about you, Shevchenko. You seem to have definite leadership abilities."

"I serve the Soviet Union, sir!" Ihor said.

"You're doing a good job of it," Azarov replied. "Vsevolod didn't send you back here only because you can do such things, though, did he? You make your home around these parts, isn't that right?"

"Yes, sir." Ihor nodded. "On a kolkhoz not too far from the city."

"You have a family there?"

"My wife, sir. We don't have children, not yet. We might have started if I hadn't got called back into the Red Army."

"Ah." Nikita Azarov had a round, fleshy face. With another ten years to work on his jowls and double chin, he'd look like a proper Soviet general, whether he got the rank or not. "You'd probably like to go see her, then, eh? Isn't that part of the reason why Vsevolod sent you back here?"

"Sir, I'm just a sergeant. How am I supposed to know why a colonel does anything?" Ihor might have been collectivized when he was a boy, but he came from uncounted generations of peasants. Playing dumb, especially about men of status higher than his own, was in his blood.

Like an old Russian aristocrat, Lieutenant Colonel Azarov wasn't blind to what Ihor was up to. The officer let out an expressive grunt. "Can you get to your kolkhoz from here on a bicycle?" he asked.

"Oh, yes, sir. Anya—my wife—was going to go into Kiev the morning the imperialists bombed it. But she had a horrible cold, so she stayed behind when her friends went. That's why she's still alive."

"A lot of stories like that. A whole lot more that aren't so happy," Azarov said. "All right. I'll give you a pass to go off the encampment Sunday. I expect you'll be able to scare up a bike from somewhere, won't you?"

"Yes, sir! Thank you, sir! I serve the Soviet Union, sir!" Ihor came to the stiffest attention his bad leg allowed. He snapped off a parade-ground salute. An officer who was a human being! It happened now and again, but nowhere near often enough to let you count on it.

The bike he promoted was a beast. It weighed twenty kilos and had one speed. If it ran into a tank, the tank might have been the one that fell over. However beastly it was, though, pedaling it was faster and easier than walking.

Ihor thought so, anyhow, till it started to drizzle. He hadn't brought along a rain cape or anything. He hadn't thought he'd need one. A bicycle, water, and a dirt road didn't mix.

Drizzle turned to downpour by the time he got to the collective farm. They'd got the harvest done; the fields were full of yellowing stubble. Pretty soon, snow would cover it. By the time he reached the kolkhoz, the rain was coming down so hard that he couldn't see very far. Luckily, he didn't need to. He knew every centimeter of the ground around here.

He lowered the kickstand right outside the residential building. Mud squelched under his boots as he walked to the door. The ride back would be even more fun than the trip out here had been. He'd worry about that later. He opened the door and walked inside.

Familiar faces turned to stare at him. They all looked closed and wary. To the kolkhozniks, he was a stranger, an outsider, a danger. *What does the Red Army want with us now?* That was what they had to be thinking. They didn't know him soaking wet and in uniform, especially with his cap pulled down low on his forehead against the rain.

"*Bozhemoi,* Comrade Sergeant, what made you come out here in weather like this?" Of course Petro Hapochka read his shoulder boards at a glance. The kolkhoz chairman—in the old days, he would have been a village headman—had returned from the Great Patriotic War with only one foot.

"I'm putting you all in khaki, that's what!" Ihor growled.

They looked horrified for a moment. Then Petro recognized his voice. He limped over to Ihor on his artificial foot and folded him into a bear hug, no matter how wet he was. "You son of a bitch!" he roared.

"You damn near made me piss myself! Now what are you really doing here?"

"They sent me back to this military district to be an instructor. Crazy, isn't it?" Ihor said. "But never mind that. Where's Anya?"

"In your room, as far as I know," Hapochka said. One of the women nodded.

"I'll see you later, then." Off Ihor went. Fear made his own limp worse, the way it did when he went into combat. What if Anya wasn't alone in the room? What if she was pregnant out to there, or nursing a baby that wasn't his? *I'll kill her,* he thought. *I'll kill the bastard who got her, and then maybe I'll kill myself.*

The door stood open. Anya sat on the bed, darning socks. No pregnancy. No little bastard in a cradle. A great stone of dread fell from Ihor's shoulders. He stood straighter; he could feel it.

Anya looked up when the footsteps stopped outside the door. Like the other kolkhozniks, she needed a second to recognize him. Then her face lit up like sunrise. "Ihor!" she squeaked, and ran to him. She plastered herself against him, even though that meant her whole front got soaked. Between kisses, she managed to ask, "What are you doing here, darling?"

"I came back," he said. "I didn't even get shot this time, but I came back." He propelled her from the hallway back into the room. Then, quietly but firmly, he closed the door behind them.

Luisa Hozzel wandered around Fulda like a woman caught in a bad dream she couldn't wake up from. The town had been bombed during the last war, but not so badly as this time around. American and English planes must have hit it day and night after she got shipped off to Siberia. Too many roads and railways went through here. To keep the Russians from sending men and machines farther west, they had to wreck those roads and railways—and the place that held them.

The money the clerk gave her at the border seemed a cruel joke now.

Her apartment was gone, along with everything it held. There were no rooms to be had. Almost half the people were living in shanties or tents or caves. Fall was in the air. Winter would be coming soon. She had a cot in a tent for herself. How much fun would that be in the middle of a blizzard?

She ate at a soup kitchen, along with swarms of others. Actually, it wasn't soup most of the time, but American military rations. They filled her belly, but the flavors screamed how foreign they were.

Gustav would have eaten rations like that. The Amis seemed to have no trouble feeding as many people as they needed to. Spam and canned corn and fruit salad and cigarettes, enough for a whole planet—even if no one but an American could want that kind of food. But what difference did wanting make? When you chose between Spam and hunger, Spam won every time.

Yes, Gustav would have eaten these rations, but Gustav was dead. She'd heard that at the border. Max had confirmed it. He'd seen Gustav's body.

Max was alive. What was he doing, being alive when Gustav was dead? What were he and Trudl doing, being happy when Luisa was miserable? True, their flat and Max's printing business were wrecked, too. They were living in a lean-to, little if any improvement over Luisa's tent. They had each other, though. She had nobody.

Where was the justice in that? Nowhere she could see.

She had no idea how she could ever be happy again. On the contrary—the temptation to use her body to get herself out of trouble was as strong here as it had been back in the gulag. Of all the things she hadn't imagined when she climbed into the train that took her out of Russia and back to the civilized world, that stood high on the list.

Even if she didn't know how to make herself happy, she knew perfectly well how to make other people unhappy. All she had to do to make Trudl and Max as miserable as she was would be to tell him how his wife had wound up keeping her belly full while she was in the gulag.

Trudl would deny everything, of course. Could she deny everything well enough to make Max believe her? Before the MGB men came for her and Luisa, Luisa wouldn't have believed it for a minute. Now . . . Now she wasn't sure. The gulag was a postgraduate course in deceit. If you somehow got your hands on extra food or *makhorka* or anything else, you deceived your fellow *zeks* so they wouldn't steal whatever you had.

And deceiving the guards was as natural, and as vital, as breathing. You made them think you were working hard in the taiga when you were really goofing off. You made them think you weren't so strong as you really were. Every once in a while, you helped them get the count wrong.

So yes, Trudl would have a lot of practice at spinning convincing lies. Max would want to think she was telling the truth, too. He'd be happier doing that than thinking his wife had opened her legs for a camp guard so she wouldn't have to cut wood and so she could get extra helpings of swill.

Every once in a while, Luisa reminded herself that Trudl and Max were her friends. Friends didn't hurt other friends for the fun of it, not if they wanted to stay friends. But whoever'd said misery loved company knew what he was talking about, down to the last millimeter.

Luisa fitfully tried to find work. She could be a shopgirl or a clerk or even a secretary, as long as she didn't have to take much dictation. But none of the few business open in Fulda seemed the least bit interested in hiring her or any other outsiders. They were family concerns, and didn't want to take on anyone who wasn't a sister or at least a sister-in-law.

For that matter, Max found his own unhappiness without any help from Luisa. When he ran into her on Fulda's cratered main street, he looked as if he'd just bitten into a lemon. "What's the matter with you?" she asked.

"The print shop is *kaput*—you know that," he said. She nodded. He went on, "I applied to my insurance company. If they would have paid off, I could have used the money to get back on my feet, maybe even get the shop started again."

"If they would have . . . ?"

Max's nod was sour as vinegar. "That's right. The policy excludes acts of God and acts of war, they tell me. So I'm stuck. I'd like to give them an act of war, is what I'd like to do."

"You sound like you mean it," Luisa said.

"Which is only because I do. I bet I could still get my hands on a bazooka. I know plenty of guys who wouldn't ask any questions. Go to Frankfurt in the middle of the night, send a rocket or two into the pig-dogs' building . . . They'd find out about acts of war, by Jesus!"

"They'd know who did it," she pointed out.

But the printer just snorted. "The devil they would! You think I'm the only one the insurance company's shitting on? Fat chance, Luisa. Fat chance. There were acts of war all over the *Bundesrepublik.* How much you bet they don't want to pay off on any of them? The line of people they're screwing forms on the left and winds around the block three or four times."

He sounded perfectly serious, as he had when he said he knew how to get hold of a bazooka. For all Luisa knew, he was perfectly serious. A stretch in the gulag had taught her more about lying and cheating and stealing than she'd ever dreamt she'd learn. What would two long stretches of fighting the Russians have taught him? Something like, if anybody gets in your way or gives you a hard time, you kill him? She wouldn't have been a bit surprised.

He eyed her. "I'm sorrier about Gustav than I know how to tell you. He was a good fellow, your man. He worked hard, and he was fun to work with. And he was a good *Kamerad,* too—the best. Nothing we went through got him down. Just like me and Rolf, he'd seen worse the last time around."

"Who's Rolf?" Luisa asked.

"Who was, you mean. He's dead now, too, poor bastard. A guy in our squad—a piece of work, and then some. A *Waffen*-SS veteran—LAH, no less. An officer then, I think, but he stayed an ordinary soldier with us. Crazy brave, I'll say that for him. But he was one of those guys who hurt things for the fun of it, so I wouldn't have wanted anything to do with him away from the front."

"What happened to him? Do I want to know?"

"He was clearing mines after the ceasefire—I told you he was brave. His luck ran out—he wound up in the middle of one of our old fields left over from the last war. I don't think he knew it was there till too late. He blew himself up. Hoist by his own petard, you might say."

Luisa had only a vague notion of what a petard was. She didn't ask Max; she got his drift. She said, "It's a shame he got killed after the fighting stopped."

"It's always a shame when anybody gets killed," Max said. "But you could see it coming with him. He was happy when he was fighting, and I don't think any other time. So he would have caught something sooner or later. You go looking for trouble, you'll find it."

"Or it'll find you," Luisa said.

"*Ja.* If he'd lived, I bet he would have wound up in the French Foreign Legion, even if he couldn't stand the frogs. Or maybe the Spanish one instead. He could have kept on soldiering in Africa or Indochina."

"It could be." Luisa knew a lot of Germans with shady pasts or a taste for blood had put on the white kepi after the Third *Reich* went down in flames. The French asked few questions of men who'd never seen Europe again.

Max touched the brim of his beat-up hat and wandered off. Luisa felt proud that she hadn't blurted out anything about Trudl. Not this time, anyway.

ISTVAN SZOLOVITS PUNCHED OUT at the Blue Front warehouse and hurried toward his old Hudson. He still wasn't much of a
driver or much of an English-speaker, but he'd managed to convince
the California Department of Motor Vehicles that he deserved a license. The C-note the car had set him back made it overpriced.

"*Nu*, where you heading with your pants on fire like that?" Aaron
Finch called after him.

"Night school," Istvan answered. "Sorry, but I've got to hustle. Don't
want to be late."

"Go. Go," Aaron said. "An awful lot of *Yehudim* have taken that road
before you. Oh, you bet they have."

Into the car Istvan slid. The front-seat upholstery split a little more
under the weight of his *tukhus*. That was one more thing he'd worry
about some other time. He worked the choke and turned the key. When
the motor caught, smoke belched from the tailpipe. The Hudson guz-
zled oil the way a man crawling through the desert would guzzle water
at an unexpected oasis.

Still laying down his own smoke screen, Istvan piloted the car east,
toward Pasadena Junior College. It combined the last two years of high

school and the first two years of college. Since he was a legal resident of California, taking classes there didn't cost him anything. The Communists had introduced free public education for everybody to Hungary after the Second World War—one of the good things they'd done. Somehow, Istvan wasn't surprised to find out it had been around in capitalist America for years.

He was taking basic English and an English-literature course. Once he had a better grasp of the language, he figured he'd go on to other things. The car got him to the college much faster than the disappointing local bus system would have. He bought something to eat at the little cafeteria that sold the same kinds of goodies as UCLA's Gypsy Wagon.

His stomach still full and rumbling, he hurried to the classroom where a patient man taught basic English. Some of the students were brown-skinned and black-haired, and spoke Spanish among themselves. Some were ordinary Americans who'd bailed out of high school for one reason or another and were coming back for a second crack at education. And then there was Istvan.

Mr. van Zandt waited till the clock on the wall said it was seven o'clock. Then he said, "Let's get started, shall we?" It was far less formal than a Hungarian classroom would have been. The instructor went on, "Turn in your homework assignments, please, and I'll give back the ones you did on Monday."

This latest assignment was three paragraphs about work or family. The one van Zandt returned was a similar composition about hobbies or games. Istvan noticed not everyone turned in a paper, and not everybody got one back. That baffled him. Why enroll in a class if you didn't want to do the work?

The sheet that came back to him was measled with red marks. He'd written about his time on the POWs' football side. His command of the verb *to be* was still shaky. He'd called people *it* twice; Hungarian had no genders at all. Mr. van Zandt showed him several places where his word order was wrong. Istvan saw what his trouble there was, too. English and German might be cousins, but they weren't identical twins.

At the bottom of the paper, under the B- grade, van Zandt had written *This is not bad at all. You write English better than you speak it. What you are trying to say is always clear, even if you don't say it the way someone who grew up speaking English would. Keep working and you will learn that, too.*

That made Istvan feel good. As far as he was concerned, making yourself understood in a foreign language was more important than getting all your grammar perfect. He knew his German, while better than his English, wasn't anything to write home about. Yet he'd used it with Poles and Czechs (whose *Deutsch* was also apt to have holes) and with Germans, and he'd managed to get his meaning across.

They went through the night's lesson on possessives and on the differences between *its* and *it's* and *whose* and *who's*. "Some of you will make mistakes on these," Mr. van Zandt said. "You'll try not to, but you will. Try hard, because these are the kinds of mistakes that will hurt you if you're looking to get a job or something. Someone will go, *If this person does that, he can't know much.* But I'll tell you something. Some people with college degrees don't know when to use *it's* the contraction and *its* the possessive."

Istvan could see that. Most of the time, English used the apostrophe to show possession. *Its* was an exception. Exceptions to rules led people into mistakes.

"For your assignment for next time, I want you to do the exercises on possessives at the end of Chapter Four, and to give me three paragraphs—three well-organized paragraphs—about where you hope to be twenty years from now," van Zandt said as the hour wound down. "I'll see you then. Good night."

Out they went. Some people headed for their cars or the bus stop. Istvan had another class at eight. He walked to that room. Twenty years from now . . . That would be 1972. It seemed a million years off, not twenty, when you thought of it that way. Whatever he'd be doing, he'd be doing it here, not in Hungary. That was as much as he could see at first glance.

He hoped he wouldn't still be delivering stoves and washing machines for Blue Front. He was glad to have the job, but he didn't want it for a career. He couldn't see any future in it. Aaron Finch seemed contented enough, and he was no dope, but Aaron had his wife and little boy to support. He also had a gift for using his hands that Istvan lacked.

Here was the classroom. Istvan sat at the desk he used most of the time. A few seconds after he walked in, a young woman who was also in his basic English class came in. She sat down just to his right. Recognizing him, she smiled and said, "Hi. How you doing?"

"Hallo," Istvan said. "I am fine. How are you?" You said *I am fine* even if you weren't, unless you were talking to a close friend or something. It was a response to a greeting, not an answer to a real question.

"I'm fine." She hesitated, then said, "You have an interesting accent. Where are you from?"

"Hungary," he answered. *Interesting* probably meant *thick enough to slice*. He knew how much his spoken English left to be desired.

"How funny!" she said. "How did you get here?"

Before he could tell her, the teacher tapped her lectern with a pointer to call the class to order. Mrs. Valentine taught more interesting things than Mr. van Zandt did, but she was a less interesting person. "How many of you read Hamlet's soliloquy before you came in tonight?" she asked, sounding as if she expected the worst.

Istvan raised his hand. So did the young woman from the other class and about half the students in this room. The others just sat there. The instructor looked unsurprised. Again, Istvan was. Why take a class if you didn't care enough to keep up?

Then one of those students raised his hand for a question. "Yes, Rodney?" Mrs. Valentine asked. She'd made a point of quickly learning everybody's name.

"Why do we got to learn this weird stuff at all?" Rodney said. "*Thee* and *thou* and *'tis* and all like that. Nobody talks like that any more! And it makes the rest of the story hard to understand, y'know?"

Mrs. Valentine breathed out through her nose. If she wasn't irked, Istvan would have been amazed. He was more surprised. All of English seemed strange to him, Shakespeare no less than what he heard in the

Pasadena Junior College eatery. If anything, Shakespeare might have been a little easier; his word order was closer to the German that Istvan had studied in Budapest.

After a long moment, Mrs. Valentine said, "I don't suppose the fact that it may be the most magnificent poetry anyone's ever written has anything to do with the way you look at it."

Rodney shook his head. "Nah. If I don't get it, how great can it be?"

"Well, let's see if I can help you get it—you and everyone else in here." Mrs. Valentine did her best. Istvan was sure he understood the soliloquy better at the end of the hour than he had at the start. He'd fought through it in his apartment with a dictionary and a lot of patience. He wasn't sure how much help the instructor gave some of the other people in the classroom, Rodney among them.

As he was getting up to go back to the parking lot, the young woman asked him, "What's your name?"

"Istvan." He repeated it so she'd get it right. *Ishtvan* was how it would have been spelled in English. Then he thought to ask, "Uh, what yours is?"

"I'm Gina," she said. "See you next time, Istvan."

"See you," he said, and a silly grin spread across his face.

Regardless of temptation, regardless of provocation, Max Bachman didn't go looking for a bazooka after the insurance company feathered its nest instead of his. He knew damn well Rolf would have done it, though he had trouble imagining Rolf running an insured business. Rolf got even when he got mad. Max made sour jokes and tried to go on with his life.

It wasn't easy. He'd never dreamt Fulda would be so battered when he finally came back to it. It had fallen fairly fast. But air power counted for even more in this war than it had in the last. No flat to go home to; no business to restart. Nothing except his mustering-out pay and the clothes he had on his back.

The shape poor Trudl was in made everything else seem inconsequential by comparison. He'd *really* never dreamt the damned Russians would haul ordinary women whose only crime was to have patriotic husbands off to the other side of the world and stick them in camps. He would have fought them even harder if he had dreamt any such thing.

I would have been more like Rolf, he thought. Then he shook his head. No matter what happened, he didn't think he could ever have been like Rolf. He hoped not, anyhow.

But Trudl . . . He wanted to fatten her up like a Christmas goose. American army rations weren't good for much—as someone who'd eaten too damn many of them the past couple of years, he could cite chapter and verse on that—but by God they'd give you a double chin in nothing flat.

She didn't want to talk about what had happened in Siberia. Max knew several people who'd come out of German concentration camps after the Nazi collapse. She wasn't quite so scrawny as they'd been then, but she shared with them the desire to forget everything that had happened to her while she was inside.

The only trouble was, you could not talk about something like that, and you could not think about something like it, but not talking about it and not thinking about it didn't make it go away. Now Max had two wars' worth of things like that. When he came home after the last war, Trudl told him he used to wake up shrieking. After a couple of years, he stopped. Now he'd got some new memories to have nightmares about.

From things Luisa'd told Trudl and Trudl'd told Max, he knew Gustav had had those wake-up-screaming dreams, too. He wouldn't have been amazed if the same news channel, working in reverse, had informed Max about his nightmares. Poor Gustav! He'd been a good soldier. If your luck ran out, though, how good you were stopped mattering.

And poor Luisa! She'd come home all happy at getting out of the labor camp, only to find, almost the second she got back into West Germany, that her husband was dead. That had to be the hardest thing in the world. No wonder she seemed halfway around the bend these days.

She was less shy than Trudl over talking about what it was like in the labor camp. She always called it the gulag—the ugly Russian name seemed to fit the ugly kind of place it had been. Little bits of Russian flavored her speech these days, too. Trudl had to know the same things, but she didn't use them. Her attitude was the same one the Victorians had had about sex: if you didn't mention the horrid thing, maybe it would disappear.

He walked on. A big American bulldozer, painted yellow as a lemon, cleared away wreckage that might include chunks of his old apartment block. Sooner or later, something new would go up where the old place had stood. Fulda wouldn't look the same once all the new buildings rose.

Max's mouth twisted. And what would happen here in, say, 1975 or 1980, when some new hotshot Russian leader decided it was time to send his panzer divisions through the Fulda Gap and see if he could make it all the way to the Rhine? That day might not come. The threat of A-bombs and H-bombs might make even a Russian think twice.

Or, of course, it might not. Who in politics ever remembered anything for very long? Rolf's precious *Führer* hadn't. He'd dragged his *Reich* into a two-front war, the same way Kaiser Wilhelm did with his. Hitler's war hadn't turned out as bad as the Kaiser's. No—it had turned out worse. No one who'd lived through the First World War would have believed it, but there it was.

He lit a cigarette: an American Old Gold. The German brands had come back to life after the defeat, but now their factories lay in ruins again. Max puffed. American tobacco was all right, not like the horrible harsh black stuff the French smoked. And he could smoke his cigarettes whenever he wanted. They weren't currency, the way they had been after the collapse.

An old woman with a cloth-covered basket waved to him. "I've got prunes for sale," she said. "Prunes and sun-dried apricots, too."

"No, thanks," Max said. "Not today."

Her scowl turned her into something scary, a witch straight out of one of the Brothers Grimm's grimmer fairy tales. "You cheap bastard!" she screeched. "Hitler should've thrown you in the oven with the rest of the kikes!"

He wanted to cross himself to ward against evil, and he wasn't even Catholic: just a Lutheran who hadn't gone to church in years. Germany wasn't the place it had been when Hitler called the shots. Rolf had understood that, no matter how much he'd hated it. But not all the poison was gone yet. Max shuddered. Would it ever be? Could Germany ever become a nice, quiet, ordinary country?

He shrugged. He had no idea.

Down the street was a sort of makeshift market where people sold whatever they had. Farmers in from the country had vegetables and eggs. Fishermen who'd been lucky sold bream or carp. And townsfolk sat behind blankets and battered tables displaying ashtrays and light-bulbs and cooking pots and books and anything else somebody might want to buy. Maybe those were desperate people selling off their worldly goods so they could live. Or maybe—and, Max judged, more likely— they were scroungers who pawed through the wreckage in the middle of the night and grabbed whatever was still in one piece.

That skeletal figure in the quilted jacket . . . That could only be one of the recently returned prisoners. When she turned, he saw it was Luisa. He'd thought so, but she'd changed so much he hadn't been sure. When their eyes met, he waved and walked over to her.

"Can I get you anything? What do you need?" he asked, adding, "Insurance or not, I think I've got more Deutschmarks in my pocket than you do."

Her face twisted; he needed a moment to realize she was laughing. "How about a time machine, like the one in the book that Englishman wrote?" she said. "Then I could jump on it and go back to when none of this had ever happened."

"That would be nice, but I don't know the shop where they sell them," Max said. "How about a duck and some potatoes? Then you won't need to open ration tins for a few days."

"I don't like the rations—who would, who isn't an American?—but eating them isn't what bothers me so much. Queuing up to get them bothers me," Luisa said. "It's humiliating. When I was in the gulag, I had dreams about food like you wouldn't believe. People there would do anything for food, anything at all."

"I'm sorry." Max remembered too well how wonderful half-rotten horse (or maybe it was dog; you quickly learned not to ask too many questions of the guys with the *Goulaschkanonen*) was when you'd been chewing on snow for two days so you'd have something in your mouth.

But Luisa said, "You don't know what it's like for us, Max. It isn't the same for women as it is for men."

"No, I don't suppose it would be." During the last war more than this one, Max had seen and done some things he'd never talked about with Trudl.

"Some women, they would do anything at all to get more food, better food," Luisa said again. Max thought she was about to come out with some confession, but she went on, "I wasn't one of them, thank heavens."

"All right, Luisa," Max said gently.

"Some women I knew were, though," Luisa continued as if he hadn't spoken. "Some women you know were." She turned on her heel and walked off: walked quite fast, in fact, with her head thrown back. Max stared after her. Was she laughing? He opened his mouth to call to her, then closed it again. If he didn't have to know, he didn't want to know.

After years of hating his father's trade, avoiding it, running from it, Vasili Yasevich found himself in that trade once more, helping out at Witold's. He knew enough to make a pretty tolerable druggist. The way the art was practiced in Warsaw was close to the way his father had brought it out of Russia and into Harbin.

But his father had learned from Chinese druggists after he went into exile. He'd shown that side of the practice to Vasili, too. Some of the herbs the Chinese relied on didn't grow in Poland. Sometimes, though, he could find equivalents because his father had trained him in both schools. *Ma huang*, the Chinese stimulant, was known in the West as *Ephedra sinica*. No one on this side of Eurasia could get it. He found out that other species of *Ephedra* did grow in Europe, though.

"Oh, yes, jointpine. We put that in medicines now and then," Ewa said. "It helps tired people get through a day."

"That's the stuff," Vasili agreed. "They use it all the time in China."

"Do they?" The druggist's daughter sounded interested. "It's a once-in-a-while thing here."

"If fighters use it, they can keep going longer than if they don't," Vasili said. "That might help against the Russians."

"It might. Let me talk to my father about it," Ewa said. "You may have something there."

"I hope so," Vasili said.

But he turned out not to. "They make pills that do the same thing," Ewa reported. "Benzedrine, they call one of them. It's almost like ephedrine, the stuff that comes out of jointpine. We can buy or steal plenty."

"Oh," Vasili said, crestfallen.

"It was a good idea." She sounded serious. She usually did. "It shows you mean it about giving the Reds trouble."

"Of course I do," Vasili said.

Ewa just looked at him. With Casimir dead, no one in Warsaw could vouch for him. Ewa and Witold trusted him with the work of a druggist. That involved people's lives, too, but not so dramatically as the war against the Soviet Union. As a druggist, he couldn't expose other people who were conspiring against disease and malnutrition.

So here he was, on the side where he'd wanted to be since he got to Poland, even if they didn't fully trust him. The only reason he hadn't deserted to the rebels right away was that he'd feared the Red Army would squash them the way a nasty little boy squashed caterpillars under his shoes.

And his fears seemed all too likely to come true. Russian heavy bombers came over Warsaw almost every night. Vasili crouched in the cellar of the cheap, battered block of flats where he had a room. The Russians had bombed Harbin before they took it, but not like this. These explosions seemed to shake the very fabric of the city.

Of course, the Russians could hit Warsaw with an A-bomb. That would settle the city for good. The Poles insisted that Molotov had promised Truman he wouldn't A-bomb any more cities. They were sure he wouldn't bomb Warsaw that way. Then again, they were also sure he was a prime liar.

Whatever had been rebuilt in Warsaw went up in flames or fell down in the explosions. Like other healthy young people in the city, Vasili stood in line in bucket brigades that did not nearly enough to fight the fires. And then the Red Army pushed up from the south and started shelling the Polish capital. The rebels did all they could to hold the tanks and soldiers away from the city. All they could wasn't nearly enough.

People began to give up on the uprising. The government of the People's Republic—the government of Russian puppets and stooges— had Soviet planes drop leaflets promising amnesty to anyone who came out and pledged loyalty by the end of October. *Your freedom will continue undisturbed if you do,* the leaflets said.

Vasili thought that was funny. So did Ewa. "What kind of freedom do they give us if it runs out at the end of the month?" she asked anyone who would listen. Vasili listened a lot, since he worked at the drugstore.

"You would think running away from their own capital with their tails between their legs might have given the people in the People's Republic a clue about how much everybody loves them," he said.

Love was one thing. Fear was another. Bombs and shells had a brutal logic of their own. The Communists had sabotaged Radio Warsaw's transmitter before they fled. The rebels had a station with lower power that worked intermittently, in between explosions and losses of electricity. They broadcast appeals for aid to England, France, and the USA.

No aid came. Not a soldier, not a rifle, not a cartridge, not a can of beans. As far as the Western democracies were concerned, the USSR was welcome to Poland.

On Sunday the twenty-sixth, Poles filled their battered churches to pray for deliverance from the enemy at the gates. A young priest up from the south, a firebrand named Karol Wojtyla, preached an impassioned sermon of courage and defiance. Vasili went with Ewa to hear him. He cared very little for Catholicism, but he was coming to care more and more for the girl.

Wojtyla pounded the pulpit as he cried, "God has made us free souls! What God has made, man has no power to take away from us! Anyone who dares to try will burn in hell forevermore!" What he said was the usual thing that came from the mouths of patriots around the world. The way he said it . . . When he said it, people who listened to him believed. Even Vasili, who didn't share his faith and understood him only imperfectly, felt his back stiffen and his blood heat while he listened.

But Father Wojtyla hadn't finished when the Red Army started shelling Warsaw in earnest. People went running out of the church before the priests offered Holy Communion. Vasili grabbed Ewa's hand and pulled her toward the door.

"*Deus vobiscum!*" Father Wojtyla called to the emptying crowd. Then he switched to Polish: "Get out! Get safe! God knows why you're doing it!"

Vasili's heart jumped when Ewa squeezed him back. They quickly discovered they'd fled the frying pan for the fire. Shturmoviks roared in just above the rooftops to bomb and strafe and rocket and napalm the Varsovians. Vasili used what was practically a rugby tackle to throw Ewa down behind a pile of bricks and stones that might offer some shelter from the attack planes. To make sure she didn't try to stick her head up and see what was going on, he flopped on top of her.

"What are you doing?" she yelled in his ear. To her, it must have seemed close to criminal assault.

"Trying to keep you alive, dammit!" he shouted back over the roar of the Shturmoviks' engines and the explosions going off close by. A cannon shell slammed into the rubble heap a moment later. It didn't get through, which went a long way toward making his point for him.

"They can't attack now!" Ewa said. "The propaganda the Red Poles dropped gave the city till the thirty-first."

"They're Russians. They're Soviet Russians." Vasili didn't want her connecting him to the Red Army, even if he'd been an unwilling part of it. "They can do whatever they please. It's all for the proletariat, right?"

"Right," Ewa said. "When can we get up?"

"When this eases off a little, we can try," Vasili said.

But it didn't ease off. The Shturmoviks came over in waves, one after another. The artillery fire went on and on. The only blessing Vasili could see was that the Russians weren't close enough to throw Katyushas into the heart of the city. Cries and shrieks of mortal agony gave high notes to go with the bass thunder of explosives.

The church fell in on itself with a rending crash. A shell fragment struck sparks off the broken brickwork bare centimeters above Vasili's head. That made up his mind for him. "We'd better find a cellar if we can, if it doesn't take too long," he said.

"Christ have mercy, it's about time," Ewa said. "You're squashing me flat."

"Sorry." He tried to hunch over as he got up. "Stay low, for heaven's sake."

Seeing someone disappear into a hole in the ground, Vasili and Ewa followed. It was more a cave than a cellar, but it was better than nothing or the junk pile they'd used before. As Vasili ducked into it, he heard another note joining the symphony of destruction: the rumble of God only knew how many diesel engines, all growling forward at once. That could mean only one thing. The Red Army and its tanks were moving on Warsaw.

. . .

Harry Truman eyed a badly printed leaflet in a language full of consonants in combinations so rich in Z's, they would have sent a Scrabble player straight to heaven. His gaze swung to a typed translation. "The Polish Communists said they would give the rebels till today, till Halloween, to give themselves up?" he said.

"That's right, sir." Omar Bradley nodded.

"But the Russians stormed into Warsaw last Sunday? Five days early?"

"Yes, sir," the Secretary of Defense said.

"Pretty low even for the Russians, don't you think?"

"Do I think so? Of course I do. But, considering all the agreements they've danced up and down on when they saw some gain by doing so, this is par for the course. They didn't even break an agreement, not in the legal sense. They just had their Polish stooges say they'd do one thing but then did something else instead."

"I don't like it, not even a little bit," Truman snapped. "I've got a good notion to give Ambassador Zarubin a piece of my mind. He'd understand me when I did it, too. More direct than it would be with Molotov."

"Mr. President, forgive me, but I recommend that you hold back here," Bradley said. Truman looked at him in surprise. The former general went on, "I do, sir. We agreed to give the Russians a free hand in Eastern Europe. The ambassador will throw that in your face and say it's none of our business. Unless you're ready to back up your protest with military action, making it only dissipates our strength. A threat you don't back up is a wasted threat."

Truman chewed on that for a second. Then he sighed. "Well, when you're right, you're right. I won't miss meeting Zarubin face-to-face; I'll say that."

"He's an ugly bruiser, isn't he?" Bradley said.

"As a matter of fact, yes," Truman replied. Georgi Zarubin looked like a middle-aged ex-prizefighter. He had a widow's peak with deep wings of bald scalp to either side. His eyebrows beetled. His Tatar cheekbones were scarred. His mug, in short, was not an advertisement for Bolshevism.

But he was smarter than he looked. He'd been Stalin's ambassador to the UK till this new war broke out. Now that peace was back, Molotov had sent him here to Philadelphia. Unlike Hitler, who'd had a jumped-up champagne salesman for a foreign minister, the Soviet leaders were careful about who carried out their foreign policy. Neither Litvinov nor Molotov was lovable, but they were both capable. The same held true for Gromyko, the Soviet ambassador to the UN. And it also seemed to be true for Georgi Zarubin.

"Elections coming up Tuesday," Bradley remarked.

"Yes. That's the big trick or treat, isn't it?" the President replied. "It will be good to have Congress back in working order, anyhow. I'm afraid the Republicans will pick up a boatload of seats, though."

"They'll work with you on our foreign policy, anyway," Bradley said.

"Oh, yes. Politics stops at the border, pretty much. Even the worst isolationists rallied round the flag after the Japs bombed Pearl Harbor. They'll give me a hard time on things we have to do at home, though. Some of those people barely think the Federal government's entitled to coin money, let alone spend it."

Omar Bradley's visage was less stern and craggy than George Marshall's had been, but not by a great deal. "If they vote against funds for rebuilding in their own districts, they won't stay in office long," he said, and that forbidding face showed a smile for a moment.

"Yes, but a lot of them will come from the Midwest, which wasn't touched," Truman said. "The way it'll look to them is, Washington—I mean Philadelphia, dammit—wants to tax them till their eyes pop to rebuild the coasts. They don't miss Manhattan or San Francisco. A lot of them think the country's better off without places like that."

"How do you aim to get around them?" Bradley asked.

"It's simple. I'm going to veto any bill that has money for the Midwest unless there's money for the coasts in it, too. I don't think they'll be able to override me. If they can, the country's really gone to hell in an atomic handbasket."

The Defense Secretary coughed discreetly. "What about your successor, whoever that turns out to be?"

"If it's Stevenson, there's no issue. He'll do what's right." Truman didn't think Stevenson stood a chance against the Republicans, but he was damned if he'd say so in public. He might have said it to Marshall; not even Marshall's face suspected how much the man behind it knew. But Marshall was gone.

Omar Bradley wasn't George Marshall; he was just as close as Truman could come to Marshall. He did know the question he had to ask: "Suppose it isn't Stevenson, sir?" He stated no opinion about how likely he thought that chance was, or about whether he thought it would be good or bad.

"Eisenhower understands that it's all one country. I give him that much," Truman said. "Nixon . . . Nixon is an ugly piece of work, and I don't just mean when he looks in the mirror. But he's an ugly piece of work from California. He would see the need—I hope he'd see the need—for getting the coasts, the ports, in full working order again. Los Angeles isn't nearly so much without its port. Same with Seattle. San Francisco is already a going concern again."

"That's all true, Mr. President," Bradley said.

Truman pointed a finger at him. "You served with Eisenhower, under Eisenhower, in the last war. What did you think of him as a general?"

Bradley blinked. He might not have looked for such a blunt question. If he hadn't, he only proved he didn't know the man he served under very well. After a moment's pause for thought, he said, "He'd never make anyone forget Rommel or Zhukov as a strategist. But that wasn't really what he had to do. He held us and the English and the French and the Poles and all the other little contingents together and kept us all going the same way. For that, he deserves as much praise as you can give him. I'll tell you, sir, *I* wouldn't have wanted to ride herd on Montgomery and Patton and de Gaulle at the same time."

"Mm, there is that," Truman admitted. Bradley's appraisal was more generous than he'd expected. Then again, Bradley might have penetrated to the heart of the mystery. Eisenhower hadn't been in a position where he made policy. He'd carried out orders from FDR and Marshall, and got all his partners in the anti-Hitler coalition to do the same thing. As Bradley'd implied, some of those partners had strong opinions of their own, too.

"The other thing I have to give him is, he doesn't panic if something goes wrong," the Secretary of Defense said. "He just tries something else. If we'd failed at D-Day, he had a statement ready that took all the blame. And he would have started working on a different way to invade Europe, or at least telling the people who worked on things like that to get busy. He would have got results from them, too."

Truman had always thought of Eisenhower more as a corporate executive than a soldier. Bradley changed his perspective of the man who'd probably succeed him. When you had an organization as large and complex as the American military had become, perhaps you needed some corporate executives at the top, to keep everybody below them working smoothly.

With a sigh, Truman said, "I wish this would have turned out better. We followed the best intelligence estimates about what the Red Chinese would do if MacArthur advanced to the Yalu, and they turned out to be wrong. And we followed the best intelligence estimates about what Stalin would do if we A-bombed those Manchurian cities, and they turned out to be wrong, too. So this is what's left now that most of the dust has settled."

"Mr. President, we won the war," Bradley said. "Don't you think Molotov would be happy to trade places with you?"

"Molotov's never happy," Truman said. "I don't know if he has a wife and children, or if they're still alive. If they are, I might want to trade places with him. That's me talking as Harry Truman, of course, not as the President."

"Yes, sir," Bradley said. "Molotov was married to a Jewish woman. Stalin sent her to a labor camp four years ago. Beria turned her loose.

The report that reached me said she asked how Stalin was, and fainted when she heard he'd died. Children? I don't know. But she's still with us."

"Then I won the war and Molotov won the battle." Truman sighed again.

24

BRUCE MCNULTY HAD to cross the San Francisco Bay to look for work in his chosen profession. The airlines' offices in San Francisco itself remained out of commission. The ones in Oakland, though, were still operating at something close to normal.

"Well, well," said the nice young personnel man who interviewed him for United Airlines. "You have a very impressive record." He'd gone through the papers that showed Bruce had flown B-25s in the last war and B-29s in this one. "I'm sure you'd have no problems with any plane in our fleet."

He didn't sound all that enthusiastic, no matter how nice he seemed. "But . . . ?" Bruce asked. "There's a *but,* isn't there?"

The nice young man—a plate on his desk said his name was Dave Simpkins—looked faintly embarrassed. "I'm afraid there is, Mr. McNulty. We're fully staffed at the moment, and we have a waiting list of pilots interested in joining the airline. Most of their qualifications are as strong as yours, I'm afraid."

Bruce took himself off to Continental Airlines, whose Oakland office was only a few blocks from United's. The nice young personnel man at Continental was named Vic Torre. He had more five o'clock shadow than Dave Simpkins. Otherwise, the two of them might have been stamped from the same mold.

"I'm sorry," he said, after he, too, examined Bruce's papers. "You're very well qualified, but we aren't hiring right now. There are more pilots out there than airline slots to fill them. That's too bad, but Uncle Sam trained an awful lot of them during the last war."

"Yeah," Bruce said sourly. Considering how many men he'd trained with, he knew too well Vic Torre was right.

"I *am* sorry," the personnel man said again.

"I even believe you. But so what? Sorry doesn't put groceries on the table. What am I supposed to do now?"

"You could always go back into the Air Force. If anybody can use what you know, the people who taught it to you are the ones."

"No, thanks." Bruce violently shook his head. "Either I wouldn't do anything that matters for the next twenty years or they'd give me another plane with an atom bomb in it. You know what happened across the bay? I've done that too many times. Enough blood's on my hands now. I won't put any more there no matter what."

"I . . . see." Vic Torre looked at him as if he'd just grown another head, one that might have sprung from a werewolf's neck. Well, you didn't meet a mass murderer every day of the week. Bruce was sure he wasn't the only American murderer hustling for a job right now, though. Gathering himself, Torre said, "Some people would call you a hero."

"The Air Force did. I've got the medals to prove it," Bruce said. "I don't care. I'm never doing that again, period. Exclamation point, even."

"You might try some of the smaller airlines," Torre said. "They have more turnover than we do. Or there are other pilots' positions that don't involve passengers at all."

Bruce McNulty stared at him. "Thanks, Mr. Torre," he said. "Damned if you aren't right."

He remembered talking with Daisy about that very thing. He'd gone on about how much fun he could have flying a cropduster in the Central Valley. He also remembered how much fun he'd had in the cockpit of that Piper Grasshopper when he played air tourist over Belgium. Zooming around in a biplane low above the fields would give the same kind of kick.

Everything came with a downside, though. Cropdusting wouldn't pay the way ferrying people around the country in a big, elegant airliner did. You could sock away some serious jack if you did that for ten or fifteen years. And it would still be flying . . . after a fashion.

He wouldn't be bringing a war bride back from England. He just had to provide for himself. The big airlines did have waiting lists. He could get his name on them, so if something turned up there. . . .

After putting his name on Continental's list, and United's, and a few more, he took the ferry back across the bay and a bus to San Francisco's central library. If he was going to find out-of-town phone books anywhere, that was the place. Sure enough, the library had books for places like Firebaugh and Gilroy and Fresno and Bakersfield. He took notes.

Then he went back to the little studio apartment he'd rented and started talking with long-distance operators. He didn't want to think what this month's phone bill would look like, but that would wait. There were more cropdusting outfits than he'd guessed.

A guy in Fresno said, "What the dickens are you doing talking to me, man? How come the airlines don't want you, if you've done half the stuff you say you've done?"

"Because guys who've done the kinds of things I've done are a dime a dozen, Mr. Agajanian," Bruce answered. That wasn't strictly true. But the airlines probably didn't expect him to drop an A-bomb from a DC-6's cargo bay. He added, "And you know what else? I'm not all that broken up about it. Cropdusting sounds like about the most fun you can have with your clothes on."

Krikor Agajanian laughed. "I don't know about that, but you won't feel like a bus driver, the way you would steering an airliner all over the place. 'Course, you won't get paid like you would in an airliner, either. What I'll pay you is—" He named a figure that wasn't even within shouting distance of what an airline pilot got.

Bruce sighed. He wouldn't be able to sock away a nice piece of change dusting fields around Fresno. But he wouldn't starve, either. "Come up twenty-five bucks a week and I'm your man," he said.

"I'll come up fifteen." Agajanian sounded as if every word pained him. Bruce had no trouble getting what that meant. The boss of Consolidated Cropdusting wanted him, but was in the habit of squeezing every penny till he ground flour from the wheat ears on the back.

"Deal," Bruce said.

"Can you get down here by noon tomorrow?" Krikor Agajanian asked. "I'll show you around, show you the planes we fly, see what's what. How's that sound?"

"I'll be there," Bruce promised. *See what's what* had to mean *see if you're bullshitting me.* Bruce didn't mind. Only a fool bought a pig in a poke.

He got himself a car that afternoon: a 1947 Ford the color of a lime. He wasn't broke; he hadn't spent that much of his service pay. But he did want to have money keep coming in, not just go out all the time.

He took US 101 down to Gilroy the next morning. Gilroy billed itself as the garlic capital of the world; the smell lived up to the name. State Route 152 went east over the hills into the Central Valley. He drove southeast on US 99 to Fresno. It was November, but it felt like August there.

Since he'd never been in Fresno before, he stopped at a Flying-A station and got a road map along with his fillup. Armed with that, he pulled into the graveled lot in front of Consolidated Cropdusting twenty minutes early. A burly man with slicked-back gray hair and a big hooked nose came out to greet him. "You McNulty?" he asked.

"Call me Bruce," Bruce said, holding out his hand.

"Then I'm Greg. That's what Krikor is in Armenian—Gregory." Agajanian had a bear trap of a grip. "Come around behind and take a look at what you'll be going up in."

A big grin spread across Bruce's face when he saw the four biplanes. "Kaydets!" he said in delight. "I learned to fly in these babies." So had a million other guys; Boeing Stearman Kaydets were the first planes American and Canadian military pilots flew during the last war. These all still bore the bright yellow paint job the U.S. military slapped on its trainers.

Agajanian grinned, too, slyly. "Think you remember how?"

"Oh, I just might," Bruce said.

"How about taking me up for a little hop, then?" Agajanian pointed to the closest Kaydet. "I know that one's gassed up—I did it myself. C'mon."

Bruce followed him to the plane. A leather helmet with attached goggles, straight out of World War I, sat on the pilot's seat. Feeling like the Red Baron, Bruce put it on. "This is gonna be fun!" he said as Krikor Agajanian spun the prop and the Kaydet's little engine buzzed to life.

Armorers wheeled bombs out to the Tu-4 on carts made of steel tubing with rubber tires. Watching them, Boris Gribkov remembered that the groundcrew men at airstrips during the Great Patriotic War hadn't had such elegant transportation for their high explosives and incendiaries. They'd used whatever they could, sometimes *panje* wagons, sometimes raw muscle, to get bombs to the bombers.

Anton Presnyakov was thinking along with him. "I've seen pictures of carts like that at American airstrips in England," the copilot said.

"Now that you mention it, so have I," Boris replied. "Well, if we can borrow the design for the bomber, no reason we can't borrow the design for the cart that feeds it, eh?"

"We didn't borrow. We invented," Lev Vaksman said. "Comrade Reguspatoff is a very clever fellow."

"Reguspatoff?" Boris echoed, puzzled. It sounded as if it ought to be a Russian name, but it wasn't one he'd ever heard before.

"Of course." The flight engineer's eyes twinkled. "It's the abbreviation the Americans put on things they make. It stands for *Registered—U.S. Patent Office.*"

"Does it?" Boris said tonelessly. He shook his head. "Where in the regulations does it say every crew's got to have one crazy *Zhid*?"

"That's Chapter 47, Article 16, Section 3, Subsection 8 . . . sir." Vaksman sounded so convincing, Boris was tempted to believe him.

Chains and hooks lifted the ordnance into the big bomber's belly. The armorers worked with care Boris knew he couldn't hope for from mechanics or signalmen. No one on this crew was drunk. He'd checked them, but these fellows tended to it for themselves. If you made a stupid, brainless mistake with a wrench or a wigwag flag, you might hurt the plane and its crew, but you wouldn't do yourself any harm. If you made a stupid, brainless mistake with a 500-kilo bomb, there wouldn't be enough of you or your friends left to bury.

"Warsaw tonight," Presnyakov said. "We've finally got troops inside the city. Looks like the damn Poles are running out of steam at last. Took 'em long enough, the sons of bitches."

"*Da,*" Boris said. "We'll have to be careful not to drop our presents on our own men's heads." Soldiers hated nothing worse than getting hit by their own comrades, and who could blame them? He knew a pilot who'd got punched in the nose for bombing the wrong side's trenches west of Kiev at the end of 1943.

He was sick of bombing anyone for any reason, even if the Tu-4 carried only—only!—conventional weapons. He would have been much happier spraying insecticide over fields in an ancient Po-2, the wind blowing over the windscreen and into his face. But the state didn't care about that. It had a job for him to do, and do it he would, or else.

They went off on time. Boris had his usual moment of fear when he pulled back on the yoke. Would the bomber's nose go up? Would the beast get off the ground? If it came back to earth all at once, the crater it left would beggar any mere armorer's mistake. He kept a close eye on the throttles, and on the engines' revs. You didn't want to push them too hard, no matter how much you felt you should.

Once the landing gear went up, he breathed easier. In the right-hand seat, Presnyakov said, "Now all we've got to worry about are the goddamn Poles."

"Nobody's thrown any fighters at us since we stopped fighting the USA. Not the Poles, not the Hungarians, not the Czechs." Boris knocked his head in lieu of the wood he didn't have. "Let's hope the Poles won't tonight, either."

On they flew. Every so often, the navigator would suggest a small course correction: two degrees this way, four degrees that. Radar made navigation, especially navigation by night, far easier than it had been before. When you could "see" the terrain below, you didn't need to steer by the stars and by dead reckoning.

"We should be entering Polish territory now," Svyatoslav Filevich reported.

Looking out through the Plexiglas cockpit windows, Boris couldn't see any difference between Byelorussia and Poland. Then he did: several large fires down below. Soviet manufacturers weren't so good with Plexiglas as they might have been. The flames on the ground seemed to ripple. It wasn't too much vodka; it was windows that could have been better.

But Stalin had insisted that everything on the Tu-4 should exactly copy the equivalent feature on the B-29 that served as its model. The American plane had Plexiglas cockpit windows. Tupolev's design bureau didn't dare do anything but follow the orders it got. Tupolev himself had served a stretch in the gulag. Stalin let him out when the Great Patriotic War started, and he went back to creating new models as if nothing had happened.

Fyodor Ostrovsky had an even more panoramic view than Boris did. "They're shooting at us, Comrade Pilot," the bombardier said.

"If they want to waste ammo, that's their lookout," Gribkov said. The Tu-4 was up near 10,000 meters. You needed some serious flak guns to throw shells that high. Sure enough, tracer rounds petered out far below the bomber. Bursts from ordinary shells also failed to trouble it.

More fires on the ground showed where Soviet forces and the Polish bandits clashed. When Filevich announced that they were approaching Warsaw, Boris saw lots of fires ahead. "Do you think the incendiaries will have anything to burn by the time we drop them?" he asked.

Anton Presnyakov shrugged. "I'm not going to worry about it. We're supposed to drop them, that's all. As long as we do, and we don't drop them on our own people, our dicks aren't on the block. What happens after they hit isn't our department."

"You've got a good way of looking at things," Boris said, less sarcastically than he'd intended. That *was* a good way for a soldier to look at things. You did what your superiors told you to do and hoped they had a better grip on the big picture than you did.

Sometimes they really did. Sometimes Hitler invaded the Soviet Union, confident of another blitzkrieg victim's scalp to hang on his wall. Sometimes Stalin tried trading A-bombs with the United States, only to discover the Americans had more to trade and more ways to get them home than he did.

Things like that made you wonder about leaders in general. Unless you were a leader yourself, the smartest thing you could do was not let anyone know you were wondering. As soon as the leaders and their minions got wind of your doubts, they stamped them out with jackboots or billy clubs or labor camps or bullets.

"Nearing the target, Comrade Pilot," Ostrovsky said.

The bomb-bay doors opened. The bombs fell free. The plane bobbed in the air as they did. The doors hissed closed. Boris gave the Tu-4 more throttle and swung in a slow turn to see what he'd done to Warsaw. It wasn't full emergency power to get away from an A-bomb's blast waves. These were smaller explosions, ones that couldn't smash his airplane like a man hitting a fly with a rolled-up *Pravda*.

Big flashes of light were the 500-kilo bombs going off. The smaller, more persistent ones, the ones that looked like matches struck a hundred meters away at night, were the incendiaries. Some of those hot red dots winked out: they didn't land on anything that would burn. Others grew and spread.

What kind of fire department did the bandits have? Whatever they had, it would be tested—or perhaps broken—tonight. More flashes and sparks lit in the Polish capital. Boris' wasn't the only bomber punishing the uprising, then. A plane here, a few planes there, the USSR could still scrape together enough loyalists to do the leaders' bidding.

Was that good or bad? Boris had no idea. He suspected Molotov didn't, either. You did what you did and you saw what happened. Neither Hitler nor Stalin had dreamt he would fail. The same uncertainty applied to lesser men's deeds, too. *People like me don't get into history books, though,* Boris thought, *and a good thing we don't.*

Aaron Finch and Istvan Szolovits pulled into the Blue Front parking lot one in front of the other. They parked next to each other. When Aaron got out of his car and said, "Morning Istvan. How you doing?", he spoke English, not Yiddish.

"I am fine. How are you?" Istvan replied in the same language. His accent, though still heavy, wasn't nearly so strong as it had been when he started at Blue Front. He'd always have it, but it wouldn't stay thick enough to slice.

"I'm doing all right. And you're studying hard. I can tell," Aaron said.

Istvan still switched to Yiddish when he needed to talk about anything complicated. He did that now, saying, "English grammar is simple enough. But English spelling . . . *Gevalt!* It makes me want to cross myself, and Catholic I'm not. Why is it like that?"

"What are you asking me for? I drive a truck, remember?" Aaron said.

"You know things," Istvan said seriously. "You're another one of those people who're too smart for their own good."

That brought Aaron up short. He didn't need to think about it before he nodded. "*Mazel tov.* You just summed up the whole Finch family in one sentence. My father, me, my brothers—not my sister so much, I will say—and now my son. The lot of us are smart-alecks."

"I didn't mean to offend you," Istvan said.

"Don't worry about it. You didn't," Aaron replied. "But talk to your night-school teachers about why English spelling is so messed up. They'll be able to tell you. All I can do is make dumb guesses."

"I don't have enough English myself yet to ask the things I really want to know," Istvan said.

"Ah, okay. I get you now," Aaron said. When people said *You're somebody I can talk to,* most of the time they meant that the person they were talking to was an understanding soul. If Istvan were to say it about Aaron, he'd mean it literally. Same with *You speak my language.* Aaron didn't speak Hungarian, but they had Yiddish in common. He set his hand on Istvan's shoulder. He needed to reach up to do it; Istvan had three inches on him. "C'mon. The work won't do itself."

"Too bad," Istvan said, but he followed Aaron into the warehouse. He was willing enough; no two ways about that. But he didn't rather enjoy the job the way Aaron did. Aaron liked coming home tired from physical labor at the end of a day. It showed he'd been doing things . . . unless he came home exhausted, of course.

Istvan didn't have that. He would rather have been adding up columns of numbers, or maybe twisting a slide rule's tail. As soon as he'd learned enough to do the kinds of things he really wanted to do, he'd leave Blue Front without a backwards glance, the way a snake sloughed off a skin it outgrew.

For now, though, he was here. Aaron supposed Mr. Weissman reported back to whoever'd asked him to give the kid a job. He hadn't asked his boss about that, but it sure seemed likely. Did Istvan think of things like that? Probably. He'd lived in Red Hungary. That was the kind of place where everybody'd report on everybody else, or so Aaron imagined.

They didn't do things like that in the United States. They never had. They never would. Or so Aaron thought, till he remembered the Air Force officer who'd questioned him after he captured a Soviet flyer instead of beating the Russian to death with a tire iron or something. He'd managed to satisfy the guy that he hadn't saved the flyer because he was especially fond of Russians or anything. Even so, the idea that they thought he might have been rankled.

And he might need to look a little differently at Howard Bauman's interrogation by the Un-American Activities Committee. He'd always figured Howard had it coming, because the actor damn well *was* a Red. But the Un-American Activities Committee had been Joe McCarthy's baby, and if McCarthy hadn't dreamt of Mussolini and Hitler and Stalin when he went to bed at night, no one ever had.

Thinking such thoughts, Aaron walked right past the refrigerator he was supposed to take to Westwood this morning. Istvan had looked at the work order, too. He tapped Aaron on the arm. "Isn't this the one?" he asked.

It was a Hotpoint. It was a Model 3200. Aaron thumped his forehead with the heel of his hand. "This is the one, all right. I'd forget my head if it wasn't stapled to my neck."

"I don't think so," Istvan said. "We were going on about too smart for our own good a minute ago, weren't we?"

"Too dumb for my own good is more like it," Aaron said. "Let's get the TV and the washing machine on the truck before we load the icebox, though. They're going down to Culver City, so we'll unload them last."

Istvan nodded. "Makes sense." Aaron smiled. Jim Summers never had quite realized the last-on, first-off principle was the way to go at it. Freighters always did it that way; noticing that drilled it into Aaron. But common sense said the same thing. Jim usually wanted to do whatever was easiest right now, even if that cost him more work later.

Aaron loaded and secured the television and the washing machine. Here came Istvan with the Hotpoint on a heavy dolly. He made sure he kept it as close to vertical as he could. "Turn it around and back it up the ramp," Aaron said. "I'll get on the other side and push while you pull."

Somewhere there was a two-headed animal called a pushmi-pullyu. Was it in one of the Doctor Dolittle books he'd picked up in a second-hand bookstore? He thought so. Leon wasn't old enough for those yet, but he would be before too long.

Istvan draped a padded blanket over the refrigerator and taped it into place. He roped the icebox down so it wouldn't smack any of the other cargo. "Good job," Aaron told him. Deadpan, he added, "Anybody'd think you've been doing it for years."

"Thanks a lot." Istvan didn't sound grateful.

"Hey, it's work. It keeps a roof over your head and food on the table while you're getting ready to do what you want to do," Aaron said. "Speaking of which, feel like driving the truck down to Westwood?"

"Can I?" Istvan sounded eager, which only went to show how new he was behind the wheel. Aaron didn't mind driving, but he wasn't the kind who went out for a spin every Sunday. He'd done it two or three times after he married Ruth, but it lost its appeal in a hurry.

Istvan didn't shift smoothly, but he was still learning. He was careful on the road; he didn't make Aaron wish the truck came with seat belts. For somebody with brand new credentials, he did fine.

And he was starting to learn his way around. As he turned left from Ventura Boulevard to Sepulveda for the trip into Westwood, he said, "I came north this way on the bus the first time I went to Blue Front. I had my route memorized, but I don't know what I would have done if something went wrong."

"You'd have taken care of it. You would have found someone who spoke a language you did, or else shown a taxi driver the address. It would've been okay."

"I hope so," Istvan said. "But I was new getting around then. I had next to no English. People would have decided I was a spy."

Aaron started to laugh, but maybe it wasn't so funny. A foreigner who knew no English and plainly wasn't a Spanish-speaking Mexican? People like Jim Summers might have guessed his Yiddish or Hungarian was really Russian and called the cops. And a cop who wanted to be a hero could have put handcuffs on him and tossed him into the clink. Lots of dopes running around loose, some of them wearing uniforms . . .

The refrigerator went to a place only a few blocks from the UCLA campus. Both husband and wife were home to welcome it, which was unusual. Richard House taught medieval history; his wife Mary Ann was an administrative assistant in the history department. Their little boy looked just like Richard, including the shock of combed-back black hair. The home was shaded by trees and full of books in several languages. The Houses looked to have themselves a nice life.

"Thank you so much," Mary Ann said after Aaron plugged in the icebox and made sure it worked. She gave him and Istvan two dollars apiece and some iced tea. Richard might be the professor in the family, but his wife plainly ruled the roost. *And Ruth doesn't, with you?* Aaron thought as he got back into the truck to head south toward Culver City. He laughed under his breath. He knew darn well she did.

Marian Tabakman opened the oven and reached in with a pair of over-stuffed mittens to take out the roasting pan that held the turkey. It wasn't a great big bird—not quite eleven pounds—but it would be plenty to feed her and Fayvl and Linda through the Thanksgiving weekend.

"That smells yummy!" Linda said.

"Stay back, honey. It's real hot," Marian said. She relaxed once she put the turkey on the counter and kicked the oven door shut.

"Does smell good," Fayvl said, lifting the hand he'd set on Linda's shoulder for a moment to make sure she didn't do anything foolish. "Before I come to America, I don't think I ever eat turkey."

"How come?" Linda asked, beating her mother to the punch.

"Don't have many in Poland. Turkey is mostly American bird, not like chickens and ducks and gooses—I mean geeses—that live all over everywhere."

He had his own notions about what was good in the turkey, whether he'd had it often or not. Marian would have used the gizzard in the gravy and tossed out the heart and liver and neck. He asked her to boil them for him instead, and ate them for lunch before the rest of the bird was even close to done. He did the same thing with chicken giblets. *Poor-people food,* he called them. They were just that, but he ate them with as much relish as if they were filet mignon.

After the turkey rested, he carved it more deftly than Bill ever had. The bread-crumb stuffing inside was fragrant with sausage and chopped onions and celery. There was gibletless gravy for it and the turkey and the mashed potatoes. There were candied yams with marshmallows

(Fayvl said yams hadn't made it to Poland, either) and cranberry sauce and string beans and a tossed salad. A pumpkin pie and an apple pie sat in the refrigerator.

Fayvl opened a bottle of California white wine with a corkscrew. He poured a glass for Marian and another for himself. And he poured a splash in the bottom of a glass for Linda. When Marian gave him a look, he said, "A *bissel* won't hurt her none. Is Thanksgiving."

Marian thought it over and relented. "Okay," she said.

"Wow! Like a grown-up!" Linda was excited.

Fayvl raised his glass. "I got lots to be thankful for this year, on account of my wonderful wife and mine little girl." He clinked with Marian, then with Linda. They all drank. Linda made a face; the wine was on the dry side.

"We're thankful for you," Marian said. She and Fayvl drank again.

Linda discovered that some grown-up pleasures were an acquired taste. She didn't raise the little bit of wine in her glass to her mouth this time. "Let's eat!" she said.

Eat they did, till they were groaningly full. At the end of supper, Marian stared in disbelief at the empty big plate of Thanksgiving food and the smaller empty plate of pumpkin pie in front of her. "I can't believe I ate all that," she said. "Now I want to lie down and curl up and sleep through the winter, the way a bear does."

"Bears *hibernate*, Mommy," Linda said, so something she'd learned in school or heard in a story had stuck.

Her husband set both hands on his stomach. "You know, I don't think I eat this much the whole time I'm in Auschwitz. Not even close." *He has to be exaggerating . . . doesn't he?* Marian thought.

"What's Auschwitz, Papa Fayvl?" Linda didn't pronounce the death camp's name very well.

Instead of answering right away, Fayvl made a small production of lighting an after-dinner cigarette. He blew a stream of smoke up at the ceiling. Then he said, "It was a bad place where I went a long time ago—before you were born, even. But I'm not there no more, and the place, it ain't there no more, neither. It's *kaput*."

"What does that mean?" Linda was full of questions.

"Done with. Finished. Gone," Fayvl said.

Linda nodded understanding. She got that, all right. She said, "May I be excused? *I'm* not sleepy. I'm gonna go color."

"Go ahead," Marian told her. Watching Linda scoot away, she shook her head. "Boy, whatever kids have, I wish somebody would bottle it. I'd sure buy some."

"In a minute, I would," Fayvl agreed. Where Marian had watched her daughter, he eyed her. "I'm full, too, but you want I should wash dishes tonight?"

Part of Marian felt she wouldn't be doing her housewifely duty if she told him yes. She wasn't sure Bill had ever offered to do dishes. But she'd spent all day cooking and then eating, and it was catching up with her. "Would you? Do you mind?" she said.

"If I minded, I wouldn't say I'd do it," Fayvl answered. He set to work with Ajax and steel wool. Marian wondered if he'd make such a mess of it that she'd end up sorry she'd let him start. But he washed up at least as well as she did, maybe better.

When he started to dry, too, she said, "Just let 'em sit, honey. They'll be fine in the morning. That's what I was gonna do."

She thought he'd tell her no and keep on with the dish towel. After a moment, though, he nodded. "Hokay. I do that."

The next day, she had to go in to work. That irked her, but what could you do? Linda had the day off from school, of course. Fayvl kept his shop closed. He stayed home to take care of her. Marian didn't think he would have done much business anyhow, so that was probably cheaper than paying Betsy.

Nothing much was going on in the Shasta Lumber Company's office, either. Most of the people the company worked with stayed home to enjoy the long weekend. The phone rang once all day, and it was a wrong number. Marian and the other clerks and secretaries sat around and talked, swapping recipes and gossip. Most of them were happy the Republicans had done so well in the election. Marian wasn't, but kept quiet about it.

She yawned her way through the afternoon. When she punched out, she was glad to escape the office and get some fresh air. *If it's not too much food, it's too much nothing,* she thought, yawning again as she slid into the Studebaker. She counted herself lucky that she got home without dozing off behind the wheel and running into a mailbox or a dog.

Fayvl had leftovers heating in the oven and on top of the stove when she walked through the door. "Dinner in fifteen minutes," he said after they kissed.

"You're terrific!" Marian exclaimed.

"Is *gurnisht*—nothing, I mean." Fayvl seemed embarrassed that she was getting excited about what he'd done. Either he really thought it was nothing or he had an act plenty good enough to take it on the road.

Marian didn't eat as much as she had on the big day, but she still put away more than she usually did. She found herself yawning again. "I need some toothpicks to prop my eyelids open," she said.

"You want I should make a fresh pot coffee? I could do with some mine own self," Fayvl said.

"Make it, then, but I don't want any, thanks," Marian said. "The last cup I had at the office tasted funny." She made a face. She'd had to force herself to get it down. It wasn't just bitter, the way percolator coffee got as the day wore on. It tasted peculiar to her, almost metallic.

Fayvl studied her. "I remembering my Rivke said the same thing when she first find out she is in a family way. You think . . . ?"

"Uh—" Marian tried to remember when her next period was due. *When did I have the last one?* She had to think back. It would have been in the second week in October, which meant she'd been due before the middle of November. She hadn't been paying attention; she hadn't even noticed she was late till Fayvl asked her. In a small voice, she said, "I don't know. I could be."

"Huh. I think—no, I thought—so."

By the sound of it, Fayvl'd been keeping closer track than she had. Well, he had a male ulterior motive she didn't. But that small thought got lost in the bigger one. "A baby!" Marian breathed. "Our baby! That's wonderful, or whatever one step up from wonderful is."

"Our baby," Fayvl echoed. "I don't expect so soon, but yeah—one step up from wonderful." He kissed her. As soon as they broke apart, Marian yawned again.

25

MAX BACHMAN DUCKED OUT of the shack where he and
Trudl were staying. He had an American greatcoat in the dark green
color the Yankees called olive drab. He shivered even with it. Winter's
official start might lie three weeks away, but his breath smoked. The
bloodless sun shone pale in a gunmetal sky.

He lit an Old Gold and peered at the ruins of the town where he'd
hoped to live happily ever after, as if he were in a fairy tale with a happy
ending. He'd come back to Fulda when Hitler's regime went belly-up.
He'd got his printing business going, he'd made friends with the American occupiers so he'd get trade from them, too, and he'd hired Gustav
to give him a hand. For a while there, he'd had plenty to eat and plenty
to do and a wife he loved and who loved him back. How much more
did a man really need?

Now Fulda would be years getting back on its feet . . . again. And
the wreckage all around him struck him with the force of a Max
Schmeling uppercut as a perfect metaphor for the wreckage of his life.

He ground out the cigarette butt under the sole of his U.S. Army
marching boot. He ground extra hard, as if he had Luisa's face under
his boot. It wasn't wanting to shoot the messenger. Not quite. He

wouldn't have hated her nearly so much for telling him Trudl'd been unfaithful in the Siberian labor camp if she hadn't made it plain how much she enjoyed telling him.

Muttering, Max lit another smoke. When he felt charitable, he remembered that Luisa had precious little left to enjoy. Her life was even more completely ruined than his. The first thing she found out when she came back to the *Bundesrepublik* was that Gustav had been dead for a year. Nothing at all remained of the block of flats where she'd lived. When he felt charitable, all that came to mind.

But he didn't feel charitable very often. She could have kept her big trap shut. What he didn't know wouldn't have hurt him. If she had to tell him, she could have done it with a little compassion, a little understanding.

She hadn't. She'd enjoyed hurting him. During two wars now, he'd seen too many people who hurt other people on purpose, because it was fun for them. Not surprisingly, bastards like that congregated in the SS. Rolf was only the latest in a long line of those.

But you didn't have to be a fighter to enjoy other people's pain. Max shook his head. Wasn't life hard enough any which way? Did you need to go out of your way to make it worse for others who went through it with you?

He didn't think so. He didn't think decent, normal people did think so. But then, he'd always tagged Luisa as a decent, normal person. *Shows what I know, doesn't it?* went through his mind. He didn't believe she would have acted that way before the Russians hauled her and Trudl and most of the other women here in town whose husbands had gone to war off to the labor camp at the far end of the world.

A man with gray hair and gray stubble pushed a cart piled high with brown coal through the streets. Every so often, when a wheel didn't want to climb over a brick or a stone, he'd back up and change course a trifle. "Get your coal!" he called. "Stay warm! Get your coal here!"

Brown coal—lignite—barely deserved the name. It was a short step up from peat. It gave far less heat and more smoke than good black coal. Then again, it was a lot cheaper than good coal.

Max waved to the brown-coal seller. The cart rattled and banged over to him. He bought fifteen kilos of lignite. No scale, but he and the guy with the gray whiskers both knew about how much that was. The coal seller went on his way. Had he used that same cart in the last war? Had he tagged along after it with, say, his grandfather during World War I?

The door to the hovel creaked when he opened it. He took the brown coal inside. You didn't want to leave it out in the open, or it would disappear when you weren't looking. Or a pack of punks would steal it from right under your nose, and beat you up if you squawked.

Trudl looked up from the stew that bubbled over a fire made from more brown coal and from boards taken from the wreckage of Fulda. "Oh, good," she said. "I could see we'd need some more pretty soon."

"Me, too." Max nodded. As long as they talked about fuel or food or scrounging or how to turn the shack into something more like a real house, they were all right. It was only when they went back to talking about what they'd done in the war, and especially what Trudl had done in Siberia, that things went wrong.

She'd tried her best to deny everything. Max always knew when she was lying, though. Her ears turned red. She might not have known they did that herself, and she couldn't help it. She burst into tears when she finally admitted it. *I was starving!* she'd said. *I didn't think we'd ever come home, and I didn't want to die.*

He supposed that was even true. He knew the Russians treated German POWs about as badly as the Nazis had treated captured Ivans. They died like flies, in other words. No reason to expect Soviet labor camps to be any bargains, then.

Still . . . He hadn't wanted to touch her that way since he found out. To him, it felt like picking up some Ami's discarded chewing gum from the sidewalk and popping it into his own mouth. (That he'd spent a couple of years cadging other people's discarded cigarette butts and smoking or spending them didn't cross his mind.)

She'd asked him point-blank if he'd gone and visited any soldiers' brothels after he went off to fight the Russians again. When he told her no, he was telling the truth. She could hear it in his voice. He remembered how her face had fallen.

If she'd asked Rolf, now . . . But when Rolf lied, he would have made her believe it. Max also thought Gustav had got his ashes hauled a time or two. If he ever got mad enough at Luisa, he'd throw that in her face. He'd just never been inclined to go buy it himself.

"How's the stew coming?" he asked. Yes, that kind of question was all right.

"You can have some if you want," Trudl said. It was American Spam chopped into chunks and cooked with potatoes and turnips and greens she'd bought from local women: far from exciting, but better than, or at least different from, the canned rations the soup kitchen doled out.

They had bowls and plates and silverware. No two pieces were alike, not so far as Max could tell. They'd all been pulled from the wreckage of other people's flats and houses. A couple of forks and a spoon were heavy enough to be sterling; the rest were just cheap pot metal. Max dug in. Yes, it was something different. Trudl ate, too, after he'd taken as much as he wanted.

She washed dishes in an enameled basin. She carried water to the shack in two clean jerrycans. The place had no running water, but a few nearby faucets worked. The chamber pot boasted a tight-fitting lid.

When the dishes were clean, Trudl looked up and said, "Max?"

"What?"

"Max, I'm sorry. I wish I didn't do it. I thought I was going to stay in Russia forever. I didn't want to die there. It's not like I cared anything for him. I wanted a full stomach, that's all."

Did not caring for the guard you lay down with make it better or worse? Max was damned if he knew. Luisa hadn't slept with any guards, and she hadn't starved to death, either. Of course, when you got hungry enough you feared you'd starve well before you did.

Why couldn't Luisa just have shut up about what happened all those thousands of kilometers to the east? But he'd already figured that out. She enjoyed hurting Max and Trudl. Maybe she was also paying Trudl back for eating better and working less while they were in the labor camp.

Which meant . . . *If I stay angry at Trudl, who wins?* Max wondered. *Do I? Or does Luisa score some more points?* When you asked it that way, the question answered itself.

He let out a long sigh, then, after a moment, another one. "Well, let's see if we can patch things up," he said. "It was during the war. Everybody was crazy. You've got to be crazy to have a war."

"Women understand that," Trudl said. "Men mostly don't. I'll be as good as I can for you, Max. I do love you."

He weighed that. How could anyone be better than as good as she could? "I'll try, too," Max said. "We'll see how it goes." Something else seemed called for. He found it: "I love you, too." And it might prove true, and it might not. All they could do was go on and find out.

The doctor at the Knoxville veterans' hospital looked up at Cade Curtis from his perch on one knee. "You ready, Major?" The doc was no Southerner; by the way he talked, he came out of New York or Philly.

"I guess I am." Cade glanced at the crutches leaning against the chair he was sitting in. "I reckon I'd do darn near anything to get away from those bastards."

"You tell 'em," Jimmy said.

"I don't blame you a bit," the doctor said. "Let's see how you do with this, then." He fitted the padded cup at the top of Cade's new artificial leg to his stump and fastened the prosthetic in place with leather straps that went above his real knee. When he had it the way he wanted, he asked, "How's that?"

"Okay so far. Now comes the fun part, though—I get to put weight on it."

"That's kind of the idea. Can you stand up by yourself?"

"I think so. We'll both find out in a second." Cade used the arms of the chair to lever himself upright. His own arms were thick with ropy muscle.

Half his weight settled onto the padding in the cup. He remembered as if from a mile beyond the moon the Army doctor back in Korea bragging about what a good stump he'd made and how there was plenty of flesh below the end of the bone to act as a different kind of pad. As was often the way of the world, the Army doctor seemed half right and half wrong. No, the bone wasn't grinding against the artificial leg. But he could feel the pressure even so.

Both Jimmy and the doctor here reached for him when he took a step forward. He waved their hands away. He wasn't going to fall flat on his face. He didn't think he was, anyhow. And he didn't. To celebrate, he took another step. He felt them both—and the one thigh was weak, because it hadn't done any work after he got wounded. But he could manage.

"I know what I need," he said, standing there by himself and taking a few deep breaths.

"What's that, Major Curtis?" the doctor asked.

Major still felt unreal to Cade. He'd earned captain's rank, earned it and then some. The gold oak leaves he'd got with his discharge, though, were nothing more than a going-away present. He had to work not to let that distract him. "I need a three-cornered hat with a big red plume sticking up from it, and I need a parrot that sits on my shoulder and talks dirty."

Jimmy looked confused. "Why you need that crap?"

Korean pirates, Cade realized, must not have dressed the way their swashbuckling brothers in arms in the Caribbean had. "If I have to be Peg-leg Pete the Pirate, I may as well look the part," he said. "I should have a cutlass on my belt, too." He made as if to slash and chop.

"There you go!" the doc said. "I like it."

"Submachine gun or rifle kill better," Jimmy said. "You can smash or stab with rifle butt or entrenching tool."

The doctor eyed him. "You were a soldier yourself, weren't you?"

"Oh, you bet!" Jimmy nodded.

One more time, Cade went through the story of how they'd met, how Jimmy'd hauled him to the aid station, and how they were now related. He'd told it so often by now, he found himself using the same phrases over and over. He almost felt as if he were talking about some-one else, not himself.

"They gave you permission to legally adopt him?" The doctor sounded surprised.

"Yeah, they did." Cade also nodded. "Partly on account of what he did for me, I reckon, partly on account of I had a good record in Korea myself before I got hurt, and partly on account of I knew some people who were able to give me a hand with the papers and things."

"I got you," the doctor said. "Lots of times, you can go further on who you know than on what you know."

"Uh-huh." Cade wasn't even slightly embarrassed at Dr. Marcus' help. What else were connections for?

The doctor brought him back to the here-and-now. "Think you can turn around, walk over to the chair again, and sit down in it?"

"We'll both find out, won't we?" Cade said with a tight grin. He'd had little trouble going forward in a straight line. He hadn't been a hun-dred percent sure he could, but he saw how to do it right away. Turn-ing . . . Would the artificial leg hold him up while he rotated?

He used his arms and torso for most of the twisting motion, more than he would have if he were all in one piece. He'd been facing away from the chair. Now, suddenly, he was looking right at it. He took two steps towards it. Then he had to turn again so he could lower his be-hind into it.

"Good job, Major Cade!" Jimmy's enthusiasm, like any puppy's, knew no bounds. His grin showed white, perfect teeth. Cade grinned, too, partly in response to Jimmy's broad smile and partly because his Korean adopted son sounded exactly the way he did when he was con-gratulating Jimmy for learning something new.

"That was a good job, Major," the doctor said seriously. "I wasn't sure I'd be able to, but I'm going to send the leg home with you. Don't overdo things. Don't wear it too much. If you get persistent pain in the stump, or especially if you get any bleeding, take it off right away and go back to your crutches. Do you hear me?"

"Yes, sir. I'll do it, cross my heart." Cade made the gesture to show the doctor he was serious.

"Okay. We'll go on from there, then." The doctor turned away from him. "Jimmy!"

"Yes, sir?"

"You make sure Major Curtis doesn't act like a jerk. If he has any trouble with his stump or with the prosthetic, get him back here right away so we can take care of it. Understand me?"

Cade realized he was talking the way he might have to the wife of a patient who was liable to get obstreperous but who would let her calm him down. He wondered whether he ought to get mad about it. After a moment, he decided not to. He *was* likelier to listen to Jimmy than to anyone else on this side of the Pacific.

Jimmy got that, too. "I take care of it, sir. You betcha!"

"Outstanding! That's what I thought you'd tell me." Having dealt with higher authority, the doctor gave his attention back to Cade. "Ask you something that's got zip to do with your leg?"

"Sure," Cade said, "but what?"

"I've been in Knoxville all through this war. You took the train across most of the country. From, uh, San Francisco, if I remember your file right. What's it look like? How bad off are we? How long will we need to get back on our feet?"

"Well, San Francisco caught a bomb, of course. They'll be a while getting things back together. I have no idea how long it'll take to open up the Golden Gate all the way and turn the steel in the wrecked bridge into paper clips and steak knives and car fenders and all. And I really don't know how long they'll need to build a new bridge. We didn't go through Denver, I suppose because they got an A-bomb, too. There's a detour—I think it's new—that takes you through Colorado Springs instead. As for the rest of what I saw, it looks like it's going on the same as always."

"USA is great big country," Jimmy put in. "I know that before, here." He tapped the side of his head. "Now I know here, too." This time, he set the palm of his hand on his belly.

After they left the hospital, Cade and Jimmy waited on the corner for the bus that would take them to within a couple of blocks of Cade's parents' house. Cade was back on crutches. Jimmy carried the artificial leg in a big paper bag with the cup end sticking out of the top. Cade looked at it and said, "I can do this. Maybe I can do it by the time next semester starts. If I can, I'll go back to school."

"I come, too," Jimmy said. "I want to learn."

"I know you do," Cade said. "I bet you will, too. We may not be going anywhere real fast, the two of us, but we're going, and we won't stop till we get there, wherever *there* turns out to be. Not for anything."

"You goddamn right." Jimmy still talked like a dogface. Cade didn't care. And if anybody else didn't like it, too goddamn bad for him. The bus pulled up. The doors hissed open. Jimmy helped Cade board. Cade put two dimes in the fare box. The bus growled away.

Luisa Hozzel lined up for supper at the soup kitchen closest to her tent. It was cold and wet, with drizzle that wanted to freeze spattering down out of a darkening sky. That sky matched her mood. Her quilted *zek* jacket, made to hold off Siberian winters, kept her warm enough. It wasn't waterproof, though. She draped an old *Wehrmacht* camouflaged shelter half over her shoulders as a rain cape. Gustav must have done the same thing a hundred times.

But Gustav was gone. And ten meters in front of her stood Max and Trudl Bachman, also waiting for Yankee rations. Trudl held up a black umbrella with a couple of broken struts. *You've been scavenging, dear,* Luisa thought unkindly. Max had a shelter half of his own. He wore his as a poncho, not a cape. He must not have cared if his head got wet.

Luisa didn't care if his head got wet, either. If he caught pneumonia and pegged out before anybody could pump him full of American antibiotics, that wasn't her worry. She wouldn't shed one single tear.

What she did care about was that he and Trudl were standing there side by side, obviously still a couple. She'd told Max the truth about what Trudl had done in the gulag, even if she hadn't named names. Nothing wrong with the truth, was there? Of course not!

She'd hoped the truth would set Trudl free—that Max would walk out on her when he found out she'd laid a camp guard. Luisa knew Gustav would have if he found out *she'd* done anything like that. Knowing as much was one of the reasons she hadn't done anything like that. What she hadn't known was that Gustav was dead. She could have screwed around and eaten more and worked less without worrying about him at all.

What kind of man was Max, anyway? Didn't he have any pride? Any self-respect? Evidently not. If he did, wouldn't he have made Trudl as miserable as Luisa already was?

The door to the soup kitchen opened. The line snaked forward. Germans were almost as good as Englishmen at behaving well in a queue.

In went Max and Trudl. He stood back to let his wife precede him. That show of politeness made Luisa grind her teeth in futile fury. *She gave herself to a worthless camp guard for some extra rations and cushy work inside the barbed wire. Don't you understand that?* She wanted to scream the question at Max. Only the certainty that other people in line would stare at her and tap their foreheads and spin a finger by their ear made her keep quiet. Even then it was close.

After what seemed forever and was in fact three or four minutes, Luisa shuffled into the soup kitchen herself. They gave her American tinned beef stew poured over boiled potatoes and cabbage. That made a reasonably filling and more than reasonably uninspiring supper. A pair of hard candies—one butterscotch, the other mint—and a cup of muddy instant coffee finished the meal.

She also snagged a five-pack of Lucky Strikes from a bowl at the end of the serving table. American military rations weren't to her taste (or, as best she could see, to anybody else's), but she liked Yankee cigarettes fine. And the instant coffee might taste foul, but it packed more kick than German ersatz had during the last war. Her eyes opened wider and her heart beat faster after she drank it.

As she left the soup kitchen, she had to fight the urge to run for the closest toilet. The Russians had trained her in the gulag the way Professor Pavlov—one more goddamn Ivan!—had trained his dogs to drool whenever they heard a bell.

The only other *zek* she'd seen in the soup kitchen was Trudl. Nobody who hadn't gone through the labor camps would have had any idea what she was talking about. Trudl's bowels, though, had been through the same training program. But Luisa no longer had anything to say to Trudl, and Trudl didn't want to talk to her, either.

Why didn't Max knock out her front teeth? Why didn't he throw her out, so she could turn tricks here the way she did there? More questions she couldn't scream at him. She hadn't imagined he could be so pussy-whipped.

A jeep came up the road, slowly, dodging Germans and potholes and rubble. Both men in the rugged little machine wore American uniform, but that meant nothing these days. Both West Germans and French troops used leftovers from their patrons across the Atlantic. Only when Luisa heard the men speaking English was she sure they were Yanks.

She didn't really know English, but she did know the sound of it. Fulda had been full of Americans from the day the last war ended to the day this new one started. They'd known the Russians would charge through the Fulda Gap and head for the Rhine if fighting ever broke out again. Anybody who could read a map would see that.

Luisa gave the Amis their due. They'd fought hard to stop the Red Army. No matter how hard they'd fought, though, it hadn't been hard enough. They'd pulled back. The Ivans occupied Fulda. They decided to settle accounts with the women here whose husbands took up arms to defend their country.

And Luisa's life turned upside down and inside out because they did. Trudl's, too, but Luisa wasn't inclined to worry about that.

The soldier driving the jeep hit the brakes and tapped the horn so it made a little blatting noise. That was enough to make Luisa turn and look, which was what he wanted. "Hey, babe!" he called. "Want some cigarettes?" He took a pack of Raleighs out of his pocket and held it up as if it were the Holy Grail.

Right after the war, plenty of Amis had bought women for a couple of cigarettes. In that rough stretch, tobacco was money. And the Americans were the winners, and plump and pink and well-dressed, unlike the shabby, wretched German men coming home from a losing war. No wonder they'd had lots of fun in those days.

Things were bad now, but they weren't that bad. Luisa stuck her nose in the air. "I don't speak English," she said *auf Deutsch.*

To her surprise, the Yank tried her language: *"Willst du Zigaretten, Liebchen?"* He sounded like what he was—an American who didn't speak German very well—but she couldn't very well pretend not to follow him.

So she shook her head instead. "No, thanks. I've got my own."

He said something in English that wasn't an endearment. His pal in the passenger seat laughed at him. The driver took his billfold out of a trouser pocket. "Will you be friendly for this?" he asked, displaying a ten-dollar bill.

She'd just been thinking about Trudl and whoring. That was funny, or as funny as things got these days. She shook her head again. "Sorry. I'm not one of those. If you look around, you can probably find a brothel."

"I don't want a brothel," he said. He looked mad at her. He wanted to be irresistible, and thought that with all the money he had he would be. And chances were he would have been to someone else. Not to Luisa, though.

His friend had a grease gun across his knees. If he pointed that at her . . . *I'll scream my head off,* Luisa thought. The Russians wouldn't have cared what their soldiers did to German women. The Americans did. Some of the time. When they felt like it.

The friend poked the driver on the arm. Cussing in English, the driver put the jeep back in gear and went on to wherever he'd been going when he spotted Luisa.

He must have been desperate, she thought as she walked back to the leaky tent where she slept. She knew she looked like hell. She was still skinny, her camp jacket robbed her of any bustline, and the shelter half made her look like a demobilized soldier. But men were men. When they got the urge, anything with a pussy would do.

No doubt that was how Trudl had snagged herself the guard at the gulag. When you let them know you would, they were putty in your hands. Afterwards, they'd blame you and sneer at you, but not till they'd got what they wanted.

Luisa wondered what she would have done had the Ami offered her a hundred dollars, not just ten. A hundred dollars, that was real money. She knew more than a little relief she hadn't had to find out. Rain splattered on the shelter half as she headed off to what passed for home.

This was the second time Vasili Yasevich had watched Soviet tanks rumble into a city that didn't want them. They'd run the Japanese out of Harbin more than seven years ago now. Here they were in Warsaw. Some of them might have been the same tanks both times, too. T-34/85s weren't a measure of the state of the art, as they had been in 1945, but they were still a lot better than no tanks at all.

Some of them flew the hammer and sickle on their radio aerials. Others flew the Polish flag, white over red. Drivers and commanders on Soviet and Polish tanks all smiled and waved to the glum people who stood on the sidewalks and watched them pass. No one shot at them or flung a Molotov cocktail at a tank. The rebels in Warsaw had surrendered. Soviet brutality was a simple tool, but it worked.

Beside Vasili, Ewa whispered, "We were free for a little while. Now we're going back into slavery."

"I'm sorry," Vasili whispered back. She wasn't wrong, but Warsaw still felt freer to him than Smidovich had. It also felt freer than Harbin had under Mao's rule, or Stalin's before that, or the puppet Emperor of Manchukuo's before Stalin's.

Behind the tanks marched a regiment of Polish soldiers in the service of the People's Republic. Some of them wore Russian-style helmets, others the distinctive square-topped cap the Poles called a csapka. That told the spectators they weren't Russians. So did the big pole-mounted pictures of Boleslaw Bierut their standard-bearers carried. The jowly politician ran the country for Moscow. As long as he did exactly what Molotov told him to, he could do whatever he wanted.

Ewa sniffed. "And they have the nerve to call *us* traitors!"

"I'm a Russian White," Vasili reminded her. "The Reds have been calling us traitors since long before they got around to you people."

"Don't say 'you people,'" Eva told him. "You're one of us now. You'd better be, if you don't want the MGB to grab you."

"Nobody wants the MGB to grab him. Or even her." Vasili spoke with great conviction. Ewa didn't try to tell him he was wrong.

A military band followed the soldiers. They blared out the Polish national anthem. It was called "Poland Is Not Yet Lost," which said everything that needed saying about the country's luckless past and limited hopes for the future.

Vasili had limited hopes for the future himself. As long as he stayed out of the Chekists' clutches, he'd be happy enough. He wasn't really a Pole, of course, no matter what Ewa said. But if the choice was between pretending to be a Pole and pretending to be a Red Russian, he knew which he preferred.

"Do you want to go hear the speeches?" Ewa asked.

"Christ have mercy, no!" Vasili exclaimed. She burst out laughing. He didn't think it was funny. Political speeches were dismal enough even in one's native language. When you had to listen to them in a tongue that wasn't yours, they got even worse.

Besides, he already knew what the hacks in the square-cut suits would say. They'd talk about punishing the people at the heart of the uprising, and about how all the other Poles could get on with their lives . . . as long as they imitated their boss and did exactly what the Russians told them to. If you'd read the script ahead of time, did you need to see the movie?

He had nowhere left to run, either. He'd fled Red China for the Soviet Union. When the Russians gave him the choice between the gulag and the Red Army, he'd chosen the Army without hesitation. He'd guessed it would be easier to escape from, and he'd been right. When the Polish rebels captured him, he'd wholeheartedly gone over to them.

And here he was, still in Poland, which was not—quite—lost yet. Only it survived as a Communist country like the two he'd already found he didn't want to live in. Poland was bordered by the USSR, Czechoslovakia, and East Germany. The Reds held them down, too. No, nowhere left to run.

Or was there? He turned to Ewa. "If we could get up to the Baltic and if we could get a boat some way, we could sail to Finland or Sweden or maybe even Denmark or West Germany."

She looked at him. He didn't like what he saw in her eyes. "Those are two pretty big *ifs*," she said. "Besides, have you got any idea how to sail a boat?"

"Well, no," he admitted. The only time he could remember even being in a boat was when that drunken Russian fisherman rowed him across the Amur, out of China and into the USSR. That hadn't worked out as well as he wished it would have.

"Let's sum this up, then." Ewa ticked off points on her fingers as she made them. "We can't get to the Baltic—they'll probably be extra careful about letting anybody out of Warsaw for a while. Even if we could get to the Baltic, I don't see how we can buy a boat or steal one. And if by some miracle we did get our hands on a boat, we don't know how to use it. Is that it, or did I miss something?"

"That's it, all right," Vasili said sullenly. He looked around to make sure nobody was spying on them. He'd learned that when the Japanese still lorded it over Harbin. He hadn't even needed Communism to teach it to him. Satisfied, he went on, "I don't know if I can stand staying here."

"I understand that." The pharmacist's daughter spoke with exaggerated patience. "But if you don't stay here, you're likeliest to go straight into the gulag. I'd miss you . . . unless I went in at the same time, which isn't that unlikely, either. If they grab you, chances are they'll grab me, too."

He heard only a tiny fragment of what she actually said. "You'd miss me, Ewa? Would you really?"

"I said so, didn't I? You've known me for a while now. You know I don't usually say things I don't—"

She didn't get to finish. Vasili put his arms around her, tilted her chin up, and kissed her for all he was worth. She stiffened in surprise. She let out a muffled squawk, too. A moment later, though, she melted against him and kissed him back.

Vasili didn't want the moment ever to end. He clung to Ewa like a drowning man clinging to an oar. When he opened his eyes in the middle of the kiss, he almost fell into hers, which were also open and only a few centimeters from his. At last, though, she tapped him on the arm, more and more insistently. With vast reluctance, he drew back a little. "What?" he said.

"I couldn't breathe," she told him.

"Oh. I'm sorry," he said. Then he kissed her again. Or maybe she kissed him this time. He never could sort it out afterwards. This kiss didn't go on so long, because one of the other people who'd come out to watch the Communists reenter Warsaw broke into applause. That made Vasili and Ewa fly apart like two magnets with their north poles touching.

"I think maybe we'd better get back to the shop," Ewa said, smoothing her hair with one of those automatic gestures women used.

"I think maybe you're right." Vasili started off that way. Ewa took a couple of quick steps to catch up with him, then walked along at his side. Their hands brushed, then clung. They'd just watched the uprising they'd worked so hard for crushed. They were both smiling all the same.

When they rounded a corner, a hard-faced policeman held out his hand and said, "Your papers!"

Ewa's documents said she was someone named Maria Filemonowa. Vasili's proclaimed him to be Leszek Piskorski. They were forgeries, but forgeries from the print shop that produced genuine identity cards. The policeman examined them, gave a grudging nod, and handed them back. He waved Vasili and Ewa on.

"Just one of those things," Ewa said while the Red bastard was still close enough to hear them. Vasili nodded. He didn't want to talk within earshot of the policeman. His Russian accent would have betrayed him. He took Ewa's hand again. All right, the uprising was dead. They weren't, then. They still had lives to shape among the ruins.

COLONEL VOLODYMYR PETLYURA WHACKED the atlas page with a pencil. He should have had a big map tacked to a wall or a table and used a pointer to show the bomber crew its target. Everything in the Soviet Union seemed to be improvised these days. But he managed to make do with what he had.

"Riga," he said. "Your target is Riga. We're making progress, no two ways about it. The bandits in Poland and Czechoslovakia have gone belly-up. The Fascist retreads in Hungary won't last one whole hell of a lot longer. Once we knock the rebels in the Baltics and the Caucasus over the head, we'll be able to get on with our business without worrying about a stab in the back."

Boris Gribkov's face showed only serious attention as he listened to the base commandant. None of the other flyers raised an eyebrow or let out a cough, either. Their impassive Soviet masks passed yet another test. But, behind his mask, Boris wondered whether Colonel Petlyura remembered Hitler wailing about the stab in the back that, he claimed, cost Germany the First World War.

He wasn't about to ask Petlyura any such question. Instead, he said,

"Comrade Colonel, what kind of air defenses do the Latvians have around their capital?"

"When Riga was under Soviet control, we installed comprehensive flak rings around the city to protect it against the imperialist aggressors," the commandant replied. "They must have been successful—no A-bombs fell on Riga. Now, however, it's likely that those flak rings are in the bandits' hands."

"I see," Boris said. Those would be flak guns that could reach up and hit American B-29s . . . or Soviet Tu-4s. Had they kept the enemy away from Riga, though, or had the Americans stayed away because they were soft on the Baltic republics and wanted to see them rise against the USSR? One more query it seemed better not to put to Colonel Petlyura.

"We've been giving it to Riga pretty hard with medium bombers," Petlyura said. "Same with Memel—or whatever the Lithuanians call it these days—and Tallinn. Now it's time to get the heavies into the act."

"We aren't bombing Vilnius?" Anton Presnyakov asked.

"We *hold* Vilnius," the base commandant answered, as proudly as if he'd captured it singlehanded.

"Are the Lithuanian bandits flying night fighters?" Boris asked—the most important question to any bomber pilot.

"It's . . . possible." Colonel Petlyura didn't sound so proud of that admission. "But those are the chances of war. I got shot down over Kiev in 1943. Luckily, my 'chute blew me into a partisan-held area, so I stayed in the fight."

Getting shot down by the *Luftwaffe* was one thing. Getting shot down by Lithuanian bandits? That would be tragedy repeating as farce. *Unless I get killed,* Boris thought. Then it would be tragic all the way around.

Night came early at this season of the year. In normal times, mothers and fathers would be telling kids about the presents Father Frost would give them. Now? Who could say? Gregorian Christmas soon, and New Year's, and Orthodox Christmas. Officially, New Year's would be the celebrated day. Actually? Again, who could say?

The Tu-4 didn't carry a full load—only about eight tonnes of bombs. Maybe that was intentional, to make takeoff easier. Maybe it just meant logistics had broken down and not enough ordnance had come to Mogilev to fill the plane's bomb bay. Boris found another question he couldn't ask.

Up into the dark sky, up through the clouds, up to the edge of the stratosphere flew the big plane. It wore Soviet livery, with red stars and serial numbers. The Latvians wouldn't be deceived by American emblems, though they'd confused the devil out of the Yankees themselves.

They took antiaircraft fire from Daugavpils. That infuriated Gribkov. "The Red Army holds this place!" he raged. "Are we going to get shot down by stupid sons of bitches who happen to be our friends?"

They didn't. Those flak guns couldn't reach high enough to touch them. The ones surrounding Riga . . . If anything, Colonel Petlyura had understated how many there were and what eager gunners they had. By the accuracy with which the fire came up at the Tu-4, the bandits knew how to integrate the guns with radar direction, too.

"How soon can we bomb?" Boris demanded.

"Another half a minute, Comrade Pilot," Fyodor Ostrovsky replied.

"*Bozehmoi!* This is worse than Bratislava," Boris said. Considering that he'd been shot down over Bratislava . . . But, though the Tu-4 bucked in the air from near misses, nothing hit it before the bombs dropped away. Boris heeled the plane away from the Latvian capital with nothing but relief.

Then the radarman let out a horrified, almost girlish squeal: "Bogies on the set! Two, closing fast!"

That was the last thing in the world Boris wanted to hear. He turned hard to port and dove. As the Tu-4 shed altitude fast enough to make its wing spars groan, the radar-directed gun turrets started banging away. A hit or two from a 23mm shell would knock any fighter out of the sky. If they got lucky . . .

But they didn't. Machine-gun bullets chewed into the Tu-4. The bomber lost pressurization. "Oxygen masks!" Boris shouted. He and

Presnyakov already wore theirs. So did Ostrovsky. Boris had to hope the rest of the crew were either using them or could get them on fast.

More bullets bit the plane. So did cannon shells. One of the engines started to burn. Another quit, though without catching fire. The Tu-4 couldn't stay airborne for long on two engines. And pretty soon bullets or shells would smash into the cockpit. That would be the end of that for everybody aboard.

"Get out!" Boris shouted over the intercom, hoping it still worked. "We're going down, so hit the silk!" He tried to lower the nose wheel with the hydraulics, but they were gone. He cranked it down instead. The bomb bay wouldn't open without the hydraulics, either, so out through the wheel well was the only escape route for the men in and just aft of the cockpit.

Out they went, one after another. Bitter cold smote Boris when his turn came. The air was thin but breathable, which showed how much height the Tu-4 had lost. He yanked the ripcord. The parachute opened with a jolt rough enough to make him gray out for a moment.

Down through the clouds he fell. He could see fires in the distance when he got below the floating fog. That had to be Riga. The only trouble was, he wasn't sure in which direction it lay. He thought—he hoped—it was north of him. If he was wrong, he'd splash into the Baltic and sink like a stone.

He looked straight down past his flying boots. No, he wouldn't have seen light coming out of windows on the sea. The ground wasn't that far below, either. He gathered himself for a landing. It would happen when it happened; away from the lights, he couldn't see much.

That gathering proved pointless, because he crunched through much of the canopy of a big tree before winding up, like a hanging fruit, two or three meters in the air. "Fuck your mother!" he snarled at the tree. Then he took his knife off his belt and went to work on the lines that held him to the canopy.

He'd cut only one before an electric torch blazed into his face from below. "Hold it right there!" a man barked in musically accented Russian. "Do you surrender? We've got you covered."

"I surrender," Boris said, seeing no other choice. "Can I finish cutting myself down before I give you my knife?"

"You'll have a pistol, too," the Latvian said. "Toss that down first."

Boris did. One of the man with the torch's comrades went over and picked it up. Boris returned to hacking away at the nylon lines. When the last one parted, he balled himself up and fell. He hurt one ankle a little, but only a little. As he got to his feet, he looked at his captors. The big blond men wore Red Army tankmen's coveralls, but among themselves they didn't speak Russian.

One of them took charge of Boris. "We'll treat you as a prisoner of war," he said. "You don't do that for us, but we will for you. You can't say we don't play by the rules."

He wore rank badges that didn't belong to the Red Army. Had the bandits revived the emblems Latvia used between the first two World Wars? Boris wouldn't have recognized them if they hit him in the face. The rebel dropped back into Latvian to give his men orders. By his gestures, they amounted to *Take him away.*

One of the other bandits saluted smartly. "*Ja, Leitnants* Eigims!" he said. He and his friends took Boris away.

That horrible noise wasn't rockets screaming in from under a jet fighter's wings. It was just Istvan Szolovits' alarm clock, telling him to get up and get moving. He had to get moving to kill the damn thing. He'd put it on a shelf where he had to stand up to reach it. By the time it fell silent, he was irrevocably awake.

He still felt sleepy, though. When you worked all day and went to night school afterwards, you came home tired. He slept like a dead thing on weekends; sometimes he didn't wake up till after noon. The mere idea would have made the drill sergeants who tried to turn conscripts into Hungarian soldiers fall over and foam at the mouth from apoplexy.

He was hungry all the time, too. He fixed bacon and eggs for breakfast, and gulped two big cups of pale coffee with them. The way he ate, he should have put on weight. He didn't, though. His work clothes still fit fine.

Then it was out to see if the Hudson would start. It was gloomy outside, and chilly by Los Angeles standards. The locals said it was in the low fifties. To Istvan, it felt like ten or eleven. Getting used to Fahrenheit degrees and pounds and gallons and miles and feet and other whimsical American measures was something he hadn't thought he'd need to do. But he did—the sensible metric system was only a rumor here, and a distant rumor at that.

The Hudson's engine whirred and coughed. "Come on, you whore!" Istvan said. A moment later, it caught. *You just have to know how to talk to it,* he thought as smoke belched from the exhaust pipe.

He was only about fifteen minutes away from Blue Front. He didn't worry about the price of gasoline. The Hudson burned it as if it were going out of style, but gas was so cheap in the USA that he hardly noticed. European cars were little and cramped, which helped them sip expensive fuel. Where fuel wasn't expensive, cars were anything but little. Imperials and Lincolns dwarfed the Hudson.

He pulled into the Blue Front lot a few minutes early. Aaron Finch was there ahead of him. Aaron was another one of those compulsively early people; from what he said, Ruth was even more so. The American had been about to go into the warehouse. He waited at the door, finishing a cigarette, while Istvan hurried over to catch up with him.

"How's it going?" Aaron asked.

"I am doing all right. How about you?" Istvan said.

"Can't complain," Aaron said. "And your English is really coming along. Except for where you rolled your *r* there, you sounded like you could've been born at Cedars of Lebanon."

"At where?" Istvan frowned at the name, which sounded Middle Eastern.

"Sorry. It's a big hospital. Leon was born there."

"Oh, I see. Thank you."

When they went inside, Herschel Weissman waited till they stuck their cards in the time clock. Once they'd punched in, he said, "How'd you guys like to take a TV and a washer down near Florence and Figueroa?"

Istvan was ready to take anything anywhere. To his surprise, Aaron frowned. "That's somewhere right near the edge of what the A-bomb knocked over," he said.

"That was two years ago, Aaron," the founder of Blue Front said. "You won't start growing tentacles out of your forehead or anything."

"*Ikh vays, ikh vays.*" Aaron sounded sheepish. Returning to English, he went on, "Whether I know it or not, though, I still get nervous. I must've hung around with Jim too long before I started working with Istvan."

Istvan drove the truck through downtown. Though the Pasadena Freeway and its southern extension, the Harbor, were fully repaired, much of downtown and the area south of it remained either ruins or cleared ground where ruins had stood. New houses weren't sprouting on those vacant lots. "Would you want a house where an A-bomb knocked everything flat?" he said.

"Would I? Not unless it was really cheap," Aaron said. "The top part of my head is sure it's safe. Poke a little deeper, though . . ." He turned his thumb down.

The Harbor Freeway stopped not far south of downtown. It was years from pushing down to L.A.'s harbor district, San Pedro (which had got an A-bomb of its own). Istvan kept going south on Figueroa. Fifteen or twenty minutes later, he found Emma Watson's house. Looking north after he got out of the truck, he could see the stub of City Hall sticking up above the closer rubble fields.

Mrs. Watson opened the door as soon as Aaron knocked. "Good to see you, gentlemen," she said. She was a nice-looking woman in her early thirties, about the color of coffee before cream went in. Istvan tried to hide his surprise. No reason Negroes shouldn't buy televisions and washing machines, none at all. Money was money, no matter who spent it. He was surprised anyhow.

Aaron took it in stride. He treated Emma Watson the same way he would have dealt with a white woman. He'd done that with the colored housekeeper in Pasadena, too. But Mrs. Watson was a customer, not hired help.

She gave Aaron and Istvan lemonade—"from a tree in the back yard"—and tipped them a buck apiece as they left. Looking at the block with new eyes, Istvan saw several Negro children playing in front yards and on the sidewalk. A house a few doors down from Emma Watson's had a FOR SALE sign out front.

Aaron saw that, too. "Probably a white family moving out," he said. "The neighborhoods here are changing."

"Is that good or bad?" Istvan asked.

"Beats me," Aaron said. "An awful lot of whites don't want to live next door to *shvartzers*. I think that's silly, but what I think doesn't make it any less real."

"Captain Kovacs, the guy who chose me to come to America, he told me Negroes in America get what Jews get in Europe," Istvan said. "I'm beginning to see what he meant."

"Yeah, there's something to it, all right." Aaron paused in the middle of lighting a Chesterfield. "Captain *Ko-vach*, huh?" He pronounced the name more or less as Istvan had. Then he went on, "There's a funny guy on TV named Ernie *Ko-vacks*. That's how he says it, too. Is he wrong?"

"Maybe he was born over here. He's pronouncing it the way somebody who speaks English would if he was just reading it," Istvan said.

"Okay. I gotcha." Aaron nodded. "When I was in the merchant marine, one time I shipped with a big old Polack who spelled his name S-Z-U-L-C. In English, it looks like it oughta be *Zulk*, right? But he wanted everybody to say it *Schultz*."

"Sounds like Poles trying to spell a German name the way they're used to," Istvan agreed. "They don't do it like you or like us. With us, *s* is like English *sh* and *sz* is like English plain *s*. With the Poles, it's the other way around."

"Funny," Aaron said. "I mean funny-peculiar, not funny-haha."

Istvan had to think for a moment before he understood what the older man meant. When he did, he grinned. "Talk about funny guys! You're one, the way you put things."

"That's not me." Now Aaron shook his head. "People just say that sometimes. People who speak English, I mean. *Funny* can mean the one thing or the other, and sometimes the person who's listening can't tell which right away."

"I suppose so. It sounded like you, though." Istvan lit a cigarette of his own, blew out the match, and tossed it out the window. He added, "Girls can be funny-peculiar and funny-haha at the same time." Most of that—all of it, in fact, except for Aaron's two words—was in Yiddish.

Aaron glanced over at him. Behind the thick lenses of his spectacles, his eyes sparked. "They sure can! You find somebody?"

"Maybe. Gina's in my classes at Pasadena Junior College. We talk before and after the class time, too. I got her telephone number."

"Decent start," Aaron observed. "So you see what happens, that's all. Maybe it goes nowhere. Maybe you have some fun for a while and then it goes nowhere. Or maybe you get lucky, like I did with Ruth." He made it sound so simple. Of course, he hadn't married till he was in his mid-forties. That argued it wasn't so simple all the time, even for him. Istvan puffed hard on his cigarette. *As if I didn't already know!* he thought.

Doc Toohey nodded at Marian Tabakman. "You're in a family way, all right," he said. "From what you tell me, the baby should come some time in July. Congratulations to you and Fayvl both."

"Thanks," Marian said.

"Both of you have perked up this town since you got here," the doctor said. "It's nice you got together. I'm sure you'll spoil the kid rotten."

Marian smiled. "Fayvl will, if I give him half a chance. And you know what? I probably will."

"That's fine." Doc Toohey smiled, too. "Nothing wrong with spoiling a kid a little bit." The smile slipped. "It's a darn sight better than smacking one in the face for dropping a jar of jam or something like that. Some of the loggers, they knock their kids around when something goes wrong for them. Or they kick the cat into the wall. Or they smack their wives instead of the kids, or along with the kids."

"How awful! You should call the cops!" Marian said.

"I've done it a few times, when it went way beyond bumps and bruises," he replied. "But the wives, they mostly don't want to file charges. They tell the police 'Oh, I fell down' or 'I walked into a door' or 'Junior tripped over a cap gun and landed on his face' or ... I'll tell you, I've heard enough bullsomething to fertilize every field in the Central Valley."

He'd said things like that before. Along with policemen, doctors saw life in the raw. It left them cynical. Marian wasn't, not that way. "If somebody I was married to did anything like that to me, I sure wouldn't stay married to him for long. Either I'd get a lawyer or I'd stick a knife in him after he fell asleep. They can't stay awake all the time."

"You know what? I believe you. But a lot of women aren't like that," Doc Toohey said sadly. "I had one of 'em tell me, 'That's how I know he loves me, when he slaps me. He wouldn't do it if he didn't really care.'"

"What a bunch of bullshit," Marian said. The doctor might tiptoe around the word, but she didn't, not after her time in Camp Nowhere.

"You know it and I know it, but they don't know it." Toohey still sounded sad. "A lot of them grew up watching their fathers haul off and belt their mothers, and they think that's how things are supposed to work."

"Somebody ought to do something about it," Marian said.

He smiled again, crookedly. "You and Fayvl got Weed an ambulance. I wouldn't have believed that would ever happen, but this one would be tougher. You just had to convince a few big shots then. With this, half the guys in town think they've got a God-given right to belt Suzie if she burns the roast. And too many of the Suzies think the same way. So you can try, but looks to me like you're tilting at windmills."

Marian knew that meant *you're wasting your time* or *you haven't got a chance.* It was from some book or other. She'd run into it when she was in high school, but she couldn't remember how.

It was gray and chilly when she went outside. She gauged the clouds.

Maybe it would rain, maybe not. Wind whipped the banners and streamers plugging stores' after-Christmas sales. In spite of the hoopla, not many people were going in or out.

She walked over to the cobbler's shop to get Linda. Her daughter went in with Fayvl in the week between Christmas and New Year's when school was out. Linda didn't want to leave. She had coloring books, and she helped her stepfather do things that weren't likely to hurt her. But when Fayvl told her to go, she went.

"Am I gonna have a baby brother or a baby sister?" she asked Marian when they got out on the sidewalk.

"You sure are, sweetie," Marian answered. "C'mon. The car's in front of the doctor's office."

"I know I am. You already told me." Linda sounded impatient. "But which?"

"I can't tell you that, honey. The doctor can't tell me, either. Nobody will know till the baby comes out and we see."

"Oh." Linda looked disappointed. Marian opened the Studebaker's passenger door. As Linda slid in, she said, "They should be able to tell stuff like that. They don't know much, do they?"

"They know a lot more than they used to," Marian said as she got in herself. They had all the wonder drugs to kill germs. They had anesthetics so operations weren't something you only did if you were almost dead and had nothing left to lose.

Of course, the knowledge that led to X-rays also led to A-bombs. Maybe ignorance would have been bliss. Or maybe not. Had X-rays saved more lives than A-bombs had taken? Marian didn't know.

Fayvl came home himself not too much later. "Wasn't much business today," he said with a shrug. "Is the season of the year."

His eyes slid to the Christmas tree with the lights and the tinsel and the Santa ornaments and the big gold star at the top. He hadn't said a word when Marian put it up. It was part of a holiday important to her faith, however watered-down that was, so he respected it. Marian wondered why more people couldn't have done the same with his faith.

As if apologizing, she said, "We'll take it down right after New Year's."

"You don't got to do it on account of me. Don't t'ink you do," he said. "You don't tell much about what Doc Toohey says when you get Linda. *Nu?*"

"He says I'm gonna have a baby, like we didn't already know," Marian replied. "But the test makes it official."

"Hokay. Better than hokay," Fayvl said. "We gonna have something what is part of both of us. Is pretty good."

"I think so, too." No matter what Marian thought, she found herself yawning. She was sleepy all the time, the way she had been when she first got pregnant with Linda. "I'd better fix dinner while I can still keep my eyes open."

Dinner was a hamburger casserole, about as simple and brainless as cooking got. A good thing, too; she sleepwalked through it, and almost dozed off waiting for it to finish in the oven. Eating perked her up a little. Everything stayed down. That was great. People called it morning sickness, but Marian knew it could hit any old time at all.

Afterwards, Fayvl said, "Here. I do dishes," and he did. He didn't make any fuss about it. He didn't act as if he deserved a medal for his heroism, the way Bill would have. He just washed the dishes, the way he had at Thanksgiving and several times since. He'd got into the habit of leaving them in the drainer afterwards now, but so what? They'd dry by morning. Marian wasn't going to criticize, especially since she did it herself, too.

He fiddled with the radio, trying to get some station, any station, to come in. Static hissed all along the dial. "Sorry about that," Marian said.

Shrugging, Fayvl said, "Maybe we have some money one of these days, I get a shortwave set. Then we don't think so much we is stuck in the middle of nowhere."

"That was the camp," Linda said out of the blue.

Marian and Fayvl both laughed. "The camp was nowhere, all right," Marian said, remembering all those nights on the front seat of the Studebaker.

"They done what they could," Fayvl said. "But what you can do after an A-bomb goes off in a big city, it ain't much."

Marian nodded. And the A-bomb that had wrecked Seattle was only one of half a dozen or so that smashed most of the major towns on the West Coast, and Denver with them. No wonder relief efforts had been so spotty and so shaky. The wonder, Marian supposed, was that the government did as well as it had.

The same held true for the later attacks on the other side of the country, the ones that laid waste to Boston and New York City and Washington. The United States was like a prizefighter who'd come out of the ring with one eye swollen shut, with a cut over the other one, and with his whole face swollen and bruised—but whose hand the referee raised in victory. When he talked to reporters, what would he say? Something like *I look good next to the other guy!*

Perhaps thinking along the same lines, her new husband—the father of the baby she was going to have—said, "It ain't like I thought it was gonna be, but it ain't so bad, is it?"

"It's good, Papa Fayvl," Linda said. "It's good."

It wasn't how Marian had thought it would be, either. She nodded again even so. "It is good, Fayvl. It really is," she said. He came over and gave her a kiss. She squeezed him. Linda clapped her hands together once. Marian nodded yet again, this time against Fayvl's right shoulder. No, not what she'd expected, but good just the same.

Aaron Finch kept sticking a finger inside his collar to try to loosen it a little. He'd never liked wearing neckties. Muttering under his breath, he wondered for the umpty-umpth time why Marvin had decided to throw a fancy New Year's Eve bash. The only answer that occurred to him was, his brother didn't know the difference between doing something and overdoing it.

His wife saw him fiddling with the tight collar button. "You look very handsome, sweetie," Ruth told him.

"If you say so," Aaron answered. "We could have stayed at home and gone to bed early, or had a couple of drinks if you felt like seeing in 1953. . . ."

"Oh, come on! We'll have a good time." Ruth was used to his grumbling, and to discounting it. And maybe they would have a good time, and maybe they'd go home in the wee small hours with Aaron wishing he'd given Marvin a right to the jaw. As far as he could see, it was about even money.

From the Chevy's back seat, Leon asked, "Are we almost there yet?"

"Won't be long, kiddo," Aaron said, which was true—no part of Glendale was very far from any other part. "Now you've asked once, so *genug* already. Do it again and you get in trouble."

"Okay, Daddy." Leon took the idea of getting into trouble seriously, which was more than Aaron remembered doing when *he* was a little boy. As for Marvin—well, if *trouble* wasn't his middle name, it should have been.

They pulled up in front of Marvin's house on East Glenoaks five minutes later. Leon hadn't asked again. Aaron gave him points for that. · Ruth shivered when they got out of the car. "Brr!" she said. "It's chilly." Aaron didn't think so, but he wore a wool suit jacket over a long-sleeved shirt. Her dress left her arms bare. And he was on the male half of the it's-too-hot-no-it's-too-cold divide. That was one more thing people could argue about, but not if they wanted a happy marriage.

Leon ran ahead and knocked on the door. Not to put too fine a point on it, he banged on the door like Buddy Rich working out on the drums. Inside the house, Caesar started barking. That made Leon run back to Aaron.

Marvin opened the door. "Oh, it's you guys," he said. "I thought that was the whole Eighty-second Airborne out there."

"Nah. They would have parachuted down your chimney," Aaron said. His brother made a face at him. Remembering why he was here, Aaron added, "Happy New Year."

"Same to you, same to you." Marvin leered at Ruth. "And especially same to you."

"Oh, cut that out," Ruth said. Aaron didn't get huffy about it. His brother talked a better game than he played. Aaron suspected it was the residue of his being on the fringes of Hollywood.

"Well, come on in." Marvin stood aside so they could.

Aaron said hello to Sarah and Olivia, and to Sarah's mother, who lived in the house with them. Roxane and Howard were there, and Herschel Weissman, and a couple of second- and third-string Hollywood people, and several men Aaron hadn't met before, and women who were their wives and girlfriends. One of the men, an eager fellow in loud clothes that made him look like a racetrack tout, said, "So you're Marvin's brother? I sure hope you've got some jack in that franchising scheme of his. You'll be on Easy Street this time next year if you do. Grabbing a franchise first chance I got, it's the smartest thing I ever done."

"I'm just fine, Mr. Lefkowitz, thanks," Aaron said, and disengaged himself. It took some doing; Hy Lefkowitz was as adhesive as an abalone. But he managed. If getting in on a hot-dog chain was the smartest thing Lefkowitz had ever done, Aaron wouldn't have wanted to let him pick horses.

Howard Bauman greeted Aaron with, "You don't have your little Hungarian Republican in tow tonight?" He did grin when he said it.

Disarmed, Aaron grinned back. "Hey, he was there. He saw it with his own eyes. You don't want to listen to him, I can't make you."

"Republicans all over the place in Congress, too," Bauman said, as if he hadn't spoken. "They'll make a mess of the country—you watch. And it seems like we're dumb enough to elect one President, too." As if he had some good news, he added, "Looks like Poland and Hungary will stay allied with Russia."

"Yeah, it does." Aaron nodded, though he didn't think that was such a great thing. He'd seen a newsreel of the Red Army reentering Budapest. The city was flatter than it had been when the Russians took it away from Hitler in 1945. Now he also knew what Matyas Rakosi looked like. Not a great advertisement for Communism, as far as he was concerned. Not a great advertisement for Judaism, either. You couldn't win them all.

Howard was right that the Poles and Hungarians—and the Czechoslovakians with them—would stay under the Soviet thumb. Aaron couldn't disagree with him. But did he have to sound so cheerful about it? When Budapest fell, Istvan had stayed in the dumps for a couple of days. Aaron let it alone tonight. If he started quarreling so early, Ruth wouldn't be happy with him.

Olivia squatted next to Leon, teaching him whatever dance was popular with the hep cats these days. Leon wiggled enthusiastically, but with nothing even resembling rhythm. If he ever ended up with a girl who liked to cut a rug, he'd make her very unhappy.

Well, that was a worry for another day, another year, another decade. Leon wouldn't start alarming the female population till the 1960s rolled around. Aaron laughed to himself. When Leon was born, he and Ruth had worked out that their son would graduate from high school in the class of 1967. In 1949, it felt as if it were a million years away.

Now that 1952 was giving way to 1953, it still did . . . but then again, it didn't. Leon would be starting kindergarten pretty soon. If you were a grown-up watching it all happen in front of you, wasn't the gap from modeling clay and crayons to cap and gown little more than the blink of an eye? It seemed that way to Aaron.

He lit one more in his endless stream of Chesterfields. Right now, he could be glad that the war was over, and that it hadn't come close enough to him to do anything worse than break a couple of windows at his house and scare the bejesus out of him. Millions of people across America and Europe and Russia and China weren't so lucky. He had plenty of blessings to count.

He went into the kitchen and got himself another beer. When he came out, Herschel Weissman asked him, "So what'll you be up to in 1953?"

Aaron coughed a couple of times before he answered. The cigarettes weren't good for his wind, but he liked them too much to quit. "Sorry, boss," he said. "Main thing I hope for next year is to buy a house instead of renting. I've got enough *gelt* for the down payment. I've looked on weekends for a while. They're building a nice tract in Hawthorne, down near the airport, on what used to be a fig orchard. I may see if we can swing one of those."

"Good luck," Weissman said. "That's a long way to and from work, though."

"I'll manage. Gas doesn't cost that much," Aaron said.

Ruth tapped him on the arm. "Hon, let's get Leon to sleep."

"Okay." They settled Leon on Olivia's bed, right next to a big stuffed poodle. He might fall asleep, or he might not. As long as he didn't throw a tired tantrum and louse up the party, Aaron wouldn't worry about it tonight.

As the midnight hour neared, Marvin banged on a wine glass with a fork till everybody quieted down and looked his way. "I've got a toast, folks," he said loudly. His face was flushed and sweaty; he'd been pouring it down. "A toast," he repeated. "Here's to a peaceful 1953! Here's to hoping we've learned enough to never, ever, *ever* use A-bombs again, no matter what!"

"*Alevai omayn!*" Aaron said. Everybody drank to Marvin's toast: his family, Aaron and his family, his boss, the would-be hot-dog entrepreneurs and their ladies. Everybody. Aaron pushed his way through the crowd to his brother's side and set his hands on Marvin's shoulders. "You did good there," he told him. "I didn't know you had it in you."

"Thanks a bunch," Marvin said. "But I'm not gonna let you get me down, not tonight I'm not."

It was too bad that Guy Lombardo and his orchestra were on Eastern Time, not Pacific. The old year had gone in New York City almost three hours ago. No dropping the crystal ball in Times Square this year, though. Times Square still wasn't up to it. Marvin counted down the seconds on his expensive Swiss watch. "Happy New Year!" he shouted. "Happy 1953!"

Aaron got his first kiss of the new year from Ruth. "Happy 1953!" he said, and lit another Chesterfield.

About the Author

HARRY TURTLEDOVE is the award-winning author of the alternate-history works *The Man with the Iron Heart*, *The Guns of the South*, and *How Few Remain* (winner of the Sidewise Award for Best Novel); the War That Came Early novels: *Hitler's War*, *West and East*, *The Big Switch*, *Coup d'Etat*, *Two Fronts*, and *Last Orders*; the Worldwar saga: *In the Balance*, *Tilting the Balance*, *Upsetting the Balance*, and *Striking the Balance*; the Colonization books: *Second Contact*, *Down to Earth*, and *Aftershocks*; the Great War epics: *American Front*, *Walk in Hell*, and *Breakthroughs*; the American Empire novels: *Blood & Iron*, *The Center Cannot Hold*, and *Victorious Opposition*; and the Settling Accounts series: *Return Engagement*, *Drive to the East*, *The Grapple*, and *In at the Death*. Turtledove is married to fellow novelist Laura Frankos. They have three daughters—Alison, Rachel, and Rebecca—and two granddaughters, Cordelia Turtledove Katayanagi and Phoebe Quinn Turtledove Katayanagi.

About the Type

This book was set in Minion, a 1990 Adobe Originals typeface by Robert Slimbach (b. 1956). Minion is inspired by classical, old-style typefaces of the late Renaissance, a period of elegant, beautiful, and highly readable type designs. Created primarily for text setting, Minion combines the aesthetic and functional qualities that make text type highly readable with the versatility of digital technology.